Lock Down Publications and Ca$h
Presents

CHURCH
IN THESE
STREETS

A Gangsta's Salvation and a
Woman's Emancipation.

By
J-Blunt

First Edition 2024

Printed in the United States of America

This is a work of fiction. Names, characters, places, and incidents either are products of the author's imagination or are used fictitiously. Any similarity to actual events or locales or persons, living or dead, is entirely coincidental.

Lock Down Publications
P.O. Box 944
Stockbridge, GA 30281
www.lockdownpublications.com

Like our page on Facebook: Lock Down Publications
www.facebook.com/lockdownpublications.ldp

Stay Connected with Us!

Text **LOCKDOWN** to 22828 to stay up-to-date with new releases, sneak peaks, contests and more…

Like our page on Facebook:
Lock Down Publications

Join Lock Down Publications/The New Era Reading Group

Visit our website:
www.lockdownpublications.com

Follow us on Instagram:
Lock Down Publications

Email Us: We want to hear from you!

Chapter 1

Nephew

My name is Bobby Peterson, aka Nephew. Life been a struggle for as long as I can remember. I was born on May 6th, 1995 in Saint Paul, Minnesota at Regions Hospital. My parents, Robert and LaToya Peterson, had been married for six destructive years when they brought me in this crazy world. My mother hoped that giving birth to my father's only child would make him change his abusive, alcoholic, and cheating ways. Unfortunately for us, pop was committed to being a demon. The spark that lit the stick of dynamite happened when I was three years old. Pops got drunk and beat up his side chick. The side chick's brother came over and beat up my dad. Dad went home and beat up my mom because that's what he did when life got rough. I cried while watching him treat moms like a punching bag and that pissed him off enough for him to throw me through the living room window.

Mama picked me up off the grass and took me to the emergency room where they fixed my broken leg and bandaged my cuts. That was the last time I saw my pops. The next day we left Minnesota and ended up in a homeless shelter in Milwaukee, Wisconsin. The social workers helped us get welfare and an apartment in Westlawn Housing Projects. Moms took to the bottle to cope with depression, loneliness, and low self esteem. I explored the PJs while she was blacked out drunk. In these trenches is where I learned what it took to survive in the jungle. I was nine when a fifteen year old girl named Quanisha taught me more about sex than any sex education class I ever took in school. By the time I turned twelve I had witnessed stabbings, shootings, and even walked upon a freshly dead body after a heroin overdose. In those projects is where I would also spill blood and taste the power of someone else's fear.

Chucky was my project's kid version of D-Bo. A big, ugly, and dirty fourteen year old that didn't know his daddy and mama were dopefiends. He didn't have shit and used what he learned in the jungle to survive. His weapon of choice was intimidation and he preyed upon the smaller and weaker kids. I was small for my age but I made up for my size with my heart. It's not the size of the dog in the fight but the size of the fight in the dog. Chucky would find out what that meant. Moms had just gotten her check and hit me with ten dollars. I dipped to the store and bought all the good shit. Skittles, Starburst, Ring Pops, Pop Rocks and some penny candy. I was walking through Westlawn with my bag of goodies when Chucky came walking out of one of the buildings where they sold dope.

"What up, Bobby?" he asked, eyeing the pack of Starburst in my hand.

"Nothing. Sup with you?"

"I'm looking for my mama. Let me get that candy."

Up until this point I hadn't had any problems with Chucky so I didn't mind plugging him with some goodies. I dug in the bag and pulled out a handful of penny candy. I reached out my hand to give it to him but he didn't open his hand to receive it. Instead he was looking at me like I was crazy.

"Nah, gimmie the bag, punk."

It was my turn to look at him like he was crazy. After exchanging mean mugs I dropped the candy back into the bag and started walking. I took two steps before my world got rocked. Chucky punched me in the back of the head so hard that I blacked out for split second. When I came to my senses, I was laying in the grass on my stomach and Chucky was picking up my candy from the ground. Tears burned in the corners of my eyes as I watched him dig into the bag and drop a handful of candy near me. Then he smiled while opening the bag of skittles and walking away. What Chucky didn't understand was that I had also been learning how to survive in the jungle. I knew that a seventy five pound twelve year old would be prey and the only way I stood a chance was to even the playing field. My equalizer was a four inch knife that I never left home without. I jumped up from the ground, snatched the knife from my waist, and ran up behind the bully. I had never stabbed anyone and the thought of where to stab him flashed in my head. I didn't want to kill him, just fuck him up. I aimed high and the tip of the knife dug into his shoulder blade until it hit bone. Chucky screamed and collapsed to the ground, candy flying everywhere. I stood over him while he rolled over onto his back. The fear showing in the whites of his eyes made me feel powerful. I wanted to stab him again so I could hear him scream again. I wanted to punish him. I wanted to bring him more pain. But I didn't.

"Put yo hands on me again and I'ma kill you, nigga," I promised.

Chucky stayed on the ground until I finished picking up the candy. After tucking the knife on my hip, I popped another Starburst in my mouth and walked home feeling like a gangsta. Life changed a lot since I was that lil nigga running around Westlawn carrying a knife. For starters, my weapon changed from a four inch knife to a F&N tactical .45. I up this big bitch and make the toughest nigga turn hoe. And instead of stabbing niggas that took something from me, I do the taking. Some people say robbing a nigga ain't a real hustle or that they don't respect jack boys. I say fuck any nigga that don't like what I do. Speak my name in some ghettos and niggas get nervous and start moving around. That's how I want it. Why go through all the bullshit involved with hustling or running a business when I can take they shit with a flash from my F&N? They spend a week making a profit and I take it in thirty seconds. Who the stupid one?

"Nephew, why you gotta keep doing me like this, boo? Why can't I go? " Simone asked.

I looked up from rolling the blunt of grandaddy purp and into my ride or die bitch's slanted hazel brown eyes. My other half was beyond bad. Pop's from Trinidad and mama Japanese. She had the best of both their features. A beautiful head of long and thick hair, skin the color of sand on the beach, and a slim thick frame that demanded a nigga's undivided attention. "This a two man move, love. Me and Little gon take care of this one. Plus, this one of them broad day licks. We can't be seen and need to move fast."

"I can wear one of my wigs. You know I change it up with the best of em. I wanna go, baby. Please. "

That's what I loved about Simone. Shorty loved getting her hands dirty. Yeah, she was a baddie but she wasn't one of them pretty females that wanted to get through life on her looks. Simone was BTA, bout that action. When it was go time, she stood next to me on the front line. But this time she would have to sit this one out. "Not this time, bae. We already got it down to a science. You know I love having you next to me but I can't take you with me on this."

Disappointment and mistrust was shown by the frown on her face. "You bet not be lying to me, Nephew. Let me catch you with another bitch and I'ma catch a body. "

A vision of Simone pistol whipping my side bitch popped into my head. If I hadn't taken the gun, she would've probably killed me and Jasmine. "I ain't on that, baby. On my mama. I said I ain't gon cheat on you no more and I meant that. You all I need to get by. I know what I got in you. This just me and Little move but you know me and you gon fuck it up when I come home. We can go wherever you wanna go and do whatever you wanna do."

She was struggling to believe me. "Share yo location with me then. "

I shook my head and laughed. "You tripping, bae. Gimme a light."

She grabbed the lighter off the end table and struck it. "I'm not tripping. Only way I'ma believe you is if I know where you at at all times. If you ain't got nothing to hide, we good."

I put the blunt in my mouth and leaned forward until the tip was in the fire. Thick clouds of killa smoke filled the air as I puffed and studied Simone's serious eyes. I hated having anybody knowing my every move and tracking me in real time. Shit just didn't sit right with me. But these were my options. Take her with me or share my location. So I handed her my iPhone. "We ain't gon make this a habit. "

Excitement flashed in her eyes when she realized that I was allowing her to track me. "I can, for real? "

"Hurry up, nigga, before I change my mind."

She pulled the phone close and turned on the setting while I puffed on the blunt. After getting high with my bae, I hopped in Camaro and peeled out. It was time to take care of business.

$$$

I pulled up in front of my nigga Little's apartment about twenty minutes later. He lived in a complex on 29th and Wells with his girl, Lisa, and her daughter. After finding a spot to park, I hopped out and walked up on the porch. Little lived in 401 but I rang the doorbell for 408. A moment later a female answered.

"Who is it?"

"Nephew. Let me in. "

"Wait. Here I come. "

I took a look down the block while waiting. The neighborhood was full of apartment buildings. Shit kind of reminded me of a maze. Like the ones they put rats in. Put a piece of cheese at the end and see which rat makes it out. Only this maze was filled with shit that can get yo ass killed or sent up north with football numbers. It was a couple minutes past eleven in the morning so there wasn't many rats out. But that would change when nigga's phones started ringing and the dumpers and users started coming out. The doorknob twisting pulled me from thoughts of rats, mazes, dealers, and users. The heavy wood door swung open and I was face to face with my maroon dreadlocks wearing chocolate drop. Jasmine had dark skin like she was born in that African sun. Wide nose, thick lips, and high cheekbones. She was the relationship version of the NBA's sixth man of the year. She had the potential to be a starter but played good in her role as the first female off the bench.

"Sup, baby."

"Hey," she responded dryly before turning around and leading the way into the building.

I followed the natural sway of her bouncing booty in the blue sundress. "Why you say it like that? "

"Like what? " she asked without looking back.

"Like you mad. "

She pushed her apartment door open and stepped inside, spinning to face me with arms crossed over her breasts. "Cause I am mad. I don't like sneaking around, Nephew. Tell Simone what it is. Tell her you got two bitches. "

"Man, chill shorty. What we doing don't got nothing to do with Simone. I'm with you right now. Let's focus on the time we together cause I ain't got long. You sure you told me everything about this nigga? You ain't forget shit?"

Jasmine gave me that irritated look that females give when they love you but hate you at the same time. "Move so I can lock the door."

I stepped aside.

"That's what you care about the most, huh? Me helping you get some money? "

"Nah, baby. You know you my girl. But let's not do this right now. I need to make sure everything right before I call my nigga."

She gave me another one of those looks before heading for the couch. "Yeah. That's everything. He making the run at 3:00 like he always do and then he coming to pick me up. That's what he told me. You not gon shoot him, right?"

A pang of jealously stabbed my heart as I sat on the couch. "Why you worried about it? You act like you got feelings. "

"Nah, I don't got feelings. I'm only talking to him for you. But if it ain't no need to shoot him then don't. That's only gon make you hot and I don't want nothing to happen to you. "

I wasn't satisfied with the answer but I didn't want to pry and seem insecure or give her ammo to fire back at me. " Nah, nah, I ain't gon shoot the nigga. Long as he don't get on no bullshit. I just want that bag and then I'ma come back and me and you gon fuck up a check. "

"I don't care about the money. I already told you what I want. Tell yo bitch to get with us or get left behind. You said if I did this that you would tell her that I'm staying with you. I did what I was supposed to do. When you gon do what you supposed to do?"

Wasn't no way I could tell Simone I was still fucking Jasmine and expect to keep them both. Simone wasn't sharing. " I told you I'ma do it. "

"When?"

"Soon as I get back. "

She searched my face for the truth. I didn't blink while meeting her stare. Finally she smiled. "That's all I want, Nephew. Just to be able to be with you for real. I want to know what it feel like to go to sleep and wake up next to you."

I reached over and interlocked my fingers with hers.

"After today, you won't have to worry about that. I'ma make it right, baby. I'ma tell her that you my girl and she either gon get with it or get gone."

The words made Jasmine smile and she leaned over to kiss me. Her lips were soft and the gloss tasted like candy. "I hope she gets gone. "

"I hope you kiss me again. Yo lips taste too good."

She gave me all of the candy kisses I wanted while letting out sexy ass moans. Jasmine's moans were the best I ever heard. Like porn for your ears. Got a nigga's dick hard like I popped a Viagra. And now that she woke my nigga up, she was going to have to put him back to sleep.

"There you go. Is that enough kisses for you? " She leaned back a little, wearing a sexy smirk. She knew what she was doing. She knew her sex appeal and fuck game made the strongest nigga weak. That's why I couldn't stop fucking with her even though Simone tried to kill us.

"Wait. Come back over here. Look what you did."

We both looked at the bulge in my pants. Her smirk turned into a full grin.

"What is that?"

I pulled the .45 from my waist and sat it on the couch before unzipping my pants and unleashing the meat. She wrapped a hand around my dick and began stroking it slowly.

"What you want me to do with this?"

"I want you to assume the position."

She moved onto her hands and knees on the couch, her face inches from mine. "You want the front or the back?"

I dropped my pants and underwear to my ankles and stood. Jasmine's pussy was good enough to be bussed down, bagged up, and sold by the ounce. But her head was even better. Shorty didn't have a gag reflex and I could fuck her mouth like it was her pussy.

"I want the front."

She opened wide and I slipped my dick right down her throat until her lips was touching my trimmed dick hairs. Then I grabbed two handfuls of her dreadlocks and began moving my hips. I pulled my spit covered dick out slowly then pushed it down her throat again. She let out one of those sexy ass moans while staring up at me like I was her master and she my sex slave. The eye contact and moans put me in a zone and I started long stroking her lips. I could feel the air from her nostrils blowing over my hips and torso as she breathed harder while I increased my speed. Then she gave me that shit that I liked and went back and forth from moaning and humming. The moans were turning me on and the humming vibrated my dick and balls. I wanted to hold off a little longer but the shit felt too muthafuckin good. I started drilling her mouth as fast as my hips would move while slob dripped down my balls and spit bubbled around her lips.

"Awe shit, Jasmine! Damn, baby, " I groaned.

Tingling began in my head, neck, arms, legs, feet, and everything in between. I gave one more thrust before I was paralyzed with pleasure. Jasmine took over, sucking and swallowing while squeezing my balls. Shit felt so good that I thought I was about to have a seizure. When I was drained, I sat on the couch heavily. Jasmine stood and snatched off the sundress. She was naked underneath and her natural body looked like it could be in a plastic surgeon's book for client's to see what perfection looked like. Titties big, round, and firm. Stomach flat. Waist snatched. Hips, ass, and thighs thick, muscular, and curvy. She didn't say a word as she grabbed the back of my neck and pulled my face into her pussy while she lay back on the couch and opened her legs. I crawled on my stomach and started kissing them dark, swollen, and wet lips. She did those sexy ass moans. Then I pried those lips apart revealing that pink ass inner pussy and sucked her clit in my mouth. Jasmine reacted like I had shocked her with a taser. She tensed up, hands grabbed the back of my head, and she started pulling my face into her pussy. I kept on sucking as she moaned loudly and smashed my face against her. When I knew she was in the zone, I slipped two fingers in her pussy and one in her ass.

"Oh, my God! Oh, my God!" she cried over and over as she got closer to getting off.

She humped my fingers and face harder and faster until her body went limp. Her pussy got super wet as she released on my face. Feeling her cum on my fingers and face and listening to her moans put me back in the game. My nigga stood up straight like a soldier at attention. I was ready for round two. I put one foot on the floor for leverage and pinned her legs on her shoulders. She grabbed my dick and guided it into her pussy. I dove in deep until our pelvises was touching and then I destroyed that pussy. I hit all them spots, touched every wall, and made sure we both got ours. After we cleaned up, I ran up to the second floor to holler at my nigga, Little.

"Nephew, what's hannen, nigga?" Little greeted after opening the door and letting me in the apartment.

"You know you got it, boss. How you feeling?"

He rubbed his hands together like he was cold, a gleam flashing in his marble shaped eyes. "I'm ready to eat, my nigga. Tell me what Jasmine talking bout. Everything still a go?"

"Green light."

He gave a little fist pump. "That's what I'm talking bout. Come on in. Let's smoke something and chop it down."

I copped a squat on the Royal blue sofa and we talked strategy and smoked while listening to Mo3. Little had been my nigga since we was freshmen in highschool. We had similar family backgrounds with our dads being fuck niggas and our mother's being sole providers. Both our mothers also married super religious church niggas and converted to Christians and expected us to be choir boys. I played the role until I was old enough to be my own man.

"So how you wanna play it, Nephew. I say we kidnap the nigga and make him open the safe."

"Nah, brah. That shit won't even be necessary. We just pull up and go. The nigga make this same bank drop every week so he probably won't be expecting shit."

Little thought for a moment. "Just up banger and make that nigga give it up? You think he gon be that sweet? You know some niggas willing to die for that shit. A kidnapping might get us a better play."

"That might be a better play if that nigga don't actually got the bag. But if he got it in his hand, we taking it. Give that nigga some hot shit if he don't wanna let it go."

Little shrugged. "Yeah, that sound good but I really wanna kidnap that nigga."

I gave him a look. "What's up with you and this kidnapping shit?"

He rubbed his smooth bald head and grinned. "Shit, I just finished watching The Wash and I wanna kidnap a nigga. A nigga can't resist if I got em in the basement."

I bust out laughing. "We good, fam. No kidnapping and no basements. We gon take this nigga shit and dip."

Little gave another shrug. My phone rang. It was Simone. "Hey, baby."

"What you doing? "

"Shit. Kicking it with Little and going over the move."

"What time y'all doing it."

I looked at the time on my phone. It was almost one o'clock. "We gone slide around two. He supposed to make the drop at like three."

"Oh. Okay. You sure you don't need me to come. I'm ready."

"Nah, we got it, bae."

"Okay. I was just calling to see what you was doing. I see that you at Little apartment so at least you wasn't lying about that."

"Girl, what I tell you. You the one. Ain't nobody but you. I know what you worth. Now I need you to start trusting what I say. I ain't gon lie to you. You my Queen."

"Okay, baby. Go take care of yo business and come back to the palace. I'ma fuck you like a King tonight. Love you."

"Love you, too."

"You ain't gon tell her about Jasmine, huh?" Little asked.

"Hell nah. I can't. She a try to kill both of us. If she find out that I put Jasmine in on this, its a wrap. I had to let her track me to keep her in the house."

"Damn, nephew. You in some shit, brah. It sound like you might lose one of them."

"Yeah, it do."

"So, if you gotta choose, who its gon be?"

"I'm still tryna figure that out, fam. Simone is my bitch. She gutta, pretty, and loyal. But Jasmine would do anything for me, too. And that pussy so good, my nigga. Both of em baddies. I don't know what I'ma do. I want both of em."

Little nodded like he understood my situation.

"Guess you gotta see what happen and play it by ear. God know what we need. He gon figure it out for you."

I thought on Little's words for a moment. Why would God care who I was fucking? Didn't he have enough on his plate with the wars and people starving? My mama and her husband believed God had the answers to all of the world's problems but I didn't. If he had the power to fix the world, why was it still fucked up? "Why you always talking about God, my nigga? You really think God care who I'm fucking?"

"I do, brah. God love all of his creation and he care about what we do. And I talk about God because God is real, my nigga. Just because you can't see him don't mean he don't exist. You can't see air but you breathing. We was both baptized so God is in us. We just gotta get our shit together and link in with him. I'ma tap in with that nigga one day."

I shook my head. "I'm good on all that linking in shit. I'ma do me. My church is in these streets."

Little pulled a Glock 27 from the side of the couch and lifted it in the air. "Amen."

$$$

We left Little's apartment a couple minutes past two o'clock and hopped in my Camaro. I drove a couple blocks over to the steamer I stashed yesterday. It was a blue Nissan Maxima. Low key enough to blend in and fast enough to get us out of a jam. Little hopped in the Maxima and I followed him to Parklawn Housing Projects. The play was to park my Camero and use it to get away. After jumping in the steamer, we headed for the gas station on Sherman and Burleigh. I pulled on an afro wig and dark shades and Little did the same. I texted Jasmine to get an update and she texted back that he was about to head to the bank.

"Its go time."

Sherman and Burleigh was a busy intersection on Milwaukee's north side. Buses ran in all four directions, a Boy's and Girl's Club was inside the park, and there was a couple of small businesses nearby. At almost three o'clock in the afternoon, traffic at the stoplights was damn near bumper to bumper. Most people would think this was a bad time to hit a lic. But we wasn't most people. We was goons. Any time that bag was on the line was the right time. I pulled into the gas station and parked near the green Jaguar. There were a few cars parked at pumps getting gas and people in the store. Just a regular day to them but the perfect opportunity for us. Nobody would expect a robbery to go down. A couple minutes later an older black man walked out of the gas station dressed in tan slacks and a green polo. He was bald headed and clean shaven except for a thick ass mustache. He carried a bank bag in his left hand and keys to the Jaguar in the other. He also had a pistol in the holster on his left hip.

"He strapped," I said.

"So am I," Little said, clutching the Glock tightly. "Soon as he reach for the door we go."

My heart raced with adrenaline as I stalked the prey. He was about twenty feet away and didn't notice us watching him from the Nissan parked near a gas pump. When he started reaching for the Jaguar's driver door, we opened ours. He kept his head down long enough for us to close the distance. When he looked up again, there were two pistols pointed at him. Surprise flashed in his eyes. That surprise turned to anger when he dropped the keys and reached for the pistol.

"Bitch, you bet not!" Little screamed.

He paused, realizing that he would die if he pulled that gun.

"You bet not move or I'ma buss yo ass," I warned.

He stayed frozen as I took the bank bag while Little took his gun and car keys. We kept our pistols on him while moving back to the steamer. The robbery took less than twenty seconds.

"What we get?" I asked while driving down side streets and watching all of the mirrors.

Little brought out a handful of money. "We got them bands, nigga!"

I slapped the steering wheel and laughed. Keeping Jasmine had paid off. I drove the steamer to Parklawn so we could ditch it in one of the parking lots. The police wouldn't find it for weeks. After wiping the car down, we pocketed twelve thousand five hundred apiece, threw the disguises and the niggas keys in a dumpster, and got to stepping. We were walking out of the parking lot on Sherman when a light skinned nigga in a tan Malibu pulled into the parking lot giving us the eye.

"You see that nigga?" I asked, eyeing the car as it drove by.

"What about him?"

"Nigga was staring hard as a bitch," I said, keeping my eye on the car as it parked.

Little blew it off. "That nigga ain't on shit. I'm thinking about these Forgies I'm finna slap on my Audi."

I didn't like the feeling he gave me but I let it go and we cut through the projects. We was almost to my Camero when I heard the loud engine rev. I turned toward Sherman and noticed a police car speeding into the projects. My heartbeat sped up and eyes bucked. I got ready to run. "You see that shit?"

"We good, Nephew. They ain't on us. Don't run," Little whispered.

We quickened our steps, watching as the black and white car sped through Parklawn. Then another police car followed. And then another. I don't know what else Little needed to convince him that they was about to book our asses but I seen enough and took off running. Little followed. We ran behind the closest building, trying to get to the Camero but one of the police cars pulled in the lot and cut us off. We ran back the direction we came from but got blocked by the other cars. I ran between them and further into the projects. Little was on my heels. Tire squeals made me look back. Police cars drove on the sidewalks and grass. They caught up to us fast. Little tried to run in between the buildings but instead ran right into the path of a police car. There was a loud smack and he flew at least ten feet in the air. It sounded like he put a dent in the concrete when he landed. I didn't have time to think about what happened to my nigga because I had to get to freedom. I kept on running until I came to a short iron gate on the side of one of the buildings. I leapt that bitch like I was jumping a hurdle in the Olympics. The police car stopped and one of them jumped out to chase. I was still in a full sprint so I knew he wasn't going to catch me. I cut behind another building, ran across a field, and came out on 47th street. The projects ended and regular houses were on the other side of the street. I shot across the grass and didn't even think to look for traffic as I ran into the street. I had taken a couple of steps when I noticed something tan out the corner of my eyes. I turned my head just in time to lock eyes with the light skinned nigga in the Malibu. That bitch ass nigga hit me.

Chapter 2

Nephew (Two Weeks Later)

The nigga in the Malibu turned out to be the police. He was off duty and on his way home when he stopped to get gas and seen me and Little hitting the lic. He called for backup and followed us to Parklawn. The police damn near killed me and my nigga when they ran us down with them cars. Broke my right leg and right arm. Little broke a hip, forearm, and damn near the whole left side of his face. On top of the injuries was our charges. Armed robbery and possession of stolen firearms. We was both facing sixty years. Bail was set at two hundred fifty gs. They don't got bail bonds in Wisconsin so the only way to get out on bail was full payment. I knew I wasn't going nowhere. I had fifteen gs at home. Simone gave the lawyer ten and put twenty five hundred on my books. They took the money from the gas station and used it as evidence. Now I had to spend the next couple months fighting for my life and hope that the judge wouldn't make me spend the next sixty years in a cage.

I was sitting on the hard ass bottom bunk in a cell at the Milwaukee County Jail staring at the cast on my arm and thinking about life and how the fuck I ended up in jail. I knew how I got here. I stuck a gun in a nigga face and took his shit. That's guaranteed to book a nigga ass. But I was thinking deeper than that. Tryna figure what led me to the streets in the first place. I could argue that it was because I didn't have my pops around but it's a lot of niggas that do something with they life who don't grow up with a daddy. Plus, mom's husband, Jamie, been around since I was ten years old. He spent the last fifteen years tryna show me an example of a God fearing man but I didn't want to hear the shit he was talking about. Him and moms wanted me to be a choir boy and took me to church every weekend. I low key hated church but I loved gospel music and the girls. Even smashed Evelyn in the church basement during a cookout. But that's not what got me in this fucking cell. I don't think. I heard the preachers say that God is vengeful but I hope he wouldn't lock me up for sixty years for getting some pussy in the basement. Not with all them crooked ass preachers stealing from the congregation and them Catholic priests fucking boys. Nah, what I think led me here was living in the projects. The trenches had a bigger impact on me than my moms or Jamie realized. That's why me and Little started robbing niggas in high school. Even though I had a mama and step daddy at home that supplied my needs, I still wanted to take a nigga shit. Damn. I was a victim of the trenches.

"Nephew, you still woke?"

"Yeah. What up?"

My celly hung his head over the bed to look down at me. Dutch was a cool white nigga in his early thirties that was locked up for selling dope. He had beady eyes and always looked like he was high. Wore his black hair slicked to the back like one of them old school gangstas. "Man, I'm up here reading this letter from my bitch and it got me wondering if people understand the difference between loyalty and love. Like, she telling me she love me and how she gon be loyal but I think she just saying that shit because it sound slick because she ain't doing shit to show it. I feel like you gotta back that shit up with actions and most people don't understand that."

"I think them action words, my g. For sure."

21

"That's what I'm saying. To me, Loyalty is being trusting. You can't trust nobody that ain't loyal. And love is self-explanatory. If you love somebody, you gon show it by doing shit that let them know. I would'da did anything for my girl to let her know I love her. Seeing her happy made me happy. For real. And now that I'm in this shit, she saying one thing and doing another. This shit crazy, fam."

I could see the pain from whatever she wrote in that letter in his eyes and I didn't have the words to ease it. So I told him what Little told me the day we got locked up. "That's how it be sometimes, Brah. God know what we need. He gon figure it out for you."

Dutch gave a smirk that said more than words. He didn't believe that God was going to figure it out for him. "You still believe in God even though you might get sixty years?"

"That's all I got to hold on to."

He gave a slight nod. "Better to hold onto God than a bitch because these hoes ain't shit."

After Dutch's head disappeared, I thought about my girls. Simone acted like she couldn't live without me. We been together for two years and she wasn't used to waking up alone. Wanted to talk on the phone as much as we could and cried damn near every time I hung up. It seemed like she was taking me being locked up harder than I was. Jasmine was the opposite. She said she never wanted to talk to me again and blocked my number. The gas station nigga believed she set him up and she blamed me for getting her involved. I told her that if she didn't say shit they wouldn't know shit. I don't know what happened or if she being charged for anything. I just hope she don't snitch.

$$$

I woke up the next day feeling like shit. My body hurt like a muthafucka and the thin ass jail mattress didn't make it no better. I limped to the sink to wash my face and brush my teeth. My right arm was broken at the elbow so the cast from my wrist to shoulder made simple shit like brushing my teeth impossible. My arm was locked at a right angle and all I could move was my shoulder so I had to use my left hand. The first couple of days using my opposite hand was awkward but I managed. When I was fresh I grabbed my wheelchair and rolled into the day room. I glanced at the clock on the wall while rolling to the phone bank. It was 9:37 in the morning and Simone was probably already woke waiting for me to call. While I was dialing her number the lock on the pod door clanked loudly. I glanced towards the metal and plexiglass door as it opened. Two niggas walked in carrying bedrolls. The one that caught my eye was a short dark skinned nigga with diamonds in his mouth. I recognized him instantly. Jewels.

"Good morning, bae," Simone answered, sounding like she just woke up.

"Hey, bae. You not gon believe who just came on the unit." I said, watching the new niggas walk up to the guard desk to find out what cells they were in.

"Little?"

"Nah. They gotta keep separate on us. I only see him at court."

"Who is it then?"

"Jewels bitch ass."

She repeated the name. "How do we know him? I don't remember."

"Last year at the Hyatt."

"Oh, him. Where he at? You good? "

"He talking to the C.O right now. He didn't see me yet."

She got worried. "Damn, Nephew. You gon be okay? You still in the wheelchair ain't you?"

"I'm fucked up, bae. If this nigga recognize me, it's all bad."

"Do you want me to call up there and get you moved?"

Running from this nigga or any other nigga that I fucked over wasn't an option. "I'ma gangsta, bae. I ain't running from shit."

"But you can't defend yourself right now. What if he fuck you up?"

I watched Jewels leave the desk and head for a cell upstairs. On the way up he looked around the pod and we locked eyes for a split second, but I wasn't sure if he recognized me. "Milwaukee a little city. Whatever he do to me, I'ma do to him and everybody he love ten times worse."

"Oh, Nephew. I'm worried about you, baby," she whined. "You sure you don't want me to call? I don't want you to get hurt."

"Don't call up here, Simone. I ain't playing. But fuck that bitch ass nigga. Did you send me them pictures? I wanna see that ass."

"Yeah, I sent them a couple days ago. You should get them today or tomorrow."

After kicking it with my bae, I wheeled myself over to the TV area. An old head was watching reruns of Ghost. I half watched the show while thinking about how I was going to handle running into Jewels or any other nigga that I fucked over. Milwaukee was a small city and most of the niggas that I robbed was in the streets so it was a good chance we would meet again in jail. If I wasn't fucked up with broken bones, I wouldn't be tripping. I grew up fighting and would go toe to toe with any nigga. But having a cast on my arm and leg made me a victim. I couldn't defend myself at all. I hated feeling helpless. Worst fucking feeling in the world. As I was thinking about my enemies, Jewels came downstairs and got on the phone. During the twenty minute call a couple niggas walked over to greet him. He had numbers. After the call he wandered over to the TV area and sat a few seats away from me.

"Y'all know they made this show about me?" he joked.

The old head laughed. "I was just thinking the same thing. Back in the eighties I was a legend. I was one of the first niggas in the city with crack rock."

"Now you can't stop smoking crack rock," Jewels cracked.

I didn't want to laugh but the look on the old man's face was too funny.

"What happened to you, bro?"

I glanced over and seen Jewels eyeing my casts. "Twelve ran me over."

"Damn, they fucked you up, my nigga. Betta get a lawyer and sue they bitch asses. Pain and suffering and shit. Them Grueber niggas be on that. They be chasing them ambulances."

"I ain't really thinking about suing right now. I'm tryna get from under these charges and get my bail lowered."

"I got a weak ass P.O hold otherwise I would a been bailed out for that light ass twenty. How much yo shit?"

"Two fifty."

His eyes popped. "Damn. What you caught a body?"

He didn't figure out that I robbed him nor did I want him to connect the dots so I lied. "Yeah."

Pain flashed on his face. "Damn, my nigga. I hope you come from under that shit." Then he extended a hand. "My name Jewels."

I shook his hand. "Nephew."

"You look familiar, brah. Where you from?"

I didn't want him to know anything about me so I kept the lies coming. "The Meadows."

"My nigga, Skee, from out there. You fuck with bro?"

I robbed him too. "Yeah, I know Skee. Bro out there eating."

"Yeah, his bitch ass fucking it up in that Bentley. Shit, he the reason I went and snatched my Bentley truck."

"Ya'll killing the city with them Bentleys," the old man chimed in.

25

"I know. I gotta hit this phone again. I'ma fuck with y'all in a minute, bro."

I watched Ghost until the dayroom closed at 11:00 for lunch. After eating a nasty ass Salisbury steak and instant mash potato tray we locked down until the day room opened again at two o'clock. I was rumbling through my bag of canteen for something sweet to eat when Dutch walked in the room full of energy. "Bro, this dude Jewels tryna tell me that he got bricks of flake for twenty five. I'm calling it cap. Nobody in the Midwest got them prices. Especially for scale. Big cap."

I took sixty gs from him so I knew he had a bag. "I don't know if he got it like that but the nigga holding a lil bag."

"Bro, the only way you getting it like that is if you plugged with a cartel or something and I don't think he got it like that. He probably ain't even got twenty bands. Only reason he jacking is because he got d's in his mouth. And them might not even be real. I wish I had diamond tester."

"He got a lil bit of paper, brah. Definitely more than twenty."

Dutch gave me a skeptical look. "How you know?"

"Cause I took like sixty from him "

His mouth dropped open and eyes got big. "You lying, Nephew. You didn't rob Jewels. "

"I did. He don't even remember me."

Dutch just stared at me. And then he looked at my casts. "Bro, what you gon do if he figure it out? You fucked up."

"Shit, I'm swinging first."

"Damn, bro. That's crazy that you robbed Jewels," he laughed. "But I ain't gon let you go out like that. We live together and I fuck with you, bro. If it go up, I'm riding with you. "

$$$

(Two days later)
One thing I learned from being in jail was that niggas will gamble on anything. Jail was boring as fuck. No females,

drugs, liquor, or social media. Just TV, music, the phone, and games. To make shit interesting, niggas gambled. The possibility of winning money was exciting to everybody. And they gambled on anything. Dominos, spades, cribbage, sports, or two ants running across the gym floor. Basically anything. The craziest thing that I bet on was a dope fiend fight. Jewels was the sponsor. He bought a hundred dollar I-care package, canteen and hygiene stuff, and told two dope fiends that if they fought, the winner got the bag. Not only did the dope fiends fight, they damn near killed each other. Both them niggas was broke and didn't want to lose. They was punching, biting, and throwing each other all across the day room. We laughed from the sideline and placed bets. I won fifty dollars. After the dope fiends went to the hole and niggas seen that Jewels had money to blow, they flocked to him like heroin heads around the plug. Everybody wanted to be close to the nigga that threw money around to have a good time.

"C'mon, Nephew. Let's trunk these boys," Dutch jacked as he shuffled a deck of cards. We started a spades tournament. Me and Dutch were partners against Slim and Meech in the first round.

"You a lick, white boy. Bout to take yo money and make you wanna break Nephew other arm," Slim cracked.

"Y'all don't stand a chance, black boy. Slim, you can't even count, bro. I don't know how you got through high school cause you dumb as fuck," Dutch shot back.

Me and Meech bust out laughing.

"Keep talking, white boy. Just make sure you got my money when you get up."

The tournament was the best of three games. We won the first and they won the second. We were a couple hands into the tie breaking game when C.O Coleman got our attention.

"A'ight y'all, its mail call. I ain't about to answer a million questions about this shit. If you don't hear yo name, you ain't got no mail and that bitch lying to you. Listen up."

The whole day room went still as everyone listened for their name to be called. Mail call was a big deal in jail. Pictures and letters from loved ones kept niggas strong and showed who really fucked with you. When he called my name I rolled to the desk to get my package. I checked the address and seen that It was from Simone. It felt like the pictures I had been waiting for. I barely got back to the table before I opened the envelope. There were ten pictures and a letter inside. I went through the pictures first. I knew my girl was a dime but I hadn't been able to see her body in weeks and the pictures reminded me of everything I was missing. She wore red lingerie and worked her angles like she was an IG model. She wasn't all the way naked, but she might as well had been the way her ass and titties was poking out.

"Damn! Who is that, nephew" Slim asked, craning his neck to see my pictures.

"This my bitch, nigga," I answered proudly, loving that feeling of having a bad bitch that other niggas wished they had.

"Damn. Let me see them muthafuckas," Meech said, leaning across the table and forgetting about the spade game.

After I finished looking at the pictures, I let them check out my girl while I read the letter. A small crowd gathered around the table to see Simone flexing but I didn't pay them much attention. I was caught up in her letter telling me how she loved and missed me and that shit had a nigga feeling good as a muthafucka.

"I know her," somebody said.

I looked up and and seen Jewels pointing at Simone's picture like it was a King Cobra. A bunch of nervous energy hit me as I realized what could possibly happen. "What you talking bout, fam? You trippin."

"Nah, Nephew. I know that bitch. I won't never forget her face."

Damn. This nigga figured out who she was. I didn't wear masks when I robbed niggas so it was only a matter of time before he found out who I was. I needed to figure out a way to gain an advantage. "Let me see them pictures."

Slim reluctantly handed the pictures back and I flipped through them. "You sure you know her?" I asked, looking back and forth from Jewels to the picture of Simone.

He walked over and stood next to me while looking at the pictures. "On my mama, I know her, brah. That bitch set me up, my nigga. I don't forget no faces."

"My bitch, set you up, brah? For real?" I asked, sarcastically.

"I met the bitch at the liquor store on Capitol, my nigga. We kicked it a couple times and she was talking that money shit like she was a boss. I'm thinking she bad and boujee so I take her to the Hyatt and right when I'm finna crack, a bald head nigga and a tall brown skinned nigga come in a strip me."

I studied him as he told the story, trying to think of a way out of the jam. I didn't see one. And a glance around the day room allowed me to see all of the niggas in ear shot were interested in how this was going to end, especially Jewels' groupies.

"Matter of fact, brah, you kind of look like one of them niggas that robbed me."

When he said that, I knew shit was about to go up. And I also knew I couldn't let these niggas get the ups on me. If they got me first, they might kill me. I had to go down swinging. Cast or not, it was go time. I elbowed Jewels in the nuts with my good arm and when he bent over to grab his balls, I swung at his face as hard as I could with my cast. Pain like I never felt shot through my entire arm as I connected with his forehead. He went down and I didn't give him a chance to recover. I tipped the wheelchair and fell on top of him. When I got my balance, I got on one knee with my casted leg pointed at a crazy angle and clasped my hands together over my head. I brought my fists down together right on his nose. More pain shot through my arm damn near paralyzing me but I didn't stop. I lifted my arms to bust his shit again when I got tackled to the floor by one of his groupies. It was a nigga named Trigga. He got on my back and started punching me in the back of the head. All I could do was cover up. Then there was a loud crash and the punches suddenly stopped. I looked up and seen Dutch wrestling with Trigga. Then Dutch got on top of him and started beating his ass.

"Hey! Quit fighting! Break that shit up!" Coleman yelled and pushed the panic button on his radio.

Backup would be arriving any moment to break up the fight and take everybody to the hole. I looked over and seen Jewels struggling to get up. I was about to finish whooping his ass but more of his groupies jumped in the mix. One of them ran over and started stomping me while two more went over to stomp out Dutch. Jewels joined his friend in putting their feet on me. I covered up as best as I could and hoped they didn't break my bones again. The whole fight lasted about two minutes and when they picked me up off the floor I knew my arm was broken again. As they rolled me to the hole, I thought about all the niggas I robbed in Milwaukee. There were at least fifty maybe more. If I ran into them and they wanted smoke, I was fucked. These casts was gon get me killed.

Chapter 3

Charlene

I love nail polish. Some of my people think I'm addicted to it because I have a six quart Tupperware tote filled with different colors. It's only about 146 bottles but they act like its 500 or something. They don't realize that my collection happened over a span of almost three years. I didn't just wake up one day and go out and buy a hundred bottles of nail polish. It started when I was a freshman in college. I went to get a manicure and the way that sparkly mango looked on my nails made me want to own a bottle. Then it happened again with cotton candy blue. And the next thing I knew, I had so many bottles lining my dresser that I needed to buy something to put them in because I was running out of space.

"Cmon, Charlene. Why you acting like you can't choose? Pick one or both and let's go. I gotta pick Marquand up from Jay house."

"Its not that easy, Lana. I don't need both colors. At least not right now. I have to choose and you interrupting my process of elimination."

She rolled her eyes, put a hand on her wide hip, and smacked her lips. "You have three hundred bottles at home, girl. Make a fucking choice and let's go. I got shit to do."

"I have one hundred forty-six bottles, for your information. And why you rushing me? You know Marquand is going to make us wait. He can wait on us for a change."

She gave me that look that people give when they want to say what's on their mind but if they do it might ruin the relationship. Instead of saying it, she waved a hand and started walking away. "I'm finna go out to my car. If you ain't out this store in five minutes, I'm leaving yo ass."

"Lana, wait."

She didn't turn around or break stride. Damn. I had to hurry up. She was my ride. Mystical Blue or Punch Berry Purple? The blue went with my Air Max 90s and the purple was the same color of my Gucci tote.

"Did you decide yet?"

I looked up and made eye contact with the clerk. Her name was Kim. Fresh out of highschool and contemplating college. She was used to me seeing me in the salon and understood my dilemma.

"Not yet. I'm leaning towards the purple but that blue is hard to walk away from."

"I think you should get the blue. Blue is one of those colors that just relaxes you and makes you feel good. I get that feeling when I look at a cloudless sky in the summertime."

The image she painted jumped in my head and made me smile. "Thanks, Kim. Mystical blue it is."

"You made a good choice, Charlene. And your nails are on fleek, by the way. I like the red and white swirls."

I held out my hand and extended my fingers, showing my freshly painted nails. "Thanks, babe. I seen this on IG and knew I had to try it."

"Looks good. You want a bag?"

I grabbed the polish and slipped it in my pocket. "Nah. I'm good. Did you decide which school yet?"

"No. Marquette is looking better and better. Daddy wants me to stay close. Plus, my sister is pregnant with my niece and I want to be there to help."

"Golden Eagles is a good school, and I'm not just saying that because I go there. One of the best schools in the country. Also has a good sports program."

"I know. I know. Haven't made up my mind yet, but we'll see."

"Okay. See you around. Hopefully on campus."

I left Lady Lisa's Nail Salon and headed for the passenger side of Lana's yellow Lexus.

"I was just about to leave your ass," she griped.

I looked at this time on the dash. "I still have one minute."

"You getting on my damn nerve."

"And you need to relax. You just about ran out of nerves, ain't you?"

"Yeah. Between you and Marquand, I don't know who burned up the most of them. Give me that blunt out the ashtray, sis. I need to recharge."

"Now you talking my language," I grinned, firing up the good good. By the time we pulled up to Jay's house, we were higher than astronauts leaving the stratosphere. Lana sent him a text to let him know we were outside. He texted her back that he was going to be a few minutes and that we could come in if we wanted.

"Didn't I tell you he was going to make us wait?"

She bust out laughing. "Cmon, girl. Let's go in. I gotta pee. Plus, you know you wanna see Jay anyway."

"Whatever, heffa. I gotta man," I said, hiding the smile that threatened to spread across my face.

"That's what your lips say. But you know that I know the real."

"Whatever, " I said, reaching for the door handle.

Jay was Marquand's fine ass friend that made it difficult for me to stay faithful to Latrell. The five years in prison made his body amazing. I loved a man with muscles and he had them shoulders that looked like they could carry you around the house while he bust it wide open. And did I mention he was fine? Light brown skin, bushy eyebrows, dimples, and a smile that could open doors if he flashed it in the right direction. His problem was too many women. I heard the stories of damaged cars, clothes, and his house being vandalized. After he moved, only the people he deemed worthy knew he lived in a loft above Carlson's Steak House. Lana rang the doorbell and Marquand greeted us at the door.

"Hey, baby," he said, wrapping her in a hug and pecking her lips.

"I thought you was ready? How long you gonna be?"

"Five, maybe ten minutes. We just waiting on this nigga, Tennessee. Come on up. Sup, Charlene?"

"Sup, Marquand?" I nodded as we followed him upstairs.

Jay's loft was spacious, clean, and decorated by a man who lived alone. An autographed Giannis poster was on the wall above a basketball and Giannis's Nike's. A life sized picture of Megan Thee Stallion wearing a swimsuit while twerking was on another wall. Every man's dream TV, an 85" curve TV, took up an entire wall. There was an Xbox. Black leather furniture. Scattered throughout the living room was all kinds of things that the police would find interesting. A money counter, several laptops, a 3D printer, a couple boxes of blank credit cards, two reader/writers, and a box with different skimmers inside. Jay sat at the table shirtless, tattoos covering his muscular frame, Facetiming on a laptop.

"I gotta use the bathroom," Lana said, heading towards the back of the house.

Jay acknowledged her with a nod and made eye contact with me before going back to his call. I sat down, pulled out my phone, and jumped on Facebook while pretending not to listen to Jay's call.

"Cmon, my nigga. I gave you thirty BINs last rip. I know at least ten of em was cracking. You still owe me for that."

"Brah, it wasn't ten. On my mama. Like two or three was cracking, bro. And I only hit em one time. That was a bad batch."

Jay laughed. "See, this why I don't like fucking with niggas. Always tryna finesse. Niggas can't keep it real to save they life."

"Cut that nigga off, fam. Petty money ain't worth no headache," Marquand said.

"You right, my nigga. This ran off on the plug ass nigga just fucked up a blessing." Then he turned to the screen. "Ay, I'm good on that, my nigga. Keep that lil shit. Hope you make it last, leaking ass nigga." Then he slapped the laptop closed and shook his head. "Bro, what's wrong with these niggas? Bite the hand that feed you for peanuts. That shit crazy."

"That's how niggas is. But look at it like this. It only cost you a few bands to see who a nigga really is. That's cheap. Imagine if it was some real paper. That lil money might've saved you a lot more in the long run."

"Yeah, you right. Niggas crazy," he huffed before turning to me. "Whats up, Charlene? Came in here looking like you ready to slide in the passenger side of my Phantom. What's hannin?"

I laughed. "You got enough problems. I ain't with all that extra shit."

He picked up a credit card from the table and held it in the air. "Say the word and I'ma turn in my card."

"Jay, stop playing. You know I got a man. And I ain't about to fight none of yo nasty hoes."

"What yo man got to do with me? And what my nasty hoes gotta do with you? We don't need none of them. All we need is us."

I shook my head. "Stop."

We held eye contact for a moment before he smiled. Then, with all seriousness he said, " One day I'ma turn in my card. When that day come, I'ma find you."

I shook my head again. I didn't have any more words.

"So, you ready to go out cracking again? " Marquand interrupted, holding up a stack of credit cards. "I got a good feeling about this bundle."

"Not this week. I gotta get ready for final exams. I'm spending most of my wake hours studying."

"Fine and educated. Best of both worlds, " Jay whistled. Then the doorbell rang and his attention was grabbed by the ring camera. "Who the fuck this nigga bring by my shit?"

Marquand walked over to look at the screen. "I don't know him."

Jay reached under the couch and pulled out a black assault rifle with a long clip. I didn't like guns.

"Bitch ass nigga know not to bring no niggas to my shit. Get the door, fam."

Lana came out of the bathroom while Marquand was answering the door. She noticed the gun immediately. "Why you got that?"

"Tennessee hoe ass done brought some nigga by my house. Y'all can go in the back if y'all want."

I didn't want to be around the gun but I also didn't want to bitch up. "I'm good."

A few moments later Marquand came upstairs with the guests. Tennessee was a tall brown skinned man with gold teeth and uncombed afro. I had never seen the other man but he was big, face looked serious, and he emanated violence.

"Why you bringing niggas I don't know to my house, fam?" Jay asked, the gun resting on his lap.

Tennessee took in the situation then looked to his friend before addressing Jay. "What's all that shit about? This my brother, Klan, bro."

Jay sat up to get a better look at Tennessee's brother. His skin was really dark. Almost purple. He wore shoulder length cornrows, dark clothes, and a gold necklace with a medallion. What stood out to me was the way the shirt hugged his arms. Jay was in good shape and cut up but Klan was huge.

"Klan? On what that's you, nigga?"

"Yeah, fam. Why you clutching?" his voice boomed and lip twitched.

Jay sat the rifle at his side on the floor. The tables had turned without Klan pulling a gun.

"I didn't know that was you. I ain't seen you in damn near ten years, nigga. What's good? When you get out? "

Klan swept his gaze across at living room at the scamming merchandise. "I been out for a minute. In The City. Bro say you the plug."

"Yeah, yeah. Sit down, my nigga. Let me introduce you to my people. They all on the team. This my nigga, Marquand." They exchanged nods. "This his girl, Lana, and her friend Charlene."

Klan barely acknowledged me and Lana before turning back to Jay. "Bro say you can get new identities. Social security and all that. Can you?"

"You know everything come at a price."

"I need three. Gimmie a number."

Jay thought for a moment. "I normally charge five racks a pop but for you, gimmie ten for all three."

"When can I pick it up?"

"I need a couple weeks. How do I get in touch with you?"

"You won't. Holla at bro and he gon get at me."

Jay frowned at the response but didn't voice it. "Say less."

Klan looked to Tennessee. "I'm good. You?"

Tennessee nodded. "We good."

"Ima get at you when I know something," Jay said.

After a nod, Tennessee and Klan headed for the stairs. Jay looked relieved when they left. He gave Marquand a nod for him to lock the door. We all sat in silence until Marquand came back. The brother's had changed the atmosphere in the room. Klan spooked Jay.

"Who the fuck is Klan?" Marquand asked.

Jay shook his head like he was reliving a bad memory. "Brah, that's one nigga I didn't want to know where I lived. Nigga crazy as fuck. Damn, I hate they let that nigga out the joint."

$$$

Lana dropped me off at home after leaving Jay's house. Home was an apartment two blocks from Marquette University. The thousand dollar a month rent for one bedroom was kind of expensive, especially for a college student, but I liked my little apartment. It was close to school and a hop, skip, and a jump from the downtown life. I was able to afford rent and pay the 235 dollar a month car note on my 2016 Prius with the money I made "cracking" with Marquand and Lana. I didn't plan on getting too involved in scamming or make it a career. It was something to do to get me through college. Paying tuition, rent, car notes, food, utilities, and buying clothes was expensive. I worked part time and went to school full time for the first couple semesters of my freshmen year and there were times that I thought I wasn't going to make it. And then Lana met Marquand and he changed our lives. Once I got my bachelor's degree in business administration, I was leaving the scamming alone and focusing on my career. But, until then, a sistah had to eat and pay the bills.

I had just opened my apartment door when my phone dinged. It was a text from Latrell saying he couldn't come over because their coach was making them practice late. He was the starting point guard for the Marquette Golden Eagles. As team captain, the coach seemed to hold Latrell personally responsible for anything that was wrong on the team. Never mind that Latrell had a life and a girlfriend that needed some tender loving care. The message kind of bummed me out because I was looking forward to spending time with my man. I loved Latrell like Lizzo loved playing the flute and twerking. He was fun to be around, always made me laugh, and sex with him was the best I ever had. I've only given it up to a handful of chosen ones, but Latrell is by far the best. And when he eats the groceries... OMG! I was also bummed because we were supposed to smoke and listen to Lauryn Hill's MTV unplugged 2.0 album. We shared a common love of music and somehow we missed Lauryn's eye opening and mind-blowing album. I heard one song, The Mystery Of Iniquity, and promised not to listen to the rest of the album without him. Now it seemed like Lauryn, smoking, and getting my groceries eaten would have to wait for another day.

After settling down I decided to do some homework. There was an English 2 paper that I had been putting off for weeks. Since Latrell wasn't coming over, I decided tonight was the night to get it done. It was a short essay assignment with a prompt to write about spending your last days alive with a stranger. I turned on some Beyonce, rolled a blunt, lay on the couch, and let my mind drift. I pictured myself on a deserted island with a beautiful sand beach and clear water. Palm tree leaves swayed in the light wind while I walked barefoot in the low tide, the cool water washing over my feet as I stared up at a cloudless blue sky. The weather was a perfect seventy-five degrees and the sun warmed me from the inside out. I was trying to conjure up the perfect stranger and the perfect moment to bring them into my story when Klan suddenly popped into my head. That surprised me because I didn't find him attractive and he kinda scared me. But now that I had a picture of him in my mind, I couldn't get him out. He suddenly emerged from the water wearing only a pair of white swimming trunks. The bulge in the front of his shorts looked like he stuffed a cucumber inside. Water glistened in the sunlight while dripping from his huge muscles. The man looked like an African God as he approached and I was suddenly under his spell. He walked up and gave me a kiss that was soft and aggressive at the same time. Then he lifted me in his arms the way a husband does his wife when he carries her across the threshold. He carried me down the beach and underneath a waterfall. My feet don't even touch the ground as he manhandles and maneuvers me so that we are face to face, my legs are wrapped around his waist. He pulls the trunks down just enough to free that monster dick and slides my panties to the side. I wrap my arms around his neck and ride him under the waterfall. As the fantasy plays out in my mind, I can feel my nipples getting hard and my pussy pulsing. At that moment I decide that this paper is probably going to have to wait a little longer to be written and that Latrell is eating my pussy tonight no matter what time this coach let's him out of practice.

I grab my laptop and an overnight bag and hopped in my Prius. He lived in an apartment on the East side about ten minutes from mine. We had a keys to each other's apartment so I let myself inside. When I closed the door, I was surprised to hear sounds coming from the back. I paused to listen. It sounded like the shower. A couple questions crossed my mind. The first one was who was in the shower? The second was if Latrell lied to me? The third thought was why? Latrell had never given me a reason to be suspicious of him so whenever he told me something, I accepted it in good faith. But the text that I got from him and the shower running created a conflict. My heart thudded in my chest as I walked towards the bathroom. I began to hear voices. Latrell and a woman. And they weren't having a conversation either. Sex noises filled my ears and broke my heart. Feelings that I couldn't described filled my body as I neared what might become a crime scene.

The bathroom door was open and steam billowed into the hallway. I walked right in and what I seen stopped me like I had run into a wall. Latrell was in the shower with a big breasted dark haired white girl. He stood behind her grabbing two handfuls of her hair while he fucked her fast and hard. She was bent over, holding his wrists, screaming like one of them bitches faking it in a porno. Both of them were so caught up in the shower sex that they didn't notice me. My heart swelled and burst. For a moment I couldn't breathe. It hurt so bad that I wanted to fall on the floor and die. Then something in my mind snapped and the hurt turned to rage. I cried as I screamed his name at the top of my lungs, scaring the shit out of both of them. I lifted the laptop over my head and threw it at Latrell. All he could do was turn the opposite direction as the computer hit him upside the head. My fists followed the computer as I punched him, trying to draw blood. The woman screamed and jumped from the shower. "You punk ass bitch!" I screamed.

He grabbed me to stop me from hitting him. "Hold on, Charlene. Chill, baby. Chill."

"Fuck you, Latrell, lying motherfucker."

I tried to knee him in the balls but couldn't because he was smothering me. So I did the next best thing and sunk my teeth into the flesh on his chest. He screamed like the little bitch that he was while trying to shake loose. We lost our balance and ended up falling out of the shower. He fell on top of me and I hit my head on the floor. The impact wasn't hard enough to hurt me but just enough to make my teeth lose grip on his pectoral. I could taste the iron from his blood in my mouth.

"What the fuck wrong with you, girl? You fucking bit me!" He yelled, jumping up and clutching the wound.

I scrambled to my feet to beat his ass some more. "You fucking cheating on me, Latrell. What the fuck wrong with you?"

He began backing out of the bathroom. "That don't give you the right to bite me. Ah shit."

"Yes, it does, motherfucker. You cheated on me!" I screamed while taking a wild swing at him.

I wasn't much of a fighter so he easily dodged the punch. "Cmon, Charlene. Chill. You tripping, baby."

He backed into the living room and I gave chase taking wild swings and screaming. "I'm not the one tripping, nigga. You tripping. You fucking cheated on me."

We ended up on opposite sides of his couch. When I moved one way, he went the other. I tried to go over but he leapt onto the other side. When I realized I wasn't going to get him, I looked for something to throw. There was an ashtray on the table. I went for it but before I could get it, he jumped over the couch and tackled me to the floor. I tried to wrestle him off me but He was bigger and stronger. Somehow, he got on my back and wrapped his arms and legs around me, making me immobile.

"Get the fuck off me, Latrell," I yelled.

"Nah, nigga. You just fucking bit me. Calm yo ass down."

The tears began to pour harder. "Because you cheated on me, nigga! Let me go."

"I'm not letting you go until you chill out."

We were silent for a couple of moments and the image of him fucking the woman in the shower played in my mind. The pain felt like it was setting my soul on fire. "Why, Latrell? Why did you cheat on me, man? Why?"

"She didn't mean shit to me, baby. On my mama. She for the streets. I'm sorry."

"So, you cheated on me with a hoe? For real?"

"It ain't like that, Charlene. I mean, she a hoe but not like that."

His answers were pissing me off even more. "What the fuck are you talking about? If she's a hoe then she's a hoe. And why the fuck would you cheat on me with a hoe? What if she got a fucking disease or something? How many times have you cheated on me? How many times have you fucked her?"

"This the only time I cheated. Only with her. This the first time."

I didn't believe him. "Let me go, Latrell. I need to get out of here."

"I'm not letting you go until you chill. I ain't tryna fight you. For real."

I tried to wrestle away from him but he had me locked up tight. "Let me go, Latrell, or I'ma start screaming."

"You ain't gon hit me is you? "

I started screaming as loud as I could, hoping his neighbors would hear and come over or call the police.

"Charlene, quit fucking screaming, " he said while trying to cover my mouth.

I bit his fingers and when he moved his hand I started screaming again. Latrell pushed me away and jumped to his feet, backing away so I couldn't reach him. I glared at him angrily, wishing that I could hurt him and make him feel my pain. If I owned a gun I would've shot him dead and not felt bad about it.

"I hate you, nigga. I hope that that bitch has AIDS and that you die a slow and painful death. Fuck you."

Chapter 4

Charlene

I couldn't think of any feeling that was worse than having my heart broken. When I was seven I broke my arm jumping off a swing at the park. I used to think that was the worse pain I ever felt until I saw Latrell cheating on me. Being betrayed by someone you loved wasn't something that could be healed by a cast and a painkiller. It had been three days since I hit him in the head with my laptop and the hurt still felt the same. One year and seven months. He threw it all away for a bitch that was for the streets. I began to wonder if he ever really loved me. He said that was the only time he cheated but I didn't believe him. He lied so easily with that text message that he could've been doing it all along. If it wasn't for the English assignment and beach fantasy, I might've still been his fool. Punk ass.

The phone ringing pulled me from thoughts of heartbreak. It was Lana calling for the tenth time today. I watched the phone ring like I had the other nine times. I didn't want to be bothered. I didn't want to hear about no good niggas, her asking if I'm okay a hundred times, fuck that nigga speeches, and I can do bad all by myself. All I wanted was to lay in my bed, get high, and listen to K. Michelle's Kimberly album. The song, Giving Up On Love, was hitting the spot right now and I didn't want my music to be interrupted. When the phone stopped ringing, I reached for the blunt in the ashtray when there was loud banging on my front door.

"What the fuck?"

I let out a stressed breath. If this was Latrell at my door again, I was going to stab him. I was tired of him coming by my apartment begging, wining, and crying. He was lucky I didn't own a gun or I would've been shot his ass. After a grunt, I got out of bed and went to the kitchen. I picked out a steak knife as the banging began again.

"Charlene, I know you in there. Your car is outside. Open this door, " Lana screamed.

I didn't want to see her either but I would rather it be her at my door than Latrell.

"Hey," I said weakly.

She looked me up and down, her eyes stopping on the knife. "Why you got a knife? Did he threaten you?"

I walked towards the kitchen. She closed the door and followed. "Nah, he didn't do nothing to me. I'm just tired if his ass coming by my house crying. If that was him instead of you, I was probably going to jail. How did you get in the building?"

She gave me a searching look, trying to see if I was serious. "Girl, you better not go to jail over no dick. Don't even think about throwing your life away over a nigga. Way too many niggas out here to be fucked up over one. And you know Carter let me in. He love all of this."

I dropped the knife in the sink, rolled my eyes, and headed back to my bedroom. That was exactly the shit I didn't want to hear.

"What are you doing? How you been?"

I grabbed the American history book from the stack on my dresser and climbed back in bed to act like I was studying. "I just want to be left alone right now. I got too much shit on my mind plus I got exams all next week."

Lana sat next to me and looked around the room before staring at me until it started to feel weird. "You need to get him out of yo system, girl. I know you ain't been studying. Ain't no way you can concentrate with a broken heart. Yo ass been in here listening to K. Michelle and getting high and thinking about the good times, ain't you?"

I didn't want her to know that she pegged me so I averted her eyes and lied. "No."

"Charlene, if you don't stop lying to me. I been knowing you since we was fifteen. I know how you look when you lying. And I know how it feel to get your heart broke. I gave you a couple of days to grieve and now its time to get out and do shit that makes you feel good. So let's go. Take off them tired ass yellow pajamas and get dressed. We getting out here in these streets."

I looked down at my yellow pajama pants. "They not tired. I don't want to go nowhere. I gotta study."

She grabbed the book. "I need you to trust me, babe. Retail therapy is a real thing. I got a card from Marquand that we need to run up real quick. Didn't you say something about some Christian Lous that you wanted? This is the day, babe. And I have a surprise later tonight that you will thank me for."

The pink high heels popped into my head. Damn, I wanted those shoes. "You will get them for me?"

Lana pulled out the credit card and smiled. "Tired pajamas gotta go."

I threw my hair in a ponytail, got dressed, and hopped in the car with Lana. The retail therapy started at Macy's where I was able to get those beautiful pink Christians that I had been fantasizing about. We also bought matching Burkin bags. Next we hit Niemen's where I got a fly ass white Christian Louboutin dress and a couple gold bangle bracelets. We finished the day at my favorite nail salon where I got shimmery silver painted nails that made me feel better than the thousands Lana spent on the designer clothes. We were walking out of the nail salon and getting in her Lexus when I thought about the surprise she mentioned earlier.

"So, what is this surprise that you told me about that I'm supposed to love?"

"Girl, I know how much you love music and one of Marquand's friends is doing a reopening for his bar. You heard of Maxine's? It got shut down for a shooting earlier this year. Tonight its reopening and got one of your favorite singers performing. Guess who?"

I thought for a moment, trying to remember any concerts or performances by some of my favorite artists. Nothing came to mind so I guessed. "Don't say Ella Mai."

"Its a man. And think smaller. He not as big as he used to be but he still kinda relevant."

"Tyrese?"

"Nope. But you getting close."

"I'm tired of guessing. Who is it?"

"Ginuwine. Remember him and Tyrese was in that group, TGT, with Tank?" Then she sang part of one of his songs. "Cmon and let's do it. Ride it. My pony."

"Oh, I like him. And he still fine."

"And he gone be performing tonight. See, ain't you glad I came and got yo ass out of that apartment? Fuck Latrell and that white bitch. We out here in these streets. About to be slaying it tonight with Ginuwine. We lady bosses, babe."

We went to Lana's house to get dressed before the club opened at eight o'clock. After a quick shower I threw on the form fitting dress, did my hair, threw on a little makeup, and slipped into the 1,500 dollar heels. I did a few poses in the full-length mirror on the back of the bathroom door. I wasn't a conceited woman, but I knew I was bad. My skin had a brownish red tint from my Mama's Mexican heritage mixing with my daddy's African American blood. I got my long, thick, and curly hair from my mama as well as my bushy eyebrows. Daddy gave me the full lips, prominent nose, and high cheeks. And this body had to come from my daddy's mother because my mama was 100 pounds soaking wet with all her clothes on and her body shaped like a capitol P. Flat booty, hardly any hips with big breasts. My breasts, hips, and booty gave me the figure 8 shape that made all the boys want to taste. Latrell wanted me to become an influencer but I didn't like the thought of getting by on my looks or being treated like a sex object. I wanted to be known for more than a pretty face. So I took school serious and pushed for perfect grades and maintaining my status on the deans list. Last semester I finished with a 3.9 GPA. This semester I was aiming to finish with my third 4.0.

"What's up, girl? You ready?" Lana knocked on the door. I opened it and struck a pose. "Yes, bitch. Yeeesss."

She gave me a look from head to toe. "Ooh, if I ever get a girlfriend, I'm making you my first."

"Girl, you ain't ready for this. Mess around and put it in your life."

"Whatever," she laughed. "How do I look?"

She gave a twirl so I could get the full view of her goods. Like me, she was also biracial, her mother was Scandinavian and daddy was African American. Her blonde dyed hair was shaved on one side and the rest hung to her shoulders. She was a big boned woman with a body like a back road. You needed a map to find your way around those curves. Everything was extra-large on Lana. And I loved that she owned her body and wore what she wanted. Tonight, it was a money green body contouring dress with a deep plunging neckline that almost had the girls fully exposed. The gold red bottoms had straps that wrapped up to her knees.

"When Marquand see you, his jaw gone hit the floor and he gone have to keep them thirsty niggas away with a stick."

She cocked an eyebrow. "You coulda just told me I looked good but for overachieving I'ma return the favor. When Jay see yo ass, you gone have to beat his ass to stop him from trying to get between them thighs. And I think you should let him."

Thoughts of seeing Jay made me feel some type of way. Especially since I was newly single. And I also knew this was Lana's plan all along. "I should've known you was up to something. He gave you the card, didn't he?"

She cackled like a witch. "If somebody wanna sponsor you, let him. At least you know he ain't weird or crazy."

I just shook my head.

Marquand and Jay were meeting us at the club and since they were tight with the owner, we didn't have to wait in line. We also got a good table in front of the stage. The guys were already seated and waiting for us when we walked in. Both were dressed casually in dinner jackets, jeans, and loafers. When Marquand seen his girl all dressed up, he reacted exactly like I knew he would. Wrapped her up in his arms, grabbed so much of her ass that his hand disappeared while tonguing her down. Jay stood and looked at me like he wanted to undress me and fuck me on the table in front of the whole club. And he was looking too good. Hair and face perfectly groomed, dimples on fleek, and he smelled so fucking good that I wanted to lick the spots on his body where he sprayed the cologne.

"I see you made it worth it. Came in here looking like a bag of money, Charlene. Gimmie a hug."

"Thank you. And you looking good yourself," I said, taking a big sniff as we embraced. "What you wearing? You smell so good."

"Polo. Have a seat. You want something to drink? I heard you like vanilla Ciroc."

There was a bottle of my favorite liquor on the table. So far Jay was winning. "Thanks. You pulling out all the stops tonight, huh?"

"When you find what you looking for, you do whatever you gotta do to keep it."

The words were cliché but exactly what I needed to hear. And the way he was looking in my eyes made me want to believe him. "It sounds good."

"The truth always sound good. When I heard how your boy did you, I knew you needed to get out and fuck with a real nigga and let yo hair down. That lame didn't deserve you anyway."

I didn't want to think about Latrell so I switched topics. "Thanks. I didn't hear about Ginuwine being in Milwaukee. I used to love him back in the day."

"Yeah. And they be clowning dude on them memes. That one where he was moving that couch was super funny."

After we shared a laugh Lana wanted to use the bathroom and I couldn't let her go alone. As we were walking across the club I could feel someone watching me. I tried to be coy while I looked around until I found the person giving me the feeling. Klan. He stood near the bar holding a drink, watching me. A vision of him walking out of the water in my fantasy flashed in my head.

"Jay looking good tonight, girl," Lana said. "Said you look like a bag of money."

"Yeah. He's handsome," I said, a little distracted by seeing Klan.

"I'm just saying. You single and he single, " she grinned, giving me a nudge.

"Shut up and let's go use the bathroom."

After taking care of our business, Lana wanted to stop at the bar for a bottle of Patron. I searched for Klan as we walked over, thankful and a little disappointed that he wasn't there. Thankful because I didn't have to worry about acting all weird if he approached me and disappointed because I kind of wanted him to.

"Can I get a bottle of Patron?" Lana asked the bartender.

While she was getting the money from her purse, I turned to look around for Klan when he was suddenly standing next to me. How a man that big could move so quickly and quietly surprised me. He was huge and black and close enough for me to smell the sweet aroma of his cologne.

"Where do I know you from?" He asked.

I still hadn't recovered from him standing next to me so I stuttered a little. "Uh, I was at Jay's house."

Recognition flashed in his eyes. "Is that who you here with? That's yo man?"

"Yes and no."

"Which answer is no?"

"Kinda both."

Klan let out a chuckle. Seeing him smile made me smile. He didn't smile at Jay's house but knowing that he had a sense of humor humanized him. "Do he know that?"

I thought on my response and recycled the first one. "Yes and no."

He smiled again.

"Where I know you from?" Lana asked, giving Klan the eye.

Klan became serious. "You don't know me."

I could feel the energy shift and jumped in. "Klan, this is my best friend, Lana. She was at Jay's house with me."

His smile kind of returned. "I remember you, Lana. You look a little different with that dress on."

"You like? " she grinned, fishing for a compliment.

"Quit thirst trapping, girl. Yo man is over there."

She looked like I slapped her. "I know you didn't just say I was thirst trapping."

Me and Klan laughed.

The bartender sat the bottle on the bar a walked away.

"You killing that dress, Lana. Can't nobody wear it like you, " Klan grinned.

Lana gave me that nose in the air look. "Thank you, Klan. Now we gotta get back to our table. It was nice meeting you again."

He looked like he wanted say something but let it go. Lana grabbed my hand and drug me away.

"Why are you pulling me, girl?"

"Because I'm tryna get you away from that crazy nigga. Come on. Marquand told me about him and we don't need the type of shit he involved in in our life. Plus, Jay is right over here. He is where you need to be."

I filed away what she said about Klan for another time. I would find out more about him later. We returned to the table and didn't speak about our run in with stranger from my fantasy. Ginuwine performed all of his hit songs and a few that I hadn't heard. He also handed out red roses while he sang. I got the final rose and it kind of made me feel like I was on The Bachelor. After watching the performance, I sipped the Ciroc and kicked it with Jay while keeping an eye out for Klan. When I realized the stranger was nowhere to be found, I was able to focus all of my attention on Jay. He was very funny and had me laughing my ass off most of the night. When the liquor kicked in so did the flirting. We talked sexually, danced like we were having sex, and shared some sexy kisses that got my juices flowing. When the club closed and he drove away in the Phantom, I was in the passenger seat. He told me all the things he always wanted to do to me and I was ready for the smack down.

As soon as we walked in his loft, it went down. He gripped my bare ass cheeks while lifting me in the air and I wrapped my legs around his waist. We sucked each others lips and tongues sloppily as he carried me to the couch. His slob was all over my face but I didn't give a damn. His strength, the feel of his muscles, and all the ways he said he was going to eat my cookies had my ass horny so I didn't care about a little extra spit. He lowered us onto the couch and began kissing my neck and chest. I moaned my approval when he pulled the front of my dress down and began sucking my titties. Just when I thought he was spending too much time on my nipples, he went down for the main course. He licked my pussy lips, stuck his tongue inside me, and sucked my clit. Even went down a little further and ate the groceries. He was no Latrell with the oral skills but I wasn't complaining. He made me cum first and I liked that. Told me that he wasn't selfish when it came to pleasure.

"Damn, you taste like a starburst, baby," he grinned, licking his lips. "Can I get mines?"

"Ask and you shall receive."

He stood up and began to undress slowly, starting with the dinner jacket and T-shirt. Watching him strip was kind of erotic and I liked it. He flexed his abs a few times and made his pecs jump before sliding out of the shoes and pants. The bulge in his boxer shorts had me anticipating the final reveal. He took his time pulling them down. He was well groomed but I was a little disappointed by the semi hard uncircumcised penis. He grabbed it by the base and lifted it to my face, allowing me to see the precum dripping from the tip.

"Open wide, baby."

I was not excited to have his funny looking dick in my mouth but I was going to be a good sport since he showed me a good time and ate my cookies. "Lay down and let me do my thing."

He laid on the couch and I kneeled between his legs and sucked him into my mouth. The extra flesh of his foreskin and slimy precum made me gag and almost vomit.

"Yeah, baby. Take yo time. Don't choke yo'self."

I ignored the comment and continued to give him head. As he grew harder I noticed his dick began to curve and slide across the roof of my mouth. I heard of curved dicks but never experienced one in real life.

"Damn, Charlene. Do yo thang, baby," he moaned, putting a hand on the back of my head and pushing my head down further. When I gagged a little more he stopped pressing my head down and let me do my thing. His dick was a little bigger than average so I just focused on sucking the head and used my hand to jack him off.

"Suck my balls for a minute. Can't forget my homies."

I took him from my mouth but continued to jack him off while sucking his balls. He oohed and ahhed. Knowing that I was bringing him pleasure was turning me on again and getting me back in the mood.

"Cmon now, baby. Toss my salad," he said opening his legs wide.

It took a moment for his words to register. I know he just didn't. Wasn't no way I was licking a nigga's ass. Instead of acknowledging him, I went back to giving him head. Then he began pushing the top of my head down.

"Cmon, Charlene. Toss my salad, girl."

I stopped sucking him, unable to hide the disgust in my voice and on my face. "Dude, I'm not licking your ass. I don't get down like that."

He looked disappointed. "Why not? I did you."

"Because I don't eat ass. And I didn't ask you to. You did it on your own."

"Okay. You ain't gotta do nothing you don't wanna do. But will you stick yo finger in my ass right before I bust? That shit make a nigga go crazy."

I just stared at him, shocked that he wanted me to play in his ass. I thought only gay men wanted things in their ass. Shit. Jay did five years in prison. Is he gay? Suddenly I was turned off.

"You ain't gotta do it if you don't want to," he said reading my mood. "I just like to get a little freaky."

"I never, uh, did nothing like that. I just like to do the, uh, regular stuff. I'm not really out there like that."

"Its cool. Don't trip. Go head and finish doing what you was doing."

I didn't want his dick back in my mouth because I couldn't stop thinking about it being in another man's ass. "How about you let me get on top and ride this thang."

He knew I thought he was suspect but he didn't speak on it. "Get on up here then."

"Do you got some condoms because I'm not on birth control."

That same look flashed in his eyes again but I didn't care because wasn't no way I was fucking him raw. "Yeah. Come to my room."

I followed him to the bedroom where he grabbed a condom a slipped it on. When we climbed in bed there was no more kissing because I was completely turned off and didn't want to think about where else his lips were. Instead I jumped on top and rode him reverse cowgirl so I wouldn't even have to see his face. When he bust a nut I acted like I came too.

"Damn, Charlene. You the truth, girl. You wanna take a shower and get in another round? I got all night."

My buzz had worn off, I was turned off, and the last thing I wanted to do was spend another minute in his house or in his bed. "I actually have to do a lot of studying. You know we got final exams. You think you can take me home?"

He was surprised by my response. "You serious?"

"Yeah. I had fun and that dick is the bomb but I gotta put school first. Thanks for taking me out and showing me a good time. I really needed that but I have to get home."

He searched my face for a moment. "I didn't do nothing to turn you off, did I?"

"Nah, you good. I just really need to get home."

$$$

I was awaken by my phone. I looked at the time and the caller. Lana was calling at 9:43 and I already knew what she wanted. A quick montage of my night with Jay flashed in my head. Things were going good until we got to his house. Can't believe the nigga asked me to lick his ass.

"Hey, babe."

"Spill the tea, bitch. Was it long and strong?"

I held back. "Good morning to you too. And why is you all in my business?"

"Save the extra shit for the ones that ask for it. Now stop playing and tell me. You still at the loft?"

"No. I had him drop me off last night. Dude is real suspect."

"Suspect? What that mean?"

"This nigga wanted me to play in his booty hole. Asked me to lick his ass. When I told him no, he wanted me to finger him while he nutted. That shit had me ready to go."

"Oh my God. Are you serious?"

"Dead ass, babe. Like, what type of nigga want something in his ass? I think he got turned out while he was locked up or something. He definitely suspect."

Lana sounded blown away. "Wow. I damn near can't believe what I'm hearing. I didn't see this coming. Was the dick good at least?"

"Girl, he uncircumcised and got a bent dick. Like, he fine and all that but I'm good on all that extra shit. I damn near don't want to ever talk to this nigga again. I'm so turned off."

Lana bust out laughing.

"I don't know why yo ass laughing because ain't none of this funny. And yo man is his best friend, so..."

"Uh-uh, bitch. I know you didn't. My man ain't gay and he don't let nobody tamper with his ass. That's yo friend that like his booty cheeks molested."

"You crazy, girl," I laughed. Then an image of Klan flashed in my head. "What Marquand tell you about Klan?"

"No, school girl. If you can't handle Jay then you damn sure ain't ready for no nigga like Klan."

"I had a fantasy about him," I blurted.

"Who? Klan?"

"Yes. On the beach. We got it in under a waterfall and everything."

"Damn, bitch. Let me find out yo fake shy ass is really a closet freak."

"No, it ain't like that. It happened when I was thinking about a writing assignment. I was smoking and thinking about what to write and this nigga come out the water with a anaconda. It surprised me because he not even my type and I don't even know him like that. Then when I seen him at the bar last night it made me think about it again."

"Marquand said he a killa. Like, he really kill people. That's what he was in jail for. We don't need that kinda nigga around us. Keep that nigga out of your head, babe."

Chapter 5

Nephew (3 months later)

I hated feeling helpless. It was one of the worst feelings in the world. Even though I got my casts off two weeks ago and had full use of all my limbs, there wasn't nothing I could do to help my situation. That's how being locked up made you feel. I spent my entire life making moves and getting away with shit. When I was little my moms punished me by making me stay in the house but when she fell asleep I had my way. In middle school I got caught with some weed and got suspended. That was a vacation because I didn't have to go to school and moms was at work so I had the house to myself. I was used to wiggling my way out of situations that were supposed to be punishment. But being punished by the system was different. Wasn't no sneaking out when the guards went to sleep because they had my ass locked behind so many doors that breaking out was impossible. The courts didn't play fair. Gave me a bail they knew I couldn't pay. And the way the judge was staring down his nose at me from high on the bench told me everything I needed to know. My black ass wasn't going nowhere and when they let me out, I was going to be a lot older than I am now. I felt helpless.

"Your Honor, we ask that the court try my client separate from his codefendant. The motion I filed Wednesday outlines the reasons that it would be in the interests of justice to allow my client to proceed on his own. The magnitude of this case and charges will have a big impact on this young man's life and I feel he should be given the opportunity to be seen as an individual. He's a smart guy. Graduated from high school. Comes from a good family. I'm afraid all of this will be lost on the jury if he is seated next to Mr. Finch."

I watched my lawyer. The way he finessed his words made me feel like I might have a chance to get a small win. Anthony Higgins was a tall light skinned nigga with freshly done locks and wore a tailored blue suit that had to cost a grip. And if the suit didn't say everything about his paper, the AP on his wrist did. If I would've ran across him in the world, I would've been up a Patek and he would've been face down on the ground.

"Does the state have anything to say before I rule on the motion filed by Mr. Higgins?" The judge asked, not seeming too impressed by my lawyer's spiel.

District attorney, Maxine Fraser, stood up quick, adjusting the yellow skirt as she cleared her throat. I seen her at two other court dates and even though we hadn't spoken to each other, it was understood that I hated her and she hated me. Her being black increased my hatred. When another black person try to bam you in court it feel how them slaves in the field felt when they got told on by house niggas.

"Your Honor, Mr. Higgins's motion has no merit. Furthermore, we shouldn't traumatize the victim by making him testify more than once for the same crime. If they committed the crime together, they should be tried together. What the jury sees is the picture that Mr. Peterson created. He pulled that gun and robbed Mr. Bankton. He shouldn't be rewarded with being seen in a positive light by the jury. Furthermore, the county budget is being stretched already with covid regulations and rules. We can't afford to pick and move two juries for one case. This case needs to be tried with his codefendant. The real interest of justice lies with the victims and not the perpetrators."

If I had a gun and wasn't cuffed to a shock belt with shackles on my legs, I would've killed that bitch ten times. It felt like she alley hooped my ass. And the way the judge was looking told me that he was about to catch me like Giannis catch them lobs from Jrue Holiday and slam my ass.

"Mr. Higgins, I have read over your motion as well as the state's rebuttal and listened to both arguments. While your client is certainly within his rights to request a separate hearing and trial, he isn't entitled to such. Mr. Peterson and Mr. Finch are co-defendants. They allegedly committed the same crime and as such I believe they should be tried together. Furthermore, this covid-19 pandemic has challenged the justice system and stretched our limits. If we are to consider the interest of justice, as both lawyers have contended, the interest of justice lies with the state's representation of the victims and not the perpetrators. There will be no severed trial and the motion is denied. Please set up a scheduling so that we can proceed with pretrial. If neither of you have any more concerns, the court is adjourned."

My lawyer shook his head as the judge skirted from the courtroom. "Sorry, Bobby. I told you it was a hail Mary. I tried, brotha."

That helpless feeling wrapped around me a little tighter as the bailiff approached to escort me from the courtroom. "I know, man. It is what it is."

"Call me if you need anything."

I didn't even respond to those words. I needed to be free and it didn't look like he could help me with that. Instead, I focused on my family as I shuffled towards the exit. My moms, Jamie, and Simone had shown up to support me. Simone's teary eyes touched a nigga's soul. Being locked up was testing us like a motherfucker and we was barely hanging on. Simone wanted me free. Needed me to take care of her. I didn't even realize how much she depended on my until now. I also noticed a few changes in her attitude. She talked a little bit slicker and got mad easily. We argued constantly about dumb shit. She mouthed for me to

Homwave when I got back on the pod. After giving her a nod, I looked to moms and her husband. They were clasping their hands together, telling me to pray. Every time we talked they told me to trust God and that his will would be done. If God's will was for me to stay in jail, we probably wouldn't be seeing eye to eye for a long time.

After a short stay in the holding cell behind the courtroom, I was taken back to the pod. The fight with Jewels n'em got me thirty days in the hole and put on a new pod on the fifth floor. There wasn't much difference between the fifth and sixth floor except that Jewels and his groupies wasn't around. Being locked up taught me that jail is jail, no matter what floor you on. I got back to the pod around ten o'clock and the dayroom was in full swing. I spotted Dutch at the card table playing spades. We got out of the hole on the same day and they put us on the same pod but different cells. I had a lot of love for the white boy for riding out with me. Jewels and his groupies whooped our asses but we went down like some gangstas. He left the card game and walked over.

"Nephew, what they do for you, my dude?"

"Muthafuckas denied the motion like I thought. They tryna hang a nigga."

He shook his head. "Damn, homie. That's fucked up."

"I know, man. But ain't shit a nigga can do about it. I definitely ain't finna let them see me sweat."

"I know that's right. Gotta keep that head up like yo nose bleeding. Let me get back to this game, fool. I'ma fuck with you later."

After talking to Dutch, I went to the booth for a Homwave with Simone. She was in the backseat of Jamie's Cadillac.

"I'm sorry you didn't get what you wanted, baby. But we already knew how they was playing it so don't let it get you down."

I put on a strong face. "Anthony told me it was a hail Mary so I didn't really have my hopes up. I was more worried about how you was gon react. I know this weighing on you."

She looked away from the screen for a moment. "No matter what happens, I got your back, baby. Do the time and don't let it do you. Just keep your head up and don't worry about me. I'll figure it out."

"Let me speak to my son," my mom said. Simone disappeared and my mama's face filled the screen. My eyes were immediately drawn to the mole on her left cheek. The beauty mark had always grabbed my attention since I was a kid. "I know you didn't get what you wanted but don't let the devil make you think he won, Bobby. God got all the power and his will is being done. It might not feel like it but it is. Just hang on."

I wanted to tell her that was easy for her to say because she wasn't the one locked up but I didn't. I knew she was trying to encourage me. "If God's will is to keep me locked up, I ain't feeling that, mama. Jail ain't for me. Getting me out will get my attention more than keeping me locked up."

She looked at me like parents do when they kids talk nonsense. "Boy, that ain't how God work. He ain't somebody you can make deals with. You robbed somebody. You think you just supposed to get out of jail because you want to? If you can't do the time, you shouldn't of done the crime. God got you sitting in there for a reason."

I sucked the back of my teeth. Her words had flipped from encouraging me to pissing me off. "Ma, I know what's best for me and being in jail ain't it."

"You don't know nothing, Bobby, and that's your problem. Think you got it all figured out at twenty five years old but you don't. That's why yo butt sitting in jail for thinking you know it all and you grown."

I was done talking to her. "Can you give the phone back to Simone?"

Her eyes popped like I raised my voice at her. "Well, if that's how it is, keep it like that, Bobby. Bye."

"Let me see the phone, " Jamie said, grabbing the phone and sticking it on the dashboard. My mom's husband had smooth brown skin, a bald head, full beard, and dark eyes. Our relationship wasn't that of father and son but I respected him and he respected me. "How you holding, son?"

I let out a frustrated breath. "I'm holding."

"That's right. And you keep holding. I did my share of dirt and had to spend a little time where you at so I know what you going through. The one thing that you can't lose is your faith and hope. They took all of your money and worldly possessions but don't lose that faith and hope because that's what's gon bring you through. If you lose them, you won't have nothing. You hear what I'm saying?"

"Yeah, I hear you."

"Good. Stay encouraged and keep the faith. Keep praying and going to church and remaining faithful to God and he gon remain faithful to you. I know everything seem dark right now but it will get better. I'ma let you talk back to your girl. Hold yo head."

After I got off the Homwave with my girl, I went to the room to collect my thoughts. I grabbed the AM/FM radio that I bought off canteen, slapped on the headphones, and jumped on my bed. V-100 was a local radio station that played hip hop and R&B music. As soon as I turned on the station, Rihanna and Future's 'Love Song' flowed into my ears and traveled straight down to my heart. I was never a sucka for love but being locked up was making me one. Every song reminded me of Simone and not knowing what she was doing or who she was doing it with was fucking with me. She was also acting different. Stupid arguments over shit that happened a year ago. 'Remember when you was talking to a female in the store who complimented your shoes? You was fucking her, wasn't you?' Yesterday it was, 'why you cheat on me with Jasmine? Was her pussy better than mine?

Did you love her? Do you still talk to her?' Everything that she came at me about was supposed to be dead but she suddenly wanted to argue about it while I'm locked up and fighting for my life. Shit was stressing me out. It felt like she was pushing me away. It didn't take a rocket scientist to see what was about to happen next. I heard stories about bitches breaking bad on niggas when they catch a bid. Never thought I'd be one of the niggas telling that story.

Later that day I was in the dayroom learning to play chess and trying to keep my mind off the time I was facing. Cowboy was my teacher and opponent. He was forty something years old and had done a couple bids up north. I liked him because he didn't play around or engage in fuckery. His face was usually serious and that kept niggas away. There was a method to his actions. If you came off hostile or serious, niggas left you alone. The less people you interact with, the less chance of you having to beat a nigga ass or get into drama. I liked that he was able to keep niggas away without saying it and I wanted to learn what he knew about prison. Based on all the dirt I did in the streets, I was going to need them. But first I was about to steal a rook that he left unprotected on the chessboard.

"Let me get this rook," I grinned, snatching the piece off the board and placing my bishop where it had been. I hadn't beat him yet but now that I was up a power piece, it looked like I was finally about to get me a W.

He didn't look fazed by losing the piece or my gaining an advantage. "You ever heard the saying, 'never look a gift horse in the mouth'?"

The smile disappeared from my face. Even though I couldn't see the trap, I knew I had fallen for one. "What you talking about?"

He nodded towards the game. "Look at the board."

While I searched the chessboard for the reason behind his confident look, he gave me a lesson in history.

"In ancient Greek history they talk about the Trojan war. The Greeks and Trojans beefed for ten years because the Trojans took the king of Greece's wife, Helen. After a decade of fighting, the Greeks seen they couldn't win and gave up the fight. They sent a big ass wooden horse to the Trojans as a gift and peace offering. It was a gift horse. The Trojans bring the big wooden gift horse inside they city not knowing its filled with Greek soldiers. When everybody go to sleep, the Greek soldiers come out of the horse and get to killing everybody. In this story, you the Trojans, Nephew. You thought that rook was a gift, but it wasn't."

I watched as he grabbed the black Queen and slid it across the board in front of my white King. By taking the rook, I had opened the board and freed his Queen to checkmate me.

"Damn. I didn't see that. That was cold," I admitted.

"Chess has a lot in common with real life. Sometimes we get so focused on something that we want or appears to be free and miss the power play. Gotta keep yo eyes open. Wanna play again?"

I stored the jewel in the back of my mind. "Let's go."

I played chess with Cowboy until the C.O did mail call. The day room became as silent as a funeral home while Miss Collins called names. When she called mine, I went to collect my package. It was a small six inch white envelope. I looked at the name on the top left corner and damn near dropped the mail. Jasmine Sanders, my chocolate drop. But there was no return address. "Hell nah," I mumbled, pulling the single piece of paper out while walking back to the table. I couldn't wait to read what she wrote. A part of me was hopeful that she was about to show up and take Simone's place.

"I'ma take a piss while you read," Cowboy said before leaving.

The letter was short. The handwriting was neat with lots of swoops and easy to read.

Dear nephew, I wanted to tell you this before you heard it from somebody else. I'm pregnant. I don't think the baby yours but I'm not a hundred percent sure because I was fucking Bill too. He my man now and he taking care of me and the baby. He don't know that I know you and I want to keep it like that. That's why I'm not accepting no calls from you. I'm only writing this letter to tell you not to contact me. The police came and talked to me but I convinced them and Bill that I didn't know you. If you leave me alone, Ima keep my mouth shut. Don't come looking for me about a paternity test because Bill the daddy. I want to be with him. If you blow up my spot, I'ma testify against you. Don't try to contact me. Bye.

After reading the letter, I just sat there and stared at it like it was that black gooey shit from outer space that turned Jeff Hardy into the alien mutant, Venom. Jasmine had rocked my world. She was pregnant and didn't want me to reach out to her. What the fuck!? I was mad, hurt, and confused. How could she play with a baby like? How could she use testifying against me as leverage? This bitch was beyond scandalous. She was evil. Only an evil muthafucka would use a baby like that. All because she wanted to be with another nigga. Evil.

"Okay, nephew. I hope that letter was good news because-" Cowboy paused when he seen my face. "You good, Brah?"

I shook my head and pointed at the letter. "This bitch just fucked me up."

His face softened like he knew what I was going through. "Oh shit. Baby girl just hit you with the Dear John letter, huh?"

"Nah, my nigga. Its worse than that?"

"What's worse than your girl breaking bad when you get locked up?"

"Read it."

He picked up the letter and read. His facial expression went from curious to wide eyed and shocked. "Damn, you serious? She doing it like that?"

No words were needed.

He sat the letter down and put the chess pieces away. "You know you can't contact her, right? If you do, she gon fuck you up."

"But that baby might be mine, Cowboy. How I'm just supposed to walk away from my seed?"

"How much time you facing?"

"Sixty years."

"Shit, if that ain't enough reason to walk away then I don't know what is. You need all the breaks you can get, my dude. If she say don't come looking for her, than respect that. At least for now. Shit, you can try to find her for a paternity test after you do yo time. You can also have more kids when you get out. But don't fuck around and make her testify against you. You might never make it back home."

I got up and went in my room to think. Everything Cowboy told me was on the money but something inside of me still wanted to get at Jasmine. I didn't like not being able to raise my seed. What type of nigga would I be if I didn't fight to be in my kid's life? I didn't have a relationship with my dad and I didn't want that for my shorty. Plus, my moms would go crazy if she found out I could have a baby out there and didn't tell her about it. But I also didn't want this bitch to testify on me. The judge looked like he wanted a reason to give me 100 years. I was damned if I did and damned if I didn't. I needed some solid advice so I went to use the phone.

"What's up, Bobby?" Jamie answered. "If you looking for your mother, she out with Sister Sims."

"Nah, Jamie. I wanted to talk to you."

Although me and Jamie had a good relationship, we rarely talked about serious stuff. And if we ever did talk about something serious, it was super serious. Like when I first got suspended for weed in school or when I called from the booking room to tell him and my moms I was being charged with robbery.

"What's up, son? Everything okay?"

The part of Jasmine's letter about the kid possibly being mine flashed in my head. "Jamie, man, this female playing games with me and I don't know what to do."

"Simone is ready to cut out on you, huh?"

"It's not Simone. It's somebody that's connected to why I'm in here. She pregnant but she don't want me to be in they life."

"Whoa, Bobby. This sounds serious, man. Who is she? How is she connected?"

I thought about the phone calls being recorded. "I can't say that. You know they listening. But its somebody out there with some knowledge about me that could really do me in. She say if I try to contact her about the shorty, she will give that info to them people."

"My God," he mumbled. "Okay, son. This is what we can do. Write me a letter. They cannot open your outgoing mail. It is against the law. Explain everything to me and I will do what I can. But whatever you do, don't do anything that will get you in more trouble. I can be your eyes and ears out here. Me and your moms got your back."

"Jamie, I need you to do me a favor and not tell my moms. She won't understand like you do. Plus, its a possibility the baby not mine. I just need to have somebody out there to help me figure it out when it is time."

"Oh, boy, Bobby. Your mother is gon be real mad if she finds out we kept this from her."

"Cmon, Jamie. I need you to hold this to your vest until we find out the real."

He let out a breath. "Okay, Bobby. I got you, son. If this will take some of the burden off you, I'll do it. Just tell me what you need me to do."

I felt a little better about the situation after the call with Jamie. Just knowing that I had someone out there to help me find her when the time came made some of the stress go away. After writing Jamie a letter detailing who Jasmine was, our situation, and how to find her, I dropped the letter in the mail box. I spent the rest of the night thinking about being a dad watching my son grow through pictures.

$$$

When I woke up the next morning, my thoughts immediately jumped to Jasmine's evil ass. I dreamed that we had a son and were fighting over custody. We were in court and she was telling the judge that I robbed people and she didn't want our son around me because I would teach him to rob people too. Our three-year-old sat in the witness chair next the judge watching me and his moms fight. Then the judge asked our son what he wanted and he said, "For my mommy and daddy to stop fighting." Thats when I woke up. The dream felt real as hell. I could see our beautiful brown skinned boy and feel the love for him in my heart. I could also feel my hatred towards Jasmine as she spoke to the judge. I wondered if the dream was a sign that I was the father of Jasmine's baby. After pushing the dream from my head, I got up to get fresh. I took a piss, washed my hands, face, and brushed my teeth and then hit the dayroom to use the phone. I checked the clock on the wall as I dialed Simone's number. 9:37AM.

"G'morning, baby."

"Nah, don't good morning me, nigga. You about to have a fucking baby, nigga?"

You know that feeling you get when the worst and most unexpected thing happens to you and you are so shocked by it that you freeze up? That's what I experienced when Simone hit me with the question. My eyes bugged out like Wendy Williams and my jaw dropped like them old ass cartoons when they see a fine girl. How did she find out? Did

Jamie tell her? Nah, he wouldn't do me like that. Would he? I didn't know what to say so I did what all guilty people do.

"What is you talking about?"

"Don't fucking play with me, Nephew. I seen the shit on Facebook last night. Yo fucking girlfriend is pregnant, nigga."

Jamie didn't tell on me. Facebook did. "I don't got no girlfriend besides you. And I still don't know what you talking about. Who the fuck is pregnant and what that got to do with me?"

"Jasmine, nigga. Yo lil black ass ugly bitch. She posted it. Yolanda showed it to me yesterday."

"She pregnant? Did she say it was mine?"

"Don't play stupid, Nephew. You knew that bitch was pregnant. Is it yours?"

I didn't want to deny Jasmine's baby. I felt that denying it would be like turning my back on it before it was born. "This the first I heard about her being pregnant. I don't even talk to her. "

"You lying, nigga. I know you still be talking to her and I know that's yo baby."

After listening to Simone's explanation, she didn't know that I could be Jasmine's baby daddy. She was fishing and trying to get me to tell on myself. But I was about to flip the script. "Why the fuck is you coming at me about bullshit that I don't even know nothing about? I don't talk to her and I didn't know she was pregnant. You keep coming at me about shit that's supposed to be dead. You tryna push me away? If you wanna leave, then leave. You don't gotta be all sneaky about the shit and tryna finesse it. I'm facing sixty muthafuckin years and you keep coming at me about shit that don't matter and that I don't give a fuck about. What's really good?"

"Nah, nigga. Don't try to change it up. I didn't say nothing about leaving."

"So why you bringing up all this old shit? Why you adding to the shit that I'm already going through? You supposed to be helping me get through this, not making it harder. I put my life on the line tryna make sure we could eat and now that I'm down bad it seem like you tryna make it worse."

"That's not what I'm tryna do. I'm lonely out here. I'm mad that we can't be together or that I can't see you when I want to. I'm not tryna make yo time harder but I'm hurting, too. We got unresolved issues. I just sit here at night and think about our life and everything and I get mad at you for not being here." Her explanation was cut short by a sob. "I never had to go through this before and missing you is hard."

Even though I was mad at her for stressing me out over petty shit, I felt her pain. I could hear it in her voice. Being locked up was just as hard for her as it was for me. "Arguing with me and bringing up old shit ain't gon fix nothing. Its only gon make it worse. You making my time harder with that shit."

"Well, if I'm making yo time so fucking hard, why the fuck do you keep calling me? Why the fuck do you want me to show up at your court dates then? Huh? Why the fuck you want me to send pictures and money? Huh? Do you got another bitch that's gon do what I do?"

I had to pull the phone away from my ear for a second. "Nigga, I don't need you to do nothing for me. And you wasn't talking this hoe ass shit when I was buying you cars and bags and Gucci this and Fendi that. Now you wanna try to act like you got the upper hand on a nigga because I'm in a jam. Now you wanna try to hold this petty ass shit over my head. I don't need you, nigga. I don't need nobody. Fuck is you talking about?"

"Oh, you don't need me now? It's like that?"

The tone of her voice told me this was a loaded question. She wanted to feel validated and the only way for that to happen was to tell her I needed her. She wanted me to depend on her and kiss her ass. She wanted the power in the relationship. And if I didn't give her that, she would probably leave. I had never seen this side of Simone. She was my ride or die. We plotted on niggas and robbed them together. It was supposed to be us against the world. Jay and Bey. I never thought she would flip it up now that I was down.

"Hell nah, I don't need you. I'ma boss, baby. You know how I rock. You know how I do." Wasn't no way I would bow down to her. I wasn't about lower myself or become her bitch just because I was locked up. I was standing with my two feet on the ground, even if that meant I would be standing by myself.

"You know what, Bobby? Since you don't need me, I don't need you either. Call me when you need something. Bye."

Chapter 6

Nephew (3 months later)

Losing Simone hurt like a mutherfucker. I missed the shit out of her but my pride wouldn't let me call her. Wasn't no way I was about to tell somebody I needed them just to make them feel good. Especially when I risked my life and freedom to feed them. If anything, she owed me. In the two years that we was together, I spent over a hunnit racks on her. She got anything she wanted. Thousand-dollar clothes. New whips, and trips. Bills and rent paid. I did all that out of love. My girl didn't want for shit. And now that I was fucked up she want a nigga to beg for her to do what a real bitch supposed to do. That shit was foul with a capitol F. And the fact that she didn't write or set up a visit to check on me told me exactly how she felt. She was ready to break on nigga. She just needed a reason and me not kissing her ass was it. She lucky I couldn't bail out otherwise I would've painted the living room with her brains.

A noise outside of the holding cell pulled me from thoughts of Simone. The bailiff was probably coming to get me. I was locked in a small room behind the judge's chamber. Today was the first day of pre-trial. Me, Little, our lawyers, and the bitch ass district attorney would begin picking the jury. We had to pick twelve men and women from a pool of twenty and they would decide whether me and Little was guilty. I was still contemplating the latest deal from the district attorney. If I plead guilty, she would recommend twenty years. Ten years in prison and ten years on parole. It was her second offer. The first was for me to plead guilty for twenty-five years. I quickly denied that because wasn't no way I was about to agree to do twenty-five years. My lawyer told me to reject it too. He said she would come down but it would take some negotiating. The bailiff's face appeared in the small plexiglass window on the steel door.

"They ready for you."

When the door opened, he and his partner put shackles on my legs and cuffs on my wrist before putting me in a wheelchair and rolling me into the courtroom. The judge wasn't in yet but there were about twenty people spread out in the gallery wearing facemasks. Men and women of all ages and races, but mostly white. This was the jury pool. The district attorney ignored me as she spoke with a man sitting next to her. My lawyer looked cool in the powder blue tailored suit as he whispered to the chubby white man sitting next to him. The white man was Mark Daffles, Little's lawyer. Little sat next to him in a wheelchair wearing the orange jumpsuit and chains like me. When the bailiffs rolled me up to the table our lawyers arranged us so that me and Little sat next to each other on the inside and our lawyers were on the outside.

"How you doing, Bobby?"

"I don't know. It all depends on what you gotta say."

"Well, me and Mark spoke to the D.A and she wanna make a deal. She don't want the county to waste time a resources on your case when she got a video of the robbery. She want you and Mr Finch to plead guilty and let these people go home because these covid rules is making the criminal justice process difficult and expensive."

"Is she still talking about twenty years? Because I'm not accepting that. I'd rather have all these people stay here and make them spend whatever it takes to get through the trial."

"Nah, we were able to get her down to ten years. Five in prison and five on parole. I think that might be as good as it gets but its up to you. We can deny it and see if she will go lower."

I ran the number around in my head. Five years didn't seem bad, especially since I was facing sixty years. I would get out when I was thirty years old. I would still be young enough to live life. But if we could get it lower... "You think she will drop it lower?"

"I don't know. Considering that you on video, probably not. But the only thing that beats a failure is a try. But whatever you decide, you and Finch have to agree so you might wanna talk to your guy."

I spun to my boy. He was speaking to his lawyer. "Holla at me, bro."

"What's up, Nephew. I'm talking about this deal with my lawyer."

"Yeah. They talking about five years. What you wanna do?"

Something like hope flashed in his eyes. "It don't sound that bad. Especially since they got us on tape. She dropped it down from twenty-five to five. My lawyer thinks this is the best deal and for us to take it."

I took a moment to think. I looked to the D.A. She was still talking to the man next to her. They didn't seem to be paying us any attention so I wasn't sure if they were talking about us. I glanced at the jury and most of them wore bored faces, like they'd rather be anywhere than the courtroom. "I think we should try to get it lower."

Little looked uncomfortable. "My nigga, you tryna play with fire. What if the bitch renig? I can do a nickel. I been up north already and its way better than the county jail. If we try to deal she might make us sit a couple more months and I'm tired of this jail shit. Plus, I ain' tryna lose the deal."

I had never been to prison so I didn't understand how it was better than jail. I was still locked up and to me being locked up was the same no matter where you was at. "I think we should try to get it lower. If she don't go, then we deal. But I feel like we gotta give it one more try."

He let out a frustrated breath. "I don't know, Nephew. Let me holla at Mark."

While Little spoke to his lawyer, I turned to mine. "I think we should take one more shot at a better deal. See if we can get it a little lower."

"Y'all in agreement?"

I turned to Little. He was wrapping up the conversation with his lawyer. I waited. "Take one more shot?"

I nodded to Anthony. Our lawyers got up and walked over to the D.A's table. I watched them intently, trying to guess what they were saying and wishing I was in the conversation. The D.A and the man next to her looked at us a couple times during their conversation.

"You think they going?" Little asked.

"I don't know. The bitch keep looking at us though. But I can't tell if that's a good thing or bad thing."

While they were in the midst of their discussion, the door to the judge's chamber opened and in walked the Judge. The lawyers ended their conversation and walked back over to us and sat down.

"We might have something," Anthony whispered

"What?"

"Hang on. Wait until the judge speaks."

"All rise for the Honorable Judge John Warner," the bailiff said.

The lawyers stood.

"You may be seated," the judge said as he sat down and looked out over the court. "You all seem to be in a spirited discussion. Care to share?"

"Your honor, we were discussing the possibility of a plea deal," the D.A said.

The judge looked surprised and interested. "Really? Do you need more time?"

The D.A shared a look with our lawyers. "Yes. If we could have a recess, it is possible that we could resolve this case this morning."

"That sounds good. Shall I dismiss the jury pool?"

Our lawyers shared another look and exchanged nods."Yes, your honor. We can dismiss them. A deal is in the works."

"As you wish," the judge said before turning to the court reporter. "This case was scheduled for a pre-trial and jury selection but let the record show the jury is being dismissed and the court will have a twenty minute recess for plea discussion." Then he turned to the people in the gallery. "Jury members, thank you for honoring your civic duty but your services are no longer needed. Have a good day. Court is in recess."

And with a bang of the gavel the judge and jury left the courtroom leaving our lawyers, the D.A and her partner, and the bailiffs. Maxine walked over and got right down to business. "They are not getting off without doing prison time."

"We're fine with them doing time. Just a matter of how much. We feel that five years is too much. Especially for a first time offender like Bobby," my lawyer said.

"Five years is low considering what they did. And it was in broad daylight. We have witnesses that will testify," her partner jumped in.

"We never said our clients weren't guilty. You have it on tape," Mark said. "We just don't want our clients to spend that much time behind bars. Nor do we want to continue to stress the states already stressed budget. Covid rules are making the logistical side of things very difficult. Our clients will plead out right now for one year of initial incarceration followed by one year of parole."

Maxine looked like she wanted to throw up. "You can't be fucking serious. Four years inside and four years on parole. And that's because Bobby is a first time felon."

My lawyer countered. "Two and two."

"This is my final offer or we will call the jury pool back and have a trial. Three years in and three years out, with a ten year stayed sentence if they violate parole. Both men will also owe ten thousand dollars in restitution. That's the best I got. If you deny, we go to trial and when they lose I will push for them to get the max."

I watched the negotiation on the edge of my seat and when she made the final offer I hoped the lawyers didn't deny it. That was as good as it was going to get. I was ready to plead guilty.

"You heard her, fellas. Final deal. What do you want to do?" Mark asked.

Me and Little spoke at the same time. "Deal."

$$$

The State Pod was a unit in the county jail that housed inmates after they were sentenced to prison time. This is also where I learned that there 'are' differences in jail pods. Unlike the sixth floor, and the rest of the pods in the Milwaukee County Jail, there was no C.O on the floor with us to keep order and babysit. On the state pod the C.Os were outside the unit behind big ass glass windows. They watched the pods from the outside for their own health and safety. Somebody with a fresh life bid wouldn't have a problem sticking a guard in the eye with a shank made out of a toothbrush. They already got life so more time for fucking up a slick talking guard wouldn't matter. The only time they came onto the state pods was when we were locked in our cells or there was an emergency. After we were given our three-year sentences, they moved me and Little to the State Pod to await our transport to prison. There were a few niggas sitting around playing board games. A few more on the phones. We were sitting at a table near the TV area watching music videos on BET and talking about life.

"So, Simone cut out on you, huh? I definitely didn't see that coming," Little said, shaking his head in pity. "I thought she was a rider, for sure. Especially since she was on the front line holding heat. That just goes to show you that you don't really know nobody. Remind me of that Boosie song, 'Trust Nobody'."

"Or 'Betrayed'. I trusted her with my life, brah. Wasn't nothing I wouldn't have did for her. And then she do me like this. The chocolate drop fucked me over too. She fucking with the nigga we licked. Pregnant and telling me not to contact her or she gon testify. Brah, I don't think I'ma do the love thing again. Muthafuckas got larceny in they hearts."

"I don't think you should go that far, brah. Still a few good ones out there. Lisa holding a nigga down like ankle weights. You just gotta find the right one. God got that virtuous woman out there for you. I was just blessed to meet mine a lil earlier than you. But I think she out there, fa sho. Just gotta go through."

"I hear you, fam, but I don't know. Right now I'm just focused on getting through this time. I hope this shit go smooth and these niggas just let me be. I just wanna do my time and go home."

"I hear you, Nephew. I ran into a nigga that we hit on my pod but he didn't want no smoke. You remember Chinchilla? We robbed him at the lakefront. Took his Benz and Chinchilla coat."

"Yeah, i remember him. You gave Lisa daughter the coat, right?"

"Yeah. She still got that, too. Nigga didn't say nothing to me but we knew who each other was. "

" Jewels and his clique of groupies tried to get down on me but I held my own. Casts and all. I took off on that nigga first."

"I heard about that. They said you and the white boy tore that bitch up. Niggas went down swinging."

"That was my nigga, Dutch. White boy is a rider. For real," I laughed as visions of the fight flashed in my head. I got my ass beat but I made sure to get mine in.

"I wish I was there with you, my nigga. We definitely would'da fucked them niggas up."

We went silent for a moment and watched a throwback of Mary Mary's 'God in Me' video.

"Lisa wanna get into the church. She thinks God answered our prayers. We prayed for me to get 3 years. God answered."

I gave him a look. "On what?"

"That's my word, brah. We knew that I wasn't gone come home so we just prayed for mercy. We agreed on three years and kept praying on it. That's why I jumped on it when Maxine said it. I think that was God at work. I'ma use this time to get closer to God. I'm finna put the guns up, Nephew. I ain't coming back. "

I knew Little believed in God but I was surprised to hear that he was putting the guns up. " That's what's up, my nigga. I don't know what I'ma do but that ten year stayed sentence got me a lil shook. No way I'm finna do a dime. Moms nem talking that church shit but I don't know. I gotta do something different but I don't know what to do. I guess I'ma play it by ear."

"I hear you, Nephew. That's all we can really do is play it by ear."

We hung out in the dayroom watching videos and playing a little chess until it was time to serve dinner. Mashed potatoes, gravy, and undercooked green beans was on the menu. I took a couple of bites but mostly played in the food. Getting a fresh three years had taken my appetite. Plus, the instant mashed potatoes were dry and hard and the gravy was so thick that it didn't even move. It looked more like a greyish brown paste than something you put on top of food. Little didn't seem to have a problem eating. He smashed all of the food on his tray and looked like he wanted seconds.

We were putting our trays away when the locks on the pod door popped. I turned and seen a short brown skinned nigga with cornrows walk on the pod. He carried bed sheets and a couple brown paper shopping bags with his property inside. The redness and swelling around his eyes told that he just got a fresh sentence.

"Monday through Friday, from eight to five they be bamin niggas," Little said, quoting Plies'100 Years'.

"They don't want our money they want our freedom," I added.

We had to lock down until the swampers cleaned the unit so I headed to my room. The new nigga seemed popular as he spoke to a few niggas that were still eating. I was walking up the stairs when I made eye contact with him. He nodded so I nodded back. He turned to go his way before doing a double take. Recognition flashed in his eyes. We exchanged long looks before I started mugging him. I was about to start barking but he looked away. I kept my eyes on him until I was in my cell. When the door closed, I racked my brain trying to think of who this nigga was. And then it hit me. Tike. Me and Little caught him slipping at the gas station and took his 300C on 24s, some money, and jewelry. Damn. It looked like my hopes for niggas to leave me alone was about to be tested. I hopped on my bed and turned my radio on V-100. Lil Durk's 'Viral Moment' took me out of the cell and put me back in my Camaro. I was speeding down Sherman Boulovard smoking something good. I could taste the backwood and smell the green burning. Damn, I was going to miss riding and smoking. I dozed off but was awoken by the lock on my door being popped. That meant the dayroom was open. I stepped onto the tier and looked towards Little's door. He stepped out his room and looked towards me.

"What you on?" I asked.

"I gotta hit Lisa real quick."

"Okay. I gotta holla at you when you get off the phone."

I was walking down to the TV area when Tike's door opened. I watched his eyes search the dayroom until he found me. We exchanged mean mugs before he looked away. I sat down and kept one eye on the TV and the other on Tike. He walked around speaking to the niggas that he knew while sneaking peeks at me. Some of the niggas he spoke to turned to look at me. I could feel the animosity in the air and knew it was about to go up. We all had fresh prison sentences with nothing to lose. When Little got off the phone, I filled him in what was going on.

"That nigga that came in after dinner is Tike. You remember him?"

"Tike? Tike? What we do to him?"

"The white 300C at the gas station on 27th. He over there by the windows with them dread heads. "I nodded in their direction.

"Yeah, I remember that nigga now. Took that Cuban from him too."

"Yep. And it look like he recruiting. Niggas been sneaking peeks since the dayroom opened. I think they building courage."

"One thing we not finna do is let these niggas get the ups on us, Nephew. We hittin first. You got something in yo room to even the odds? Its more of them than us."

"Shit, I got a couple tooth brushes. "

"Me too. Lets go put our shit together and come back in like an hour. If them niggas still on they fake mugging shit, we gon move on they bitch asses."

The plan sounded good to me. Wasn't no way I was about to get my ass whooped and stomped again. This time I was taking the advantage. "Say less."

I went to the room and grabbed my toothbrush from the holder and the extra one from my brown property bag. Then I found a rough spot on the floor under the toilet and began rubbing the handle across it until it was sharp. To get one toothbrush sharp enough to penetrate skin took about thirty minutes and my fingers and wrists was sore as hell. But Tike and his groupies kept me focused on the agenda. At least four niggas that he spoke to looked at me so counting Tike, there were five potential threats. All of them was about to get something sharp in they life if they acted like they wanted smoke.

After sharpening the second toothbrush, I tucked them in my waistband and went to find Little. I stepped out of my cell, pausing to look over the dayroom, checking the temperature. Tike and the three niggas he was sitting at the table with looked up wearing mean mugs. I took a quick survey of the entire dayroom to see if I was getting any more hostile looks before turning back to them wearing my own mean mug. I didn't look away as I walked down the stairs and into the dayroom. They exchanged words with one another and nodded at me like it was about to go up any moment. And that was the sign that I needed to get it cracking. I was walking to Little's room when he stepped out.

"Them niggas acting like they want it, fam. They been mugging me and whispering since I came out here."

Little looked towards the table of ops and then back to me. "Well, lets get it popping one last time. Ain't no sense in waiting on these niggas to kick it off. Lets take it to em. I got Tike."

No more words were necessary. We walked towards the table on a mission. I took one side and Little took the other. I could see questions forming in the eyes of some of the niggas at the table. They wasn't sure of our intent, if they should send it up, or wait to see what happened. And that hesitation cost them. A tall skinny nigga with dreadlocks was closest to me and he became my first mark. I upped both shanks, one in each hand, and swung the one in my left hand at his neck. He jerked and that movement probably saved his life because the shank pierced his shoulder instead of his neck. He screamed and jumped away from me so I went to my next vic. A short light skinned nigga with rainbow colored dreads. He tried to run but stumbled over the chair. I reached out and stabbed him in the middle of the back. He kept on running like the stab didn't phase him. I chased him and tackled him on the ground like we was playing football. I lost one of my shanks in the scuffle but stabbed him in the arm with the other. While I was doing my thing, Little was getting down on Tike. My nigga was chasing Tike around the dayroom swinging the shank at him like it was a machete. Tike was ducking and dodging while screaming for the C.O. The forth nigga at the table ran in his room and closed the door.

The light skinned nigga grabbed my arm holding the shank with both of his hands to stop me from stabbing him again, so I used my free hand to start busting him in his shit. He rolled over to cover up, pulling my arm with the shank underneath his body while pulling me down on top of him.

"Let me go, bitch ass nigga. Let me go!" I yelled, giving him a couple of hard blows to his ribs. He didn't let me go and a loud crash made me look up. C.O's were rushing the pod with cans of pepper spray and tasers.

"Everybody lock in right now! Lock in!"

"Stop fighting! Stop fighting! Drop the shank and get on the ground!"

When the goon squad came in, the fight was over. I wasn't about to be tased or sprayed with mace so I let go of the shank and lay on the ground. The C.Os handled me rough while putting on cuffs but I didn't fight back because that would've made it worse. On the way leaving the unit, I looked at Little and smiled.

Chapter 7

Charlene

There were a lot of perks to being an only child. I got all the toys I wanted and my favorite Bratz Dolls and Barbies were still in my bedroom at home. I had lots of pets growing up, too. My favorite was our German Sheppard, Pinky. She was an old lady now but when I was younger she was my best friend. And I also liked that I didn't have to compete with siblings for my parents' time but the downside to that was my parents were always in my business. Talking to my dad about getting my period was super weird but he insisted that it was healthy for our relationship and that I would thank him when I got older. Still haven't thanked him yet. The sex talk with him at thirteen was even worse but thankfully I talked to my mom about it when I began my period a year earlier and she was able to explain to me how my body worked to compliment my dad's, "Your body is a temple" speech. And when I fell in love with Latrell and brought him home to meet them, they agreed that he was a good one and wanted me to marry him, after college of course. When they found out he cheated on me, my dad wanted to beat him up and swore there was always something about Latrell that he didn't like. Wish he would've given me the heads up before I watched him fuck Sharron in the shower. My mom wanted to spend as much time with me as possible to make sure I was healing. Like smothering a twenty-one-year-old woman with 'love and affection' was the cure for a broken heart. She had been at my apartment all day. After binge watching All American, I decided to try to paint her nails.

"I like the sparkly neon pink. I think you should go with it. Dad might even notice it and give you a compliment," I teased as we searched my box of polish for a popping nail color. My dad was notorious for missing the changes to my mother's styles or for noticing them way too late. He would have to notice Sparkly pink nails. He just had to.

"Your father is always too busy with work or on the phone. The only way he notices anything is if I put it in a text message."

My father was a workaholic with a capitol W. He worked ten hours a day as the number one salesman and manager at a hot tub store and then came home and worked from his phone until he went to sleep. His working too much, specifically bringing work home, had been causing problems in their marriage since I was a little girl. Twenty years later and dad was still bringing work home.

"That's why you need these sparkly neon pink nails, mom. He won't miss these when you take the phone from him."

She laughed a little. "No, all the colors are too much for me. I'm a simple lady. French pedicure is enough. All those colors are for you young people."

I rolled my eyes. I didn't like when my mother acted like an old lady. She was forty-nine but acted like she was sixty. "You're not that old, mom. I think age is a mental thing. If you act old then you'll be old. You're not even fifty yet. I bet if you dye your hair and get them nails popping that dad will notice."

Her brow wrinkled and a frown spread across her face. "What's wrong with my hair?" She asked, the Spanish accent heavy. When she was irritated or angry the accent and Spanish words came naturally.

I looked at her hair while trying to find the right words. Her hair was sandy brown with streaks of gray all over. She was the only women I ever met that didn't want to dye her hair. And coupled with the gray hair was her plain style of dress. She wore clothes that covered most of her skin and hardly ever wore anything form fitting. She also had nice boobies but refused to show any cleavage. She dressed like a church mom and could use a makeover. "Your hair could, um, use a little, um, dye."

She shook off the thought. "I wasn't raised to wear makeup, dye my hair, and dress provocative. My parents were Catholics and raised us a certain way. Being conservative is not a bad thing."

"But dating a black man is?"

My comment made her pause. She always spoke about the way my grandparents raised her to be a Catholic but never about how the entire family disowned her for getting pregnant by my dad. "Why do you always do that?"

"Because you talk about them like you have to live by the things they taught you when you obviously didn't. There is nothing wrong with dressing the way you want or loving who you want. If doing something different will make dad notice you, I think you should do it."

She smiled how parents do when they realize their kids are grown up. "You are so beautiful and so smart. And you look so much like your dad."

The compliments threw me off and I didn't know where the conversation was going. "So, you're saying that you agree with me and want me to paint your nails sparkly neon pink?"

She shook her head. "No. My nails are fine." Then she paused.

I waited. Something was up and it looked like she was trying to figure out a way to tell me.

"I've been speaking to your father."

I was waiting for her to tell me what she was talking to my dad about but the way she was searching for my reaction told that she wasn't talking about her husband. "You spoke to Roland?"

She nodded. "His sister reached out to me on Facebook about a week ago. I gave her my number and he called. We've talked a couple of times and he wants to speak to you."

I was speechless. The one topic that we never discussed was Roland Ford, my biological father. He got locked up when my mother was six months pregnant with me. I didn't find out that Kevin wasn't my father until the day after my eighteenth birthday. My parents decided that I was old enough to know the truth and sat me down to tell me that Roland was doing life in prison for murdering a pregnant lady. It was up to me to decide if I wanted to meet him. I declined because I had a dad. Kevin was all I knew and there was no room in my heart to love another man as my father.

"I don't want to talk to him. I already have a dad."

"Okay."

We sat in silence for a moment and Roland filled my thoughts. I didn't know anything about him. What he looked like, if I had any siblings, or cousins, or grandparents. I've never met anyone on my mom's side of the family. My dad has a sister who has one daughter, my cousin Neesy, who was like a sister growing up. That was the extent of my family and it never mattered that we didn't have a big family. Not until my mom told me that she talked to Roland's sister.

"Are you okay?"

"I don't know. I never really cared about knowing him. But now... I don't know."

She reached out and grabbed my hand. "It's okay, hija. You don't have to do anything you don't want to do. I love you and Kevin loves you. The only reason I am telling you this is because I don't want to keep anything from you. You needed to know."

"I need some time to think about everything. Thanks for telling me."

"Take as much time as you need, sweety."

My phone dinged. It was a text from Lana telling me she was outside. "Lana's here."

"Good, because I need to get home and make something for your father to eat."

"Just gon ditch me like that, huh?"

She stood and kissed me on top of my head. "You'll be fine, sweety. Now you have someone's nails you can paint."

I walked my mother to the door. "Still think this sparkly pink would've helped you and daddy get it popping."

If looks could talk, hers would've said, 'Girl please'. "Don't worry about what we are popping. I know how to turn him into a papi chulo when I need to. Keep the nail polish for somebody who needs it." Then she winked at me while stepping into the hallway. My mouth dropped open and I didn't have a comeback. Mama did that.

"Bye, sweety. Love you."

"Love you, too, mommy."

Lana walked into the building as my mother walked out. They greeted each other with a hug before mama left.

"Hey, girl. What Silvia was doing over here?"

"Trying to help me get over Latrell," I said dryly as we stepped into my apartment. "Its been three months and I'm so over him that I can't get over him any more."

She scrunched up her face. "You still thinking about him?"

"No. I just told you I was over him. What are you up to?"

"I'm ready to go get this money, girl. You wanna go cracking?"

Summer was ending and school was starting in a couple of weeks so I needed the money. Then Jay's face popped into my head. "Who's all going?"

"The usual. Me, Marquand." She paused. "And your boyfriend that like it in the booty," she laughed.

"Stop saying that. He is not my boyfriend. I wish I wouldn't have even went out with him. I liked him better when everything was a mystery. Now that I know, I wish I didn't."

"Some niggas just freaky like that, girl. That don't necessarily make him gay because he like to get his ass tampered with."

I gave her 'the look' followed by one word. "Girl."

She bust out laughing. "But he got money. A lot of it. And he about to put some in our pocket right now so lets go."

I let out a gust of air. "Okay. I hope he don't try me cause I sho hate to have to read him."

"I think he got the hint. He don't even try to flirt with you no more. Strictly business."

"Good. Where we going today?"

"Menomonee Falls. Jay got some people that want some electronics. We in and out for a thousand dollars."

$$$

We went to Lana's house to 'dress up' for our shopping spree. Dressing up was putting on a disguise. Wigs, colored contact lenses, and make-up. I threw on a red haired wig with side swept waves, green contact lenses, and light makeup. Foundation on my face and concealer under my eyes. A little bit of blush on my cheeks and some red lipstick and I was ready to go. Lana picked a purple curly wig, big Cartier glasses. When satisfied with our looks, we left for Jay's condo. We smoked a blunt during the drive and when the weed kicked in I started thinking about Roland.

"My dad wants to talk to me."

"So. What's the big deal about that?" Lana said, not giving my words much thought.

"Not Kevin. Roland."

Her eyes grew wide and she turned to look at me for a moment before focusing on the road again. "Your biological dad?"

"Yeah. Me and my mom were talking about it right before you came over."

"Is he out? I thought he got life?"

"He do. But his sister contacted my mom on Facebook and her and Roland talked a couple of times. He told her that he wants to talk to me."

"Damn. That is crazy. So, what are you gonna do?"

"I don't know. I never wanted to know him because Kevin is my dad and I didn't feel like I was missing anything. But when my mom mentioned him having a sister, it made me think about his family. What if I have a whole family? What if I have brothers and sisters? What if I met some of them and didn't even know it?"

"I mean it's possible." Then her eyes grew wide like she discovered something. "What if you slept with a family member like Kevin Gates?" she laughed.

I didn't think that was funny. "Shut up, Lana. I'm being serious."

"So am I. What if you slept with your cousin? What if you and Latrell are kin?"

I shook my head. "See, this is why I can't talk to you about serious stuff."

"Okay. I'm sorry, babe. How do you feel about talking to him?"

"I don't know. It kind of feels like I'll betray Kevin. I feel kind of obligated to only love and acknowledge him as my dad. But I also want to know if I have more family out there."

"It sounds like you should probably talk to Kevin first. I mean, I get you feeling obligated to him but you also owe it to yourself to find out where you come from. You can't talk to your mother's side of the family so that limits what you can find out. But Roland's side might unlock a lot of things. And who knows. Maybe you'll find out that Latrell is your brother."

$$$

"Ya'll look like ya'll going to the club instead of scamming," Marquand laughed as we hopped out of the rented Cadillac truck.

"You can tell us that we look good, baby. I know that's what you really want to say," Lana said, striking a pose.

"Fine, fine," I added, blowing her a kiss.

Jay looked like he wanted to comment. He had been eyeing me since we arrived at his house and during the drive to the Bud's Electronics but hadn't said much since we exchanged greetings. Which was fine with me. I just wanted to get my money and get gone. Instead he gave us a quick pep talk. "Ya'll know the move. Five thousand limits on each one. Grab them TVs. In and out. Y'all good?"

I nodded but Lana did a little extra. "We know, nigga. We ain't rookies."

"Can't never be too safe, baby," Marquand said. "And don't forget these facemasks."

We threw on the black N95 masks and got on with our mission. The store was practically empty of customers because of covid rules and lockdowns. That worked in our favor because businesses wanted customers and didn't ask many questions or harass people for fear of running them away. Jay had already checked the store's inventory online so we knew what to look for. We grabbed shopping carts and checked out the TVs that were on stands in the front of the store. There were all sorts of smart TVs that did everything imaginable. We looked around until we found the 85" Samsung. They were 4,500. I threw one in my cart and Lana threw one in hers before we made a beeline to the checkout. The white man behind the counter wore a facemask with the store logo.

"That's a nice TV," he commented, smiling with his eyes. "What's the method of payment?"

I flashed the card I got from Jay. "Credit card."

He pointed to the credit card reader and I said a silent prayer before I swiped. There was a beep and then our eyes went to the display. A second beep almost made my heart stop. The cashier studied the screen and began typing on the keypad.

"I'm sorry, but there seems to be something wrong with your card. Is it expired?"

This was the first time that a card didn't work and I began to panic. "Um, no. I just used it this morning. What is it saying?"

His brows furrowed while trying to decipher the information on the screen. "I think it says something about not being registered."

I looked to Lana, pleading for help with my eyes. My friend was more savvy than I at scamming and jumped to my rescue. "Sometimes cards do that. Just clear the screen and swipe it again. Its fine."

The clerk shrugged and cleared the screen. "Do it again."

I held my breath and said another prayer before swiping the card.

"Okay. There it goes. Turns out she was right. All it needed was a reset."

I exhaled loudly. Lana shook her head and giggled. After getting the TVs back to the Escalade Jay gave us a thousand dollars apiece and we hit the highway back to Milwaukee. The coronavirus lockdowns kept people at home and made traveling easy. When we pulled up to Jay's house, he got my attention.

"Can I talk to you for a minute?"

Alarms, bells, and whistles went off in my head. Why did he wait until we were back at his house to ask to talk? What was he up to? "Uh, sure. What do you want."

"Let them get out. I want to talk to you in private. Matter of fact, let me take you home."

I gave Lana the same look that I had when the card didn't work. But this time she didn't come to my rescue. Instead she smiled and a devious look flashed in her eyes. "That would be so cool if you could drop her off because me and Marquand got something to do."

I was mortified. I wanted to bust her in her shit.

"Call me later, babe," Lana giggled.

I gave her the middle finger.

"You don't gotta be here if you don't wanna be. I can call you a ride," Jay offered.

I didn't want to be rude to the man that just gave me a thousand dollars. "No, its not like that, Jay. You can take me home. I just didn't like the way Lana did that. It felt like she was setting me up."

"That's exactly what she just did," Jay laughed as he drove away. "She been tryna hook us up forever. And that's what I wanted to talk to you about." The energy shifted quickly and I knew what he wanted to talk about. "Shit been icy for a few months. How we go from fucking around to not speaking? Did something happen? Did I do something to kill the vibe?"

I tried to think of a nice way to tell him that asking me to stick my finger in his ass killed any chance of there being something between us. "So, um, I don't really know how to say this so I'ma just say it. Asking me to tamper with your booty was a super turnoff. That's never happened to me and it made me feel some type of way about you."

"So, you think I'm gay?"

I shrugged. "I don't know. I never had someone ask me to stick my finger in their ass so... I don't know."

He laughed and shook his head before focusing on driving. We rode in silence for a few minutes and I was hoping that he didn't take offense to me being honest.

"I think you shallow and closed minded as fuck," he blurted.

"What? Shallow?" I scoffed.

"When I was licking yo ass it was cool but the minute I want the same a nigga is gay? Fuck outta here. I ain't gay. I ain't never fucked another nigga and ain't no nigga touched me. People is different and muthafuckas like what they like.

94

You should feel blessed that I even let you in my presence or in my world. You know how many bitches a kill to lick my ass? Do you know that I can charge hoes for my dick? I'm really that nigga out here. Fuck outta here with that gay shit."

I wasn't sure how to feel about his rant. The anger was understandable but the arrogance was unnecessary. "Okay, man. Um, I don't know where this is going but I was just being honest with you. You the one that wanted to talk to me. What, you wanted me to lie to you?"

"Hell nah, I didn't want you to lie. But that fag shit is some ass bitch ass shit. I'm a boss. In real life I'm him."

It seemed like the more I said the worse things got. "I don't know what else to say but you getting madder is making me a little uncomfortable. I think we should just stop talking."

"You know you in my truck, right? That means I can say whatever the fuck I want to say. And if you don't like it, beat yo feet."

The snarl spreading across his face, lip twitches, and heavy breathing told me that it was probably safer for me to start walking. "You can pull over right here. I'm good."

He pulled over quickly, jerking the truck to a stop. "Get the fuck out, bitch."

I was shocked at how quickly things went wrong. Me and Jay had never been disrespectful to one another. I was trying to remain calm but him calling me a bitch took me there. "Don't be calling me out of my name because yo ego can't handle being bruised, nigga. And wanting something up your ass is gay. You gay. Come out the closet already. Its 2020. Just be you."

I recognized the threat of violence in his eyes and jumped from the truck before he could lay a hand on me. He climbed over the passenger seat and hopped out behind me. I knew I couldn't outrun him so I didn't even try. Plus, if something was going to happen to me, I wanted to see it coming. So I spun to face him, lifting my hands defensively. I had never had a fist fight with a man but if he hit me, I was hitting him back.

"What are you doing, Jay? You about to hit a girl?" I asked while back pedaling.

"Nah, I ain't about to hit you. I'm finna beat yo ass!" He lunged at me, tackling me in the grass.

"Get the fuck off me!" I yelled while scratching and kicking.

An engine revving and tires screeching made us both look up. I hoped it was the police but what I seen was worse. Three men wearing black masks jumped out of a green truck with guns. They ran towards us and started beating up and pistol whipping Jay. Then two of them dragged him towards the green truck. The third one grabbed me by the arm and snatched me off the ground.

"Get up, bitch. Let's go!"

Even though I just fought Jay for calling me a bitch, I knew better than to do that to a man with a gun. I allowed him to drag me to the truck and throw me in the back seat next to Jay. There was a man in the driver's seat also wearing a face mask, one jumped in the passenger seat, another next to me, and the third one hopped in Jay's truck.

"What y'all want? What this about?" Jay asked.

The man next to me lifted a gun to Jay's head. "You say one more word and I'ma put yo brains on the floor, nigga. Both of y'all put y'all heads between y'all legs and don't say shit"

I kept my head down and prayed for God to intervene as we rode in silence. I was so scared that my teeth chattered like I was freezing. The silence made it ten times worse and I began to play out different scenarios in my mind. I didn't know if I would be raped, killed, held hostage, or sex trafficked. I had lost track of time but I could feel when the truck slowed down and rode over what felt like an alley bump. A couple moments later we parked inside a garage. The man next to me grabbed my arm and pulled me from the truck. I tried to find an identifying marker in the garage but it was abandoned. The only thing I remembered was a busted window. I was taken through a backyard with a tall wooden gate around it and led towards the back door of a small green house. I could make out houses on both sides as I was taken inside. There was a short hallway, a small empty kitchen and almost bare living room. I was thrown down onto a dusty brown couch. The man that sat next to me in the backseat of the truck stood in front of me holding a gun while the others took Jay into a bedroom. I kept my head down until I heard footsteps and then a familiar voice.

"You wasn't supposed to be with him, Charlene."

I looked up and when I heard the voice. He wore dark clothes, a black ballcap covering his braids. I couldn't believe he was here. Then I remembered what Lana said. He was a killer. I wasn't sure if I should be relieved to see his face or even more scared. In the movies, the only time someone that is kidnapped sees the kidnapper's face is when they are about to die.

"I don't have anything to do with him. He was giving me a ride home."

Klan just stared at me, his eyes reflecting the indecision.

"What we gon do with this bitch?" the man with the gun asked.

"Why did you even bring her?"

"The nigga look like he was finna beat her ass. We had to make a play before somebody called twelve. She collateral damage."

Klan shook his head and let out an angry huff. "Come with me, Charlene."

The man who kidnapped me intervened. "What you doing, fam?"

Klan looked at him like a boss does a worker when they speak out of line. "I got this." Then he looked at me. "C'mon."

I followed him through the kitchen and out into the backyard. "Why the fuck is you with this nigga?"

"He was giving me a ride home."

He shook his head like I had given the wrong answer. "Nah, why is you with this nigga?"

He wanted to know everything. So I told him. "Me and my friend help him crack credit cards. That's where we were coming from. We just bought TVs and he gave us a thousand dollars."

"That's what you do? Scam?"

"I guess. I'm in college and I need the money."

He stared at me for a moment like he was judging my worth. "You fucking him?"

I didn't want to tell him the truth because it might get me killed. But I also didn't want to lie because that might get me killed too. So I answered his question with a question. "What?"

"Y'all was fighting. It was some domestic shit, huh?"

Klan was smart and I didn't want to insult his intelligence. So I kept it real. "Yeah. He wanted to know why I ghosted him. When I told him, he got mad and tried to fight me."

Curiosity flashed on his face. "Why did you ghost him?"

"Because... He wanted me to..." I couldn't say it. Klan waited, impatience growing in his eyes. "Can I tell you the whole story?"

He pulled out a cellphone to check the time. "Tell it fast."

"I never messed around with him until the night I seen you at the club. That was the only time. I ghosted him afterwards because he asked me to toss his salad and stick my finger in his ass."

Klan's eyes grew wide and then he laughed. "What the fuck?"

"That's what I was saying. That shit was weird. I didn't want to talk to him anymore and when I told him, he tried to fight me but your boys stopped it."

He went quiet and began staring at me again. I gave him the saddest puppy dog eyes, silently praying that he spared my life. "Can I trust you?"

I took my time answering. "Yes."

He searched my face for the truth. "Its something about you. I don't know what it is but I'm not gon let nothing happen to you. I'ma make sure you get home but I need you to keep this between us. Don't tell nobody about this conversation or that you seen me. Not yo mama, daddy, best friend, boyfriend. If you Catholic, don't even tell the priest at confessional. Nobody. This is street shit, Charlene, and niggas get whacked for this shit. After we finished with this nigga, we gon leave y'all in the house with y'all phones. I'ma follow you home to make sure you get there safe and also make sure you don't get on no bullshit. Now gimmie yo word that you gon do what I said. I take people's word serious. It means everything to me and I don't break my word for nobody."

"You have my word."

He stared at me again. "A'ight. I'ma put you in a room by yo'self until we done. Keep yo word."

Chapter 8

Charlene

I still couldn't believe that I got kidnapped. It had been two days since the incident and I was still in shock and probably suffering from Post Traumatic Stress Disorder. I was getting water at three this morning when the refrigerator's motor turned on and almost gave me a heart attack. Every noise put me on edge and had me checking the windows to see if Klan was out there watching. I was constantly making sure the door was locked, too. I even slept with a knife and thought about buying a gun. I didn't want to go outside because I didn't feel safe so I just sat around my apartment, smoked, and replayed how it all happened.

After talking with Klan, he put me in an empty bedroom where I sat on the floor and waited for a sign that we could leave. It took almost two hours. The room door opened and Klan told me that I could come out in five minutes. The house was quiet when I came out. I went into the living room and found our phones on the couch. Jay was in another bedroom tied to a chair and blindfolded. Besides being scared, he was okay, which I found a little disappointing. I kinda wanted Klan and his guys to beat him up for trying to fight me. I untied him and we went outside to find out where we were and I called Marquand and Lana to pick us up. Jay checked his home surveillance. The kidnappers had taken his keys and robbed his loft. We watched the different cameras inside and outside of his house as the men took scamming equipment, guns, jewelry, and a safe. They wore masks so we couldn't see their faces. I watched for someone that fit Klan's appearance but none matched his size. When I asked Jay if he knew who did it, he said no. I spoke to Lana this morning and she hadn't heard anything about the kidnappers either. I wanted to tell her what I knew. She was my best friend and we told each other everything. But I couldn't risk her telling Marquand. I didn't know what Klan would do if he found out that I had told on him.

My doorbell rang, interrupting my thoughts. I wasn't expecting company nor did I feel like being bothered so I lay in bed hoping that whoever was outside would go away. They didn't and the doorbell rang a few moments later. I got up and drug myself to the intercom.

"Who is it?" No one answered but the doorbell rang again. I got funny feeling. "Hello? Who is it?"

"It's me."

I knew the voice and the sound of it made my blood boil. "I told you not to come by my house again."

"Cmon, Charlene. Just open the door so we can talk. Please. I miss you. I just need-"

"I don't have anything to say to you, Latrell. Get away from my house. Stop trying to contact me. I'm done done."

"But, Charlene, just open the door. Or at least unblock me so we can talk."

"No, Latrell. I don't want to talk to you and I want you to leave. Bye."

I took my finger off the intercom so I didn't have to hear his voice anymore. The bell rang two more times but I didn't answer. I waited to see if he would ring the bell again. If he did, I was going to threaten him with the police. After about a minute of no rings, I walked away. And that's when the bell rang again.

"Latrell, I'm not playing with you. Leave me alone. Get the fuck off my porch or I'm calling the police."

"Who is Latrell?"

The new voice sent an instant chill up my spine. Holy shit! It was Klan. My mind went into overdrive trying to figure out why he had come to my house. Did he think I told Jay that he was behind the kidnapping and robbery? Did he come to kill me? Should I call the police?

"Charlene?"

"Um, yeah. I'm here. Uh, what's going on?"

"I need to talk to you."

His voice didn't sound threatening but that didn't mean I wasn't in danger. "Okay. What's up?"

"You gon let me in?"

I began to jump up and down and wave my hands in panic. He wanted to come in. Oh shit. If I didn't let him in, he might send his goons to kidnap and kill me. If I did let him in, he still might kill me. I thought about calling the police again but what if he really wanted to talk? He said it was something about me. That meant he liked me, right? But I wasn't sure. Shit. I had to find out more.

"I didn't say nothing to Jay."

"I know. This ain't about that. I just want to talk to you. I'm not on no bullshit. That's my word. And I don't break my word for nobody."

Dammit. I was scared as hell but I believed what he said about his word. He said he would let me go and he did. So I buzzed him in. During the couple of seconds that it took for him to make it to my door I went back and forth about whether to let him in the apartment, call Lana to tell her that he was here, or keep the door locked and call the police. I couldn't make up my mind fast enough and the knock on the door forced me to act. I checked the peephole to make sure he was alone and then opened the door. The first thing I noticed was his scent. Vanilla, lemongrass, and good weed. He filled the entire doorframe and I had to lift my head to look in his face. His facial hair was trimmed and beard shinning like he sprayed it with a sheen. His nose was wide like the ones in the African carvings, his lips full and moist.

He wore dark clothes, Balenciaga runners, and a black ballcap over his braids. I searched his eyes for his intentions. His irises were dark and hard like blackened metal but held no malice.

"Hey," he nodded.

"Hey."

"Can I come in?"

I stepped to the side. He took a couple steps inside and looked around while I locked the door.

"Can I sit down?"

Having him ask me to come in and sit down made me lower my guard a little. If he wanted, he could've barged in and did whatever he wanted. "Yeah. Have a seat."

He took up most of the loveseat. I sat down on the lounge chair across from him.

"You got some nice lil digs here."

"Thanks."

We made eye contact for a heartbeat and in that instant his intentions became clear. Desire. He wanted me.

He dug in his pocket and pulled out a stack of money and sat it on the table. "This yo cut for keeping my secret."

"I don't need the money. You keep it."

He lifted one eyebrow and tilted his head to the side. "You really gon turn down five thousand dollars? You in school, right?"

I nodded. "Yeah, but you don't have to pay me to be quiet."

"In some cultures its disrespectful to deny a gift. Take the money. "

I didn't want to disrespect him. Plus, I needed the money. " Okay. Thanks."

"Latrell is the nigga that was leaving as I was walking up, huh?"

"Yeah. My ex. "

"Why is he yo ex?"

" I caught him cheating. "

His eyes grew wide with surprise. "Like, caught in the act?"

"In the shower with a white girl."

He shook his head. "Damn. Some niggas don't know what they got until they lose it. Salt look like sugar."

The simile surprised me. "Look at you getting all philosophical."

"I know a lil something something."

"Have you mistaken salt for sugar?"

He paused for moment. "Experience is the best teacher."

"What does that mean?"

"It depends?"

"On what?"

"On whether or not we can be friends."

We held eye contact for a moment and a scene from my sexy daydream flashed in my head. He was walking out of the water with those little shorts on and it made my temperature rise. "You want to be my friend?"

"I want to be more than friends but we can start there."

My living room got even hotter and I needed to cool down. "Do you want something to drink?"

"Now that's how you treat a friend," he grinned. "Yeah, I'll take some water unless you got something hard."

Hearing the word made me think about his dick getting hard. I wondered If it was as big in real life as it was in my fantasy? Dammit, Charlene. Calm your ass down. "I'll be right back."

I had to stick my face in the freezer and take a couple deep breaths to cool down. Then I opened the fridge and grabbed a bottle of water, my eyes lingering on the Jamison whiskey. What would happen if we took a drink? I shook the thought and went back to the living room.

"No liquor? " He asked after taking the water. "What college student got a dry house?"

"Its not dry. Its just early. Ain't even five o'clock yet."

"So, your college experience ain't been all about partying and experimenting?"

"My early years were but now that I'm about to graduate, I'm focused on grades."

"What you going to school for?"

"Business. Tell me about your experience with salt and sugar."

He took a slow sip of water and got comfortable. "I'm a very trusting person and I trusted some people that I shouldn't. My day one and my girl betrayed me. I also know what it feel like to be cheated on. Hurt like a muthafucka. "

Seeing and hearing this giant and dangerous man become vulnerable touched my heart. I was so used to seeing street niggas in a certain light. They didn't show sensitive emotions and acted way harder than necessary. But Klan didn't have a problem talking about the pain of betrayal and I respected that.

"When I seen Latrell fucking her, I thought I was having a heart attack. It literally felt like I was about to die."

"I don't know what I would'da done if I'dda caught them in the act. I found out because she left her bracelet in his car. I got it for her for Valentine's Day. Rose gold with her name etched on the back. When I found it and asked him about it, he started acting funny and stuttering. Right then I knew. And I snapped. They was sneaking around for a year. He said she came at him first."

"What did you do to them?"

"Everything but kill em."

An image of him throwing people against walls like rag dolls popped into my head. "I thought about killing Latrell, too. I was surprised because I never thought about killing nobody before. I was just so mad and hurt and I wanted to hurt him like he hurt me. Even more."

"That's the thin line between love and hate. Make you do some things that you never thought you would."

The look on his face when he said those words sent a chill through my body. It was time to lighten the mood and switch the subject. "Do you smoke?"

"Like a chimney," He grinned, pulling out an ounce of weed. "And I keep a pocketful of that strong."

"I got some Jamison in the kitchen. I'll be right back."

When I grabbed the bottle of liquor, I knew that I was sleeping with Klan tonight. I wanted to know him in every way. The danger and desire was sexy and intoxicating as hell. I grabbed two glasses and threw a couple ice cubes in each. When I walked back into the living room, I brushed against him as I sat next to him on the loveseat. He eyed the bottle of liquor while rolling a blunt. "That's that good shit."

"I love to smoke and drink a glass of Jamison on the rocks while listening to music. It is so relaxing and calming."

"I like to ride around and smoke while listening to music. When I'm high, I can feel the words."

I felt his words. "Oh, my God. I'm the same way. What do you like to listen to?"

He gave me a funny look. "Don't laugh when I say this."

"Why would I laugh?"

"I love country music."

My eyes grew wide with surprise. I didn't want to laugh but I couldn't help it. He nudged me with his knee.

"I told you not to laugh."

"Oh, my god. I wasn't expecting you to say that. Country? Like, trucks and beer and honky tonks?"

He let out a chuckle. "Not the old twangy shit but the new pop type of country. Its good music and its real. It ain't like rap where everything is cap or niggas talking about drillin and gettin money and drugs. Country is about real-life shit."

I was surprised by his passion for country music. "This is one of those situations in life that you don't see coming. You look so intimidating. Everybody and they mama would peg you as a hip hop head. Wow. I didn't expect this."I grabbed the remote off the table and gave it to him. "Show me something."

He looked up 'Stay' by Florida Georgia Line. Then we smoked and drank while watching the video. The song was about heartbreak, regret, and wanting another chance at love. I felt the lyrics "I'd sell my soul just to see your face and break my bones to heal your pain".

"Damn, that was deep."

"They got a lot of good shit. Even did some shit with Nelly. Check it out."

We sat and listened to country music for hours and I liked it. The songs were about real life and love and regret and not the honky tonk shit that I seen on commercials or heard on the radio while growing up. We talked about everything and laughed like old friends as the weed and alcohol relaxed us. We closed all the distances between us and allowed the chemistry to dictate our actions. I was sitting the length of the couch with my back against the armrest and my feet in his lap. He was rubbing my feet, slowly making his way further up my leg.

"I can't believe I'm listening to country music with you. How did you even get into this?"

He laughed at the memory. "Man, you ain't gon believe this. So, I was in maximum security at Columbia Correctional Institution. We up north and you know the rap stations don't come in like that out there so a lot of niggas listen to pop stations or this lil hip hop station out of Madison, 93.1. Well, they put me in the cell with this nigga from the treys named Red. A jack boy. My type of nigga. He was locked up for a couple robberies so we clicked on that. The nigga also loved country music. Every time a song came on the radio, he knew all the words and he had hundreds of country songs on his tablet. At first I was like, "this nigga trippin" but then I heard a song I liked. 'Take your time' by Sam Hunt. That led to a couple more. Next thing I know, I'm in. Now I'm a fan."

"Wow. I thought prison was so crazy and violent. I didn't know robbers and killers sat around listening to country music."

He stared at me for a moment, danger and desire swirling in his eyes. "Its a lot about me that you don't know."

It seemed like a challenge. "Oh yeah? Like what?"

His hand moved up my calf, stopping behind my knee. "I got two degrees?"

That surprised me. "What did you study?"

"My first degree is in arts. The second is in pleasure. You have erogenous zones behind your knee."

While he was saying the second degree, he was rubbing and applying a little pressure behind my knee and I swear it was feeling good and turning me on.

"You also have them on your inner thigh, pelvis, elbows, armpits, neck, lips, and ears."

He was touching all the places he spoke of and my clit pulsed every time he laid a finger on me.

"But the biggest erogenous zone is the brain." He pressed fingers at both my temples while staring in my eyes. "When you get your mind fucked, that's the best orgasm you'll ever have in your life."

My body was reacting to everything he was saying and doing. My heart was racing, breathing heavy, I felt higher than I had ever been, my clit felt like it was twice its normal size, and my pussy was so wet that juices were soaking my panties. "How do you fuck someone's mind?" I whispered, wanting my mind fucked.

"That's what I'm doing right now."

He leaned forward and gave me one of the best kisses I'd ever had in my life. His lips were big and fluffy and soft. His mouth warm, tongue wet and juicy. He kissed me gently and sucked on my tongue and then my bottom lip. Then he pulled his face away to look at me. Seeing the fire in his eyes was so erotic.

"Take the top off."

I did as he asked. He licked his lips while staring at my breasts. "You got some pretty titties."

Then he lowered his head and began sucking my nipples. When I purred, his suck turned into a nibble, the sharp pain sending a jolt of electricity through my body that exploded at my clit. He went back to sucking my nipples while sliding a hand inside my panties. His fingers slipped over my clit, between my lips, and then slowly into my hole. It felt so damn good! I closed my eyes and allowed him to do his thing. Then he stopped. My eyes shot open and I watched as he opened his mouth and sucked my juices from his fingers. The shit was so damn sexy.

"Take these off."

He put his hands inside the waistband of my sweats and tugged. I lifted my hips and he snatched my pants and panties off in one motion. I hadn't shaved in a couple of days so there was a little stubble on my kitty. But he didn't seem to care because he was looking at me like one of those lions in Africa do when watching they gazelles. I knew he was about to tear me up. He stood up and began to undress slowly. He removed the shirt revealing his massive chest and arms. He wasn't ripped nor did he have a six pack like Jay but there was no mistaking his strength and power. The shoes and socks were kicked off next, and then the jeans. Excitement rushed through me as he revealed black boxer briefs. His hard dick made a thick outline going down his thigh, the dark head peaking out the leg of his underwear. It was huge and my excitement turned to fear. I was a little scared to have something that big inside of me. Then he slid the underwear down and the little fear turned into full blown terror. It was the biggest thing I had ever seen.

"You good?" He asked.

I shook my head. "Hell nah. Your dick is... Oh my God."

" I got a degree in pleasure, remember?"

I just shook my head in fear and awe. I didn't think I would feel any pleasure.

He lowered himself on top of me and gave me some more tongue, kissing his way down my neck, to my breasts, stomach, pelvis, and stopping when his face was between my legs. I squirmed from his beard brushing against my skin as he licked and kissed both of my inner thighs. Then he gave me the tongue. He licked around my labia a few times before focusing on my clit. He flicked his tongue rapidly across my pearl tongue before sucking my button between his lips. I rode the waves of pleasure as he sucked me good. Then he slipped a finger across my slit and used some of the juices to wet my ass. Two fingers went into the pink and one in the stink. The sensations that I got from having my clit sucked and holes plugged made my body vibrate. And when I came, it was loud and messy and great.

He climbed up my body and gave me more kisses. I knew what was coming next. He pushed the head of his monster against my lips and I instinctively tensed up, expecting to be ripped open. I lowered a hand to press against his pelvis so I could stop him if it hurt too bad. Then he thrust. A bolt of lightening flashed from my coochie to my brain and I pressed my hand against his pelvis to stop him. He didn't move anymore. Just continued to kiss me and rub my titties. When things started to feel good, I relaxed and allowed him to push more in. I stopped him again after a couple more inches. He continued kissing me while rubbing my breasts and then started thrusting slowly. He took his time, never rushing or getting impatient. Then it started feeling really good and I wanted more. He gave it to me, too. Every thrust was a blissful pleasure. I screamed as he went deeper and deeper. When the base of his dick brushed my clit, pleasure exploded inside me. I wanted his base to kiss my clit again so I could recreate the sensation again. That's when I realized I had taken all of him inside me. Knowing that I had taken that monster turned me on even more. He sucked in a couple of shallow breaths and held me tight while nestling his head against my neck. The kissing was over. He wanted to get his so I braced myself for a rough ride.

He increased his thrusts slowly until his hips were pistoling forward hard and fast. He rocked my body as our flesh smacked. I held onto him as he dug into me, the pleasure and pain almost unbearable. My pussy was so wet that I could feel the juices dripping down my ass crack and hear them sloshing around his pole every time he pushed into me. A swirling wave of goodness began bubbling up inside of me. This was going to be a big one.

"Oh, God! I'm about to cum," I warned.

"Me too," he echoed.

He pumped into me hard and fast, no longer restraining himself but allowing me to feel his strength. He was heavy, strong, and powerful. I screamed as the orgasm gathered up in me and forced its way out. Klan thrust into me one last time, biting my neck as he came. Klan was right. The orgasm was mind blowing and amazing. And somehow I knew that sleeping with him was going to change my life.

Chapter 9

Nephew (3 years later)

Waupun Correctional Institution, aka "The Walls" was a maximum-security prison in Waupun, Wisconsin. It was built in the 1800s and was the oldest max in the state. The prison looked like an old ass castle from the outside. It was also known as "The Walls" by those who lived there because it was surrounded by a thirty-foot concrete wall. Guard towers lined the three-foot-wide wall every twenty or thirty feet to make sure that anyone crazy enough to attempt to climb it would be shot down. Waupun held about 1,200 inmates, most of them minorities from the hood who didn't respect authority. They housed us in six cell halls; North Cell Hall, Northwest Cell Hall, South Cell Hall, Southwest Cell Hall, Health Services Complex (the hole), and Behavioral Health Unit (for the crazy niggas on medication). I had been in Waupun for three years and had been on every unit, except the med unit. I was moved so much because of my institution record. Fighting kept me in the hole. At least a year and a half of my three had been spent in solitary confinement. My latest scrap got me six months in the box. Today I was being released.

"Peterson, you ready?" the intercom in my cell buzzed.

"I been ready."

"Sergeant Bauer is on his way to get you."

"Already."

I sat on the thin ass mattress waiting to be released from my cage. The cell was ten paces long and two paces wide. I knew that because I walked and did pushups for an hour every day during the many months I spent in this dungeon. Being in the hole in a maximum-security prison made you feel like a caged animal. Two showers a week, the food was pushed through a small slot in the door, and at night, the demons came out. Niggas screamed and banged on their doors for hours upon hours every night. The first time I came to the hole I thought I was going to go crazy. It was loud and it stank. But I refused to break. I learned to ignore the smell and sleep during the daytime. And while niggas behaved like animals, I escaped through reading. My favorite book to read is the Bible. It is the reason I haven't lost my mind. The reason I haven't given in to the urges to turn into an animal when the sun goes down. Keys jingling grabbed my attention. That was my ticket. I walked over to the door to look through the small plexiglass window. Sergeant Bauer was a bald white man with a big ass beard. He stopped at my door and used a key to unlock the trap.

"You ready?"

"I stay ready so I won't have to get ready."

"C'mon and cuff up."

I stuck my hands through the trap so he could put the cuffs on my wrist. Any time an inmate was out of the cell while in the hole he had to be cuffed, even when being released. After he put the cuffs on, he waved towards the camera at the end of the hall and my door was buzzed open. I grabbed the bedroll and brown shopping bag with my books and hygiene items in it and stepped into the hall.

"A'ight, Nephew. Be smooth, my nigga," my neighbor, P-Wood called. He was also in the hole for fighting. We clicked because we were a part of the minority of niggas that didn't turn into an animal when they came to the hole.

"Okay, P. I'ma see you in gp."

113

Sergeant Bauer led me down the tier and locked me in a strip cage. I was wearing the standard orange hole clothes and had to give them back. I also had to be strip searched and given a set of greens.

"You want the same cell when you get back?" Sergeant Bauer cracked.

"It don't matter where I do my time at. Time is time. Let me get a good set of extra-large greens and size twelve boots."

"That's true," he said before grabbing my sizes from the shelves next to the cage. "You know the routine. "

I took off the hole clothes, allowed him to look at my nuts, and then threw on the greens. When I was ready, he led me to the side door.

"Alright, Peterson. See you next week."

"Yeah, fuck you, too," I mugged before grabbing my shit.

"You'll get one shower a week for that when you come back," he chuckled. "You're going to the south cell hall. Good luck."

I was released from the hole at ten o'clock in the morning. Recycled air and artificial light was no substitute for the real thing. The sun was bright in the sky and I had to squint for a moment to let my eyes adjust to the rays. I hadn't seen real light in one hundred and eighty days. The spring breeze felt good on my skin and the fresh air tasted good in my lungs. It felt good to finally be out of the hole. I walked down the concrete ramp and towards the metal gate that separated general population from the hole.

"Nephew, when you gon keep yo crazy ass out the hole?"

I looked to the left of the gate and seen a tall brown skinned nigga with brushed waves. Dre. I met him while working in the kitchen when I first got to Waupun. He was locked up for a shootout gone bad. A fourteen-year-old girl was killed, and he was given life. That was seventeen years ago.

"Man, these niggas keep testing me. I'm TTG."

"Don't forget the H. You trained to go to the hole," he cracked.

I stepped through the gate and we embraced and shook hands.

"When you gon stop putting yo'self in the belly of that beast? Ain't you tired of being around all them crazy niggas over there?"

I looked over my shoulder at the Health Segregation Complex sign. "You get used to it after a while."

"You know you sound institutionalized, right? I been locked up for seventeen years and I ain't been to the hole as much as you. You can stop when you want. Despite our surroundings, you still in control of you."

"Easier said than done, Dre. I'ma street nigga and ain't nothin sweet. Ain't no nigga finna treat me."

He stared at me like big brothers do little brothers when they say something stupid. "Really, Nephew? That's yo answer?"

I stood on what I said. "Yeah. I'ma street nigga. Live and die a gangsta."

He let out a frustrated breath. "What cell hall you going to?"

"Dirty south."

He shook his head. "Damn. I was hoping you was going to the Northwest so we could get a chance to chop it up. That south probably gon get you put back in the box. I'ma walk with you because ain't no telling when I'ma get the chance to holla at you again. Have you thought about what I said about going to church?"

I smirked at the question. I knew it was coming. Dre was one of the few people that knew my background of being raised in the church. He also knew that I read the Bible a lot in the hole. We had a few in depth conversations about scriptures and he always pushed me to go to church.

"I ain't tryna be one of them niggas that run to church or God when they get locked up. That shit feel fake."

"But what if that's what God want you to do? What if he put you in jail so that you learned to depend on Him? What if all this is part of his plan?"

"Then I would tell him to come up with a better plan. Locking me up ain't the way."

"Man, you know how many young brothas that I seen come through here with two or three years and then get out and get right back in the streets and get killed or come back with more time? Y'all be acting like getting locked up and doing time is cool. Like y'all don't mind these people looking at yo nuts or putting you in a cold ass dark room for weeks and months. You can't play with pistols forever, Nephew. You got a mama that love you and want to be there for you. I was in here when my moms died. Couldn't go to the funeral or have that last goodbye. I don't want you to be like me or end up in a grave like them other niggas that couldn't see that God was tryna tell em something. Take this time seriously, lil brah. This time is not meant to hurt you. This is an opportunity for you to do better."

I could hear the pain in his voice from losing his mother while he was locked up. I couldn't imagine losing mine. "I hear you, Dre. I do. Shit just ain't that easy. I robbed a lot of niggas and they ain't letting that shit go. I'm tired of going to the hole, brah. I'm tired of missing visits. But niggas won't let me chill."

"Don't you go home soon?"

"Yep. Three months."

"Before you go home, come to church and learn something else. Get some new friends."

I shook my head and laughed. "Man, can we talk about something else?"

He stared at me for a moment, and I could tell he didn't want to change the subject. "Okay. Yeah. Just think about what I said. So, what happened with them girls you was telling me about. They come back around yet?"

Jasmine and Simone's faces jumped in my head. I hadn't talked to either one of them since I left the county jail. "Nah. I heard Simone is getting it how she live. Jasmine, I don't know. I tried to have my people find her but they couldn't."

"That's crazy that she playing with the baby like that. Hopefully its not yours. And Simone, man, if she couldn't stick it out for three years then she definitely ain't no rider. You can do better. God got somebody for you. Just trust him."

I parted ways with Dre outside the South Cell Hall. He had to go to work at the welding shop and I had check in. I walked up to the steel gate and rattled it a few times to get the sergeant's attention. He looked up from the computer screen and buzzed me in. I stepped into the cell hall and was met by a bunch of smells. Weed, tobacco, shit, and stale air. There were about three hundred inmates in the South cell Hall spread out on four tiers. One hundred fifty on the front side and the other half in the back. Three hundred people in one building and stacked on top of each other meant that it was always noisy. Niggas hollered from tier to tier and cell to cell, playing chess, having conversations, or arguing over bullshit.

"You just get out of seg?" the sergeant asked as I approached the desk.

"Yeah."

He checked the computer screen. "Bobby Peterson?"

"Yeah."

He nodded towards the front side. "You're in F-46."

"Can I pick up my stuff from property?"

"They know you're here. I'll pop your door when they call for you."

The tiers were labeled E-H. E was the bottom, F on the second floor, G on the third, and H all the way up top. I took the stairs to the second floor and found my cell. It was smaller than the cells in the hole. 8'X15'. I could lift my arms and touch both walls. The length of the room was only four paces. Inside was a bunk bed with shelves at the foot of each, a metal table, toilet sink combo, a piece of polished metal screwed to the wall for the mirror, and an old ass push button light on the ceiling. The room was empty and the door was already open. I stepped inside and the steel door clanged loudly as it locked. I sat my stuff on the table and began making my bed. The mattress was the Department of Corrections' standard hard ass piece of plastic and the pillow was of the same standard. After tying the sheet and folding my blankets, I lay down to await being called to the property room where I could pick up my TV, tablet, clothes, shoes, and canteen.

The conversation with Dre popped into my head. His mom was a crackhead and alcoholic that allowed him and his brothers to run the streets. He was fifteen years old when he got locked up and might not ever step foot in the free world again. He wanted me to learn from him. I had a mom that loved and supported me. Her and Jamie had been my rocks while doing this time. They accepted my calls, sent money, and used to visit once a week but my constantly being in the hole made regular visits hard. Now they came to see me about once a month. The only thing that I didn't like about my moms and Jamie was them constantly pushing me to go to church. I thought about going several times but what they, or niggas like Dre, didn't understand was there was a negative stereotype connected to Christians in prison: they was soft or running from something or someone. I didn't want that shit connected to my name. I was a gun slinger, and I didn't want niggas mistaking going to church as soft. Niggas preyed on the weak and I didn't want nobody thinking I was prey. Plus, there was that saying, "If you scared, go to church." How would it look if I went to church?

I began listening to niggas talk over the tier to take my mind off Dre, my moms, and the church. There were several conversations taking place but the one that caught my ear was an argument about whether or not Wendy Williams was a man. One nigga said she was thick with some big titties and he wanted fuck her. The other nigga called him gay and said she was a man. I laughed as they went back and forth talking about beating each other's asses when the doors popped. One of them was going to end up in my old cell before the day was done. When the lip boxing match was over, I started reading the writings on the wall in the room. A bunch of niggas left their names, blocks, and different gangs etched in the paint. What caught my eye was a verse from the bible. "Let your requests be made known to God; and the peace of God, which surpasses all understanding, will guard your hearts and minds through Christ Jesus."

I took a moment to think on the scripture. The peace of God which surpasses all understanding sounded good. I hadn't known peace since... I couldn't remember the last time I'd felt at peace. Had to be when I was a kid. I definitely hadn't felt it since I got locked up. I had been fighting since I got arrested and had to constantly be on my Ps and Qs. But deep down inside I wanted peace. I was tired of having to watch everybody and listen for hidden messages. I didn't want to fight. I didn't want to go back to the hole. I was tired of listening to niggas turn into animals. I didn't want to get out and get killed or come back to prison with a life bid and miss my mama's funeral. I wanted a different life but the life I lived before prison made trying to find a new way to live impossible. If only I could find a better way.

I dozed off thinking about peace and dreamed that I was standing on the basketball court in the middle of the big rec field at Waupun. The sun was shining bright, there were no clouds, and the sky was clear and blue. And I was all alone. I spun around looking for an inmate, guard, or somebody. But there was nobody. Just me. It felt eerie like a scene from The Walking Dead. Like I was the only human alive and a bunch of zombies were out there waiting to eat me.

"I can give you that which you seek, Bobby."

The voice boomed all around me like thunder, scaring the shit out of me. But nobody was there. I moved towards the rec exit while looking around to find out who had spoke to me.

"I formed you in your mother's womb, my son," the voice thundered, knocking me to the ground.

I rolled onto my back as a fear I had never felt entered my bones. Something was surrounding me. I couldn't see it but I could feel the power. It made the hairs on my arms stand up and goose bumps pop all over my body.

"Your life is not your own. Arise and follow me."

The cell door clanked open, pulling me from the dream. I shot up in bed and seen that I was still in my cell. The smells and sounds of prison filled my senses reminding me that I was no longer dreaming. I let out a relieved breath as the dream played back in my head. Everything felt so real. The voice. Being knocked to the ground. The power surrounding me. Replaying it in my head made the hairs on my arms stand up and goosebumps return. I got up from the bed and walked to the sink to splash water on my face. After wiping away the water, I stared at my reflection in the mirror trying to figure out if God had spoken to me in my dream. That was how he spoke to some of the prophets in the Old Testament. Was this some type of calling? And what would happen if I didn't accept the call? Before I could get answers, a C.O. showed up at my door.

"You Peterson, right?"

"Yeah."

"They want you at property. Go pick up your stuff."

$$$

When Saturday came around I found myself walking in a crowd of thirty something Bible toting inmates on our way to the chapel. I felt out of my element in the midst of the holy rollers. I heard God this and God that. Everybody was smiling and seemed to be in a good mood. I wasn't sure if the smiles were a front or the real thing. How could they be so cheery in a maximum-security prison? Amongst the questions that swirled in my head was the meaning of the dream. Was God trying to get my attention? I had been raised to fear God and the dream left me terrified. Which is why I was going to church. I needed answers and the house of God seemed like the place to go.

The prison chapel was a big triangle shaped wooden building with tall stained-glass windows. It had the look and feel of a church in the free world. There were about twenty wooden pews stretching from one side to the other. Each pew looked like it could seat ten to fifteen people. White fans spun from the ceiling, a book of Bibles was on the table near the door, and there was even a live band and choir. A few inmates played instruments while two others stood near the alter and sang a gospel song. I found a seat in the last row to listen.

"I-iiiii, I'ma living testimony. Lord knows I should'da been dead and gone but Jesus let me live on. Whoaaa, I-iiii, I'ma living testimony and I thank God I'm still alive. When I was packing pistols every day, I should'da been dead and gone, but I thank God I'm still alive. When I was disrespecting my mother, I should'da been dead and gone, but I thank God I'm still alive. C'mon, y'all. Help us sang it."

The congregation rose and began to sing along. I watched the inmates around me lose themselves in worship. They closed their eyes and lifted their hands while singing along. The scene took me down memory lane and visions of being in church with moms and Jamie flashed in my head. The words about packing pistols and disrespecting moms made me think about my life and relationship with my mama. I had been in plenty of shootouts and robberies, but I always made it out alive. I had disrespected my mother so many times but she always forgave and loved me. I didn't know where they came from, but suddenly and unexpectedly there were tears in my eyes. It surprised me because in all the years I had been going to church, I never had the urge to cry. And I wasn't about to start now. I began blinking rapidly to hold them back. I kept on blinking until my eyes dried. After they finished singing, the guest preacher got up to introduce himself. He wore a plain black suit, black shoes and a white priest collar. His neatly trimmed afro was sprinkled with grays and face was clean shaved.

"Good morning, church. For those of you who don't know me, my name is Pastor Greg Sims and I come to you from The City of God Church out of Milwaukee, Wisconsin."

Hearing the church name got my attention. That was my mom's church. Her and Jamie started going there after I got locked up.

"I haven't been up here in a while, but God put it on my heart to come today. I have a special message for a special person. I want you to know that we've been praying for you son and today is your day." Then he looked directly at me. "Today is the day that you will be set free."

The look and the message made me a little uncomfortable. Was he really talking to me? Did my mama and Jamie send him up here? Could they do that?

"Choir, come up and give us an a selection. Do y'all know that song by Kirk Franklin, 'Your Change Will Come'?"

A brown skinned man on the piano spoke up. "Yeah, we do. We got you, rev."

The choir was made up of twelve prisoners that I had seen around the prison. They stood in front of the congregation and tore the house down with their version of Kirk Franklin's song. While they sang, I thought more about the preacher. I didn't even tell my moms nem that I was coming to church so how did he know I would be here today? Plus, churches had to go through a process to get people from the outside to come inside and preach to us and knowing an inmate in the prison probably wouldn't get them approved to come in. I started to get that 'is this really happening to me?' feeling. After the song, Pastor Sims got up to speak.

"That's what I'm talking about, choir. Y'all have ushered the holy spirit up in here and I feel it moving. The Bible says that where the spirit is, there is liberty." He paused to let his words sink in. When he spoke again, his voice was louder and filled with energy. "My brothas, liberty is freedom and where the spirit of God is, there is freedom. I'm feeling a whole lot of God in here today so that means, hallelujah, there's a whole lot of freedom in here, too!"

Some of the inmates broke into clapping and shouting Amens. While they clapped, Pastor Sims looked amongst us like he was searching for somebody.

"I came here today because I have a message for somebody. I don't know what you look like and we have never met before, but it don't matter because God knows and he sent me here to tell you that today is your day." He looked out at us again. "Is there a Bobby Peterson in here?"

I froze up. I looked to my left and right to see if somebody would point me out. For a moment I thought I was having another crazy dream. When I didn't get blown out of the building by an invisible voice or experience something supernatural, I realized this was real life. And that made me trip out a little. This was my first time coming to church and I had never met the preacher but he was standing up here calling my name. I didn't know what to do so I didn't do anything. I didn't speak up or acknowledge that he called my name. I just watched as the preacher eyed the crowd looking for somebody to speak up.

"If anybody knows Bobby, I want you to deliver a message to him for me. Tell him that God speaks to us in our dreams and is waiting for the prodigal son to return home."

A shiver passed through my body. Was God really trying to get my attention? For real, for real?

Pastor Sims went into his message and spent the next thirty minutes preaching about prodigal sons returning home. He was one of the best preachers I ever heard and kept niggas saying Amen and clapping. The message hit me in the heart because I knew that he was talking to me but I couldn't figure out how he knew I would be there and how he knew about my dream. After he finished the message, he called the choir back up for another song. Then he took the podium again.

"Okay, men. This is the part of the service where you have to make a decision. Right now I'm offering all you prodigal sons the opportunity to go back home to your father. All you have to do is accept Jesus as your savior and confess your sins and God will save a place for you in his mansion with many rooms. If you want a place in heaven, if you want to change your life, if you want to experience the peace of God that surpasses all understanding, then I want you to stand up."

I heard the alter call hundreds of time while growing up but I never had the urge to be saved. Until now. Something inside urged me to stand but the thought of all eyes on me kept me in my seat. I snuck a peek around to see if anyone would accept what the preacher was offering. Nobody stood.

"Now ain't the time to doubt God. He is a keeper of his promises and can't lie. Don't worry about what the person next to you thinks. This is a decision for you to make with God."

I wrestled with the decision to stand. The dream and everything the pastor said made it seem like God was trying to get my attention. I couldn't get out of the joint and rob people again because that would lead me back in here or a grave. I didn't want either. I needed to change. I needed a new life. I needed that peace.

"Brotha, God knows your name and today will be the first day of your life," Pastor Sims said to a man that stood up in the third row. "Is there anybody else?"

I closed my eyes and stood.

"Praise God. God knows your name and today is the first day of the rest of your life. Is there anyone else that wants to receive the free gift of salvation?"

When no one else stood, Pastor Sims led me and the other man through prayer and confession. While reciting the words with the pastor, an indescribable feeling washed over me. I had never experienced it before and I felt tingly.

"Make sure you brothas are baptized in Jesus' name when you have the opportunity. If you give me your names, I will make sure to add it to our churches prayer requests."

"Robert Patterson," the man in the third row said.

Pastor Sims looked at me expectantly. I hesitated giving my name and that brought more attention from the church goers. Everybody was waiting on me to say my name. Beads of sweat popped out on my forehead and my palms got sweaty. I didn't realize I was holding my breath until I couldn't breathe.

"What's your name, brotha?" Pastor Sims asked.

I cleared my throat. "Bobby Peterson."

The pastor's eyes shown a confidence that comes from experiencing supernatural things. "Hallelujah! Praise God," he celebrated.

The inmates began clapping and shouting Amens. That was the moment I knew God was real.

"Alright, men. The service is over. I'm praying for you guys. Hey, Bobby, can I get a word with you?"

I walked to the front to shake the pastor's hand.

"Congratulations, son. God put it on my heart to come and give you a word. We've been praying for you for a long time."

"We? How do you know me?"

"Your mother and father are members of my church. They've been sending in prayer requests for you for a long time. I check the request list every now and again and your name jumped out at me. When I found out you were here, I turned to God and he gave me a word. I'm faithful to God because he is faithful to me. I came here for you, Bobby."

I was blown away by the words and didn't know how to respond. Couldn't believe he traveled all this way for somebody that he never met. "Man, how did you get in? Y'all been having people come up here all this time."

He smiled like he was about to tell me a secret. "Bobby, the beautiful thing about knowing God is that he will give you access to whatever you need when you need it. Our church has a prison ministry but it has been dormant for a while because of neglect. Brother Jovan used to be in charge of it but once he left, the ministry fell to the wayside. That was a little over two years ago. Then I got a call yesterday from the Chaplin here at Waupun asking if we had someone to come today. I had already gotten a word from God about you. Once I seen that God provided a way, I walked it out."

Everything he said had me speechless. It sounded too good 'not' to be true.

"Mr. Peterson, let's go!" the guard called.

I didn't want to leave but I had to. "I gotta go, man. I don't even know what to say."

"Call your family and rejoice with them. And when you come home, just know you have a church family waiting for you."

I left the church with a feeling that I've never felt before. It was a type of high, but not the kind you get from weed. It was a spiritual high. I felt like a different person. Like I had been changed on the inside and made new. Like my life was starting over. I walked into the South Cell Hall wearing a smile that I never wanted to leave my face. And then I seen Dino. He was walking on the lower tier talking to one of the inmate workers. When we locked eyes, a snarl spread across his face.

"Fuck you lookin at, bitch ass nigga? I'll set this bitch off right now," he spat and began walking towards me.

The spiritual high crashed like a drone being flown by a drunk flier. I lifted my hands ready to go back to the hole.

"Chill, fam. Chill. Not right now," the cell hall worker said while holding him back.

"Hey, do we have a problem?" Sergeant Shimmel yelled, bouncing up from the officer station.

I dropped my hands to my side and took a step backwards, making sure to keep my eyes on Dino. "I'm good, sarge."

"All of you guys lock in right now. If I hear any bullshit, you're going to the hole."

I walked up the stairs feeling frustrated and angry. Dino was the reason I went to the hole the last time. Me and Little robbed him a couple years ago and when he seen me at rec we set it off. I beat his ass but he still wanted more. Since there were only four cell halls and I had enemies all over, there was nowhere for me to go where I wouldn't run into somebody that wanted smoke. This is why I stayed in the hole.

"How was church?" JB asked when I closed the door. He moved into the cell a few hours after I did. He was in his early forties but we hit it off good since we were both from Milwaukee.

"Everything was going good until I came back in this muthafucka. Brah, you wouldn't believe what just happened to me."

He looked interested. "What?"

I filled him in on Pastor Sims, the message, and my encounter with Dino. "Fam, I ain't no religious ass nigga but that is definitely the devil. You try'na do something righteous and boom, just get attacked like that as soon as you step in the cell hall. Yeah, fam. That's Satan."

I gave his words some thought. "That's crazy, brah. Soon as I try to do the right thing I get tested like this. I don't even know what to do."

"I think you only got two choices, fool. You gon have to go to rec and beat that nigga ass. Or pray for a miracle."

A knock on the door got my attention. It was the range worker, Fresh. "Y'all want the phone?"

"Yeah. Let me see that."

He plugged the phone into a jack outside my cell. "Ay, bro, was that you that got into it with Dino downstairs?"

My spidey senses started tingling. "Yeah. What up?"

"Bro, he a real life goofy. Don't even waste yo time on that nigga. He a fuck boy. Locked up for raping a ten-year-old girl. Its a nigga upstairs that wanna put it in his life. Bro, if you got something going on, don't fuck that off going to the hole over dude, for real."

The information surprised me. "He a tree jumper? On what?"

"On everything I love. He just got out the hole this morning so niggas think he tellin' because niggas don't usually get out the hole on the weekend. That shit spreading all over the cell hall right now. Fuck that nigga, bro. I gotta hand out this ice. Be smooth."

I looked at JB. "This nigga a fucking pervert, bro."

"Talking all that shit like he really in the streets," he laughed.

I pulled the phone in the room and dialed my mother's number. "Hey, son."

"Hey, ma. How you doing?"

"Fine. Just texting Pastor Sims back."

Hearing the name brought a smile to my face and made me forget about Dino for a moment. "He already told you, huh?"

"Told me what?"

"Stop playing. I know he said something."

"He just sent me a text saying God is good. I was texting him back. Is that what you talking about?"

"He didn't tell you about coming up here?"

"Pastor Sims came up there?"

I laughed. She really didn't know "Pastor Sims came up here to preach today. I got saved."

"What you just say?"

"I said, pastor Sims came up here today and I got saved."

"Don't be playing with me, Bobby," she said, the excitement bubbling up inside of her waiting to be released.

"I'm not playing, mama. I'm serious."

My mother started screaming like she was catching the holy ghost. "Oh, praise God! Hallelujah! Thank you, Jesus!"

"What's going on?" Jamie asked in the background.

"Bobby got saved, baby! Bobby got saved!"

"Bobby got saved? When?"

My mother continued praising God and it sounded like she was running through the house.

"Bobby, what's going on?" Jamie asked.

"Pastor Sims came up here today. I accepted Jesus."

"That's great, Bobby. Oh, my God. Thank you, father. Congratulations, son. We been praying for you for a long time."

"I know. Pastor Sims told me."

"You said the pastor came up there? How? When?"

"Church just ended about ten minutes ago. Pastor Sims preached a word. He said that God sent him to save me. I believed him."

"Good God."

"Put it on speaker, baby. Let me talk to him," moms shouted. "Tell me what happened, Bobby. Tell me everything."

I explained everything from my conversation with Dre when I got out the hole, the writing on the wall, the dream, and then everything that happened at church. My mom and Jamie screamed and shouted like they won the lottery. Then I told them what happened with Dino.

"Don't go to rec, Bobby. Don't go out there and do nothing stupid. That's the devil, baby. You hear me? He is trying to take your joy. Don't let him," mom warned.

"I know, mama. But I don't know what to do. I gotta go to rec to shower. Plus, if I don't go they gon think I'ma coward."

"Just skip the shower. And if they think you a coward, so what. They called Jesus worse names."

That's the kind of shit that made talking to moms difficult. She didn't understand the real world. "It ain't that easy. What people think matters. I can't have nobody thinking I'm sweet or everybody gon try me. Plus, this our only shower until Monday night. I gotta go."

"Bobby, me and your moms is concerned about you, son," Jamie cut in. "I know how it is not wanting to look weak but I don't think you should willingly put yourself in the lion's den. You know you gon have to fight if you go to rec. I think you should stay back and read the Bible and pray. This is a spiritual test, son. You can't win this with your fists."

Jamie's response made more sense than my mother's but I wasn't sold. "I hear you, Jamie, but I don't know. I'ma play it by ear."

"Bobby, do you hear what we are telling you? Do not go to rec," moms said in a demanding voice that I would've obeyed when I was a little boy.

"I hear you, ma."

"Bobby, just allow us to pray with you for a moment, okay?" Jamie offered. "We gon pray for God to intervene. If it's his will for you to go to rec, go. If he gives you a sign, Bobby, make sure you take heed because God is not to be played with."

I prayed with my moms and Jamie and when the phone call was over, I turned on my tablet and sat on my bunk and thought about what it meant to be saved. According to the Bible, I couldn't smoke, fuck random females, get drunk, curse, and I had to go to church and read the Bible and pray a lot. I didn't know how I was gon make all of those changes. I wasn't even sure if this being saved thing was going to work out because wasn't no way I was turning down some pussy after being locked up for three years. But first things first. I had to make it through this night without ending up in the hole because if they called rec, I was going.

I played games on my tablet and listened to music for the rest of the day, every now and then thinking about whether or not God was going to somehow intervene on my behalf and help me with my situation. When 5:30 PM rolled around and they started buzzing tiers for rec, I knew that I was going to have to figure out a way out of the situation with Dino on my own. I grabbed my shower bag with my soap and change of clothes inside and waited for my door to pop. When it unlocked, I followed JB out of the cell and made my way to rec. Big Top recreation was being held in an upstairs gymnasium next to the cell hall. There was a line of inmates going down the tier, outside, and upstairs to rec. I followed the man in front of me, all the while keeping my head on a swivel looking for potential threats. I made it all the way to rec without an incident, but that didn't mean I was safe. I was in a maximum-security prison surrounded by niggas that wasn't never going home. It could pop off at any time and for any reason.

I made my way to the weightlifting area. It was next to the showers, and I could also see everybody coming up the stairs and see everybody that was already at rec. Dino's tier hadn't been released yet and I wanted to see him before he seen me. A few moments later he walked through the door. He wasn't carrying a shower bag and was searching the crowd with a serious face. Then we locked eyes.

'If you gon do something, God, you betta do it now.'

Dino headed right towards me and I could see the intent in his eyes. We was about to get it on. My heart started beating faster as I clenched my fists. As soon as he got in arms reach, I was swinging. But he never made it. Dino was so focused on me that he never seen the Jamaican nigga getting up from the game table with the shank. It was made from the lid of a can, sharp and jagged like a Christmas tree. He swung the blade and it went through the right side of Dino's neck, the point poking out the left side. Then he snatched the blade out, spraying blood on everybody and

131

everything within a few feet of the scene. Dino grabbed his neck, his eyes growing wide with fear as reality settled in. He was about to die. He took off running and the Jamaican chased.

"Punk faggot raped my niece! Bet you won't rape another muthafucka!" He yelled in between swings, stabbing Dino in the back and arms.

Everybody at rec watched the cold blooded murder, knowing better than to try to stop it. It took a moment for the C.Os to realize what was happening. By the time they reacted, Dino was laying on the handball court shaking, blood pooling around his body.

"Everybody get back to the cell hall and lock in!" A guard yelled as the alarms started going off.

I felt a numbness growing inside of me as I grabbed my shower bag and headed towards the stairs. I had just witnessed a gruesome murder and part of me felt responsible. I prayed for God to intervene. If I didn't come to rec, would that nigga still be alive?

"Damn, youngin. Looks like we about to go on another three-month lockdown because that nigga ain't gon make it," an old head walking beside me chuckled. "Hope you got some good books in the cell."

Chapter 10

Charlene

My life changed a lot in the past three years. For starters, I graduated from college with a 3.972 GPA. I was disappointed that I didn't get the overall 4.0 but I'm over it. Kinda. I still don't respond to any comments on social media about my English 2 professor. If his car just so happens to be swallowed by a sinkhole or get stolen when he leaves the keys in the ignition while paying for gas, I'm not saying that I wouldn't care that something bad happened to him. Definitely wouldn't shed a tear though. That's just karma for not allowing me to redo the finals paper. Besides graduating, I got a job, too. I'm a project manager at Lang Brothers & Sisters.

Just two years in and I've already gone from an assistant project manager to lead project manager. If I keep going at this rate, I'll be a project coordinator in five years. Five years after that I'll be managing coordinators. I also put a down payment on a house and moved out of the apartment. It isn't in the best neighborhood but forty-nine thousand dollars for a two-bedroom single family home seemed like too good of a deal to pass up. The plan is to live in it for a couple years and then sell for profit. Then do it again. When I explain these parts of my life to people, they think I have it so good. They congratulate me for buying the house and graduating with honors. They say how lucky I am to have a job that I like and am really good at. But they all miss the disappointment in my voice and in my eyes as I'm explaining it all. It doesn't matter how good you have it in life if you're not happy. I haven't been happy in almost two years. I hate the house that I live in and I'm scared of the person that I live with. My family and friends tell me that I need to make changes but those things are easier said than done. They aren't the ones that have to sleep with Klan every night.

For starters, my man in controlling, possessive, and crazy. I don't even remember how he gained so much control over my life. It happened slowly and then the next thing I know, I'm checking in with him like he's the warden and I'm a prisoner. He wants to know who I'm with at all times, I can't have male friends, and he doesn't want me wearing anything sexy or too revealing. Literally went through all my clothes and had me throw away the things he didn't think were appropriate for his woman. I even have a curfew. If I am ever out past eight o'clock without him, he throws a fit when I get home. I barely see Lana anymore. She hates Klan so she doesn't come by the house. We get together once or twice a month, whenever I can get away from Klan for a few hours. She says he's fucking up my life and that I need to get away from him. She wants me to just pack up and leave. Like me and this man haven't started building a life together. Like I can just pack up my feelings in a box and lock them up in a storage unit. Like he would just let me walk away. So I do what I can to try to make it work. I hang on to the good times that I've had with Klan and hope that one day he will wake up and see how good we can be if he returns the love and devotion that I give him. Which is why I was hoping we could go out for dinner.

"I heard about this new restaurant at work today. Want to come?"

Klan kept his attention on the video game. Nothing got between him and Final Fantasy V. "What restaurant?"

"It's called Vincent or Vinny's. Something like that. It's downtown."

"Oh, you talking about Vinny's over there on Oakland. It ain't that new."

"Yeah. Vinny's. They said they have a bomb crab broil and I'm hungry. Wanna come with me?"

"Why don't you just order something. I wanna play my game and chill."

"Because I don't want to eat at home. I want to get out of the house. We don't never go out to eat anymore. All we do is stay in the house."

"So. In the house is where its safe. Ain't gotta worry about gettin shot in the house."

"In this neighborhood we do. Plus, I want to go out sometimes. I'm bored. And hungry."

He didn't respond. Gave all of his attention to the game.

"You really about to ignore me for a video game?"

He kept ignoring me, moving the stick and pressing the buttons like the battle was heating up.

"Klan?"

"Hold on. Wait."

I raised my voice. "Cedric?"

He exploded. "Damn, Charlene, you just made me die. Fuck."

"Sorry. Can we go eat now?"

He stared at me for a moment. "Why you so eager to leave the house? Is somebody s'posed to be meeting you there or something?"

I was surprised by the allegation. "Why every time I want to go out you accuse me of something?"

"I ain't accusing you of nothing. You guilty or something?"

I took a moment to calm down and stop from getting worked up. Then I realized what he was trying to do. "You think you slick, huh?"

"What?"

I shook my head and laughed. "You trying to start an argument so we stay in the house. Nope. I'm hungry and I want you to come with me so let's go."

"You think you know me, huh?" he chuckled

"I do. Plus, who is stupid enough to bring their man to a spot they planning to meet someone else? I got a 4.0 remember?"

"A 3.9, babe," He corrected.

My mouth dropped open. "No you didn't just rub that in."

"I wasn't rubbing it in. Just stating facts."

"Here's another fact, Klan. If you don't buy my food, you will be jacking off for the foreseeable future."

His mouth dropped open. "You gon weaponize the pussy on a nigga?"

I got up and patted my ass, putting an extra switch in my hips as I walked towards the door. "Weapon of mass destruction."

$$$

Vinny's was an Italian and Mexican restaurant that served amazing and authentic food from both countries. I experimented with a dish called Huevos Con Migas and discovered the most delicious meal of all time. Eggs whisked with crema acida and scrambled with fried tortillas, topped with salsa and sliced avocados. Every bite was a flavor explosion and I swear that I came in my mouth while I was eating.

"That food was so good, baby." I patted my stomach as we walked towards Klan's Audi.

"It was a'ight. It would'da been better if all them white people wasn't staring in my face."

"You ate like you was a bear. Most people don't eat like that. You're a messy eater. Just saying."

"So. It's my food. I paid for that shit. I can eat it how I want."

136

"And those are their eyes."

He gave a look that made me stop talking.

"Damn! She got a fat ass!"

It came from our left. Two men were getting out of a red Lexus with chrome wheels. One was short with dirty dreads. The other was tall and bald. The short one had the big mouth and both were looking at my ass like it was a solar eclipse.

"Aye, watch yo mouth, nigga," Klan said, stopping to give them his signature mean mug.

"In my hood niggas take that as a compliment," the tall one said.

"Well, I don't, nigga. keep it pushing."

"Cmon, Klan. Let's go home. Forget them."

"Yeah, nigga. Listen to yo bitch," the shorter one said, adjusting the gun in the front of his pants.

I grabbed his arm to pull him to the car. "Come on, babe. Forget them. Let's-"

"Or what, nigga? Listen to my girl or what, nigga?" Klan asked, pushing me out of the way and walking towards the Lexus.

The men were momentarily stunned by Klan's boldness. The tall one shook it off and moved towards Klan with an arm cocked back to swing. He never got the punch off. Not only was Klan bigger and stronger, but he was also faster. My man's fist caught him right on the chin, making his head snap back like his neck was broke. He fell and was out like a light. The other man was moving towards Klan tugging at the gun in his waist but he couldn't pull it out because it was caught on his belt. Klan didn't have that problem. His gun came out like he was in a gun duel in an old western movie that my dad liked.

"Get cho hands off it, bitch ass nigga," Klan demanded, pointing his gun in dirty dread's face.

His hands flew in the air like he was at a concert and the performer was asking people in the crowd to wave. "C'mon, bro. I ain't on that."

"Say you sorry, nigga," Klan said, roughly pulling the gun from his pants.

"I-I-I'm sorry."

"Gimmie the keys."

He went in his pocket to get the keys and held them out. Instead of taking them, Klan slapped him in the face with his own gun. "Ayy, get out of here. Meet me at home," Klan said, tossing me his keys.

"What? What are you doing? Let's go."

Klan bent down and started going through the man's pockets. "I got a ride. Take yo ass home!"

$$$

(Two days later)

"Charlene, hold on. Where you finna go?"

I was moving down the hall so fast that when I tried to stop, my ankle almost gave out. Stuart Weitzman sandals looked good but they weren't meant to keep you balanced while making quick movements. After saving my leg and sandals, I backtracked towards the breakroom. Yolonda met me at the door.

"What's up, Yo-Yo?"

"Wondering why you running up outta here like you Marion Jones."

"Who?"

"The fastest bitch in the world about twenty years ago. You really don't know who she is?"

"No. And I gotta get home and get ready to go out with Klan. You know how he get if I'm late. He will swear up and down that I'm cheating on him."

"I don't know why you keep putting up with that fool. Last time you went out you was almost an accomplice in a armed robbery. You my girl, Lene, and I'm telling you that you need to leave that nigga alone."

I met Yolonda when I started at Lang Brothers & Sisters.
. She was a gum popping, loud mouthed, neck rolling mess
but we hit it off instantly. We were the only black girls at the
job and the fact that she thought my nail polish obsession
was cool made us instant besties. But right now I didn't want
to hear her words of wisdom about my relationship.

"I don't got time to hear this right now. I'm grown. Is that
why you called me? To give advice on who I should be
sleeping with."

She frowned like something offended her nostrils. "Since
you getting an attitude, I don't want nothing. Call me when
you need some bail money."

We rolled our eyes at the same time before I stepped off.
I left wok and hopped in my Prius and headed home. I felt
kind of bad for how things went with Yolonda but I needed
her to get out of my business. Klan was waiting for me at
home. We weren't going out but I didn't want to tell her that
I had a curfew. Klan said the incident at Vinny's put some
heat on us and he wanted me to come right home from work
for the next couple of days. Twenty minutes later I pulled up
to our house on 25th and Townsend. I hated the
neighborhood and only agreed to stay because Klan swore
we weren't staying long. It was the Hood with a capitol H.
Shootings and high-speed chases was an everyday thing. I
grew up in a middle-class neighborhood where you could
leave the door unlocked but none of that was happening on
Townsend. The first night that we moved in someone was
killed a couple houses away. I wanted to move out the next
day but Klan convinced me to stay. Said it would be our first
flipper house. He had some of his people come by and fix it
up. That was almost two years ago. After locking my car, I
walked up the stairs searching my keyring for the key to the
three-hundred-dollar security door that looked like a prison
gate. I had just unlocked the door when my phone rang. It
was Klan.

"Hey."

"Where you at?"

"I'm walking in the house right now and hi to you too."

"Oh, hey, baby. I'm out right now and I probably won't be back until late. I gotta handle some bidness out here. Don't wait up for me."

Every word that he said pissed me off. "What you mean you gon be home late? You said we needed to stay in the house to let it cool down. I don't want to have to stay in the house if you don't."

"Cmon, Charlene. We talked about this already. I can handle mines but if they run up on you, fuck you gon do? Just chill. I'll be home later. Bye."

"Grrrr!" I grunted in frustration, slamming the door as I walked in the house.

I flopped down on the couch and stared at the fifty-inch screen on the wall wondering why I didn't take the advice of my friends and family and leave him. It wasn't like I was overly attached to the house. I hated it and would put it on the market tomorrow if necessary. I wasn't madly in love with Klan to the point that I couldn't live without him either. In fact, my life would be better without him. We also didn't have any kids to keep us attached forever and the implant would make sure that didn't happen. But I knew that if I left, he wouldn't just let me walk away. He would find me. If I got the police involved, we would become enemies and I didn't want to be on his shit list.

My eyes roamed around the living room and landed on a picture that we took under a giant red fern during our trip out west last year. We wore huge smiles as we embraced. We looked happy and in love. He took me to California for my birthday and we had a great time. He treated me like a queen that day. We even went to a Sacramento King's basketball game. And the birthday sex was amazing. We switched roles like the Usher song and I fucked his brains out.

"What the hell, Charlene?" I said, disgusted that I went from thinking about leaving him to remembering how great the sex is. I needed some air. If he was going to be outside, then I was going out too. I grabbed my bag and phone and got in traffic. I didn't have anywhere to go so I just drove and listened to Ella Mai. Then my mom called.

"Hey, momi."

"Hola, mi amor. Como esta?"

"I'm okay. Just got off work. I was thinking about coming to see you."

"Oh, yes. Come on. Someone is here to see you," she said excitedly.

The excitement in her voice got me a little anxious as I wondered who would show up at her house looking for me. "Who is it?"

"I am not telling. Hurry up."

Fifteen minutes later I pulled into the driveway of my parents' house and parked behind my mother's Ford Fusion. I was hoping that whoever had come over would have a car parked out front to give a hint as to who they were but the only car in front of the house was my dad's old school Cadillac Fleetwood. I was giddy with excitement as I walked in through the back door. The kitchen was empty so I headed for the living room. My cousin was sitting on the couch with my parents.

"Neesy!" I squealed, running by my parents to hug my sister-cousin.

"Charlene!"

We hugged and jumped up and down like teenage girls. I hadn't seen her much since we started college. She went to Spellman and I stayed home and went to Marquette. After school she got started building a family down in Atlanta and wasn't able to come back home that often.

"Dang, gurl. Look at you," Neesy said, stepping back to look me up and down. "Last time I seen you, you didn't have those curves. And you wearing that pink suit, gurl. Yes."

141

I had filled out a little since we last seen each other, and I was proud of my curves. Even struck a few poses. " I try, baby. I try."

Neesy acted like she was holding a camera. "Okay. Now it's my turn. Watch yo girl work."

I held up my phone and acted like I was recording while she worked it. My cousin was fine too. Shoulder length curly dreadlocks, beautiful dark chocolate skin, a gorgeous smile, and an amazing little body. She had the short, muscular, and thick build of a gymnast.

"Y'all ain't got no sense," my daddy chuckled.

"Hey, daddy."

"You not see me here?" My mom asked with a little attitude.

"You know I was saving the best for last," I smiled while bending to hug her.

"Okay, baby. I did my part. I'm gone. Game is on," dad announced before vanishing down the hall.

"Bye, daddy," I called after him before sitting down and turning to Neesy. "So, what's up? Why didn't you tell me you was coming to Milwaukee?

"I just wanted to pop up and see the look on your face. My husband's cousin's funeral is tomorrow."

"Jay is here, too? Where is Janay?"

"They are with his family. They doing some serious grieving over there and I didn't want to be a part of all that. Murda Mike got killed trying to rob some dope boys and they acting like he was a saint. Like he got killed for no reason. The boy was a thug. His name was Murda Mike."

"Charlene know all about thugs," mom said, wearing a sneaky smile.

"Really, mom? She talking about somebody dying."

"What you talking about, Silvia?"

"Charlene got-"

"Nothing. She ain't talking about nothing," I interrupted before mom could put my business out there. "This ain't about me. What you been up to? And how is you keeping that figure after having Janay? Wasn't she a big baby?"

"Yes, girl. Ten pounds five ounces. Ripped me open and gave me stitches. I told Jay we ain't having no more kids. He think I'm playing. I had to do all kinds of diets and workouts to get my body back. Plus, now that I got my legal assistant job, I'm not taking no maternity leaves. I need to move up in the legal world, not be stuck at home changing diapers."

"I heard that. I'm trying to crash that glass ceiling in the banking world. Lord knows I ain't having nobody's baby no time soon."

"Do you still go to church?"

My mom sucked the back of her teeth loudly. "Charlene hasn't been to church in years. Ever since she met-"

"No, I don't go to church. Don't really have time. Since when do you care about church?"

"Since I got saved. We got to church twice a week. Jesus is the reason that me and Jay's love is so strong. I swear that praying together brought us closer."

My mouth hung open for a little while. "Say what? You in the church like that?"

"And she got a man to pray with?" Mom added.

"Nothing is more intimate than prayer. Plus, I think a man that loves God is sexy."

"Wow. I'm surprised. I always thought church was for older people."

Her and my mom looked offended. "Old people? For real? Girl, stop. Church is for everybody."

"You need to take Charlene to church with you," mama cut in. "Her and that diablo that she lives with."

I gave her the look. "Ma? Really? At least let me tell her about him before you start bad mouthing him."

"Charlene, you got a man?" Neesy asked.

"He' s not a man. He's a crook," mom continued.

I just stared at my mom. If she was anybody else, it would be on and popping.

"Hmp," she shrugged. "Tell her."

Neesy could see the controversy surrounding my man and leaned forward, ready to drink the tea. "Oh, tell me about him."

I crossed my arms over my chest and shut down. "Ain't nothing to tell."

"What is aunty talking about? Tell me."

I raised my voice. "I don't want to talk about it."

They were surprised by my anger and we sat in silence for a moment.

"Okay. We don't have to talk about it. So, what do you want to do tonight?" Neesy asked.

I thought about the curfew. "I don't know. I don't really do much."

"So, you don't have nothing to do, right?"

The question was loaded and I wasn't sure how to answer. "No, I don't. Why?"

"Because I heard you bought a house and I want to see it. Plus, I want you to see Janay. They're by Jay's cousin's house. Let's go."

After saying by to my mom we hopped in my Prius. As soon as the doors closed, she started with the questions about Klan. "What's up with your man? Silvia hates him, huh?"

I thought about how to describe my relationship with Klan. "He is a mistake that I can't get rid of."

She gave me a concerned look. "What does that even mean?"

"Neesy, I've been judged, lectured, called stupid and all kinds of other names concerning my relationship with Klan. But nobody-"

"His name is Klan?" she interrupted.

"His real name is Cedric but they call him Klan. Please, don't judge me. Neesy. Just listen."

Her eyes showed the mouthful of words that she wanted to scream at me but she swallowed them and nodded. "Okay. I won't judge you. Go ahead."

"I used to do a little scamming in college to make ends meet and I met him at a friend's house. I ended up getting kidnapped and it turns out it was Klan behind it. They didn't mean to kidnap me. They wanted my friend Jay and I just so happened to be with him."

Neesy's mouth hung open. "You were scamming and got kidnapped?"

"I did. It was just going to the store and buying stuff. Nothing serious. Well, when Klan found out that his friends kidnapped me, he made sure that I got home safe. Literally followed me home. Then he showed up at my door one day and has been in my life ever since."

"Damn, Charlene. Why would you get with somebody that got you kidnapped?"

"I don't know. He was dangerous and sexy. And smart. He was a street nigga that listened to country music. He was soft and hard. He was different from anyone I've ever been with."

She stared at me for a moment. Then her eyes grew wide with clarity. "He dick-matized you, didn't he?"

I didn't want to admit that I was dick whipped. "No. I don't even know what that means."

"Yes you do. That's when he put it down so good that you do all kinds of dumb stuff to keep him. You know he ain't no good for you but you can't let it go. You dick-matized."

I blew her off. "Whatever."

"Girl, you think you the only one that's been dick-matized? Shoot, Jay did it to me. Best I ever had. That's why I married him. I want that thang forever and I'm not sharing it with nobody. But the difference is Jay is a good one. He is a good man and Klan sounds like he is headed to jail or a casket. I don't want you to go through that, cousin. You're too pretty and smart to be with somebody you will have to bury or send money for the canteen. And what if you get pregnant by him? I know you don't want to raise a baby around all of that?"

"I'm not getting pregnant by him. Believe that. I got the implant."

"Why are you with a man that you don't want to have a family with? And what happens if you do get pregnant? Accidents happen."

The thought of taking my kids to visit Klan in prison made a shudder pass through me. "Damn, Nessy. Why you have to put that out there? Got me scared to sleep with him again."

"Because you need to hear this. He is headed in the wrong direction and I don't want my only cousin going down with that sinking ship."

"I know I need to leave him but it's not that easy. That's what everybody doesn't understand. It's hard to walk away from someone you love and care about. He has become a big part of my life."

She reached over to grab my hand. "I hear you, sis. I know it's hard to do but you have to do it. You know what you need?"

I took my eyes off the road to give her my attention. If she had the secret for making break ups easier, I wanted it. "What?"

"You need to go to church."

The words were a let down and the look on my face let her know it. "Neesy, that ain't no kind of help."

"Just hear me out, sis. Going through something like this, you're going to need strength. Whenever you decide to leave Klu Klux Klan, it's going to hurt and you're going to need all of your strength and a little bit of somebody else's. Sometimes you not gon even want to get out of bed. But you'll have to. And the only person that I know strong enough to help with something like that is Jesus. I'm not telling you to go to church so you can get to heaven. That's on you. But I am telling you to go to church so you can find the strength to do what's best for you."

I thought about her advice and the heartache I felt when I ended it with Latrell. I knew all to well what it felt like to not want to get out of bed. Neesy was right. About everything. Her words affected me differently than all the other people that told me to leave Klan. It sounded like she was speaking from experience. "How do you know about getting strength to leave someone? What happened down in Atlanta?"

"Girl, I ain't always been no Christian." she chuckled.

Now it was my turn to get in her business. "What does that mean?"

She looked out the window while collecting her thoughts. "Going to an all-girls school is a different experience than going to co-ed schools. There is more experimenting with your sexuality. Girls know what girls like. And this girl Tanisha was my first girl crush. Had me thinking about coming out and telling the world."

My mouth dropped open. "You're lesbian?"

"No. I was experimenting. I thought I loved her but now that I'm with Jay, I realize it wasn't love but lust. I was thinking with my coochie because she knew how to do things. But I knew I wanted a man and a family, and I couldn't have that with her. Leaving her was the hardest thing I ever did. I needed help and I got strength from going to church. That's also where I met Jay. What if the man that God made for you is waiting for you in church, too?"

That was funny. "I don't know about a church man. I'm not ready for all of that."

"Girl, you don't know what God got for you. Is there a church close to your house?"

"I think so. It's called God's City or something like that. But I don't know if it's open this late."

Neesy grinned like she knew something I didn't. "Let's find out."

After parking my car at home, we walked a block over to see if the church was open. The City of God Church was a huge brick building on the corner of 24th and Auer. It had tall stained-glass windows, a big steeple on top, and the church's name was in big block letters across the front doors. I could hear singing as we got closer to the door. I was hesitant about walking in the church on a Thursday evening, but Neesy didn't hesitate to try the door. She smiled back at me when it opened. We followed the sounds of music into the sanctuary where a choir was singing. It looked like they were practicing so we had seats in the back and listened. The choir was good and we were immediately bouncing our heads and snapping our fingers. I had always liked gospel music because it was uplifting and made me feel good. About ten minutes later Neesy grabbed my hand.

"Cmon, cousin. Let's pray."

Chapter 11

Charlene

"I can't believe that you been in Milwaukee all your life and you never knew about this little boutique. They have nice clothes and reasonable prices. And if they don't got it, you can tell them what you want and they will find it for you."

I looked around the black owned business in awe. Monique's Boutique was a small upscale clothing store that had everything from high end Gucci to affordable clothes by lesser-known designers. I was standing in front of a full-length mirror holding up a black and gold Alexander McQueen dress. "I'm amazed, Neesy. They got stuff in here that Macy's don't."

"That's all I'm saying. This is exclusive stuff, for real. And that dress is cute. You buying it?"

"Uh-uh, girl. I don't got 2,500 to spend on a dress that I won't ever get to wear. Klan ain't taking me nowhere classy enough to wear something like this. His idea of having a good time is sitting in the house watching hood movies and eating Churches."

She gave me a pitiful look. "That is sad, cousin."

"I know. But it is what it is, " I sighed, putting the dress back on the rack. I started perusing through more dresses when I felt Neesy watching me. "What?"

"You know you have to leave him, right?"

"I know. I just don't know how."

She shook her head. "I can't believe you had to ask him if you could kick it with me after you got off work. He is the one that robbed them and created the whole situation. Everything is his fault but he still leaves the house whenever he wants. I don't like him, cousin. He is controlling you."

"I know. I know. Trust me, I know."

"You gotta kick his butt like J-Lo did that white man in Enough," she joked. " Learn how to fight and bring the pain."

I pictured me knocking out Klan and bust out laughing. "You crazy."

Then she became serious. "It's something else I didn't tell you, Charlene."

"What?"

"I was in an abusive situation before. That's what made me try to be with a woman."

My eyes popped. "Seriously?"

"Yes, girl. His name was Terrance. I messed with him during my sophomore year. He sold dope. A lot of it. I thought it was cool because he bought me whatever I wanted. But then he got controlling and started trying to tell me what to do, what to wear, and who to be around. Then one day we got into an argument and he hit me. And that's when I left his butt. It was hard because I cared about him and was going to miss being wined and dined and not having to worry about money. But I knew I couldn't let no man have control of me or put his hand on me."

"Damn, I didn't know. "

"I didn't tell nobody. I was ashamed. If my daddy found out I was dating a drug dealer and that he was hitting me, he would've drove to Atlanta and killed both of us."

"Yeah. Uncle Lonny don't play."

"So that's the story of my thug love. If I would've stayed with Terrance, I probably would've missed out on Jay. What if keeping Klan around for so long is keeping you from meeting the man you're supposed to be with?"

"Dang, girl. Why you had to get all deep on me and shit? How I'm supposed to respond to that?"

"I don't know. Just giving you something to think about."

Janay's cry from the stroller got our attention. She had been sleeping for the last couple hours and now she was awake and wanted her mother's attention. While Neesy tended to her daughter I went back to looking through the racks of clothes and thinking about Klan stopping me from finding my soulmate. Ever since we went to church, I found myself thinking about the man and the life that God had for me. I wanted so much more than I was getting out of life and love. I wanted to be with a man that I could feel secure with. Someone who didn't put my life and freedom in danger. Who didn't want to control me. Who I could pray with. And when I looked over and seen Neesy bouncing Janay on her hip and heard the way the baby was laughing and giggling, I realized that I wanted a family too.

$$$

"I don't understand why you gotta kick it with her every night that she been here. She got a husband. Why she just don't go out with her nigga?" Klan asked, angry that I wanted to hang out with my cousin.

"Because we haven't seen each other in years. I told you that. And you can come too. Her husband is coming. We can do a double date."

"Man, I ain't tryna be around that square ass nigga. That fake ass Christian shit. Them muthafuckas sin more than everybody and be tryna act holier than thou."

"They are not like that. Everybody isn't defined by who you think they are. They are cool. This is their last night in town and we want to see a play, baby."

He waved me off, keeping his attention in the game. "What ever, man. Go do you. If them niggas from Vinny's see you out there and get on yo ass, don't call me because I told yo ass not to go out but you wanna be hardheaded."

I glared at him from the couch across the room. "Really, Klan? It's like that?"

"Yep. And don't think you finna be out all night either. You need to be back by eleven o'clock."

I looked at him like he was speaking another language. "Eleven o'clock? I'm not on a curfew. I don't tell you when to come home."

He took his eyes off the TV to give me a serious look. "You ain't me. You don't run shit. Eleven o'clock. I ain't playin either."

His response pissed me off. "What the hell is that supposed to mean? You don't run me or own me. I'm grown and my daddy is at home with my mama."

"Nah, yo daddy up north   doing life. That nigga living with yo mama is one of them stupid ass tender dick niggas that let females call the shots. We ain't on none of that up in here. I run this and what I say goes."

I didn't want to go there with him but I wasn't about to let him disrespect me and my family. "You better watch how you talk about my family. You didn't have a real family growing up so you don't know that family ain't blood. It's love. And my daddy is my daddy. You don't even know your daddy and your mom was a dope fiend hoe that died from an overdose so you shouldn't even be talking about somebody's parents."

He jumped up from the couch and threw the controller against the wall. "What the fuck you say about my mama, bitch?"

He stood over me with clenched fists, threatening violence. I was too scared to respond. This was as close as he had ever come to hitting me and I didn't want to say anything that would get my ass kicked.

"Like I thought, soft ass nigga. Talk that shit now that I'm in yo face if you so fucking tough. Matter of fact, for that, you ain't going nowhere. You staying in this house with me. You got all dressed up for nothing. Now say something about that."

I tried to be brave but my voice came out in a whine. "Klan, I'm not staying in this house with you."

He pushed me back onto the couch. "Oh, you not? You think you finna leave? Okay. Leave this muthafucka if you want to and I'ma act a fool. Watch. I dare you to try me."

I didn't know exactly what he meant by the threat but I knew that he didn't make idle threats. If he said it, he was going to do it. But I also didn't want him to control me. The conversation with Neesy popped into my head. This is what she was warning me about. If I let him keep me in the house, he would gain control over my life. Then my phone dinged. He grabbed it off the table and read the text.

"That's yo cousin. Tell her to fall back."

I grabbed my phone and read the text. Neesy and Jay were outside. I had to make a decision. Klan hovered over me with a threatening stare. If I left the house something bad would happen. If I stayed, I would give all of my power to him. Tears spilled down my face as I sent the text.

I can't go. Something came up.

Klan smiled. "That's right, nigga. Stay in yo place."

He had conquered me and taken my will. My life was his and he knew it. When Neesy called my phone, I didn't answer. I couldn't face her. I didn't want her to know that I was a coward and was staying home because I didn't want something bad to happen.

"I hate you," I told Klan as the tears burned down my face.

He grabbed another controller and sat down to play the game. "Shut up, nigga."

When the doorbell rang, we looked at each other.

"I got it," Klan said.

I got up with him. "No. Its my cousin. I got it."

I wiped the tears from my face and Klan stood next to me as I opened the door. Neesy gave me a once over to see if I was hurt before snarling at Klan. "What's going on, cousin? Why can't you come with us?"

I felt like such a coward standing there with Klan over my shoulder. "I just can't. We'll do it another time."

"Don't let him do this, Charlene. If you let him tell you where you can go, you are giving him all of your power. You have to stand up to him."

I tried to hold back the tears but couldn't. "I don't want nobody to get hurt. I don't want to fight. Just go without me."

Fire roared inside Neesy's eyes as she turned to Klan. "Why you tripping on my cousin? This my last night in town. We just want to go to a play."

"What did she tell you, Neesy. She can't go. Now go mind yo business and don't worry about what go on in my house."

"I am worried about what go on in your house if it got something to do with my family. You a bully, Klan. Leave her alone and let her come out the house. You ain't her daddy."

"Get away from my house, bitch. I ain't finna argue with you."

"Bitch!? I got yo bitch. You a coward, Klan. A punk and a coward. You won't face nobody that ain't scared of you. C'mon, Charlene. Get away from this insecure boy. You need a real man."

Klan shoved the door open and stepped onto the porch, towering over Neesy like the Incredible Hulk does every human on the planet. "Get the fuck away from my house before I beat yo ass, lil punk ass bitch!"

"Neesy, just leave." I yelled, stepping between them and holding Klan back. I couldn't let him hit her. "Don't do this, Klan."

Neesy didn't back down. "I'm not scared of you, punk. I dare you to hit me. I dare you."

"Aye, what's going on?" Jay called, heading for the porch.

Neesy's husband wasn't a little man. He was a little over six feet with a lean build. He had brown skin and wore some kind of texturizer kit in his philly fro. He carried himself with confidence and self-assurance but I knew that Klan would take his confidence.

"I'm not leaving without my cousin," Neesy continued.

"What's going on, baby?" Jay asked as he closed the distance.

"He out here disrespecting me and won't let my cousin leave. I ain't scared of him. Just because he big and ugly don't-"

"Bro, come get yo bitch before I beat her ass. I ain't playing," Klan promised.

"Ay, man, don't talk to my wife like that!" Jay said, stepping onto the porch.

"Well, check yo bitch, nigga."

Jay pointed at Klan aggressively as he spoke. "If you disrespect my wife one more time we throwing some blows, man. For real."

I seen violence flash in Klan's eyes before he shoved me out of the way. Jay knew what was about to happen but was powerless to stop it. When Klan started swinging, all he could do was try to cover up. The punches were heavy and fast. Every time a blow landed, Jay's body folded. He backed up until he lost his balance on the step. When his arms began flailing to keep his balance, his guard dropped giving Klan a clean shot at his face. When somebody as big as Klan gets a free shot, you might as well call the hospital because something in your face is about to be broken. And I'm pretty sure Jay's jaw would need to be fixed because I heard a crunch when Klan hit him. Jay rolled down the steps and fell into the grass and didn't move.

"Baby!? Baby!?" Neesy yelled, running down the stairs to check on her husband.

"Why did you do that?" I yelled at Klan angrily.

"Shut the fuck up, nigga. I told that bitch to get the fuck up outta here. If you wouldn't of never been fucking with her shit talking ass, none of this wouldn't of happened. Now tell them muthafuckas to get off my grass. If I come out here and they ain't gone, I'm puttin both of em in body bags."

Klan stormed in the house and I went to check on Jay. His jaw was twisted and he was still knocked out. "Neesy, you gotta leave right now. He going to get a gun."

"Look what he did to his face." She cried. "He won't wake up."

I felt sorry for what happened to him but I knew if they didn't leave before Klan came back outside, something worse was going to happen. So I slapped Jay on his broken Jaw. He screamed as his eyes few open.

"Charlene, why you do that?" Neesy yelled, looking like she wanted to fight me.

"We have to get him in the car before he comes back out here. He will shoot y'all. You have to go."

I grabbed one of Jay's arms and Neesy grabbed the other as we pulled him to his feet. His legs wobbled like a newborn deer as he tried to walk.

"Charlene, you have to leave him, He is crazy." Neesy said, through terrified eyes.

"I know. But I can't right now."

"Yes you can. Get in the car with us and leave. Let's go."

I entertained the offer for a moment but knew that if I got in the car, Klan would get even madder. "I can't. Just go. I'll call you."

Neesy continued her pleas as we sat Jay in the passenger seat of their rental car. "Please, Charlene. Get in. Don't go back in that house."

"Charlene!?"

I turned and seen Klan standing on the porch holding a gun. I couldn't leave now. I looked at Neesy. "Leave."

Chapter 12

Nephew

Most people in prison say that time moves too slow. When you count minutes, hours, and days the clock seems to stand still. But for me time went by in a blur. After Dino was killed the prison was put on lockdown for three months. I knew that God had answered my prayers and revealed himself to me. I needed to make a decision with how I was going to live the rest of my life. I chose to ride with God and used the time that we were locked down to get closer to him. My mom signed me up for a correspondence Bible study course that helped me understand the Word of God. I also signed up to be in the Waupun Choir officially known as The Mighty Men of Valor. After we were taken off lockdown, I went to a couple choir practice sessions to meet the brothers and learn how to sing a little. I had never been in a choir nor had I ever sang a note but the choir leader, Rev, showed me how to blend my voice with the others. After two weeks of practices and two official services with the choir, other inmates around the prison had begun to talk about my change and I was officially known as a Christian.

I thought that changing my life would make me prey to all of the wolves around me, especially the people I robbed. But I was wrong. To my surprise, most people respected that I changed and my enemies left me alone. I guess that was the peace of God that the Bible talked about. There were still people that talked bad about me but there weren't many. I chalked it up to having haters. Some people will always talk about you no matter what you do. Being called a Christian and trying to do the right thing was taking some getting used to. I had been in the streets for so long that I never pictured doing anything other than robbing people to eat. Now my life had changed and I had to figure out another way to get paid. And I had to do it fast because I was getting out in two days.

"Aye, Nephew?"

I was sitting on the front pew collecting my thoughts before the next service started when someone called my name. I turned to see Roland, our choir leader, walking towards me.

"What's up, Rev?"

"I just wanted to come and talk to you while we are waiting for the next service to start. How you doing, son?"

"I'm good. Just thinking about getting out on Tuesday. I have to figure out a new way to live since the old me is dead and gone."

"Yeah. That is a big day. How long you been gone?"

"Three long years."

He laughed. "Three years is nothing when you think about how long life is. And that is nothing compared to the eternity that we get to spend with God in heaven. You're still young enough to put this behind you and do great things. Do you have a plan?"

"Not really. All this is new to me. If you would'da asked me that question three months ago I would'da said I'ma get it how I live. But after God showed me those signs, I don't know."

"Well, I know you've heard this before but I'm going to tell you again as a reminder. If you don't have a plan, you've already planned to fail. If I were in your shoes, I would focus on finding a church home and using their resources. Lots of churches have outreach programs that help people recently released from prison. That could be the beginning of your plan."

I nodded at the advice. "Yeah. That don't sound half bad. So, what's your plan when you get out?"

He gave me a long look. "In my father's house there are many mansions. When I go home, I plan to live like a king."

I wasn't expecting a Bible quote. "I'm not talking about heaven. What you gon do when you get out of here?"

He looked me right in my eyes. "I'm never getting out of here, Nephew. I got letters."

I didn't know what to say. I was going home in two days and he was never getting out.

"Don't feel sorry for me. God don't make no mistakes. Everything that happens to us is supposed to happen. Just focus on getting out and being the best version of you. Put God first and remain faithful to him because he will always remain faithful to you. Okay?"

I nodded. 'Yeah."

"Alright. Let me say a prayer for you before we run out of time. The next group should be coming in at any moment."

The next cell hall started filling in while we were praying. After an Amen, Rev went back to the piano to get the music started so the praise and worship team could begin the service. I was watching the inmates from the North Cell Hall file in when I seen a face that I never expected to see in the crowd. He didn't look much different from the last time I'd seen him except putting on a few pounds of muscle. Still had the shiny bald head, neatly shaved goatee, and cool swagger. He was so deep in the conversation he was having with another inmate that he didn't see me approaching.

"Little!?"

He looked up and Surprise lit his eyes when he seen me. "Nephew, what's good, man?"

We embraced like long lost brothers before I stepped back to look at my best friend. "I'm good, man. What's up with you? "

"I'm good. Just came to get a word. How long you been here?"

"Little over two years. I came here from Dodge. What about you? When you get here? I heard you got sent to a medium."

"I did. I was at RCI for a minute. Got jammed up and had to do six months at Boscobel. I just got here on Monday."

I was surprised. "You went to super max?"

"Yeah. Got knocked for a lil weed and got a month added on."

I shook my head. "That's messed up. But you still finna get out soon. A month is light."

"I would'da been getting out this month but now it's pushed back. It is what it is. You should be getting out soon, right?"

"I go home Tuesday."

"That's what's up, brah. Sit down and chop it up with me before the service start. Is you in the North Cell Hall too? What side you on?"

He was asking because only inmates from the North Cell Hall were allowed to attend this service. Each cell hall had their own church time. I lived in the South Cell Hall but members of the choir attended all services. I was kind of nervous to tell him about my change. We had been partners in crime since we were kids and I didn't know how he would react to me being a Christian. "Nah, I'm in the south. I'm here with y'all because I'm in the choir."

He looked surprised. "You in the choir? On what?"

I smiled nervously. "For real."

He grabbed my hand and shook it. "Praise God, saint."

It was my turn to be surprised. "You saved, brah?"

"Fa-sho, Nephew. I told you I was gone hang up my guns. I been rocking with the lord for almost a year now. I went to

Boscobel because I got caught up backsliding. But the lord admonished me and I'm done with all that. Now I'm focused on living righteous."

Hearing him talk about righteous living and being saved was different. "Wow, man. I don't even know what to say. I can't believe that we both saved. Man, that's crazy"

"God is good."

"All the time. And all the time, God is good," I finished. When the music started playing that was my cue to join the choir up front. "Little, I gotta go, brah. I'ma give you my mom's number when the service is over. I should have my own phone on by Tuesday night. Make sure you call so she can give you my number."

"I will, Nephew. It was good seeing you."

$$$

(Tuesday morning)

Being released from prison was the best feeling I had ever felt in my entire life. Better than losing my virginity. Better than the first time I hit a blunt. Nothing could compare to having the power to make your own decisions. No one telling me when I could take a shower, when to eat, or to lift my balls and spread my butt cheeks during a search. Living in a small closet for three years with a bathroom a few feet from where you lay your head at made you feel inhuman. Like an animal. And in the hole some people became animals. I had seen a lot during my three years in the box and I knew for sure that I wasn't ever putting myself inside the belly of that beast again.

"Mr. Peterson, I just want to congratulate you for earning your freedom back," Captain Varley said, extending a hand.

I reached for his hand and shook. "Thanks."

"Don't come back, okay?"

"You ain't gotta worry about me no more, cap. I'ma new man."

"Good to hear. Get on out of here."

He opened the door to the holding cell and two blue shirts helped carry my property boxes to the front lobby. My mother stood in the waiting area wearing a smile as big as mine. LaToya Peterson was hands down the most beautiful woman to walk this planet. And I wasn't just saying that because she was my mom. Okay maybe I was. But who isn't biased when it comes to their moms? Her thick and curly hair framed her face like the perfect natural picture frame. Her skin was a bronze color, eyes light brown, beauty mark on her cheek, and smile perfect. She wasn't that tall, just 5'3, but that never stopped her from being a giant in my life. She wore a black T-shirt with 'blessed' across the front in white letters, black jeans, and white sandals.

"There go my baby!" she sang, barely holding back tears.

I dropped the box and wrapped her in a tight hug. "Hey, mama."

"You did it, Bobby. You made it. Welcome back."

I held onto my mom like I was a newborn and shed a few tears of joy. The nightmare was finally over. "Thank you, mama."

"Thank you, Jesus." She stepped back to look me over. "Look at you looking all handsome in your street clothes."

She bought the clothes I wore. The same black t-shirt with 'Blessed' across the front, Christian Dior jeans, and a pair of Giannis' Greek Freak Nikes. "You didn't do bad, ma. I like the touch of Milwaukee with the shoes, too."

"I told you I got style, boy. Now let's get these boxes and get up outta here because our Waupun days are over."

We piled my boxes in the backseat of her blue Rav4 and put Waupun in the rear view mirror.

"So, when is we going to the church?" Pastor Sims sent a message for me to check in with him as soon as I got out and I was looking forward to seeing him.

"We going a-sap. Please believe it."

"You still saying that? That's from like early 2000s, ma."

162

"I know. That's my thang. Y'all young people got y'all sayings and I got mine."

"Oh, so you admitting that you old?"

She looked like she wanted to hit me. "Keep playing and you gon need that captain to come get me off yo butt. I'm still twenty-five years old."

"That means I'm older than you. Is you my mom or sister?"

"With God all things are possible, son. Remember that."

After sharing a laugh, things turned serious. "So what are you going to do now that you out? You're sticking with the program and getting your life together, right?"

"Yeah, ma. I was serious when I told y'all I was done with the streets. I wanna live for God and see what this life has for me. I don't wanna die before it's my time or end up back in Waupun. I wanna live. I wanna go to church. I wanna eat some of yo good cooking. I wanna take a bath. I wanna stay free."

She looked over at me and smiled. "I'm so happy to hear you say all of that. And we got your back. Me, Jamie, and your new church family, too. I'm so happy that you home. Thank you, Jesus."

We pulled up at our house on 66th and Capitol an hour later. I took everything in as moms parked the car. We lived in a yellow and red two story one family house in the middle of the block. Bushes lined the front and there were purple irises along the sides. The grass was freshly cut and an 'Obama for President' sign was in the middle of the lawn.

"You know Joe Biden is president now?" I cracked as we climbed from the car.

She waved me off. "Barack will always be president."

We grabbed the boxes from the backseat and took them in the house. The first thing I noticed was the smell. Vanilla plug ins. It was my mom's favorite scent. The living room hadn't changed much since I left. White carpet, white leather furniture and a flat screen on the wall above the fireplace.

The only thing that had changed were the pictures on the wall. Black Jesus, mom and Jamie in different places wearing smiles, and a big one of us on a visit in Waupun.

"Why you put this one up?"

"Because it was the only recent picture I had of us together as a family. Now that you out we can take some more and hang them up." Then she pulled out her phone "Smile."

After a couple pictures, I went to put the boxes in my room. It looked the same as the last time I was in it. TV on the wall with my XBox still hooked up. The scratches on the headboard for how many girls I smashed in my bed. Still at thirty-four. The screw was still missing from the vent where I hid my drugs, guns, and money. And the bullet hole in the ceiling from when I was playing with a Desert Eagle while I was high. I lay on my back in bed and closed my eyes, allowing the memories to flood my brain. Being back at home felt like a dream.

"You wanna lay there or go meet the people that have been praying for you?" Mom asked from the doorway.

"I got lost in the memories, mama. I can't believe I'm back at home."

"Well, it's real. You here. Now let's go meet the family."

I took a moment to think about the word family. The only family I had ever known was my mom and Jamie. "We got a real family, now?"

She nodded. "A real family, baby. They been praying for you and can't wait to meet you."

We hopped back in the SUV and headed to The City of God Church on 24th and Hopkins. I watched as the neighborhoods went from middle class to the hood. There were more potholes in the hood, as well as trash and abandoned houses. The people looked like zombies walking aimlessly and mindlessly amongst the rubble. I forgot how messed up the inner city looked until I was back in it. But one thing about the hood was it had the best church services.

For some reason the anointed preachers and choirs were in the ghetto. Pastor Sims kept the stereotype alive with his fiery sermons. Mom parked in the lot behind the church and I finally got to see the building. It was huge compared to the small church that I had gotten used to worshipping in at Waupun. Big stained-glass windows and the steeple atop looked to be a hundred feet in the sky. I followed mom through the huge double doors and into the foyer. The hallway had red carpet and white walls. She led me down the hall to another set of double doors. I could hear music coming from the other side. When she opened them I got a glimpse of the sanctuary and about fifty members of the congregation. They were spread out amongst the pews but when the doors opened all of their eyes turned towards us. The scene left me speechless. I couldn't believe that all these strangers had shown up for me. They even had a 'Welcome Home' sign on the wall.

"There he is," Pastor Sims shouted. "The prodigal son has returned home."

Everyone began clapping as my mom led me down the aisle towards the stage. Jamie stepped out of the crowd and gave me a strong hug.

"Welcome home, son," he beamed.

"Thanks. It feels good to be free."

"C'mon up here, Bobby, so you can introduce yourself," Pastor Sims said.

I walked upon the stage to receive a warm hug from the church leader.

"Everybody, this is Bobby Peterson, Brotha Jamie and Sister LaToya's son that we have been praying for for almost three years. Today we are officially welcoming him into our church family and he is the newest member of the City of God Church."

The people began clapping again.

"I had the honor and privilege of reciting the sinner's prayer with him while he was in. I heard how this young brother has grown in Christ and went from the pews way in the back to in front singing with the choir. Tell me God ain't good."

The church yelled, "Amen."

"Now, I'ma turn this mic over to Bobby and let him say a couple words. Here you go, son."

I was never good at public speaking and the fact that I was about to talk in front of a lot of strangers made my anxiety worse.

"I just wanna thank God for bringing me through and allowing me to be here. Um, I thank everybody for their prayers, and um, I really don't know what else to say. I been through a lot and I seen a lot. I'm just glad that I'm out and can be here with y'all."

After stuttering my way through the short speech we went downstairs for the banquet. I was sitting and talking to Junior Pastor Greg when a pretty brown skinned female walked over. I tried not to stare but her body was cold.

"Bobby, I want you to meet my fiance, Tasha. She is Pastor Sims daughter," Greg introduced.

"Hey, Bobby. It's nice to meet you. Welcome home," she smiled.

"Thank you. It's nice to meet you, too."

There was an awkward silence as me and Tasha continued to stare. I could feel the spark and attraction.

"Um, Tasha, Don't you have to be at work?" Greg asked.

She snapped back and looked to her husband. "Yes, I do, baby. I just wanted to come and welcome Bobby to the church. Nice to meet you again."

She kissed Greg and we both watched her walk away.

Chapter 13

Nephew

"Bobby, I'm about to go to work."

I opened my and seen My mom standing in the doorway. "Okay."

"I left my keys on the table in the kitchen. Don't sleep all day. You have to see your P.O at 8:30."

"A'ight. what time is it?"

"A little after six-thirty. Don't forget to renew your license, too."

When moms left, I stared at the ceiling trying to decide if I should get up. The first night in a real bed made me want to spend the day sleeping. My Serta felt like a cloud compared to the mattress that I slept on in Waupun. I went back and forth in my head for a few minutes before deciding to get up. I had spent the last three years stuck inside a prison. No way I was spending my second day out in bed. I threw off the sheet and got down on my knees to say a morning prayer. After talking to God, I rolled on my stomach to do a light workout; 100 pushups and 100 sit-ups. I had been doing the routine for two years and was done in a few minutes. I grabbed a pair of boxers from the drawer and some towels from the closet in the hallway before hitting the bathroom. Twenty minutes later I stepped out so fresh and so clean then went to get my grub on. Moms had the fridge and cabinets stocked with food but all I wanted was cereal. In Waupun they served mostly wheat flakes for breakfast and I was fiending for some Golden Grahams. I grabbed the biggest bowl that I could find, a mixing bowl, and dumped in half the box and went to work.

After getting full on cereal I rummaged through my closet for something to wear. I had a couple fits from before I went to prison. I pulled out a black and red Balenciaga fit and got myself together. For the final touch I hit mom's room to search Jamie's cologne collection. There were about twenty bottles on the dresser. I searched the scents until I found something my speed. You could never go wrong with Jordan. I gave myself a once over in the mirror to make sure the philly fro, lining, and goatee was fresh before going back to my room to get my phone and debit card. Moms and Jamie put 1,500 on the card for me to go shopping. I still had an hour before the meet with my P.O so I decided to do some social media surfing. I got a lot of welcome home messages and friend requests on Facebook. None of that was of interest to me. I was looking for a comment or request from one person. Jasmine. I needed to see if the baby was mine but she was hard to find. After sucking up my disappointment, I hopped in mom's RAV4 and went to see my P.O.

The Probation & Parole Building on East Capitol was a big white building with lots of windows. I followed the signs and entered a small hallway with big doors on both sides and an elevator at the end of the hall. I took the elevator to the fourth floor. There was a big white door at the end of the hall with a Probation and Parole sign. Inside was a small waiting room. Across the room was a window being manned by a heavy-set white lady wearing bad make-up. There was a large arrow in the window pointing to a clipboard with "sign in" written on it.

"How can I help you?" She asked, flashing yellow stained teeth.

"I have an appointment with Linda Weaver."

She began typing on the computer. "Who are you?"

"Bobby Peterson."

"Sign in and have a seat."

I watched from the bench as she picked up the phone and spoke a few words. "She'll be out in a moment."

I took in my surroundings while waiting. The room was plain. Nothing on the walls. No plants. Nothing. I figured it was by design. They were reminding us not to get comfortable. I got the message. A couple minutes later the door next to the office opened and out walked a slim brown skinned woman.

"Bobby Peterson?"

"Yes."

"Come on. Follow me."

I didn't mean to check out my P.O but I couldn't help it. She was fine and looked to be around my age. The jeans hugged her small frame in all the right places and showed off her slim figure. I followed her down a hall with lots of small offices on both sides. We turned a corner and her office was the first door on the right. It didn't look much bigger than a cell at Waupun. Only had enough room for a desk and a couple chairs.

"Come on in and have a seat. Welcome back to the free world."

"Thanks. It feels good to be back."

"So, I'm your parole officer for the next couple of years and if all goes well you won't see my face again after discharge. I don't like locking up black men because I know the statistics. Prison is overcrowded with you guys. But if you force me to do my job, I will. I'll help you out in any way I can but if you don't help yourself, don't expect nothing from me. Are we clear so far?"

"Yes, ma'am."

"Stop with the ma'am, Mr Peterson. I'm only thirty. Linda is fine."

"Okay, Linda."

She opened a file and brought out a piece of paper. "These are your rules. I need you to sign them. There are a lot of them so I'll give you copy. Take a few minutes to read them."

I skimmed the twenty-five rules. They were pretty basic and common sense. No guns, drugs, or committing a crime. If so, I will be sent back to prison. I signed them and handed the paper back.

"Do you have any questions?"

"Nah. It's all pretty basic. Don't do nothing that will get me in trouble."

"Exactly." She pulled a check from the file. "This is your institution check for 632.28. Your parole fees will be ten dollars a month until you get a job. When you get employed they will increase to thirty. By the way, do you have any jobs lined up?"

"I have some options. Working with my stepdad or finding something with the church."

"Okay. Let me know if you need any help. I have some resources. I'm going to set it up for you to see me again in thirty days. Hopefully you will have found a job by then. If you don't have any questions, you can get on your way."

After seeing my P.O, I headed for the DMV to renew my license. It took about two hours but I eventually got my picture taken and card issued. I walked out of the government building a little after eleven o'clock. I was supposed to go shopping but decided to put that on hold. Instead I headed for the hood to see some old faces. I knew I was playing with fire by visiting my old stomping grounds but I picked up the lighter anyway. When I pulled up to the gas station on 35th and Hopkins, I seen the same things that I'd seen before I'd gone to jail. A crackhead offering to pump gas and wipe windshields, a pregnant teenager walking away smoking a cigarette, and a man with nappy hair and dirty clothes panhandling near the door. "Some things never change," I mumbled as I climbed from the car.

The man near the pump approached me. "Hey, young brotha. Yo windshield look like it need to be washed. Let me take care of that for you."

"I'm good, man. I don't need it."

"Come on, brotha. Don't be like that."

"I don't got no money, brah."

He blew me off and went to the next car that pulled up and ran the same script. When I got to the door, the panhandler approached.

"Brotha, can you spare some change?"

"I don't got no money, brah," I said before stepping into the store. I was walking towards the coolers when I spotted a tall light skinned brotha with brushed waves and gold teeth. It was my boy, B-Eazy. He noticed me too.

"Nephew, what it do, nigga!?"

"B-Eazy, what's good, fool?" I asked as we embraced.

"Shit. Just out here gettin it how I live. What up wit chu, fam? When you get out?" He slurred, talking in slow motion. That was the lean.

"Yesterday. I was just sliding through to see who out here."

"You know I'm always out here, nigga. Tryna catch me a lic. You tryna get down? I know a nigga we can strip. Catch a couple pounds of loud."

"Nah," I laughed. "The kid is on something new. Don't do the things I used to do. I'm living a new life."

He frowned, looking me up and down like I had done something wrong. "Fuck you talkin bout, boy? That corn ball ass shit."

I didn't want to explain myself because I knew he wouldn't understand but I gave it a shot. "I got saved while I was in, brah. I'm tryna do the right thing now."

His eyes grew wide in surprise and then he bust out laughing. "Awe, shit! You went to the bing and got sanctified? For real? Praise God ass nigga."

My body grew warm with anger. I didn't like being the brunt of his jokes. "Ay, chill, fam. I know you didn't expect this but don't clown me, my dude."

"My bad, Nephew. I'm just surprised, fam. You was out here fucking shit up and now you flipped the script. I wasn't expecting this. Not from you."

"I wasn't expecting it either. But I seen some stuff, B. I can't go back to that old life."

He shook his head and looked at me like I sold out. "I hear you, fam. If that's what you on, who am I to judge. If yo ribs start touchin though, you know where to find me at."

I shook his hand and we hugged again. "When you ready to find what you been missing, get at me."

"Right. Right," he smirked and walked away. "Wait to niggas in the hood hear this."

I knew that coming to the hood was a bad idea but B-Eazy confirmed it. The way he looked at me like I sold out and being the butt of his jokes was humiliating. I didn't want to experience that again. The people that knew me before I went in would always see me as a jack boy. The hood didn't respect change. After buying a cherry Coke and a pack of Listerine strips, I headed for my mom's truck. A red Cadillac on chrome was parked near the door. When I seen the driver, I wished I had never come to the hood. He didn't see me at first but when the door chimed, he turned and we made eye contact. Jewels. Recognition flashed in his eyes and he immediately went for his waist.

"Move, nigga!" B-Eazy yelled.

I turned just in time to see B-Eazy pulling a gold pistol from his waist. Jewels took aim at me while B-Eazy opened up on him. I took off running as gun fire erupted behind me. The thought of Jewels walking me down made me run further than necessary. I ran two blocks before slowing down to catch my breath. I looked around nervously as my life flashed before my eyes. I had almost died on my second day out. If it wasn't for B-Eazy, I would've been gone. I looked in the sky and wasn't sure if I should be thankful to be alive or mad that I had almost died. But the one thing that I did know is that I was scared. Three years ago I would've wanted revenge but now all I wanted was to go home and be with my family. I was leery about going back to the gas station but I needed to get my mom's truck. If she found out I was in the hood, it would be on. I figured that B-Eazy and Jewels would be gone or laying on the ground bleeding. As I was walking back, I remembered the parole rules. I couldn't be around criminals, crime, or have police contact. Any violation could put me in jail. I needed to hurry up and get away from the scene.

I walked quickly back towards the gas station, keeping a lookout for the red Cadillac. When I was across the street from the Citco, I checked the scene. Jewels and B-Eazy were gone. I was about to cross the street when a black Buick Lacrosse jerked to a stop in front of me. I thought Jewels was coming back and my adrenaline surged. I was about to take flight until I heard a female's voice.

"Nephew, get in."

I looked in the car and was shocked to see the driver. Simone. She looked even better than I remembered. She had matured and filled out. I literally got stuck as memories of our last conversation played in my head.

"Hurry up. Get in," she rushed.

Her voice and the seriousness of my situation brought me back. Shooting. Police. Jail. I jumped in the passenger seat.

"When did you get out?" she asked while driving away.

"Yesterday." I gave a one word answer as the heartbreak set in again.

I couldn't believe that I was sitting in the car with her. It was so much I wanted to say to her when I was in that cell but now that she was next to me, my mind was blank. I just stared.

"Oh, my God! You look so good. Welcome home."

"Thanks."

She glanced at me to see why I was hitting her with the one word answers. I couldn't hide the pain in my eyes and she couldn't hide the sadness in hers. There was so much that we needed to talk about but neither of us wanted to bring it up.

"I heard shooting and seen you running. You good?"

"Yeah. That was Jewels."

Her eyes grew wide with surprise and then dimmed to deviousness little slits. I remembered the look. "You want me to help you find him?"

I found it crazy that she would put her life on the line to help me get revenge but wouldn't ride out the time with me. "Nah. I gotta get out of here before the police come. I can't have no police contact."

Her expression changed to a frown. She never heard me duck smoke. "You for real?"

"I changed, Simone. I'm done with the streets. That was just some karma. I gotta live with it."

She looked at me again, mouth hanging open a little. "You really did change. What happened?"

"I really don't got time to tell you everything right now. I need to get back to the gas station to get my mom's car. I don't want her to know I was over here."

"Okay. I'll turn around up here."

We rode in silence for a few moments. Then she broke it. "I'm sorry I wasn't there for you."

Her words stirred up emotions and memories that I wanted to leave in the cells at Waupun. "That was foul, Simone. I did everything for you. You didn't want for nothing. I thought it was real. I thought you was real."

Tears began rolling down her face. "I loved you, Nephew. With everything inside of me. You was good to me. I know I'm foul. I didn't want to face you. I figured it would be easier to push you away when I got pregnant. I didn't know how to tell you so-"

"You had a baby?"

"Two."

Her words felt like a stab to the heart and I needed a moment. "Two kids?"

"It got hard for me. I had to get out here and get it how I lived."

"What that mean?"

She hesitated. "I started stripping and selling pussy."

"While I was in the county jail?"

She wiped the tears away and let out a long breath. "Do you got time to talk to me?"

As bad as I wanted to get out of the hood before the police came, I couldn't leave before we talked. I wanted to know how she could dip on me like that. "Yeah."

She pulled up to the gas station and parked on the side. "I started fucking with this nigga, Ken, while you was in the county jail. I told him about you but he wanted to take me from you. He wanted to be with me but I wanted to see what was going to happen to you. All that shit changed when I got pregnant. I was on birth control but somehow it still happened. I didn't want to tell you so I started pushing you away. Ken ended up getting killed when I was seven months. I was a street bitch and I wasn't about to let me and my baby starve so after I had lil Ken, I started stripping. You know what come with that. Then I got pregnant again with Sinclair."

"That's crazy," was all I managed.

"I'm sorry, Nephew. I really am. I don't regret having my kids but I do regret how it all happened. I wish it could've been different."

I didn't have any words. "It is what it is. Nothing we can do about it now."

We got quiet again.

"Tell me about you and this change. What happened in there?"

A police car pulled into the gas station and two officers got out to talk to the gas station owner.

" I'm a Christian."

Her eyes grew wide and mouth dropped open. "Yeah right."

"I'm serious. I'm done with the streets."

She stared at me like she was finally seeing the real me. "I knew that you grew up in church but I never thought that you would do that." She paused. "I'm proud of you for changing. I wish I could'da been there to witness this."

I wished she would'da been there too but I didn't want to tell her that. When we became silent again, I took that as my cue to leave. "Well, I gotta go. I need to get out of here before they start asking questions."

"Wait. You just gon leave"

"I wasn't expecting to see you and hear all this. Then running into jJewels and almost getting shot. This is all too much for my second day out. I need some time to process all this."

I could see the hope of there being an 'us' shatter in her eyes. Then she began searching my face for something. Maybe the love we used to have or to see if it had changed to hate. It reminded me of how she used to stare at me before I went to prison. Then she dropped a bomb.

"I got HIV."

I heard what she said but it took a moment to register. "What?"

She looked down at her hands. "I got HIV. I guess that was my karma for everything that I've done. You went to prison and I got a disease."

She didn't look like she was sick. Her skin was glowing and body looked amazing. I wondered if I had it too. I got tested while I was in prison and came back negative but they said it could lay dormant for years.

"How you get AIDS?"

"Not AIDS, HIV. I got it from Sinclair's daddy. Nigga was out here passing that shit out. Got me too."

I realized she wasn't searching my eyes to see if I loved or hated her. It was to see if I was going to judge her when she revealed her secret. "Damn, Simone. I don't even know what to say."

"Nothing you can say. You don't have to live with this. I do."

I tried to think of something encouraging to say but all the words that passed through my head would do nothing to help her situation. It was time to go. "I'm sorry for what happened to you. And I forgive you. We good."

Tears welled up in her eyes again. "You a good nigga. And I really am sorry. Get at me on Facebook. Just because we can't fuck don't mean we can't be friends."

"Okay. I got you."

"Don't look back, Nephew. Ain't nothing out here for you. Niggas is crabs in a bucket and can't wait to pull you back down. Take care of yourself and don't think for a moment that I ever stopped loving you."

We shared a long hug before I climbed from the car. My heart shattered as I watched her drive away. Despite everything that happened between us, I still loved her. But I wouldn't act upon it. Her bed was already made and I was moving on with my life. As I stood in the lot watching the police search for shell casings, I realized that God had used prison to save me from everything that I had seen this morning. It was time to let go of the things I used to know and receive the new life that God had for me.

$$$

Charlene

It was a little past 8:30 on a Sunday morning and I was wide awake. I sat on the couch staring at the TV, letting it watch me. Had been sitting in the same spot since I woke up at six. Reruns of Chicago PD were showing but I wasn't paying it much attention. The weekends were normally days for rest and relaxing. Sleep in late and lounge around the house all day. But I couldn't sleep because of Klan. We spoke around eleven last night and he said he was coming home. I stayed up until one waiting for him. I woke up around six to pee and he still wasn't home. I tried to call him but he didn't answer. A bunch of emotions flowed through me; mostly anger and worry. I was worried that he could be hurt or in trouble. He was a street nigga and there was a real possibility that he could be in the hospital or in jail. Another part of me knew better. Klan was perfectly fine and just decided not to come home. It wasn't like he hadn't done it before. The double standard pissed me off. If I stayed out all night I would come home to world war three. He was going to come home and act like everything was all good. His explanation would be the same as it had been the last couple of times. Something happened and he had to lay low for the night. Oh, and his phone died, that's why he didn't call. Then he would get mad because I was mad. That would lead to more arguing.

Why did I let this no good, jealous, and controlling nigga take over my life? I deserved more out of life and love. I was educated, had goals, and came from a good family. Klan was all of the opposite. And this was the man that I gave sole possession of my will. My family was mad at him for what he did to Neesy's husband. My parents threatened to disown me if I didn't come home. Neesy sent me a message saying not to speak to her until I left Klan. And even though I knew things between me and Klan would get worse and that he was pushing away everybody that loved me, I stayed with him. I was scared to leave. Some nights I found myself hoping that he would get caught up in the streets and go to jail. That would make breaking up so much easier and I wouldn't have to worry about him coming after me.

Something on TV caught my attention. The police were raiding a church. The scene made me think of going to church with Neesy. We sat and prayed while listening to the choir practice. Listening to gospel music and praying had touched something within me. I felt hopeful. Almost like a spiritual healing. And that was exactly what I needed this morning. Healing. So I decided that instead of sitting on the couch feeling bad about my life, I would go to church. I took a quick shower, put on a green sundress, sandals, threw my phone in my tote and walked down to The City of God Church.

There were lots of cars parked around the church and I felt a little nervous to be going alone. That disappeared when I heard the choir singing. It felt like the music was pulling me inside. I walked through the big double doors, down the hall, and into the sanctuary. The church was filled with about three hundred people. Lots of them were standing with their eyes closed, hands in the air, singing along with the choir. The scene was touching and I could feel something in the air. It was indescribable. I hadn't been to church in years but I don't ever remember feeling what I was feeling at that moment. I was about to go find a seat when an usher came and led me to a seat three rows from the back. I looked around the church until my eyes found a sign telling us to turn off our phones. Klan's face flashed in my head. If he tried to contact me and I didn't answer, he would get mad. Then I thought about him not coming home and turned off the phone.

The choir sang 'Taking me Higher' and I felt the words in my spirit. When they were done, a handsome older man in a dark suit walked up and introduced himself as Brother Jamie Andrews. He asked everyone to bow their heads before going into a fiery prayer that brought 'Amens' and applause from the congregation. He read a scripture, 2nd Thessalonians 3:1-5. The words about being delivered from unreasonable and wicked men touched me. That's exactly what I needed. After Jamie finished, the choir sang again before Mother Sims got up to say prayer and introduce her husband, Pastor Sims. Although he wasn't an imposing man, he spoke with an authority and confidence that made me listen.

"Good morning, church. Let me first start off by thanking God for His grace, mercy, and protective presence. If you haven't heard, God has done some amazing things in some of our members lives and I want to take the time to speak about one particular brotha who God has been working on. For those of you that don't know the newest member of The City of God family, let me introduce brotha Bobby Peterson, Jamie and LaToya's prodigal son. Stand up for a moment, son."

The church applauded as a man wearing a blue suit, yellow tie, and yellow shoes stood. The brother was Fine with a capitol F. He was tall with a nice build, his hair and face neatly trimmed. He spun around to wave at everyone. We locked eyes for a moment.

"Bobby's story is a true testimony to the transforming power of God. Three years ago he was a hard-core gun carrying criminal that robbed, stole, and destroyed. He did the devil's work with a smile on his face. But God."

"Amen preacher, " someone shouted.

Go head and tell it," another said.

"Watch me tell it," the pastor grinned. "He was eventually arrested and sentenced to prison time at Waupun, a maximum-security prison with some of the worst criminals in Wisconsin. Now for those of you that remember, Sister Toya and Brotha Jamie always asked us to pray for their son, Bobby. And we did. Then one day God spoke to me. He told me that it was time to go get Bobby. Y'all ain't gon believe what happened next. My phone rang the next day and it was the chaplain at Waupun asking if we had a team to come and preach."

The congregation erupted with more Amens. I sat up, eager to hear the rest of the story.

"That call was the conformation that God had already worked it out. So I got on the highway like a good and faithful servant of the Lord. And while God was showing me signs out here, He was showing Bobby signs on the inside. Bobby was a problem child. Stayed in the hole for fights. Never went to church. But God spoke to him in a dream. That dream made him go to church for answers. God sent me with the answer. I had never spoken to Bobby before so I had no idea what he looked like. When I called his name during the service, he didn't answer. I preached the word that God gave me and then offered salvation at the end of the service. And do you know who stood up and gave their life to the Lord?"

The church started shouting and clapping. I joined in the clapping, amazed by the story.

"Do you see the awesome power of God, church? He is still doing miracles. Sometimes we get stuck living in the now and can't see what God has done or is about to do. None of y'all are here by happenstance. You didn't come here because you wanted to. You came here today because God called you here. This is exactly where you are supposed to be. Somebody praise God."

The church went wild and people started catching the holy ghost. I was amazed by the message and it tugged at my heart. For the next two hours I clapped, laughed, and had the best church experience of my life. Time went by in a blur and before I knew it the service was over. I stood and pulled my phone from my purse to check messages and realized I had done something that I hadn't done in years. I forgot about Klan. He didn't cross my mind once during the service. Maybe there was something to this church stuff.

"I never seen you here before."

I jumped at the sound of the deep voice. I spun to see Bobby standing next to me. "Man, why you sneaking up on people?"

"I'm sorry," he laughed. "I didn't mean to scare you."

"Apology not accepted. You have to make noise when you walk up on people you don't know."

"I'll remember that. My name is Nephew, I mean, Bobby."

"Hi, Nephew, I mean, Bobby. That's a really long name but it's nice to meet you. I have just one name. Charlene."

"It's Bobby. Nephew is my nickname. Old habits die hard. Are you a member of the church?"

"No. This is actually my first time coming to a service."

"This is my first service, too. What did you think?"

"I had a good time. Pastor Sims is great and you have an amazing story. Was all that true?"

"Yeah. I used to be a wild child," he grinned.

We became silent for a moment. I was waiting for him to tell more about his transformation but instead we ended up staring at each other. That saying about windows being the eye of the soul popped into my head. Bobby's soul reflected an honest, gentle, and caring man. His energy felt good. I liked him instantly, which surprised me. I hadn't liked a man in a long time. I wondered if he kidnapped and shot people like Klan. Dammit, Klan. The thought made me realize that I was smiling in another man's face. It was time to go. Plus, I suddenly had to pee.

"It was really nice to meet you, Bobby, but I have to go."

Disappointment flashed across his face. "Okay. Will you come back again?"

I wanted to say no and put as much distance between me and Bobby as possible. Whatever this connection was between us could get us both in a lot of trouble. But I didn't want to see the disappointment on his face anymore. I wanted to see him smile again. "Yes. I'll be back. I have to go now. See you later."

He smiled and nodded and I swear it was worth it. "See you later," he waved.

I spun and walked away with a bunch of feelings and emotions bouncing around inside of me. On the walk home I tried to make sense of it all. The church service did what I hoped it would do and healed me. I felt good and my spirits were lifted. I also thought about the pastor's words about

God calling me to church. I was supposed to be here. Why? And then there was Bobby. I liked him. I wanted to get to know him but knew I couldn't. Getting to know another man was dangerous. Thinking of Klan made me check my phone. There were four missed calls and three texts from him. Damn. This could turn bad. The impending doom seemed to make me have to pee worse and I put some pep in my step wishing I would have peed at church but I was too busy trying to put distance between me and Bobby. I called Klan back as I high stepped across the street but he didn't answer. I wanted to text him but stopping my bladder from exploding was taking all of my energy and concentration. I ran upon the porch and did the 'I gotta pee' dance while unlocking the door. I stepped into the house about to make a dash for the bathroom when Klan appeared, blocking my path. And he was big mad.

"Nigga, where the fuck you was at?"

"Move. I gotta pee," I said, trying to get by.

He grabbed my arm. "I don't give a fuck. You ain't goin nowhere until you tell me where the fuck you was at. I been calling you and texting you all morning."

My spiritual high came crashing down and the anger that I felt all night and morning took over. "Really Klan? You're the one who didn't come home. I was calling you and texting you all night. Where were you? And let me go. I have to pee."

I tried to yank away from him but he grabbed me again and pushed me against the wall and got in my face.

"Nigga, what the fuck is yo problem? You done lost yo mind? Don't be snatching away from me. I told you yo ass wasn't goin nowhere until you answer my question. Where the fuck was you at?"

My anger turned down a notch when I seen how mad he was. "I was at church. Now where were you?"

"Don't worry about me. Since when you start going to church and why didn't you answer the phone? You had some nigga with you or something?" Jealousy and anger swirled in his eyes.

"No. I went by myself." I tried to get away from him. "Let me go. I gotta pee."

His fist came without warning and crashed into the wall next to my face. I was terrified and all I could do was flinch. My bladder released. Then he wrapped a hand around my throat, his eyes bulging with anger. "Stop fucking lying to me, Charlene. Where the fuck you go and who the fuck you was with?"

Tears of fear and humiliation rolled down my face. " I'm not lying. I went to church by myself. They had a sign for us to turn off our phones."

He stared at me for a moment to see if I was telling the truth. Then slowly his face softened and he removed his hand from around my neck. "I'm sorry."

I didn't know what else to do so I stood there and cried. "You made me pee on myself."

He pulled me into his chest, wrapping me in a hug. "I'm sorry, baby."

I was confused, wet, and shaking with fear. I couldn't take too much more of this. I was terrified of him and there was no telling what he would do when he got mad. The next time he might actually put his hands on me or worse.

"Come here. I got you," he said, lifting me into his arms and carrying me in the bathroom. He sat me on the toilet, ran the shower, took off my clothes, and helped me in the water. Then he grabbed a soap and towel.

"Klan, what are you doing?"

"Sshh. I got you."

I allowed him to lather me up and then remove the shower head and rinse me. The act was so tender and loving and it confused me even more. A couple minutes ago he acted like he was going to kill me and now he was giving me an intimate bath. He was being gentle and it felt so good. He soaped the towel again and began lathering my body, taking his time rubbing between my legs. He brushed against my clit and sent a shiver through my body. Then he rinsed me with the shower head, pausing to spray between my legs. The warm water felt good on my lady parts and the sexual energy in the bathroom increased when I grabbed his hand to bring the shower head closer. The water tickled my clit and sent vibrations through my body. He stood to kiss me and I moaned in his mouth as he sucked my tongue and lips. I suddenly didn't care that he just humiliated and abused me. The danger and anger added to the passion burning all over me. I wanted him inside of me. I wanted to feel his strength. I wanted him to make me cum.

"Take this," he said, giving me the shower head.

I rubbed it against my clit while watching him undress. His dick hung down like a big black snake as he stepped into the shower. Then he dropped to his knees like he was worshipping before me. It felt powerful to have this big, strong, and violent man on his knees. He cupped my ass in his hands and kissed the v between my thighs. I put one leg on the tub, dropped the shower head and grabbed his head in both hands as he ate me. He sucked and licked me just the way I liked and it wasn't long until I was cumming on his face. He stood and put the shower head back in the base, adjusting it so that it was spraying us.

"Stand on the edge of the tub and grab that rod," he said.

I reached up and grabbed the shower rod, poking my ass out as I put one foot on the edge of the tub. He moved behind me and eased himself in until my ass was touching his stomach. It felt good to have him deep inside of me. He filled me completely and perfectly. He held my waist and started stroking me slowly. Every time he thrust up I pushed down and we created the perfect rhythm. It felt too damn good when he was fucking me. Especially when he got close to busting and started drilling me. He took control of my body and I hung onto the shower rod and let him have his way. I could feel all of his strength and it was so intoxicating. I came again and it felt so good that I wanted it to last forever. Then he thrust into me one final time and growled as he released. When he let me down, he washed my body again before carrying me into the bedroom for round two.

Chapter 15

Charlene

When I awoke, the first thing I noticed was the empty space next to me. I had slept so good that I didn't hear or feel Klan get out of bed. I hoped that he was gone because I needed some time to sort out everything that happened and figure out what to do next. I went from a spiritual high, to being scared for my life, to getting dick-matized. The emotional roller coaster left me exhausted. I wondered if this was what love was all about; pleasure and pains, highs and lows. I didn't see these things in the movies or read them in romance books. They always showed a perfect union and not the threat of violence or great bodily harm in the eyes of your lover. Klan had a monster inside of him and it was just a matter of time before he released it on me. I needed to find the strength to leave before it was too late. The doorbell pulled me from my thoughts. I didn't get up right away because Klan might still be in the house. When it rang again, I knew that I was home alone. I checked the time on my phone as I got up. 6:17 PM. I slipped on one of Klan's t-shirts while wondering who could be at the door. We didn't have many visitors.

"Who is it?"

"Larry's Limo Service. I'm here to pick up Charlene Anderson," a man called.

It had to be a joke. There was no way a limo was picking me up. I looked through the peephole and seen a dark-skinned middle-aged man wearing a suit standing on the porch. "Who are you here for again?"

"Charlene Anderson."

"Who sent you?"

"I'm not sure. I was told to make a pickup and that was it. Are you Charlene?"

"Yes."

"I'm here to get you."

I tried to think of who would send me a limo. It certainly wasn't Klan. I didn't think it was my parents either. Bobby didn't know where I lived. Or did he?

"Charlene, are you going to open the door?"

I clicked the locks and opened the door, keeping the security door locked. The driver looked at me expectantly.

"Are you coming out?"

"I don't know who sent you or where I'm going. I have a boyfriend and this could get me in a lot of trouble."

"Couldn't it be your boyfriend that sent me?"

Klan was a lot of things but romance wasn't exactly his thing. "I don't think so."

"Well, there is a package for you inside the car and maybe that will explain everything."

"What kind of package?"

"I don't know. A gift-wrapped box. A few other things."

Somebody was really trying to impress me. Maybe the box held a clue. "Let me get my phone and throw on some clothes."

I sent Klan a text asking him if he sent me a limo. When he didn't respond I threw on some jeans, locked up the house, and got in the limo. There was a pink gift-wrapped box on the seat. On the table was a bottle of champagne sitting on ice and a box of chocolate covered strawberries. A small pink card was on top of the box. There was one fancy handwritten line. *'This is how its supposed to be.'*

I didn't recognize the handwriting and still didn't have a clue who set this up. I opened the gift-wrapped box. A beautiful pink Dolce and Gabbana dress and a pair of gold heels were inside. Who would do this for me? I needed an answer so I found the button to let down the partition.

"You okay?" The driver asked.

"No. Are you sure this is for me?"

"Your name was on the pickup. That's all I know."

"Where are you taking me?"

"Can't tell you. Get dressed," he grinned before letting the window back up.

I took off my clothes and slipped on the dress. Whoever thought of this should've gotten me some make up and hair products. I tried to style my hair as best as I could. A curly afro was the best I could manage on short notice. Then I sat back and drank the champagne and ate the strawberries while waiting for the rest of my surprise to unfold. About twenty minutes later the limo stopped in front of a plain building somewhere deep in downtown Milwaukee. There were no identifying marks on the building, just tall black windows. When my door opened, the driver held out a hand and helped me out of the car.

"What is this?"

"Just enjoy the night, Charlene," he said as he escorted me to the door.

I walked in the building and found myself standing in a large empty foyer. I followed the sounds of jazz music around a corner where two bodyguards were standing in front of a black curtain.

"Where am I?"

"This is a private party. What's your name?"

"Charlene Anderson."

They checked a tablet and nodded. "You can go in."

"Who is throwing the party?"

"Jason Franks."

He said the name like I was supposed to know him. "Who is that?"

"You don't watch basketball?"

I shook my head.

"He plays for the Bucks."

I stepped past the security and into a large dimly lit ballroom. There were several rows of tables and booths. Couples sat across from each other smiling and talking. There was a live band on a stage. Waiters carried around trays of food. I searched the room until I found a familiar face. Klan. He wore a white blazer, tan shirt, black slacks, and tan loafers. First time I ever seen him dressed up and I was impressed. He looked really good.

"This is how it's supposed to be," he grinned walking up and giving me a kiss.

I just stared at him, wondering how he had gone from boogy man to prince in couple of hours. "Oh my, god, baby. I'm speechless."

"That's how I wanted you to be. Let me show you to our seat."

He grabbed my hand and led the way to our table in the middle of the room. There was a bottle of champagne on ice next to a candle shaped like a rose. He pulled out the chair for me to sit before sitting across from me and pouring drinks.

"You look really good tonight," he complimented.

Thank you. I love this dress. You did good. And you look so handsome. I've never seen you all dressed up. I like it."

"I tried."

"So, what is all of this? You know some Bucks players?"

"I started planning this yesterday. I know I been tripping and I wanted to do something nice for you. My nigga, Trey, uncle won these tickets and he wasn't gon use em so I bought em. I got the dress last night too. Limo a couple hours ago. I really was coming home last night but got caught up tryna bust a move. I didn't answer yo calls because I knew you was gon be mad and I had to take care of my business. After I did that, I came home to surprise you but you was gone. I snapped when I seen you wasn't home and I'm sorry for that.

I got love scars. Sometimes that shit come out in fucked up ways. But I really do love you."

I was touched by the words. I knew he spoke from the heart. "Awe, Klan. I love you, too."

"Can you forgive me for the way I acted this morning?"

I seen the regret and sorrow in his eyes. As bad as I wanted to stay mad, seeing the sincerity touched me. He had also surprised me with this dinner party and bought me a beautiful dress. But I wasn't going to let him off the hook that easy. "I will forgive you on one occasion."

"Okay. What?"

"Come to church with me."

His face scrunched up like a pug dog. "Church?"

"Yes. Church."

"So you really did go to church this morning, huh?"

"I did. And it was amazing. I was so mad at you last night but the service took it all away. And the preacher is so good. The choir too. They even had a man in there that went to prison for robbery and changed his life while he was locked up."

He laughed and shook his head. "Wow, baby. You serious about this church stuff, huh?"

I nodded.

He stared at me while deciding if he would agree to the deal. "Okay. I'll go to church one time. I'm not saying that I'm finna change my life or nothing but I'll go one time."

I couldn't believe he agreed but I was so happy that he did. "Okay. I forgive you, baby."

He smiled like a man that won a prize on a game show. "Thank you, baby. "

I just stared at him, surprised that he was being so nice. "What happened to you? Why are you being so nice all of a sudden?"

"When I seen the look on your face earlier, I knew that I fucked up. You a good woman and you don't deserve the shit that I been putting you through. I been acting like a straight up goofy. I wanna be the man that gives you everything you ever wanted, not the one who takes it all away. I wanna be better for you."

I didn't want to cry but I was so touched by the words that a few rolled down my face. "Dammit, Klan. You're making me cry."

"As long as their happy tears, its all good."

"They are happy tears, baby. You made me so happy tonight."

The rest of the night went perfect. Not only did we have a good time and eat some good food, but we also got some good entertainment. Anthony Hamilton was the surprise guest and he performed all of his hits. Even sang my favorite song, 'Charlene'.

Chapter 16

Nephew

Speed Queen was my new favorite fast food bar-b-que spot. Since moms was working late, me and Jamie decided to eat out and I chose bar-b-que. I was polishing off my second order of ribs and thinking about getting a third. The meat was juicy and seasoned perfectly. The way it fell off the bone when I took a bite made me want to salute the chef.

"So, how have you been, Bobby. Two weeks out now. You feeling anxious."

"Not really. I'm just enjoying being free. A little frustrated about not having work yet," I said, glancing at a man wearing at least twenty thousand of jewelry a few tables a way from us. If I was still in the game, he would've be a sweet lic.

"Michael said he's going to bring you in next week. It would've been sooner but the system got hacked and we're still waiting for everything to get back up and running. We're doing orders and keeping hours in a notebook. They set us back to the stone age."

"That sounds messed up."

"It is. But I'm going to make sure you get in. Its not hard work but it can be dirty. I know you never had a job so will you be okay getting dirty?"

I thought about my experience working in the kitchen at Waupun. I got paid twenty-six cents an hour to wash dishes. "Man, I used to work for a quarter an hour. Seventeen dollars an hour to put together doors is too good to be true."

"Oh, its true. They only paid you twenty-five cents to wash dishes? They treated y'all like slaves."

"That's why I didn't work there long. "

"I heard that," he grinned. "So, how's the search for Jasmine? Any luck?"

I shook my head. "Nah. Its like she fell off the map. She don't want to be found. But I did see Simone."

Surprise lit his eyes. "Did you? When did you run into her?"

I was going to leave out the part about Jewels trying to kill me. "About a week ago. She got Two kids. She dipped out because she got pregnant and figured it would be easier to leave than tell the truth."

He shook his head.

"That's scandalous. You not thinking about getting back with her, right?"

"Nah. She got HIV."

He choked on the corn on the cob he was eating. "What? Seriously?"

"Yeah. She started stripping and met some dude that got her pregnant and gave her that ninja."

"My God. That's terrible."

"I know. We talked a few times but it ain't the same, you know?"

"Excuse me. Can I ask you a question?"

I turned my head as two women approached our table. The difference in their hairstyles got my attention. One had rainbow died microbraids that hung to her waist and the other a short tan afro. Both were on the plus side of thick and eyeing Jamie like he was a snack. The one with braids did the talking.

"Sure. What's up?"

"Is you the man from the viral body wash video?"

I looked at Jamie to see how he would respond.

He laughed. "No. I don't know what you're talking about."

"I told you that wasn't him," the one with the short hair said.

"Oh. Sorry to disturb y'all meal."

"It's all good," he assured them.

The women hovered for a moment.

"You need something else?"

Rainbow hair spoke up. "Me and my sister was wondering if y'all wanted some company. "

Jamie lifted his left hand and wiggled the ring finger. "I'm married to his mother. But my son is single."

They had a little too much body for me. "I'm sorry but I got a situation. I can't."

The woman with the short hair gave me a spicy look. "Boy, you don't know what you missing."

They walked away, giving us a view of the two biggest booties I had ever seen in real life.

"You didn't want none of that?" Jamie laughed.

"I think they were fans of you. Plus, that was a lil too much for me."

"No such thing as too much for a man that just got out."

"Yes, it is. Plus, I'm not really in a rush to smash the first thing that let me. Running into Simone made me think about what's out here. I waited three years. I can wait a little more."

He nodded at me. "That's real mature of you, Bobby. When I did my time back in the day, I got out on a mission to smash everything that let me. Took a couple trips to the clinic as a result. Taking your time might help you avoid that same fate."

"You never told me what you got locked up for."

"I was a dope boy back in my day. The original certified dumper. Served an undercover four times. Did eighteen months and that's all it took for me to get my stuff together. Changed my life and never went back. God worked on me while I was in and completed the work when I got out."

I was about to respond when a woman screamed. I looked towards the door as two men wearing masks and dressed in black ran in the restaurant carrying guns.

"Y'all know what dis is. If any of you bitch ass niggas try to play hero, I'ma buss yo ass," the man holding an AK-47 threatened.

I froze and watched as the robbers surrounded the man wearing all the jewelry. The Cartier glasses, Miami Cuban link chain, and watch flooded with diamonds was an invitation for the jackers. I couldn't believe my luck. I had been trying to avoid guns and police contact since I had been home but it seemed like every time I turned around somebody was pulling out a gun.

"You know what time it is, Reno. Let's go, nigga," the man holding a pistol with a long clip said.

Mr. icy began taking off the jewelry. "Man, y'all can have this shit but I ain't goin nowhere."

Those words got him slapped him in the face with a pistol.

"Get cho bitch ass up, nigga."

Reno didn't get up. Instead he hit the ground and curled up. The men grabbed him up from the floor and were dragging him towards the door. I locked eyes with one of the robbers as they approached our table and wished I would've kept my head down.

"Oh, shit. Nephew? That's you?"

My last encounter with Trigga flashed in my head. He was one of Jewel's groupies from my time in the county jail. I tried to cop a plea. "Man, I ain't on nothing, brah."

"Let's go. We ain't got time for that," the man with the chopper said.

"Yes, we do." Trigga let go of Reno and pointed his gun at me. "Get up, bitch."

When I stood, he began patting me down for a gun. "Karma is a punk ass bitch, ain't she? "

"C'mon, brah. I ain't in the streets no more. I'ma civilian."

"Fuck that nigga. Let's go," the other jacker said.

"Nah. He know who I am. He coming with us."

Jamie stood and tried to plead for me ."Please don't take my son."

"Sit cho bitch ass down!" Trigga yelled, kicking him in the chest.

Jamie went crashing into the table, falling on the floor and taking everything on the table with him. I moved to help him up but Trigga stopped me. "You bet not move, bitch. Let's go."

If I left this restaurant with them, they would kill me. If I tried to resist, they would kill me on the spot and some of their bullets might hit innocent people. I was damned if I did and damned if I didn't. But I couldn't go out without a fight. So I rushed Trigga. I crashed into him and grabbed his arm holding the gun so he couldn't shoot me. Shots fired as we twisted and turned like dance partners. People began screaming and out the corner of my eyes I could see his partner point the chopper at us. He didn't shoot because he might hit his partner. Me and Trigga slammed into a wall and were wrestling for the gun when three quick shots near the back of the restaurant got my attention. An older bald headed black man pulled a gun and shot Trigga's partner.

"Hey, hey! Let that gun go! Put it down!" The man yelled as he approached the robber on the ground with the AK.

"Let me go. Let me go, nigga," Trigga whispered as we continued wrestling and the gun kept shooting.

"Let the gun go and I'ma let you go," I said.

Jamie moved carefully towards us.

"Fuck you, bitch ass nigga," Trigga said before headbutting me in the face. I seen stars and my legs got weak. Jamie got to us just in time and grabbed his arm, taking the gun. Trigga tried to run but the old man pointed the pistol at him.

"You going to jail or to the morgue. Your choice."

Trigga turned to mug me while lifting his hands in the air. Some of the people in the restaurant began clapping while others called 911. It turns out the bald man was an army vet with a concealed carry license. The police got to the restaurant a few minutes later to arrest Trigga and send his partner to the hospital in an ambulance. After giving statements, me and Jamie were allowed to go home.

$$$

I hated being a snitch. That was my first thought when I woke up and it had been on my mind all day. I tried to tell myself that I was a civilian and cooperating with police instigations was the right thing to do. But it still didn't sit right with me. Giving a statement to the police about how I knew Trigga and that he tried to kidnap me felt bogus. My mom and Jamie told me that I did the right thing but I still didn't like the thought of having to get on the stand and testify against Trigga if he went to trial. Doing the right thing was going to take some getting used to. Just like I was going to have to get used to being in the trenches at night without a pistol for protection. Pastor Sims wanted to talk and had invited me over for dinner. The thought of protection was on my mind because the pastor lived in the hood. 26th and Townsend was treacherous and not being from these parts made being on the block when the sun went down very dangerous. Which is why I made sure to check my surroundings and mirrors before I turned off the mom's SUV. I looked around cautiously as I walked upon the porch of the red and beige two story house. I rang the doorbell and could hear the chime sound on the inside.

"Who is it?" a female asked.

"Its Neph- I mean, Bobby."

Several locks clicked before the door opened. The smell of soul food and perfume hit me and mixed into a smell that made me hungry and horny.

"Hey, baby, I mean, Bobby," Tasha grinned.

She was the oldest of Pastor Sims four daughters. Tasha was brown skinned, wore her hair in gold and brown micro braids, had bright eyes, a pretty smile, and a body that made me sin during church services. Tonight she was wearing form fitting pink joggers and a tank top that made it hard for me to keep my eyes from wandering. Me and Tasha had a crazy sexual chemistry. Our eyes always found each other's whenever we were in the same room and that led to all kinds of fantasies in my head. If she wasn't engaged to Junior Pastor Greg, I would've pursued something.

"Hey, Tasha. Pastor here?"

"He's expecting you. Come in."

She didn't move out of the doorway to let me in. Instead she turned sideways and forced me to turn sideways to get by. Our faces were inches apart. My chest brushed against her breasts when I slid by. My soldier stirred, ready to be unleashed.

"What is you doing, Tasha?"

"You before the night is over."

I took a step back. "You about to marry Greg, right?"

"I got needs and he don't wanna have sex until we married. You don't got a girl, right?"

I wanted to lie. I wanted to be strong enough to resist her but I wasn't. "Nah. I'm single."

She closed the distance between us, pressing her soft breasts against my chest. "I'ma be your girl tonight," she whispered before craning her neck up and kissing me. I reached down to grab her fatty. It was soft and her mouth tasted like peppermint. My little head grew into a big head and threatened to bust out my jeans.

"Who at the door?" Mother Sims called from somewhere in the house.

I jumped across the room like I got shocked.

Tasha bust out laughing. "She can't see us. She in the kitchen," then she yelled to her mother. "Its Bobby, mama."

I followed Tasha's bouncing booty towards the back of the house and into the kitchen. Mother Sims stood over the stove putting some finishing touches on the food that had been tickling my nostrils since I walked in. She was a short, dark skinned, big boned woman that was always wearing a bright smile.

"Hey, Bobby!" she smiled as she walked over to give me a warm hug.

"Hey, Mama Sims. Smell good up in here."

"Taste even better, baby. Should be ready in a few minutes. Don't be too long with the pastor or you gon miss it."

I looked at the golden-brown fried chicken breasts and my mouth began watering. "Me and the pastor can talk later if you want. I'm ready to eat."

"Go talk to the pastor," she laughed. "I'll make sure to give you the biggest piece. Show him to the pastor's study, Tasha."

I followed Tasha towards a hallway at the back of the kitchen and up a flight of stairs. My eyes went directly to her swaying booty a couple steps ahead of me. It jiggled and bounced with every step. Midway up the stairs she spun around. When I seen the look in her eyes, no words were needed. I grabbed her breasts and squeezed them as our bodies pressed against each others and we started kissing again. She dug a hand into my pants and squeezed my man, making me growl.

"Okay. That's enough. Wait til later," she said, breaking the kiss.

I didn't want to stop. Her body felt so good and everything she did was turning me on. When she started walking again, I adjusted myself and followed. Problem was, I was still hard as steel. "Damn," I cursed.

She spun to look at me. "What?"

I continued trying to adjust myself. "It won't go down."

She giggled. "It better because the pastor's door is right there."

She pointed to a door at the end of the hall and my heart sank. I didn't know what I would say if I walked in there with a hard on. "You gotta get away from me."

She looked at me like I was crazy. "What?"

"You doing this to me. Leave."

Her eyes dimmed to sexy slits and she smiled. "Wait until you see what I'ma do to you later."

She gave me a peck on the lips before walking down the stairs. I continued adjusting myself as I walked towards the pastor's office. I closed my eyes and whispered a prayer. "Please, God. Help me figure this out." Conviction stabbed me in the heart, taking away the arousal. Now I felt guilty for freaking the pastor's daughter right outside his office. Especially since she was about to get married. Man, I was tripping. I pushed the guilty feeling from my head and approached the closed door. I gave a couple taps.

"Come in," The pastor called.

I opened the door and the pastor was sitting at a big, polished desk reading the Bible. "Bobby," he smiled, standing up and extending a hand.

"Hey, pastor."

"Have a seat. It's good to see you."

I sat in the lounge chair and took a look around the office. Plaques and certificates hung on the wall. A bookcase filled with books lined the wall. There were several pictures on the wall with the pastor and influential people in Milwaukee.

"I heard about the situation at Speed queen last night. Thank God you or brotha Jamie didn't get hurt."

"Man, that was so crazy. It seems like I can't shake my past. Every time I turn around I'm running into somebody or being tested. Life wasn't this hard when I was in the streets doin my thang. Now that I'm tyna to the right thing, its like everything that can go wrong is going wrong."

"Yeah, Bobby. That's what happens when you sow a lot of bad seeds. You have to reap what you sow. It is a universal law. You did more wrong than good so that's what is happening to you. But the good thing about God is that He will make a way out, just like he did last night. Despite what you may think, God has a hedge of protection around you. He protects those that he is about to use. If you stay faithful to him, he will stay faithful to you. That's a promise from God, son."

I thought about B-Eazy saving me from Jewels and the army vet saving me from Trigga. "It ain't no easier way than having people pulling guns on me?"

"You used to live by the sword, Bobby."

I laughed. "Right. Right."

"But, there is something that you can do to help with your fate going forward. You have to start doing good deeds. Your good has to outweigh your bad. If you sow good seeds you will bear good fruit. If you sow bad seeds... Well, I don't have to tell you what will happen because you already know."

"Good deeds, huh?"

He nodded. "That's right. And you can start on Sunday by becoming an usher. That's what I wanted to talk to you about."

I raised an eyebrow. "An usher? Like, helping people find a seat?"

"That's right. Simple. But those simple things can make a big difference. I believe God has a calling on your life and He is going to do great things with you. You have an amazing testimony and it needs to be told. But first, you need to learn how to walk. You need to learn the word and how to conduct yourself as a Christian man. And you need to learn how to be a leader because when the time is right, I want you to take over our prison ministry. It has been neglected for a long time and I think God sent you to us for you to take it over. You know what it's like in those places and you will be able to reach people that others can't."

I was blown away by everything he said. "Man, pastor. I don't know what to say. I wasn't expecting this."

"Say yes to my proposal. God is about to do something amazing with you. I can see it."

I decided to trust him. "Okay. Yeah, I'll do it."

Pastor Sims smiled while reaching across the desk to shake my hand again. "That's good, son. It's a couple responsibilities that come with being an usher. Mandatory Bible study on Wednesday or Thursday nights. Maintaining good conduct within the church and not doing anything unbecoming of someone with an office. And being at both services on Sunday to help out wherever necessary. Does that sound like too much for you?"

Freaking Tasha popped into my head. The office suddenly grew warm. "No, that don't sound like too much."

He smiled again. "Well then it's official. You're an usher. Now, let's go down here and see what this woman done burnt because I'm starving."

$$$

Dinner tasted even better than it smelled. We ate chicken, corn bread, yams, mac & cheese, and swallowed it all down with some of the best iced tea I ever tasted. Pastor Sims, his wife, and their children treated me like family. The only problem I had was Tasha sitting across from me giving me all kind of googly eyes and the pastor's words about conduct unbecoming of someone with an office. I was struggling with how to handle things. Before the meeting I wanted to blow her back out. Now I was trying to think of a way out. But Tasha wasn't having it. She had been rubbing her foot up and down my leg since dinner started.

"Bobby, I was just telling my wife about that brotha y'all had in the choir that could sang like he was down home. He couldn't have been no older than thirty but he sang with an old soul."

"You talking about Twan. He- whoa!" I flinched when Tasha's foot found my crotch.

"You okay?" Mother Sims asked.

I swiped Tasha's foot away. "Yeah. My burp just came up wrong."

"Yeah. Brotha, Twan. That was his name," The pastor continued. "That brotha could make you feel it in yo soul when he sang. It amazed me how you and the rest of those brothas with nothing to gain and everything to lose could get up there in front of all those hard-core criminals and sing to God with smiles on y'alls faces. Y'all must've been called all kinds of names."

"It wasn't that bad. Most brothas respected us for doing what we did," I said, taking another swipe at Tasha's foot as she tried to play with me again. "We had problems every now and then but it wasn't nothing that the Lord couldn't deliver us from."

"Amen to that. And the brotha on the piano was a musical genius. What was his name?"

"Roland. He was our leader."

"Roland. Right. He had them brothas singing like a heavenly choir."

I drifted off while the pastor went on explaining how good the choir was to his family. Tasha had taken control of me with her foot and was massaging my pole with her five toes. I wanted to swipe her foot away but couldn't. I stared at her lips and cleavage while fantasizing about drilling her. I had her legs spread from east to west and she was saying my name. It felt so good that I forgot that I was at the dinner table. A tingling began in my balls and spread all over my body. Every nerve ending was tingling. Then I exploded.

"Whoa!' I yelled, shooting to my feet. I doubled over, grabbing my stomach and crotch as my underwear were filled with nut.

"Bobby, you okay, son?" Pastor Sims asked, staring at me like I was possessed.

"I think I got a cramp or some gas. Excuse me." I rushed to the bathroom. When I was behind the locked door, I took off my pants to check my underwear. A thick load of semen filled the front of my underwear. "Man, I can't believe this," I mumbled as I stripped off the underwear.

A knock on the door made me freeze. "Bobby, let me in," Tasha giggled.

I cracked the door a little. "Man, leave me alone."

Lust glazed her eyes as she pushed the door open. "Let me in."

I tried to hold her off but when the door smashed against my big toe, I lost my strength and she barged in. When she seen that I was naked from the waist down, her eyes found the prize. She dropped to her knees.

"Let me taste you."

I wanted to shove my piece down her throat and touch those tonsils but the pastor's words popped into my head. "No, Tasha. Your parents are right out there."

She reached for me. "Just let me lick it. Please."

"Get up."

She grabbed my underwear and looked at the mess. Her eyes bulged. "Dang. That was a lot." Then she licked her tongue across my cum, paused to show me how much she got, and then swallowed. "I'm nasty, ain't I?"

I was disgusted and turned on. It took everything inside of me not to bend her over and start killing her. "Cmon, now, Tasha. We ain't finna do this."

Disappointment flashed in her eyes. "What is you on? Now you scared."

"Yo dad is making me an usher. I gotta act a certain way. I really wanna give it to you," I paused to lick my lips and look over her banging body. "But I can't. You got a fiance and I'm tryna get some good karma in my life."

She dropped my underwear on the floor and looked me up and down like I had called her a name. "You so weak, Bobby. Damn, I was gonna fuck you so good."

When she left the bathroom I looked at myself in the mirror and shook my head. I knew that I had done the right thing but it sure didn't feel like it.

Chapter 17

Charlene

I sat at my desk staring at a picture of black Jesus on a cross. I had the screen saver for about a week and loved it. It went against the stereotypical blonde hair and blue-eyed Jesus projected by the masses. And even though I was staring at a picture of the Son of God, Jesus was the furthest thing from my mind. I was thinking about how stupid I was for falling for Klan's bullshit. The gentleman that took me out on the town and bought me nice dresses lasted all of three days. Once he seen that I had truly forgiven and was still in love with him, he went back to being his no good self. We argued over the stupidest things, he stayed out all night, and he didn't go to church with me. Now I was sitting at my desk wondering how I was going to break things off with him. He would never be the man I wanted and needed. I needed to figure out a way to move on and get my life back.

"Girl, is you coming to lunch or what?" Yolonda asked, bursting into my office.

"You know that you're supposed to knock when someone's door is closed, right?"

She pursed her lips and smacked loudly while looking me up and down. "Somebody got an attitude."

"I don't got an attitude. I just want you to knock."

She rolled her eyes. "Anyway. Is you coming to lunch or not. I'm hungry."

"Yeah. Let me send Myra this contract and we can roll."

For lunch we went to Kits for gyros and sat in Yolonda's Denali to eat. "Did you see Offset talking about Cardi B cheated on him. That nigga got some nerves, don't he?" Yolonda said.

"Nah, I didn't see that. I got too many of my own problems."

She spun in the seat to look at me. "What he do now?"

"What didn't he do? I thought he really changed, Yo-Yo. The night he took me to see Anthony Hamilton was so perfect. He treated me like a queen. Now he back to being the same old no good nigga. I don't know what I'ma do. The other day we was sitting in the living room eating fried perch. He asked for the bottle of hot sauce and I tossed it to him but forgot the top wasn't all the way on. Hot sauce flew everywhere. He got mad and called me stupid. We started arguing and he threw the plate of fish against the wall and left. I ain't heard from him since."

Yolonda bust out laughing. "Oh my God. That is so stupid."

"I know its stupid but it ain't funny."

"Yes, it is," she yelled, rocking in the seat with laughter. "That nigga need a check because he crazy."

I shook my head and waved her off.

She became serious after the laugh attack. "I don't understand why don't you leave him, Lene. You pretty and smart. You can have any man that you want. What man in his right mind gon argue over hot sauce? Nah, that nigga was looking for a reason to leave. He probably got another bitch."

"I thought the same thing but I didn't want to speak it and give it life."

"Girl, every nigga in the street damn near got a bitch on the side. Let that nigga go and find you a man in that new church that you going to. I hear all the good ones in church. Shoot, one of these days, when I'm ready to settle down, I'ma get a church man. They know how to treat a woman."

Her words made me think of Bobby. I seen him last Sunday but didn't talk much. Just a hi and bye. I still had hope for Klan so I kept it cordial and took my butt home. But now everything was in the air because I was leaving Klan. I wanted to tell Yolonda about him but I knew she would encourage me to give it up to him and that's not what I wanted to hear. Plus, the less people that knew about him the better it was for me. If Klan somehow found out, it would be trouble. After lunch, we went back to work and I spent a large part of the rest of the day thinking about leaving Klan and getting with Bobby. When it was clock out time, I went home to an empty house. While in the shower I reasoned with myself that coming home to an empty house might become the norm for a while. I had done it while in college and I could do it again. It would be better to be by myself than to keep putting up with Klan and all of his bullshit. After my shower, I made a quick dinner of chicken and waffles and sat down to watch TV. I surfed the channels until I found an Atlanta Housewives marathon playing and ate while watching high fashion ratchet reality television. I laughed and had a good time, enjoying the peace of being alone. When my sweet tooth kicked in, I went to get a slice of chocolate cake. I had just taken a bite when I heard a key being stuck into the lock on the front door. A cloud of bad energy came to sit over me and I no longer wanted my sweets or to watch TV. I sat the cake on the table and waited to see what the cat was about to drag in.

"Sup, baby," Klan slurred, stumbling through the living room smelling like weed and liquor.

I ignored him.

"I said what's up?" He repeated louder, standing in front of me and swaying from side to side like he was about to fall over.

"Hey," I said dryly, not bothering to look up at him.

"Oh, so you too good to look at a nigga?"

"Leave me alone, Klan. Why don't you go back to wherever you came from."

He stood there for a moment staring at me. Then he grabbed the cake from the table and smashed it between his fingers. "Was you eating this?" He laughed.

"Klan, get-"

"Shut up," he said before rubbing the cake in my face and hair.

"Stop," I yelled, pushing him away.

He came back laughing as he fell on top of me and rubbed the cake in my hair and on my face. I tried to get him off me but he was too heavy. Then I got the shit scared out of me by a loud noise at the front door.

"What the fuck!?" Klan yelled, reaching for his waist.

"Freeze! Police!"

I looked behind Klan as six police officers ran into our living room with guns drawn.

"Get on the ground now!"

I dove onto my stomach on the floor. Klan didn't pull the gun, but he stood to face the officers, refusing to get on the ground.

"I said, get on the ground, boy," the officer repeated, tightening his grip on the gun.

"Fuck you. This my house. You get on the ground," Klan said.

"Get on the floor, Klan," I yelled, trying to talk some sense into him. I had never had this kind of encounter with the police but I had seen enough videos to know that they would shoot a black man for anything.

"Get on the ground right now. Last warning," another officer said, pulling out a taser.

"I ain't doing shit."

There was a little pop and the sound of electricity crackling. A projectile flew from the taser and stuck in Klan's chest. A moment later he was on the ground screaming as the volts ran through his body. The scene terrified me and I started screaming with him.

"Calm down, ma'am. We're not going to hurt you," one of the officers said as they slapped a pair of cuffs on my wrist.

Visions of a jail cell flashed in my head. "Wait. What are you doing?"

"Ma'am, we have a warrant to search this house and you can't be in it," he said, lifting me to my feet.

"A warrant? For what? I didn't do anything."

"I'm going to take you outside and the detectives will answer your questions. Right now I just need you to sit tight."

I was led from my house and put in the back of a police car. They brought Klan out a moment later and put him in another car. I sat wide eyed and terrified. I didn't know what was about to happen to me. I hoped I wasn't about to be framed for a crime I didn't commit. Lord knows I couldn't do jail. Just thinking about it made my body go cold and shake with fear. A few moments later a white man wearing a dark suit opened the door.

"You Charlene Anderson?"

"Yeah. What is going on?"

He pulled out the search warrant and showed it to me. "I'm detective Glasscow and we have a warrant to search your house. Is there anything in there that we need to know about?"

I thought about the guns Klan had in the closet. "I don't know. I don't have anything illegal in there."

"Well, if we don't find anything, you won't have anything to worry about. But if we do find something, you will be responsible for it because the house is in your name. So I'm going to ask you again. Is there anything in the house that we need to know about?"

I lowered my head as tears began spilling from my eyes. "I don't have anything."

"Okay. Sit tight. I'll be back in a minute."

When the detective left, the tears flowed harder. They were going to find those guns and if Klan didn't admit they were his, I was going to jail.

$$$

Jail was the worst thing that I had ever experienced in my entire life. I had been locked inside a dirty holding cell in the police station for about an hour. I spent the entire time crying, unsure what would happen next. How long would they hold me? Was I about to be framed? Would I get a phone call or bail?

"Charlene?" a man called from the other side of the door.

I shot to my feet and walked to the door. "Yes."

A tall dark skinned police officer opened the door. "The detectives are ready for you."

He led me down a short hall and turned a couple corners before stopping in front of a white door marked 'interrogation room 3'. I peered inside when he opened the door. The room was small and bare. Just a table with a recorder sitting on top and a couple chairs. A tall thin white man sat in one of the chairs. He wore a white dress shirt and dark slacks. He looked me up and down, his eyes lingering on my breasts.

"Thank you, officer. Come on in and have a seat, Charlene. I'm Detective Jacobson."

When I stepped in the room, the detective closed the door.

"What's with the make-up?" He joked, looking at the cake smeared on my face and in my hair.

"Food fight," I mumbled.

He nodded. "Is this your first time in custody?"

I nodded.

"Well, I guess you want to know why you're here, right?"

"Yes. Nobody told me nothing. What did I do?"

"Well, I don't think you did anything wrong and you're not under arrest. But all that could change. I want to ask you some questions and if you tell me the truth, everything should be fine. If you lie, then you won't be going home tonight. Clear?"

"Okay. Do I need a lawyer?"

"That's up to you. The only people that need lawyers are the ones who are under arrest. You're not under arrest. Plus, if you want a lawyer, I would have to put you back in that cell and you would have to wait for them to come. That could take a couple hours. We can talk and get this over with or you can call a lawyer. Its up to you."

I searched the detectives eyes for deceit. He seemed like he was telling the truth. "Lets talk and get this over."

He smiled. "I'm going to turn on this recorder and ask you some questions. Just tell the truth and you'll be fine. Let's start with your boyfriend, Cedric, aka, Klan. It seems he likes to take things that don't belong to him and I need to know what you know."

Alarms went off. He wanted me to snitch on Klan. If Klan found out, he would kill me. "I don't know what you're talking about. If he did something, why are you talking to me?"

"Because I'm trying to help you. We found a pound of weed, two stolen fire arms, and a thousand rounds of live ammunition in your house. Who's is it?"

"I don't know anything about any of that. I don't do drugs."

"I know that. But since your name is on the house everything in it belongs to you. If you tell us who's it is, you will be free to go. If you don't, you will be charged with the stolen guns and the weed. You could be looking at twenty years in prison."

My eyes almost popped out of my head and my heart dropped down to my ass. "Twenty years!?"

"Or you can leave as soon as we finish talking. Its up to you."

Tears spilled down my face as I thought about what to do. I didn't want to tell on Klan but I also didn't want to go to jail. "But I don't know anything."

He placed a hand on top of mine and squeezed. "Cmon, Charlene. I'm on your side. If you know anything about the armor car robbery now is the chance to say something."

That was the first I heard about an armored car robbery. "I don't know about that. He doesn't tell me anything."

"Okay. Just tell me about the guns and the weed."

I thought about telling the truth. This was my opportunity to get Klan out of my life. But what if he bailed out or beat the charges? I knew how Klan felt about snitches. "I don't know."

"Dammit, Charlene!" he exploded, slapping his hand on the table.

I jumped back, scared as hell. This was my first time in an interrogation room and we were alone. Was he about to hit me?

He took a breath and lowered his voice. "You have to give me something if you want to walk out of here. I know you're innocent but you're going to take the wrap. Don't throw your life away for a no-good thug."

"But, sir, I don't know anything. Please."

He gave a disappointed look and watched me cry. "Shit," he cursed, placing his hand on his head and staring up at the ceiling.

I continued to cry, hoping the tears would appeal to his compassionate side. Then he turned to me wearing a sad face.

"Well, Charlene. I tried to give you a way out. I'm going to have to charge you with possession for the weed and stolen guns."

"Wait! Please, don't!" I cried, grabbing his wrists.

"You have to give me something, Charlene. I can't just let you go."

My tears got bigger and spilled faster. The detective pulled me closer and wrapped me in a hug.

"Give me something, Charlene. Anything," he whispered, running his hands through my hair and rubbing my back.

I was going to have to tell on Klan. It was the only way to save myself. I was about to start snitching when he turned off the recorder and leaned back to look in my eyes. The lust in his eyes was unmistakable.

"I'll tell you what. There is something else that you can help me with." He placed a hand high my thigh and started moving slowly towards my coochie.

I was so shocked and scared that I froze. "What are you doing?"

"Its okay. You can help me in other ways." He leaned forward and kissed my neck while his hands moved up to squeeze my breasts. And that's when something inside of me snapped. I lost all fear of going to jail and the need to protect myself kicked in.

"Get your hands off me!" I yelled, pushing him away from me and leaping from the chair.

He fell to the floor, eyes wide with fear. "Calm down, Charlene. Its okay."

"No. Get the fuck away from me."

He got up and approached me with his hands out. "Charlene, relax. It's okay."

I started beating on the door and screaming. "Help! Somebody help! He's trying to rape me!"

"Shhh! Shhh! Okay. Calm down," he whispered frantically, trying to calm me down.

It didn't work. I kept on screaming until a young black female officer opened the door. "What's going on in here?"

I ran to her. "Help. He tried to rape me."

She looked from me to the detective.

"Everything is fine, officer. Just a misunderstanding. You can leave now."

I grabbed her hands and looked in her eyes. "Please don't leave. He tried to rape me."

"Its okay, officer. I got it," he said, speaking with authority.

His tone made her give him that look that only a black woman can give when somebody raises their voice and they don't like it. "Come with me, ma'am. We will talk to the supervisor."

"I'm a superior ranking detective, patrol woman, and you're hindering my investigation. Stand down or you will be on traffic duty until you retire," he threatened, face red with anger.

She gave a smirk, unphased by the threat. "Boy, please. Come on, girl."

$$$

I spoke to Captain Jones about the detective and was assured the situation would be handled. Then the captain took my statement about the guns and the weed. I told them it wasn't mine but didn't snitch on Klan. The captain said it was okay, that the entire situation was a misunderstanding, and allowed me to call a ride. I knew they were letting me go because of the detective trying to rape me. They didn't want me to press the issue.

"That's why I hate the police. Nasty lil dick motherfuckers," Lana cursed.

I didn't say much during the ride home. I was still in shock. I couldn't believe that I was almost raped by the person sworn to protect me. And it almost happened in the police station of all places. I would probably never trust the police again. And then there was Klan, the reason the door was kicked in and I was almost raped. I needed to get him out of my life.

"Here we are," Lana said, pulling up in front of my house.

I looked around and was happy to see all the police cars were gone and the block looked normal. We climbed from her truck and walked upon the porch. The security door was still in place but the big door was knocked off the hinges. I shook my head. "Damn. Who the hell is going to pay for this?"

"Girl, they don't gotta pay for nothing. They did the same thing when they ran in my sister house."

We went in the house and I locked the security door and pushed the wooden door in place as best we could. I would get everything fixed tomorrow. Then I stood in the living room and looked around. They trashed the house. Couch pillows were thrown around the living room, our clothes were scattered across the bedroom, and the kitchen was a mess.

"So, what you gon do?" Lana asked.

"I'ma clean up."

"I'm not talking about the house. I'm talking about Klan. I know you not about to let him come back here."

I rolled my eyes and started picking up couch pillows. "I don't want to talk about that right now."

"Why not? Don't you see what he doing to you? You went to jail and almost got raped. What is it gon take for you to leave? You gotta get shot next? Or killed?"

"I said I don't want to talk about it."

She grabbed a picture of me and Klan off the wall and threw it on the floor. The glass shattered into a thousand pieces. "Fuck that, Charlene. I don't care if you don't want to talk about it. I do. This nigga is fucking your life up. If you don't kick his ass out, I will. Grow some fucking balls, sis. Damn. You done let this nigga get between us and take over your fucking life. Stop being weak. Stop letting him do this."

I sat on the couch and broke down crying. "I know, Lana. I know what I gotta do but I'm scared."

"Well, you better quit being scared before you end up fucked up somewhere. Look at what this nigga just put you through. Got yo door getting kicked in by the police and you almost going to jail. Fuck that nigga."

"It's hard to leave. Where will I go? He will follow me. He not just gon let me go."

She sat on the couch and wrapped her arms around me. "You can stay with me or you can go to your parents. All you have to do is leave, Charlene. We got your back and so does your family. Stop letting this nigga take advantage of you."

After shedding a few more tears, I wiped my eyes and gathered my strength. "Okay. I'm leaving him. But I have to stay here until the morning so I can call somebody to fix the door. I don't want nobody to break in when I leave."

"Then I'm staying with you."

Me and Lana cleaned up the house and then got high and watched movies until we fell asleep. I was awaken at 4:34 AM by my phone ringing. The screen said Secure Links.

"Hello?"

"This is the Milwaukee County Jail," a robotic voice spoke. "You have a collect call from," There was a pause and then he spoke. "Klan."

"Press 5 to accept."

Chapter 18

Nephew

I turned onto 33rd and Burleigh and looked for the Audi sitting on chrome Forgiatos. A white R8 was parked in front of the second house from the corner. I checked out the expensive wheels as I climbed from my mother's SUV and walked up to the grey and white house. After ringing the doorbell, I waited.

"Who is it?" A woman called.

"Nephew."

The door swung open and a teenaged girl was smiling at me. She had pretty brown skin with red hair cut into a mohawk. "Hey, Nephew. What's up?"

It took me a second to recognize her. "Myra? You got big, girl. Look at you looking like a little woman. Gimme a hug."

After an embrace I looked her over again. The last time I seen her she was skin and bones. Now she had a few curves. "How old is you now?"

"I'm fourteen. I heard you been out for a while. Why you didn't come over?" She scolded.

"I don't know. I was waiting for yo daddy to get out."

"Well, don't do that no more. You can come over without him. We like family."

"Okay," I laughed You gon let me in now?"

She thought for a moment. "Yeah. Come in. They in the kitchen."

I followed the smell of food and found Little standing over the stove stirring a pot of pasta. Lisa stood next to him cutting up a ham. "Y'all got it smelling good up in here."

Little seen me first. "Nephew? What's good, brah?" He greeted, giving me a hug.

"You got it, man. Welcome home. Cooking Christmas hams in the summer. Y'all snapped."

"I been waiting three years to get some pork, brah. I'm finna have my way."

"Hey, Nephew. Every day is Christmas in our house. Ain't that right, baby?" Lisa asked, pecking Little on the lips.

"Eating like a King, brah. You gon stay for dinner?"

"You know it. I just got off work and I'm starving. Plus, that ham looking too good."

"Where you working?"

"I work with Jamie. We be making doors. Cool lil gig, especially since I never had a job. Start off at seventeen."

"That's slick. You think Jamie could get me in?"

"I don't know but I'll ask. I see you finally got the rims for the Audi."

"Yeah. Wifey put that together for me." He gave Lisa a loving look. "She been taking care of me and now its my turn to take care of her."

"I know that's right," Lisa said.

Seeing the look of love on their faces made me smile. "That's what's up."

"So, Little tells me that you got saved while you was locked up," Lisa said.

"Yeah. God showed me some stuff. I knew that I couldn't leave out the same or else I was gone come back with more time or end up dead. I never thought I'd be saying I'm a Christian."

"His plan is perfect," Little said.

"I know. Now I'm an usher and Pastor Sims talking about making me in charge of prison ministry in the church."

Little smiled. "That's what I'm talking about, Nephew. Look how God is moving. Our steps is ordered. He started the work in Waupun and is finishing it out here."

"You right, man. Who would've thought we would've hung up our guns to praise God? I seen B-Eazy when I first got out and he looked at me like I sold out then turned around and saved my life when Jewels tried to get at me."

"On what?"

"For real. Tried to do it to me at the gas station in the hood in broad daylight. If it wasn't for B-Eazy, I would be gone."

Little shook his head. " We sowed a lot of bad seeds. Reap what we sow. That's why we gotta stay faithful to the Lord. What church you go to?"

"The City of God over there on Hopkins. Pastor Sims is a beast too. If Y'all don't got a church, y'all should come check him out this Sunday."

$$$

When Sunday came I was standing at the back of the church waiting for people to come in so I could help them find seats. Little had shown up with Lisa and Myra. I had already shown them to their seats. I was listening to the choir sing and looking around when I locked eyes with Tasha. She was sitting next to her fiance in the first row but his presence didn't stop her from licking her lips at me. The dinner table and bathroom scenes flashed in my head. My body grew warm with guilt and embarrassment, and I looked away just in time to see an old lady walking through the church doors.

"Good morning, Sister Jenkins," I said, walking over to grab her arm and help her to her seat.

"Hey, Bobby. How are you doing?"

"I'm blessed. Every day that I wake up is a blessing."

"Amen. And when you get to be sixty eight years old, you are even more thankful."

"Who sixty eight? I thought you was every bit of thirty eight."

She laughed. "Oh, you are too kind. When you find a wife, make sure you compliment her every day. That is the key to keeping a woman happy."

"I'ma remember that."

After dropping the elder off, I turned and headed back to the back of the church when Tasha stepped into the aisle in front of me.

"Hey, Bobby."

"Hey, Tasha," I mumbled and tried to pass her.

She blocked my way. "Why you running?"

"I'm not running. I gotta help people find seats."

"We got other ushers. I need your help."

"For what?"

"Come to the office," she said, leading the way.

I looked around to see if anyone seen the encounter and locked eyes with Little. He looked concerned. I shook my head and followed Tasha. She was wearing a lavender pantsuit that hugged her frame perfectly, showing every curve of her perfect body. I checked my watch and fiddled with my suit jacket to keep myself from staring as I followed her out of the sanctuary and down the hall towards the offices. She led me to the large storage closet.

"I need to get the tambourines."

I opened the closet and stepped inside. It smelled musty and was filled with old music instruments, furniture, and boxes of books. I hit the light switch and began looking for the tambourines when Tasha stepped in and closed the door. She pressed her body into mine while reaching around me to grab my piece. I pushed her away.

"What you doing?"

"I wanna know when you gon give me what I want?"

"C'mon, Tasha. We in church. Chill."

"This is only a building. We are the church. Don't you pay attention at Bible study?"

"Yo future husband is out there. You tripping."

She closed the distance between us, pressing her breasts against my chest, face inches from mine. "I tasted yo cum, Bobby, and now I want it all. Just one time and I'll leave you alone. I promise."

Lust and deceit swirled in her brown eyes. Then the door opened. Little's eyes grew wide when he seen Tasha in my face. "Nephew, what you on?"

Tasha looked him up and down. "Excuse you. Can't you see that we talking in private?"

I stepped out into the hallway. "I ain't on nothing, brah. That ain't nothing."

"Bobby, grab this box," Tasha ordered like she was talking to a worker.

"Yo arms work. I gotta do my job. Let's go, brah."

"Nephew, what was that about? Who is she?" Little asked as we headed to the sanctuary.

I shook my head. "Man, that's Pastor Sims daughter. She engaged to the junior pastor but she want me bad. Trying everything to get me to hit that."

"Did you?"

"Nah. But she won't take no."

"Dang, bro. What you gon do?"

"I don't know. Keep avoiding her I guess."

"Don't give in to that temptation, my boy. Stay strong and steadfast and God gon reward you."

Charlene walked through the doors while Little was talking and stole the breath from my lungs. She was finer than fine and the white dress that she wore made her look like an angel. "I gotta walk her to her seat. I'ma see you in a minute," I told Little before making my way to Charlene. "Good morning. Glad you could make it."

"Good morning to you too. And I'm happy to be here as well."

I lifted my arm for her to take. "Can I show you to your seat?"

She hooked her arm in mine. "You can."

I spun towards the sanctuary doors just in time to see Tasha walking down the hall carrying a big dirty box. She gave me a nasty look which I ignored as I showed Charlene to her seat. "Here you go. If you need anything, just let me know."

"Okay. Thank you."

When the service began, I found a spot in the front of the church facing the doors so I could keep watch just in case someone showed up and needed to find a seat. The choir sang, Mother Sims prayed, and then Pastor Sims took the podium. My eyes roamed the church during the service and accidentally found Tasha's. She gave me the meanest look and that was the first time in my life that I had been scared of a woman. I knew she was plotting revenge on me. I just hoped that the Lord would continue to defend me. If things got too crazy I would have to talk to her fiancé or father. I hoped it wouldn't get to that but a woman scorn was capable of anything.

After shaking Tasha's angry mug, my eyes found Charlene. I didn't know much about her but we had a connection. I felt it the first time I laid eyes on her. I wanted to ask her out but talking to females in church wasn't my strong suit. I was still unsure how to approach. She must've felt me watching her because she gave me a smile. My heart beat faster and I felt like a boy with a school crush. Then she wagged her finger and pointed at Pastor Sims. I nodded and turned my attention back to the bringer of the word. At that moment I decided that when the service was over, I was taking my shot. Two hours later, Pastor Sims said a final prayer and ended the service. I headed for Charlene to get a moment before she left.

"What did you think about that word today?"

"I always enjoy Pastor Sims messages. That was messed up that Jesus' own friend turned him in for some money."

"That was supposed to happen. It was prophesized. If Judas hadn't turned on him, we wouldn't be here having church this morning. All of that was a part of God's plan of salvation."

"If I was God, I would'da messed him up. I don't know if I would'da gotten crucified for all of y'all," she joked.

"Well, I thank God that your name is Charlene and not Jesus cause you ain't got no sympathy. You would let us all go to hell."

"I'm sorry but some people probably need to go to hell. They evil."

"Yeah. Gotta work out our own salvation. So, you planning on coming every Sunday?"

She looked me up and down. "Why you all up in a sistah business?"

I laughed. "Because I want to be."

"Didn't you hear the saying about nosy people getting messed up?"

"You heard my testimony. I ain't always been a Christian so I can handle the smoke."

"You don't want this smoke," she challenged.

"What if I do?"

We held eye contact for a moment, reading between the lines.

"Nephew?" Little called.

I spun to see my friend and his family walking in our direction. "What up, brah?"

"We about to go get something to eat. You wanna come?"

"Yeah. We got a little time before the next service. Jakes, right? I can go for some corn beef."

"That's what I'm talking about, Nephew," Lisa smiled.

I spun around to Charlene and made the introductions. "Charlene, this is Little, his wife, Lisa, and their daughter, Myra."

After they exchanged greetings, I took my shot. "We about to grab a bite. Wanna come?"

225

She gave it some thought and then her face softened with the apology. "I'm sorry, but I have somewhere to be."

The rejection stabbed me in the heart. "Okay. Maybe next time, right?"

"Yeah. Maybe next time. But we can exchange numbers if you want."

I tried not too seem to eager. "Yeah. Let's do that."

It felt awkward getting her number in front of Little and his family. "Okay. See you next week, right?"

"Yeah, Bobby. See you around," she said before walking away.

"So, that's the one, huh?" Little asked.

"I want it to be."

"Awe, Bobby gotta crush!" Lisa teased.

We jumped in Little's Audi and went to Jakes to get our grub on. After making our orders, we hopped back in the car to wait for our food to get done.

"So, how was my boys in the choir doing when you left?"

"Them brothas up there moving in the spirit, Nephew. I heard Twan got PRC'd to a medium, too."

"That's what's up. I gotta write that brotha. I been meaning to get at him but life been so hectic out here."

"Oh, and that brotha Dre about to come home, too. They said some lawyers picked up his case and filing papers to get him out. You know he been locked up since he was fifteen or sixteen."

"I know. I hope they get him out here because they did him bogus. He spent more time in prison than he did on the streets."

"That's how they do us. Throw away the key if you black."

"That's so wrong but true," Lisa said.

I didn't want to talk about jail so I switched topics. "So, y'all really got married, huh?"

"He didn't have no choice," Lisa said, holding up her ring. "I wasn't finna spend three years of my life waiting on a man that wasn't gon marry me."

"Yeah. My queen is a rider. When you find a good one, you hold on to her."

"What ever happened to Simone?" Lisa asked. "I thought y'all would get married."

"Wow. Simone," I said, trying to think of words to describe everything that happened between us. "She broke bad while I was locked up and the streets got hold of her and set her on fire."

"Set her on fire?" Little asked.

"Man, she started stripping and prostituting. Somebody gave her HIV."

Lisa grabbed her chest. "Oh my Lord."

Little shook his head. "Damn, brah. She got a crucial judgement."

"She doing okay, though. Despite what happened, she tryna live her best life."

"You know where she live?" Little asked. "That was my dawg and I wanna see her. You don't mind, do you?"

"Nah, we cool. I still got love for her. She on 45th and North. We can shoot over after we get our food."

When our food was done, Little drove over to Simone's house. She lived on the lower level of a brown duplex. Her car was parked out front so me and Little walked upon the porch and I rang the doorbell. We waited for a few moments before I rang the bell again.

"You think she here?" he asked.

"That's her car." Then I put my ear to the door and listened. "It sound like a baby crying."

Little put his ear to the door and listened. "That is a baby."

I knocked on the door and called her name. Still no answer. So I tried to door. It opened. I looked at Little. He shrugged. "Simone, you in here? This Nephew," I called.

When no one answered, I stepped into the house.

"Simone, you good?" Little called as he followed me inside.

No one answered but the child's screams got louder as we walked into the living room. When I stepped into the dining room, I almost threw up my corn beef sandwich and curly fries. It looked like one of those scenes that you see at the beginning of the cop shows that set the premise for the episode. Simone lay on the floor, eyes wide open, staring up at the ceiling. A pool of blood surrounded her body. A big chrome pistol lay nearby. There was a swollen burn spot on her temple where blood dripped from. Simone's daughter kneeled next to her dead mother, covered in blood, crying her eyes out. I wanted to pick up the little girl but the HIV made me keep my distance.

"I'm finna call 911," Little said.

I just stood there frozen as the tears welled up in my eyes. I couldn't believe she had gone out like that.

Chapter 19

Nephew

I lay in bed watching Wakanda Forever but couldn't focus on the movie. The anger and sadness of King T'Challa's sister over his death made me think of Simone. I was pissed that she had taken her life in such a way. And to leave her kids like that was a coward move. I wished that I could bring her back to life and tell her how bogus she was. To bring kids in this world and then abandon them because of bad choices was wrong on every level. When I had kids, I was going to do whatever it took to be there for them. I wouldn't abandon them when life got hard like Simone did or give up on them like my father had done me. My phone dinging pulled me from thoughts. It was a text from Charlene.

'hey'.

I smiled as I dialed her number. We talked a couple of times since Sunday and every time we hung up the phone I wanted more. "Hey, Charlene."

"Hey, Bobby. What you up to?"

"Watching Wakanda Forever."

"Oh, I love that movie. Kind of sad though."

"I know. All of that emotion had me thinking about all kinds of stuff. I been zoned out and in my thoughts."

"What's on your mind?"

"Mainly my ex committing suicide in front of her daughter. We found her after service on Sunday. I couldn't believe that she went out like that."

"Oh my God, Bobby. I'm sorry to hear that. What happened?"

"She shot herself. Me and Little went to check on her and found her on the floor. Her daughter was covered in her blood crying her eyes out. She got HIV while I was locked up and I guess she couldn't deal with it no more."

"That is so sad, Bobby. Imagine what kind of trauma that did to her kid."

"That's what I was just thinking about. I don't understand how people can do certain stuff to they kids. My pops never looked for us after we left Minnesota. I don't understand how you could let your seed grow up without you."

"I've never met my real dad. He went to prison while my mom was pregnant. I was raised by my stepdad but I don't love him no less because he isn't my biological dad. Just because we don't share the same DNA don't mean we ain't family."

"That's crazy because I was raised by my stepdad too. Jamie is my dude. When I have kids, I'ma be a great dad. I'ma put my kids first."

"How many kids do you want?"

"I don't know. Probably two. What about you?"

"I want two. A boy and a girl. I want to have the boy first so he can protect his little sister."

"You see all of this stuff we got in common? We both only kids, raised by our step dads, and we want two kids. When do you want to make it official?"

"Boy, stop," she laughed. "You probably got too many girls."

"What makes you think I got a lot of girls?"

"Because you have a penis."

"Damn. That's bogus. Lump me with every man in the world."

"Did I hurt your feelings?"

"A little. But just so you know, I haven't had sex since I got out. I'm basically a virgin. Been out a month and still ain't touched a woman."

"Wow. Really? Why?"

"I guess I'm just waiting on the right one. What about you? When was the last time you got some?"

She was quiet for a moment. "Hey, uh, can I call you back? Someone is calling on my other line and I need to answer. It's important."

I didn't like the note we were ending on but I didn't want to press. "Yeah. It's cool. I need to get some sleep anyway. I got work in the morning."

After hanging up the phone, I thought about what just happened. Was it a coincidence that she got an important call while we were talking about sex or was she hiding something? We hadn't talked about relationships but I figured she was single since she gave me her number. Was she a female player? Another Tasha? Guess I still had a lot to learn when it came to women in the church. I tried to watch Black Panther again but I was suddenly feeling restless. It was almost ten o'clock at night and I wasn't tired. I felt the need to do something. To get out of the house. To blow off some steam. I decided to take a drive. Maybe hitting a couple corners would curb my need to do something. I threw on a pair of shoes and grabbed mom's keys from the living room table and got in traffic.

I was stopped at a red light, listening to Lecrae when I noticed a female standing by one of the pumps at the gas station on 27th and Capitol. She wore a white tank top, tiny blue cotton shorts, and a pair of black Nikes. Her body had crazy curves and there was barely enough clothes to cover up. But that wasn't what got my attention. There was something about the way she arched her back and knees bent backwards a little that looked familiar. I couldn't see her face because she was facing the opposite direction so I pulled in lot to get a better look. I parked one pump from where she was standing. She turned to me as I climbed from the car. Memories flooded my brain the instant that we locked eyes. Her hair was no longer done up in maroon dreadlocks. Instead she wore a lace front wig with blonde streaks. But I would never forget my chocolate drop. Her chocolate skin glistened under the bright gas station lights and her body was killin it. Neither of us could look away as I approached. In her eyes I could see the same disbelief that was in mine.

"Jasmine? What's up?"

She covered her mouth, eyes growing wide. "Nephew?"

"Damn. I been looking for you. How you been?"

"I'm okay. How are you?"

"I'm free so I'm good."

She shook her head, still surprised to see me. "When did you get out?"

"A lil over a month ago. I been trying to find you. What happened with the baby? Is it mine?"

Sadness flashed in her eyes and she looked down at the ground. "I lost the baby."

Relief and disappointment hit me at the same time. "I'm sorry to hear that. What happened?"

"I had a miscarriage. Something is wrong with my tubes and it makes it hard for me to keep a baby to full term."

I didn't know what else to say. "Damn."

An awkward silence passed between us. Then it hit me that she was standing at a gas station without a car. "What's going on with you? Why you out here? You need a ride."

She looked around before looking back to me. "I was, uh, waiting for somebody."

I knew she was lying. She was probably out here selling herself and didn't want me to know. Simone's face flashed in my head and I didn't want Jasmine to kill herself because she ended up with a disease. "Let me give you a ride. I'll take you wherever you need to go."

She looked around again like somebody was watching. "I'm good, Nephew."

I took a quick glance around to see if someone was out there. "You sure you good?"

"Yes." Her eyes said something different.

"Let me give you a ride. And I'm not taking no for an answer. I'ma stand here until your ride comes or you can get in the car."

She took a moment to think it over. "Okay. Take me to my sister's house."

"I never met your sister. Where she live?" I asked as we climbed in my mother's SUV and pulled from the gas station.

"On 37th and Clarke. And you never met her because you didn't want to commit to me." She smiled when she said it but I didn't think she was trying to be funny.

"I wasn't ready to grow up back then. But don't act like you don't got some blood on yo hands. That letter cut me deep."

Regret flashed in her eyes. "I thought you wasn't coming home for a while and he wanted to take care of me. I did what I had to do." Then she reached over and put her hand on my lap. "But if you let me, I can try to make it up to you."

My lil man had a mind of his own. Her touch made images of our past flash in my head. Simone was a sex goddess and she knew how to keep me coming back. "You ain't gotta do that. We can leave the past in the past. We both did some wrong."

She sucked her bottom lip and moved her hand further up my leg, brushing against my hardness. "What if I want to do it?"

I cleared my throat and adjusted in the seat. "Simone, I'm trying to walk a different path. You look real good but I can't go there with you."

She grabbed my piece and squeezed it. "Why yo dick so hard then? And what that mean? You tryna be faithful to your girl?"

I adjusted in the seat again and pushed her hand away. "Nah, I don't got nobody. I'm single. But I'm in the church now."

She leaned back in the seat and looked at me like I just told her I was an alien. "Say what? For real?"

"Yeah. I got saved while I was locked up. I'ma usher at the church."

She bust out laughing. "Oh my God, Nephew! I can't believe what I'm hearing. For real?"

I nodded.

She just stared. "So, that means you have to forgive people when they do wrong to you and all of that, huh?"

I nodded. "Yep. Jesus forgave us. We gotta be like him."

She shook her head in disbelief and looked out the passenger window for a moment. Then she came back at me more aggressively. She grabbed my pole again and started kissing my neck. "I wanna fuck yo brains out, Nephew. Couldn't nobody hit this pussy like you used to."

I tried to wiggle away but I was secretly loving the feel of her touch. "C'mon, Jasmine. I'm tryna drive."

She climbed into the driver's seat and onto my lap and started kissing me.

I swerved. "Jasmine!"

"C'mon, Nephew. Pull over and fuck me. I missed you so much and yo body feel so good."

"Jasmine, chill," I said, trying to watch the road.

She straddled me and started grinding on my lap while reaching under my shirt to feel on me as she kissed me. "I want some dick right now. Pull over."

I didn't know a man alive that could resist this much temptation. My balls were demanding to be drained and my dragon was so hard that the only way it would go down is if it got slayed. I turned onto a side street and into an alley. I threw the truck in park, killed the lights, and got it on.

"Let's get in the backseat," she said, leading the way.

I was riding a sexual high and would've followed her into hell with gasoline boxers. I kissed her while rubbing and squeezing breasts and booty. Then she pushed me backwards. "Let me suck it."

I kicked off my shoes and snatched my pants down. My stick was pointing in the air like a missile. She grabbed hold of me and was about to put me in her mouth when the passenger door opened. A dark-skinned man with dirty dreads climbed in the passenger seating pointing a big black pistol at me. The back door opened a moment later and Jasmine got out and was replaced by another man holding a pistol. I froze and lifted my hands.

"Damn, she was finna suck on that mu'fucka, huh?" the passenger laughed.

"You know what dis is, boy. Don't move," the one next to me said.

"Can I pull up my pants?"

"You move and I'ma buss yo shit," the one next to me said as he began checking my pockets, taking the 57 dollars.

The other began searching the console and glovebox. "Where that shit at, nigga?"

"I ain't in the game, brah. I'm a civilian."

"Next time you see a bitch standing at a gas station all alone, keep driving." the one next to me said.

"Shit. Five-oh," the one up front yelled.

They took off. I looked up and seen head lights down the alley. I couldn't tell if it was a police car, but whoever it was, they had come at the right time. I had just zipped my pants when the car pulled along side me. Sure enough, it was the police. They flashed a light in my face.

"You good?" the driver asked.

"Yeah. I'm good."

He shined the light towards the passenger window and revealed Jasmine standing close by. "You and your friend should probably get out of this alley."

"Okay. Thanks, officers."

They drove away slowly.

I got out of the car and just stared at her. If I wasn't in the church, I would've blew her down. "That's how you gon do me for real? You set me up?"

She kept her head down. "I tried to tell you to leave."

"How about just telling me that you out here licking tricks? You bogus."

She didn't say nothing. Just kept her head down.

"You ain't got nothing to say now?"

She looked at me with tears in her eyes. "I'm sorry. What else you want me to say?"

She wasn't sorry. She was sorry that she got caught.

"You foul, shorty. And you lucky I changed otherwise they would be picking yo brains up off the ground. Punk ass bitch."

I hopped back in the truck and peeled out of the alley. Not only was I pissed off that they took my money, but it hurt worse that someone I loved set me up. These streets was grimey and I was happy that I was done with them. And I was also relieved that Jasmine lost the baby. I could only imagine what type of baby mama she would've been. She was a slave to whatever man she was with and I didn't doubt that one of them jackers was her guy. And the fact that he left her on the scene said a lot about him. They were going to get Jasmine killed. And I wasn't going to feel sorry for her. Lecrae's 'song' *cry for you* came through the speakers and started speaking to me. The Bible was filled with men who had fallen because of their lust for women. I could add my name to that list. That fifty-seven dollars had taught me a priceless lesson and I wasn't going to fall like that again.

$$$

When Friday came, I got off work and went to kick it with my boy, Little. Our new lives didn't allow us to kick it as much as we used to before we went to prison. We both had jobs, I was in church, and he was married. The adult life came with responsibilities and priorities. Plus, my moms and Jamie were spending a couple days in Chicago and being home alone on a Friday night didn't seem that appealing so I went by Little's house to get some more of Lisa's good cooking. We were sitting in the living room eating plates of pork chops, spaghetti and talking about Jasmine.

"I still can't believe that she tried to set you up. That was crazy," Little said.

"Man, who you telling. And she played the role so cold. I really thought she missed how we used to get down. All that time she was keeping my attention off the set up. And the dudes was rookies because they left her when twelve pulled up. If I was still in the streets we could'da got on demon time and put everybody down."

"They blessed and don't even know it," Little chuckled.

"Amen."

"So, you really gon get off into that prison ministry that pastor Sims was talking about?"

"I'm thinking about it. I feel like everything that I been through is setting me up for it. Him saying its my calling is kinda like the icing on the cake."

"I was talking to my wife about it the other day and whenever you put the team together, we wanna be a part of the movement. I wanna put the same energy into the kingdom that I put into emptying they pockets. From poppin pistols to spittin that word."

I smiled at the thought. "Yeah. I like it. It might be a while but I definitely think we should make it happen."

"Say less."

Lisa poked her head into the living room. "Do y'all need anything before I go in here and start watching TV?"

"I'm good. You already fed me. I can't ask you to do nothing else."

"Nah, we good, baby. But Nephew said he gon put us down with the ministry whenever he get it poppin."

"That's good. Y'all going from doing the devil's work to doing the lords work. Hopefully you have you a wife by then and we can create some teams. And that'll keep you out of them dark alleys at night," she cracked.

"Where that come from."

She pointed at Little. "Your friend."

"I tell wifey everything," Little said.

I shook my head. "I'm still waiting on God to bring me that virtuous woman."

"I know one thing. You ain't gon find her in an alley," She laughed before walking away.

"Lisa got jokes, huh?"

"She was throwing em at you. But you do need to find somebody though. Stop you from burning with lust."

I thought about Charlene. "I thought it was gon be Charlene but I think she might have a man."

"What make you say that?"

"I asked her when was the last time she had sex and all of a sudden she had to get off the phone."

"She played that card?"

"I know, right. I wanna ask her again but at the same time I don't want to make it seem like I'm sweating her about it. What if she really did have a call?"

"Have you talked to her since?"

"Just once but we sent a few texts."

"I think you should ask if she got a man the next time y'all talk. You need to know so you won't be wasting yo time. This not about her. This about you finding what God got for you. And if she got a man, she ain't the one."

I nodded. "Yeah. You right."

I turned my attention towards the TV to think about what he said. Then my phone rang. It was a text. I looked at Little. "Dawg, you ain't gon believe who this is?"

"That's her?"

"She want me to call."

"So call her."

She answered on the first ring. "Hey, Bobby."

"Hey. What's up?"

"Nothing. Bored so I thought I'd call you to see what you was up to."

"So, you called me because you bored? You sho know how to make a brotha feel special."

"Cmon, Bobby. Don't do that. You know it ain't like that."

"Tell me what its like then."

"I know you not about to do this."

"Do what? I'm just making conversation. I want to know what its like. See if we on the same page."

"Why are you being so extra today?"

" Because you was bored."

She laughed. "So, you're really not going to let that go?"

"Not until you tell me what its like."

She paused for a moment. "It's like this. I like you and I called you because you normally do a good job holding a conversation but today you're being extra."

"You like me, huh?" I grinned.

"I do. Now you tell me what it's like. Just to make sure we on the same page."

I decided to go for it. "I would rather show you."

"How are you gonna do that?"

"By taking you out. Tonight."

She got quiet. "Charlene?"

"Yeah. I'm here. Um..."

The hesitation made me think she had a man. "You got a boyfriend?"

"No. I have a... situation."

"Does he have a penis?"

"Yes. But he's in jail and I'm breaking up with him."

"So, are y'all still together?"

"He's in jail and he might be there for a long time."

"And you not gon wait."

"No."

I let all the information run through my head. It reminded me of my situation with Simone. I didn't like the thought of her leaving her man while he was on lock, but I also didn't want to let the opportunity to get to know her better pass. What if he was locked up for abusing her or was facing life and would never get out?

"So, can I show you what it's like?"

She took her time answering. "Yeah. You can show me."

I couldn't stop smiling. "I'ma go home and get dressed. I'll call you when I'm on my way."

"Okay. See you later."

I looked over at Little. "He in jail and she ain't waiting."

"Simone did that to you. You wanna do that to another brotha?"

"I thought about that. I need more information. If she bogus, I'ma cut her off. If the situation is in my favor... I'ma move accordingly."

Little studied me for a moment before nodding. "Okay, brah. Do you. Take her wine tasting. Them spirits is like a truth serum."

Chapter 20

Charlene

I stared at my blank phone screen wondering why the hell I agreed to go out with Bobby. Why didn't I just say no? Why would I bring someone into all of the drama that I had going on in my life? I wanted to call him back and cancel but I wasn't strong enough to dial his number and say the words. So I sat and stared at the screen trying to figure out my next move. Before I could make up my mind, the phone rang. The number that flashed across the screen made me groan. It was Klan. He was the last person I wanted to talk to but if I didn't answer he would send one of his friends over. He had already sent them once. I didn't answer the first night that he called and got a visit from J-Rock the next day asking questions. He also gave me ten thousand dollars to get Klan a lawyer. Klan showed me that he could get to me even while he was locked up. That's why I was so confused about going out with Bobby. If it got back to Klan, someone was going to get hurt. My life was so screwed up.

"Hey," I answered.

"Sup, baby? You hear from my lawyer?"

I rolled my eyes, tired of answering the same questions. "No. The last time I talked to him he said he couldn't do anything about the P.O hold and that you have to wait for your parole officer to finish their investigation."

"What he say about the pistol case? Can I get bail yet?"

"We already talked about this. He said you can't get bail because of the P.O hold."

"Why you sounding like you don't care about what I got going on? Like I'm bothering you or something? Like you don't want me to get out?"

I let out a frustrated breath. "Because I'm tired of every call always being about what you need. I talk to you five times a day and you keep asking me the same questions. Why don't you ask about me? How I'm doing? I almost got raped. I went to jail too."

"Man, get out of here with that weak ass shit. You didn't go to jail, you went to the police station. You ain't the one facing twenty years. I am. I'm tryna get the fuck outta here. Hell yeah I'ma keep asking you what the lawyer say until I get out. Fuck wrong wit chu, nigga?"

"You what's wrong with me. I'm tired of this. I'm tired of you treating me like I ain't shit. You don't appreciate me. You don't love me. You haven't apologized once for me getting arrested or getting our door kicked in and the police putting guns in my face. I'm tired of everything being about you."

"You tired? So what that mean, Charlene? You gon break on a nigga while I'm locked up? You gon get tired when I need you the most?"

"Klan, I'm not-"

"I don't give a fuck what you tired of, Charlene. You mines. You gon always be mine. And let me find out you fuckin some nigga while I'm locked up. Think its sweet. Think I'm playin and my niggas gon be on demon time. You already know."

I had already been kidnapped by his people. They were just as violent as he was. I couldn't win with this man. I felt helpless and couldn't believe that I was being controlled by someone in jail. I was so frustrated that I began to cry. "What do you want me to do? What do you want from me?"

"I want you to play yo part. I want you to be here. I don't want you to get tired."

I didn't want to argue or be threatened anymore so I agreed. "Okay. I won't get tired. I'm here."

"That's what I'm talkin bout. Now look, I got a ace up my sleeve but I'ma only play it if I can't get out. One way or another, I'ma get out of here. I ain't goin back up north."

I spoke to Klan for fifteen minutes and when the phone hung up, I was thankful that he couldn't call back. They had to lock in at 9:00 and he couldn't use the phone again until tomorrow morning. I went back to staring at the phone while playing out different break up scenerios in my head. I told him it was over and then he sent Jax to kidnap and kill me. He caught me with Bobby and then shot us. Or, Bobby's street side came out and he beat Klan's ass. The scenerio that gave me the most relief was hearing the judge sentence him to twenty years in prison. That would make everything so much easier. Damn. Wishing he spent two decades in prison made me feel bad. I needed to woman up and leave him and stop trying to put it in someone else's hands. My phone rang and Lana's face flashed on my screen for a Facebook call.

"Hey," I answered.

"Hey, girl. Why it look like you been crying?"

"I hate my life."

Her eyes dimmed into angry slits. "You still accepting that nigga calls?"

"He sent Jax over here. He still got some power."

"Girl, that's why I told you not to go back to that house. Sell it and move in with your parents so you can move on with your life."

"I just want him to stay in jail. Maybe he'll leave me alone if the judge give him twenty years."

"Or you can just stop accepting calls from his ass and not wait for the judge to do shit. Its up to you, sis. A nigga only gon do what you let them."

I sighed. "I know."

"In the mean time, I wanna go out tonight. What's up?"

My eyes grew wide and I jumped up from the couch and headed for my room. "Shit. I have to get dressed. Bobby is supposed to pick me up."

"You talkin about the nigga from church?"

"Yeah. I talked to him thirty minutes ago. He is showing me how much he likes me."

Lana smiled. "That's what I'm talking about, sis. Go get that thang. And make sure you tell me how good it is."

"Shut up. I'm not sleeping with him."

"Well, if you do, let me know. I'ma find somebody else to go out with. Have a good time."

I dug through my closet and pulled out a blue Versace satin dinner dress and a pair of Beauti soles floral printed slingback stilettos. When I was satisfied with my clothes I went to shower and rubbed some Kinky Curls in my hair. I had just thrown on my clothes when Bobby called.

"Hey. Why are you interrupting my beautifying process?"

"I thought you woke up like that?"

"Ooh, you smooth. That was a good one. Two points for that one."

"I try," he laughed. "I was calling because I was about to get in the car when I realized I don't know where you live."

I didn't want to give him my address just in case Klan was having the house watched? "I thought about that after we hung up earlier. I was going to text you but I forgot. I live on 71st and Brentwood. Beige and yellow house in the middle of the block. Look for my daddy's old school Caddy in the driveway."

"You stay with your parent's too? Another thing we have in common. Not that I'm keeping track."

"I think you are. But its all good. I think its cute."

"I live on 66th and Capitol. I'll be there in about ten minutes."

He was closer than I expected. "Um... I'm still at the hair salon and she's finishing up right now. I might be a few minutes late."

"That's cool. I'll just enjoy the scenery til you get there. What do you drive?"

"A blue Prius."

"Okay. I'll be in the RAV4. See you in a minute."

I sped up my process and was able to get to my parent's house in fifteen minutes. Bobby's car was parked in front of the house. I pulled into the driveway and hopped out quickly, hoping our cars didn't get my parents attention. I hadn't told them about the police running in my house, Klan getting arrested, or meeting Bobby. I didn't want to have those conversations tonight.

"You don't look like the RAV4 type," I joked as I climbed in the passenger seat.

"When you don't got no money to buy a car, you do what you gotta do." He looked me over. "You look like you just stepped right out of heaven and you smell like everything good."

"Thank you." He wore a tan dinner jacket, jeans, and shoe that matched his jacket. "And you look GQ yourself. That's a nice color."

"You know yo boy stay fresh," he laughed and did a little shoulder bounce. "Ready?"

I buckled my seatbelt. "Ready. Where to?"

He smiled and gave a wink as he pulled away from the curb. "It's a surprise."

"What if I don't like surprises?"

"You will."

I believed him. He turned up the music and we vibed to Chris Brown and Rick Ross's *'New Thang'*.

"I like this song. Are you trying to send me a message?"

He held my eye contact, allowing me to see his intentions. "Of course."

"Playing spades with the cards up?"

"Only way to play."

"So you say."

We listened to the song and I checked him out as he drove. He was very handsome. His lining was sharp, hair freshly cut, goatee neatly trimmed, and his brown skin had a healthy glow. His dark brown eyes were soft and hard, revealing two sides of his character. He had nice fluffy lips and I found myself wondering if he was a good kisser. He was also tall and lean. And even though I had never seen his body, I knew there were muscles underneath his jacket. If I ever had an ideal man, Bobby fit the script.

"Can I ask you something?" he spoke.

"What's up?"

"I don't wanna beat a dead horse but I also don't want to spend all night with these thoughts in the back of my head. I got some questions about yo situation. I try to always do the right thing and I don't want to make a mistake."

"Playing spades with the cards up?" I asked.

He nodded. "My ex left me when I got locked up because she figured it was easier than telling me she was pregnant. I don't want to be involved in nothing bogus."

I thought about how to describe me and Klan's situation without making myself seem weak or like I was doing something wrong. I also didn't want to get all emotional and break down crying so I tried to keep my explanation simple. "Our relationship has been over for a long time but it took him going to jail for me to get the strength to leave. Sometimes you get used to something and think you can't live without it. Even when it's not good for you. He isn't good for me. He was very controlling and abusive. Our lives are headed in two different directions. Him getting locked up was the best thing that could've happened to us."

He nodded. "So, it's really over?"

"Yes. I have to leave so I can get my life back."

He nodded again. "Okay. I can see talking about that put you in a bad place and I won't dampen the mood with questions about whatever his name is. We about to do a new thang."

We ate dinner at a restaurant called Rick's. I had never heard of the place but their food was the bomb. The braised short ribs were so good I wanted to slap the chef's mama. Dessert was a warm chocolate cake with powder sugar sprinkled on top. When I dug my fork in, creamy chocolate spilled out. After filling our bellies we went to a winery and did some wine tasting. They told us not to swallow the wine but I did. Now I was on my second glass and feeling really good.

"You know, for a guy that used to be a robber, you are cultured and pretty cool to hang out with," I said while swirling a sparkling white wine around in my glass like the host showed us.

"I'm always on my best behavior for the first couple of months. After ninety days is when the real me comes out."

"Well, the real me comes out after my third glass of wine. This is number two. Be careful," I warned.

He laughed. "You always figure out a way to one up a brotha. You won that round."

I took a sip of wine and swished it around my mouth before swallowing. "That was good. Tastes airy and bubbly."

He took a sip from the wine glass he was holding and swished it around before spitting. "Taste like wine to me. I think we should just drink it."

I raised my hand for a high five while bringing the glass to my lips for a drink. "So, what kind of plans do you have for your life? Career? School? Settling down?"

"I'm still trying to figure all of that out. If you would'da asked me that a year ago, I would'da told you I was gon get out and get it how I live. I didn't plan on going to school or get married or work. But now everything is on the table. I'm just kinda seeing where God leads me. Right now its towards ministry. I want to do prison ministry where I go to prisons and introduce those brothas to the word. Lot of hopelessness in them places. I wanna be an example of the power of God.

Show them brothas what redemption and salvation look like."

I stared in his mouth like I was trying to swallow the words as he spoke them. I had never met a man like him and he intrigued the hell out of me. He was one of those special people that could probably change the world or at least have a great impact. His story was so powerful. I wanted to root for him and be there to watch him succeed. And he was getting finer by the minute. "That is so cool. I really admire you. I think you're a great guy and you are definitely going places. I'm happy that I met you."

He gave me one of those looks that men give when they want to kiss a woman. He got that twinkle in his eyes and licked his lips. I leaned in a little, giving him the green light. And that's when I heard a loud cracking noise from the wine barrels. They were stacked about twenty feet high near a wall a few feet from us. It sounded like one of the barrels broke and we looked up just in time to see one of the wooden barrels tip over. It bounced off another barrel before hitting the ground and exploding. Bobby stepped in front of me just in time to block me from the spray of wine.

"Oh, my God! Are you okay?" I asked. Although he only protected me from wine, the gesture meant a lot more. He was a protector. I liked that.

"Yeah. You?"

"I'm fine. Let me get something to wipe you off." I went in my purse to look for napkins to wipe his face and hair. That was about all I could do because he was drenched from head to toe.

"Sir, are you okay? I'm so sorry," the host said as he rushed over.

"Yeah. I'm good. Nothing a dry cleaner cant fix," Bobby said, taking the jacket off and wringing it out.

I liked that he reacted so calmly. Klan would've threatened to shoot somebody. It was nice to be around a civilized man.

"I'm sorry, sir. This has never happened before. If there is anything I can do, please let me know," the host apologized again.

"Its fine, man. Accidents happen. I'm good." Then he turned to me. "I need to change."

"I understand. Let's go."

He looked uncomfortable sitting in wet clothes as he drove. I thought it was funny and laughed my ass off.

"What you laughing at?"

"You look really uncomfortable." I laughed again.

"So, I'm soaked all the way to my socks and drawers and you think its funny? Last time I be a human shield for you."

"Its not like that. I'm laughing with you not at you."

"Why you the only one laughing?"

"Cause it's funny. But you're my hero, Bobby. Thank you for saving me from the wine." I leaned over to peck his cheek to show my appreciation.

"You mean all I had to do was spill some wine on me to get a kiss? If I'da knew that, I would'da just bought a bottle from the store and poured some on my head."

I laughed and pushed him playfully. "Not the same."

"So, what do you want to do? This don't have to end our night. My parents are out of town until tomorrow so you don't have to worry about running into them."

It was almost eleven o'clock but I didn't want my night with him to end. "Let's get you out of these wet clothes and see what other surprises you have up your sleeves."

He left me in the living room while he went to change. I looked at the family pictures on the wall. There was a big one of him in prison greens standing next to his parents. They wore smiles and looked happy. There was another one of a group of about fifteen inmates dressed in greens. They were all shades and all ages. Bobby was in the middle. "Mighty Men of Valor " was inscribed in the frame.

"I need to take a quick shower. Make yourself at home. Do you need anything?" Bobby asked, appearing shirtless and shoeless. The sight of his chiseled frame made me stop and stare. He looked like he could be a personal trainer. Arms, chest, abs, and shoulders like pow.

When I realized I was staring, I snapped out of it. "Oh, um... Yeah. I'm fine. I was just looking at the pictures. Mighty Men of Valor was the choir in prison?"

He smiled and looked at the picture like he missed being there with his guys. "Yeah. Roland had us moving in the spirit. I miss those brothers. But hey, I'ma hit this water. Gimmie a minute. Make yourself at home."

Hearing the name made me pause. I wondered if it was a coincidence that he was locked up with a man that had that same name as my biological father. I turned back to the picture to find Roland. I had never seen him but I still looked to see if I could recognize him. Maybe I had his eyes or his nose. I took my time but didn't see any distinctive features on anyone that I could point to as a possibility. But the thought of him knowing my father set off a chain of thoughts in my head. Was God was trying to send me a message? The conversations with Neesy's popped into my head. Was Bobby the one? I sent my mom the text to see if Roland was still in Waupun.

She texted me back. 'why?'

I texted back. 'bcuz I want to know.'

She texted back. 'Yes.' 'where r u?'

'with my friend. call u in the morning.'

My insides bubbled as I looked back to the picture. There were four older men with gray hair. Two had very dark skin, one brown skinned, and the other light skinned. Roland had to be the brown skinned or light skinned man because I was light skinned. I sat down and turned on the TV but my mind remained on the picture and thoughts of destiny and fate. Bobby came back into the living room ten minutes later dressed in a short sleeved coogi sweater, jeans, and boots. He sat next to me, giving me a whiff of some good smelling cologne.

"You ready?"

"Um, yeah. Hey, what prison were you in?"

He looked towards the pictures on the wall. "All that was in Waupun. Why?"

My heart started beating faster. "I think you know my dad."

His eyes popped in surprise. "Yo pops in Waupun? Who is he?"

"His name is Roland."

His eyes got bigger and mouth hung open. "Roland is yo pops?"

"I think that's him. I've never seen him before but that isn't a common name."

He got up and grabbed the picture from the wall before sitting back down. He pointed to the brown skinned man. "This is Roland. Now that I think about it, you have his nose and eyes."

I just stared at my father. He didn't look like a murderer. He was tall and handsome with a bright smile. His short curly afro was streaked with gray. "He doesn't look like how I imagined him to look. I thought he would be a big mean looking man. My mom said he killed a pregnant woman. Only a monster would do something like that."

"Roland ain't a bad dude. And I'm not saying that because he yo dad. He is a genuinely good dude. Gave me some good advice and treated me like a son or little brother. He prayed for me before I left. He was our spiritual leader. We call him Rev because he is an ordained minister. I don't know what you know about him, but I didn't see nothing negative in his character. I have a pretty good judge of character, too. Roland is stand up and a righteous brotha."

I continued to stare at my father while thinking about what Bobby said. Roland is a minister and the choir's spiritual leader. I never expected to hear that about him. "He called my mother three years ago and asked if he could call me. I said no. Kevin is my dad and I didn't feel I had any room in my heart to know another man as my father. Especially someone who killed a woman and her baby. But now I'm wondering if I made a mistake. What are the chances of you doing time with him and then us meeting? And then to hear about your change and him being a minister. I don't know what to think."

"I don't believe in coincidences. I believe what happens is supposed to happen. I was supposed to meet your pops and I was supposed to meet you. Why? We don't know yet."

I continued to stare at my father and wonder why God had allowed these meetings to happen. I no longer wanted to go back outside. I wanted to stay on the couch with Bobby. "Can we stay here and chill? Maybe watch a movie or something? . I just want to stay here with you."

"Yeah. For sure. What do you want to watch?"

"I don't care. Whatever you want to watch."

"Okay. How about I make some popcorn and get us some drinks and we can watch that BMF show?"

"Let's do it." When he left, I sat the picture of my father on the table and kicked off my shoes to get comfortable. Then I found the show and waited for him to come back.

"Look what I found," he grinned, walking into the living room with an arm full of goodies. A bowl of mixed popcorn, a box of nutty bars, and two Pepsis.

"Somebody got the munchies."

After kicking off his shoes, we snuggled up on the couch to watch season one of BMF. Being with Bobby felt as natural as breathing. I was at ease and comfortable. I knew that I was safe with him and that he respected me as a woman. He wouldn't pressure me to do anything or try to control me. He was a real man. He was looking for a partner. An equal. He was the man I had been looking for my whole life. I was attracted to him on every level. And I couldn't stop staring at him and wondering if God put us together.

"Why you looking at me like that?" He asked after catching me staring.

I touched the side of his face. "You're a beautiful man."

He grabbed my hand and kissed the knuckle and stared into my eyes. "I never made a list of things I was looking for in a woman. But if I ever made a list, it would be you."

His words made my heart melt and ooze all over my insides. I no longer cared about watching the BMF story, feeling guilty for cheating on Klan, or the consequences of being caught. I wanted him and everything that he was. I leaned forward to taste his lips and he met me halfway. The kiss was sweet, salty, and sexy. Our tongues slipped and twisted and danced. Our hands caressed and squeezed. I lay back on the couch and he fell on top of me. He grinded his hardness against me, thrusting like he was trying to push through the layers of our clothes to get inside me. I was dripping wet, my panties becoming soaked. He broke the kiss long enough to pull off the Coogi and then we made out some more. I rubbed his arms and back, loving the feel of his muscles flexing every time he moved. When I was way beyond being turned on and tired of the foreplay, I pushed against his chest.

"What?" His eyes low and glossy like he was high.

"I'm ready."

No more words were needed. He stood and began undressing. I didn't find a flaw from the top of his head down to his feet. He was well groomed and didn't have any body hair. Muscular upper body, rock hard abs, toned legs, and a nice bubble booty. The package was my favorite body part. It wasn't too big but it wasn't small either. Just the right length and thickness and I couldn't wait to have it inside of me. I slipped the dress over my head and pulled off my panties. He climbed on top of me and didn't waste time getting what he wanted. My coochie sucked him in like she was trying to eat him. He went slow, pushing deep, pulling out slowly, and then went back deep.

"Mmmmhh. Damn, Charlene," he moaned in my ear.

Hearing my name turned me. I wanted him to go ham in it. "Do it, Bobby," I whispered back, biting and licking his ear. "I wanna feel it all. Give it to me."

My words must've turned him on too much because two pumps later he went deep and erupted.

"Oh, my God. Awe man, Charlene, " he grunted.

His dick spasmed inside of me and it felt like he shot out a gallon of cum. I thought it was over and I was about to be disappointed until he started thrusting again. His lips found mine and we kissed as he went slow and steady. I pushed my hips up and matched his stroke. He grabbed my breasts, squeezing and rubbing his thumbs over my nipples. It felt so good and an explosion began to bubble up inside me. When he started to speed up, so did the race to my orgasm. He squeezed my breasts harder the faster that he thrust. The gentle lovemaking came to an end along with the kisses when he started going ham in it. I dug my nails in his shoulders and called out to God. When my orgasm came, a light flashed in my head and I got the tingles all over my body. He came right behind me, filling me with more cum. And he was still hard. We lay there for a moment, cheek to cheek, breathing heavy and trying to catch our breath. When I was ready for more, I started kissing his neck and sucking his ear.

"Let me ride," I whispered.

When he lifted up and pulled out, I could feel his sperm seep out of me. When I stood, even more spill out and dripped down my leg. "Look what you did."

"That's three years," he grinned. "You wanna take a shower?"

A vision of our wet bodies under the water flashed in my head. "Later. Right now I just need you to stay right there."

I straddled his lap and guided him inside. I sucked on his bottom lip while rocking my hips back and forth. We established a rhythm so perfect that it felt like we had known each others bodies for years. And he had stamina. I rode him until a second orgasm forced me to slow down. Then I got on the floor on my hands and knees and he drilled me from the back until he came again. We went from the floor to the shower. After we cleaned each other, we had sex in the shower. From the shower we went to his bedroom where we spent the rest of the night talking and having sex.

Chapter 21

Charlene

The first thing I seen when I opened my eyes was Bobby's face. We slept facing each other, his arm wrapped around my waist. He was so cute. I wanted to lean over and kiss him but didn't want to wake him. So I lay there and watched him and thought about last night. I came so many times that I lost count. We literally had sex, took a break to talk and catch our breath, and then went at it again. Did that all night. I didn't even remember falling asleep. I also didn't know a man could get hard so many times. Bobby was a sex machine and he knew how to work that magic stick. My body was sore in places that I didn't know I could get sore. It felt like I worked out or ran a marathon. Then Klan's face popped into my head. I had to leave him. I thought about what Lana said about selling the house and moving back in with my parents. That way Klan couldn't get to me. Shoot, I would give him the house if he left me alone. He paid the most for it. All I knew is I needed to leave. Meeting Bobby couldn't be a coincidence. He was so perfect for me and I adored everything about him. When he stirred, I closed my eyes so he wouldn't catch me watching him sleep. Then I opened them again and seen him staring at me.

"Hey," he smiled.

"Good morning."

"Waking up with you is definitely a good morning."

The compliment made me smile. "Awe, thanks. But I am so sore."

"Sexercising will do that. It's like a work out. Your body gotta get used to it."

"Mmmh. I like the thought of getting used to you."

"So do I." He leaned over to peck my lips.

"You want to pray with me?"

I was a little throwed by the question. "What?"

"It's my morning ritual. I pray as soon as I wake up and then a lil workout."

"Oh. Okay."

"That's a yes?"

"Yes."

He grabbed my hands. "Close your eyes."

I closed them as thoughts of Neesy praying with her husband popped in my head. I got a little tingly inside. It was so intimate.

"Dear heavenly father. I'd like to thank you for waking us up this morning. I know the things we did last night wasn't right in your eyes, but you brought us together for a reason and I pray that you forgive us and show us the reason."

I opened my eyes at the comment. He kept his eyes closed and continued praying.

"I ask that you continue to watch over us and guide us. Bless us with knowledge, wisdom, and understanding, as well as the strength to overcome anything that is not of you. In Jesus name we pray."

I closed my eyes and said Amen with him. We opened them at the same time.

"Did you want to add anything?"

"No. I think you said it all."

"You wanna work out with me real quick?"

I frowned. "No. I don't have any clothes on."

"Neither do I. A hundred pushups and a hundred sit ups. It's easy."

"For you. How about I watch and cheer you on."

He shook his head before rolling out of bed and onto the floor. I moved to the edge of the bed and watched him do pushups. I counted as he pushed. His butt was poking in the air a little and I couldn't help but grab it.

"What is you doing?"

I gave him a couple light spanks. "You have a nice booty."

"Stop. You supposed to be counting."

"I am. You're on twenty-six."

After doing a hundred pushups without stopping, he rolled onto his back and started doing situps. He did those without stopping too. Then he lay on his back and we looked into each others eyes for a moment.

"What are you doing today?" He asked.

I thought about the calls I was going to get from Klan. I had to answer. "Nothing much. Run some errands. What about you?"

"I planned on relaxing. Kinda hoped that you wanted to do the same."

I would've loved nothing more than to relax with him. "Sorry. I have some important stuff. Can we get together later? Like, after eight?"

That made him smile. "It's a date."

"Hopefully we won't get wine bombed tonight."

"You mean me get wine bombed right because you stayed dry?"

"Yeah. You," I laughed.

We went silent and stared at each other again. I read his mind. "My parents won't be back until later. You wanna?"

I reached my arm down to grab his hand. "Kevin Gates said I don't get tired."

We had a morning sex marathon that started in his bed and ended in the shower. Then he cooked me bacon, cheese eggs, and grits before dropping me off at my parents' house. I checked the time on my phone as I unlocked the back door. 8:32. My phone rang while I was stepping in the house. It was Klan. I pressed 5.

"Good morning," I answered.

"You already woke?"

He was suspicious but I knew how to erase that. "Yeah. I'm at my parents house."

"Oh. What you got going on over there?"

"Nothing. Just hanging out with my mom. We're going out and doing girls' stuff. Probably go get our nails done, too."

"That's what's up. What time you gon be done with that?"

"I don't know. Around two or three probably."

"Aight. When this call over, I'ma fall back and let you kick it wit cho moms. I'ma call you back around three o'clock."

I sat in the kitchen and talked with Klan for fifteen minutes before going to find my mom. She sat up in bed looking at her phone. My dad was sleeping next to her.

"Good morning."

"Hey, baby. You're up early. What's going on?"

"Can we talk?"

My dad stirred and looked up at me. "Hey, baby. What you doing over here so early?"

"Hey, dad. I just wanted to talk to mom. You can go back to sleep."

He fluffed his pillow and closed his eyes. "A'ight."

Mom got up and we walked to the kitchen. I sat at the table while she turned on the coffee machine.

"I need some coffee. Want some?"

"Yeah."

"What did you want to talk to me about?"

"Roland."

She sat the coffee filter down to look over at me. "What about him?"

"I seen a picture of him yesterday at my friend's house. Apparently Roland is a Christian. Actually, he is the spiritual leader of the choir at Waupun and an ordained minister."

She nodded and went back to making the coffee. "He told me that when we talked. He's changed a lot. He isn't the same man I knew back in the day. He's gotten older and wiser. Who is your friend? How does she know Roland?"

"His name is Bobby. I met him at church. He was in the choir at Waupun."

She gave me that concerned motherly eye. "Your friend was in prison? And since when did you start going to church?"

"I started going to church right after Neesy left. The first time I went was with her. We listened to the choir and she prayed for me. When Bobby got out of prison, the preacher introduced him to everybody and told us his story."

She cocked her head to the side. "You were with him last night?"

I nodded.

"Where is Klan?"

I hadn't told her about the police breaking our door in and taking him to jail. I was hoping to avoid talking to her about it but now I didn't have a choice. "Klan is in jail, mom. He's been in for a couple of weeks now. He might be going to prison."

Surprise lit her eyes as she walked over to sit across from me. "Why are you just now telling me this?"

"Because I was trying to figure out what to do."

"What is he in jail for?"

"A gun. His P.O has a hold on him."

She smiled. "Good. You're not going to stay with him, are you?"

I shook my head. "I spent the night with Bobby."

She gave me a knowing look. "You slept with him?"

"Yes."

Her smile got bigger. "Tell me about him."

"He's a Christian and wants to be a minister. He did three years and gave his life to God while he was locked up. He works full time but still lives with his parents because he just got out a little over a month ago."

"Does he have kids?"

"No."

"How long have his parents been together?"

"They're like us. His mom married his stepfather. He's an only child too."

"And you're sure that you want to be with him?"

"I think so. I feel like God brought us together. We have so much in common."

"And he knows Roland."

I nodded. "I think I should talk to him. How do I get in touch with him?"

"I haven't talked to him in two years. Kevin didn't like it so I ended all communication. But I have all of his contact information in my phone. I'll find it and send it to you. Write him a letter and give him your number. I'm sure he'll call."

"Okay."

She studied my face for a moment. "Are you really going to leave him?"

"I have to. I want a better life. I don't want to be controlled. I want my life back."

"Have you told him that its over?"

"No."

"Why not?"

"I'm a little scared."

She grabbed my hand. "Stop procrastinating. Do what you have to do. And so what if you're scared. Be scared and do it anyway. Take your life back, sweety. Stop letting him control you. He's in jail and can't do nothing to you."

Her words gave me a little strength. "Okay."

"What are you going to do about the house?"

"I don't know yet. I think I should sell it and give him his money back. I also thought about giving it to him if that will make him leave me alone. He put the most money down anyway. I just want my life back."

"Well, you can always come back home if you need to. I just want you to be happy. Whatever you decide, me and your father will support you. We got your back, baby."

$$$

After talking to my mom, I went home to rest, and figure out my next move. The first thing that I did was write Roland a letter. It was short and to the point. I told him that we should talk and gave him my number. I was going to mail it as soon as I got the information from mom. I was laying in bed thinking about my love triangle when Lana called on Facebook.

"Hey, girl."

"Did you give it up?"

I bust out laughing.

Her eyes got wide. "You little slut. Was it good?"

"It was better than good. I didn't even know I could have sex that many times in one night. We did it at least twenty times."

Her mouth hung open. "Damn. He like an Energizer Battery."

"In real life."

"So, that means that Klan is gone, right? You got re-dickmatized so we out with the old and in with the new."

"I was talking to my mom about it earlier. I'm done. I'm going to tell him when he calls later. I can't do it anymore. Plus, I really think Bobby is my person. He knows my biological father and everything. I seen a picture of him for the first time last night on Bobby's wall."

"Why does Bobby have a picture of your father?"

"Roland is the choir director and was his spiritual leader at Waupun. He has a picture of the whole choir."

"For real? That's crazy."

"I know. I decided to get to know Roland. He sounds like a good guy. I just finished writing him a letter."

"Awe, that's cool, Charlene. Bobby came and brought some good stuff in your life. When do I get to meet him?"

"Uh... I don't know."

"When the next time you seeing him?"

"Later tonight."

"Ooh, he got you sprung on that thang already."

"Shut up, Lana," I laughed. After talking to my girl, I fell asleep but was awoken by the phone ringing at 3:00 on the dot. It was Klan.

"What you doing?" He asked.

"I just woke up."

"Why you sleeping late?"

"Because I was tired."

"What you tired from?"

I let out a frustrated breath, tired of the Q and A. It was time to end it. "I'm selling the house."

"Selling the house? For what?"

"Because I don't want to live here anymore. I want to move on with my life. I'll give you your money back with interest and then we can go our separate ways."

His end of the phone went silent. My heart thudded as I waited for him to connect the dots and respond.

"Oh, you on that? You tryna leave a nigga?"

"I need to move on with my life, Klan. You're too controlling and abusive. I don't want to fight you. I just want my life back. Just let me go. Please."

"What!? Nigga, is you fucking crazy? Gon wait to a nigga get locked up to get on this bitch ass shit? After everything I did for you?"

"All you do is control me. You don't treat me like I'm your woman. You treat me like I'm your slave and I'm not happy. I'm tired of being treated like shit."

"Hold on, hold on. Where the fuck is all this shit coming from? Just the other day you said you wasn't tired and now you on this bitch ass shit. You letting yo family and friends make decisions for us?"

"I'm making this decision for me. I'm tired, Klan. I can't do this no more."

"Nah, fuck that. You can't get tired of me. You don't get to choose when you can leave. Think I'm playing and I'ma send my niggas over there to get active. You-"

I hung up the phone. I didn't have any more words and I didn't want to listen to him threaten me. When he called back I blocked the number so he couldn't call me back. Then I cried. I cried because it broke my heart to leave him while he was in jail. He didn't have anyone and leaving him felt wrong. But I had to do it. I also cried because a part of me was going to miss him. We had some good times together, but the bad times outweighed the good. When I was done crying, I called Bobby. I needed to get out of the house before his friends showed up.

"Hey, angel. I was just thinking about you."

Being called angel made me smile. "Oh yeah. Tell me what you were thinking."

"I can't go into too much detail because my moms is close. But just know that you was the star of the show."

"Ooh, I like being the star."

"You will always be my star."

"Always?"

"Always."

I believed him. "Since I'm the star, that means I get to decide what happens next, right?"

"Tell me what you had in mind."

"Oh, I don't know. I was thinking that since our date got cut short last night because of the wine explosion that we could hang out for the rest of the night. What do you think?"

"Are you coming to me or am I coming to you?"

"I'm coming to you. See you in a minute."

Chapter 22

Bobby

After hanging up the phone I went back to shampooing the driver's seat of the RAV4. The truck smelled like wine and my mom didn't like it. Now I had to clean the entire truck. My mom was in the backseat pulling out the floor mats and giving directions on what to clean and how to clean it.

"What you smiling like that for?"

"Like what?"

"Like you about to go on a date. I heard your conversation. She the reason my truck smell like a brewery?"

"Kinda, sorta, but not really. I told you a wine barrel exploded on me."

"Was she with you when the wine exploded?"

"She was."

"Tell me about her. Who is she and how long you knew her?"

"Her name is Charlene. I met her at church a couple weeks ago."

"She go to our church? Is she a member?"

"Not yet. She just started going."

"Well, that's good that she in the church. Are you dating or just hanging out?"

"Just kinda hanging out right now."

She raised an eyebrow. "You know Christians just don't do no hanging out, right? I'm not telling you to propose to the girl but you can't be just sleeping around. And you also can't be a player. Find you a good one to build a life with."

"I'm not trying to be a player, mom. The pastor told me not to do things unbecoming of an usher. I'm taking what he said serious."

"That's good to hear. So, is she someone you can get serious with?"

"I think so. She has a good job and graduated from college. I also know her pops. He was our spiritual leader in the choir in Waupun. I thought it was crazy that I got out and met his daughter. He never even mentioned her and come to find out they never met. I had to tell her about him because she thought he was a monster because of what he was locked up for. I guess he killed a pregnant lady or something."

"Oh, my God. He is a monster. He killed a pregnant woman? That means the baby died, too."

"I'm not saying what he did wasn't bad because it was. But God is using him in there. He ain't the same man that he was when he did that. Just like I changed, so did he. He helping a lot of people. He a good dude."

She smiled at me like parents do when their kid says something smart. "You're right, Bobby. People can change. Cause you was a handful when you was out there robbing people. Now you ushering people and talking about being a preacher. God is good. So, when do I get to meet this Charlene?"

"She'll be here in a little while. I guess you can meet her then."

Me and mom finished cleaning the truck and were putting the mats back in when Charlene pulled up.

"Jamie, come out here and meet Bobby's girlfriend," mom yelled in the house.

I gave her the look. "Can we not make a big deal or call her my girlfriend?"

"Bobby got a girlfriend?" Jamie yelled outside.

I shook my head and walked towards Charlene's car. She lowered the passenger window and I leaned in.

"Hey."

"Hey. Is that your mom?"

"Yeah. She wants to meet you."

A nervous look passed over her. "Oh my, God. Are you serious?"

"Yeah. But its cool. She not one of those overprotective moms that don't think nobody is good enough for her son."

"Oh, man. I was not ready to meet parents."

I laughed at her nervousness. "You good. Ready?"

"No," She groaned, pulling the key from the ignition and getting out of the car.

We were walking up the driveway when Jamie came outside. He gave an approving nod after looking Charlene over. Mom extended her hand and made the introduction.

"Hi, Charlene. I'm Toya and this is my husband, Jamie."

"Hi, Toya. Hi, Jamie."

"Hey, Charlene. Nice to meet you," Jamie said before turning to me. "This is your girlfriend, Bobby?"

"Friend, Jamie. She is my friend," I clarified.

He lifted his hands. "Okay, son. Sorry."

"She goes to our church, baby," Moms told Jamie. "Charlene, are you thinking about joining our church officially?"

"Um, I don't know. I haven't given it much thought."

"You know what? You do look familiar," Jamie said. "I think I've seen you in the pews before. You should give some thought to joining us. You need that spiritual home. Are you saved?"

Charlene winced a little. "I got baptized when I was a kid."

"That's good, but that was involuntary," mom said. "You have to make a conscious decision to serve God as a grown up."

"If you join the church, the pastor will explain everything to you," Jamie added.

"Okay, that's enough interrogation," I jumped in. "Y'all treating her like a criminal."

"Chill, son," Jamie said. "We're just trying to make sure she understands the importance of saving her soul."

"It's fine, Bobby," Charlene said.

"Let's talk more about it on Sunday. Right now we have somewhere to be."

Mom looked me up and down like I was a sell out before turning to Charlene. "It was nice to meet you, sweety."

"Hope to see you in church on Sunday," Jamie added.

We jumped in Charlene's Prius and got away from my parents as fast as we could.

"Where are we going?" She asked.

"It don't even matter. Just drive. That wasn't that bad, was it?"

"No. They were cool. They seem like they really care about our souls though. How were you so bad with parents like that?"

"I moved out as soon as I graduated high school so I dealt with them on my time. Which was hardly ever. I didn't wanna hear nothing about Jesus back then."

"Now you got dreams to be a preacher. Baby boy is all grown up now."

"Something like that."

"Guess what I did today?" She asked, giddy with excitement.

"I don't know but you seem happy about it."

"I wrote Roland."

"For real?"

"Yeah. I feel like I should give him a chance. Listening to you talk about him made me want to meet him. I sent my number."

"That's so dope. For real. That letter is probably going to make his year."

I drove around and hung out with Charlene for the rest of the day. We ate fast food, watched Avatar at the movies, and went bowling. She was the coolest chick I ever met. She was funny, smart, and beautiful. I couldn't keep my eyes off of her. We clicked easily and our connection was super strong. We enjoyed each other's company so much that we didn't want to go home when the sun went down. Instead we spent the night in the hotel. And just like the first night we didn't get much sleep. The sexual chemistry between us was clicking so hard that all we wanted to do was explore each others body into the wee hours of the morning. We were awakened at six by the alarm on my phone.

"Good morning."

"Hi," she smiled.

"You ready to go to the house of the Lord and ask forgiveness for our sins?"

She wrapped her arms around me and snuggled up against me. "Do we have to? I would rather stay here."

"I would love to stay here with you but I'm an usher and I kinda got a job to do."

"Okay."

I rolled onto my stomach and clasped my hands together. "Cmon, lets pray."

After morning prayer, I did my usual workout before we took separate showers. Knowing that I had to do the Lord's work had me feeling guilty so we decided to keep our hand to ourselves. She dropped me off at home so that I could get dressed and she went home and did the same.

$$$

"I was wondering if you was coming home," my mom said, giving me the eye when I walked in. She was sitting at the table eating breakfast and drinking coffee.

"Why wouldn't I? I gotta be at church."

"You wasn't thinking about church last night, was you? Where did you sleep?"

"Ma, you know I'm grown, right?"

She looked at me like I said something disrespectful. "Well, excuse me, Mr. I'm grown. I was just tryna be a concerned mother. Make sure you wasn't out doing the devil's work. But gone head with yo grown self."

"I'm sorry, ma. I didn't mean it like that. I spent the night with Charlene. I just didn't want you to judge me. You was giving me that look."

"I can give you whatever look I want. You my son. And I also wanna know that you safe at night. A call or a text wouldn't hurt."

"I'm sorry I didn't let you know. I'ma do better."

She gave a half smile. "Good. Now gon in there and wash that sin off you so we can get to church. Remember what I said about just hanging out."

After another shower to make my moms happy, I got dressed and hopped in the car with her and Jamie. The service didn't start until eight but we always got there early. I had to be ready to seat the people. I kicked it with Little and his family for a moment before seating a few new comers. I kept my eyes peeled for Charlene but she hadn't shown up yet. When my bladder demanded to be emptied, I dipped off to the bathroom. After taking care of my business, I stepped into the hallway and spotted Tasha talking to a couple of women near the offices at the back of the church. I kept head down and put some pep in my step. She seen me coming and stepped in my path.

"Hey, Bobby."

"Hey, Tasha."

"Hold on for a second. I want to introduce you to some ladies in the church."

The three women looked just as good as they smelled. And the way they were smiling told me they were probably just as freaky as Tasha.

"Hey, " I waved.

They waved back.

"This is Shawntale, Tina, and Tracy. They are apart of the church family and are all single."

I nodded. "Okay. That's good."

"Your single, too, right?"

"Um, yeah. But I have to get back up front. Gotta get my usher on. It was nice meeting you ladies."

I tried to step away but Tasha grabbed my arm and stopped me. "Wait. I need your help with something."

I didn't want to help her with anything but I also didn't want to be rude in front of the other women. "What's up?"

Tasha dismissed her friends. "Ladies, I'ma be up front in a minute. Give us a moment." The ladies waved at me as they walked away. "Why you acting like that?"

"What is you talking about?"

"You acting like you too good to say more than hi."

"What else you want me to say?"

"Mingle a little bit. Flirt. Act like you looking for a woman."

"Man, look. I don't got time for this right now. Do you want anything else?"

She looked around to see if anyone was watching us before licking her lips and sliding her hand across my chest. "Yeah. I wanna taste that D. When you gon let me have it?"

That's when Charlene walked in. She seen Tasha hanging on me. A fire or jealousy lit in her eyes and she mean mugged me.

I snatched away from Tasha. "Watch out, man."

I walked towards the sanctuary and looked around for Charlene. She was sliding down a pew close to the front. I was walking towards her when I noticed Junior Pastor Greg watching me. I acknowledged him with a nod but he turned away. That was weird but I didn't have time to think about it because I needed to talk to Charlene.

"Hey. You looking good."

She looked me up and down and rolled her eyes. "Don't you have a job to do or are you too busy with the church hoes."

"Its not like that. Tasha engaged to the junior pastor."

She crossed her arms over her chest and gave me that 'yeah right' look. "You talking about the one that was hanging on your arm rubbing your chest? "

"She wasn't hanging on my arm. She grabbed me and held it. But It wasn't like that."

"Whatever, Bobby."

"Cmon, Charlene. Don't do this. It ain't what you think?"

She stared at me for a moment before her eyes cut to something behind me. "Yo girlfriend tryna get your attention."

I turned and seen Tasha standing next to an elderly woman waving for me. "Charlene, its not like that."

"Bye, bobby."

I let out a frustrated breath before going to see what Tasha wanted. "What's going on?"

"I need you to help me escort my fiancé's aunty. Can you take her to a good seat up front? I told her she would be in good hands with you."

Pastor Sims was tearing down the house with his preaching but I spent most of the service thinking about what to say to Charlene. I didn't want her to think I was some type of player. I wanted her to know that she was important to me and that I only had eyes for her. I didn't want to do a full disclosure of my run ins with Tasha but I would if necessary. So when the choir sang their final song, I made a beeline to where she was sitting. When she seen me walking up, she turned and walked away. "Charlene?"

She turned to look at me when two of the women that Tasha introduced me to suddenly appeared.

"Hey, Bobby," Shawntale waved, stepping in front of me. "You got a minute."

Charlene shook her head and kept on walking.

"Not really. I have something important to do."

"Well, just take down my number real quick. I was hoping that we could talk."

Shawntale was fine-fine. Had I met her three years ago, I would've tried to have my cake and eat it to. But I was a different man and the only cake I wanted to eat was leaving.

"I can't. I gotta go." I ran outside and seen Charlene walking across the street. "Charlene, wait up. " She didn't slow her stride so I ran after her. "Where you going? Can we talk?"

Anger and disgust swirled in her eyes. "I don't got nothing to say to you, Bobby. I'm going home. Leave me alone."

"Just let me walk you to your car. Where you parked at?"

"I don't live with my parents, Bobby. I live right down the street and I'm walking home."

That surprised me. "Where do you live?"

"Leave me alone, Bobby. Go back to all of your hoes at church. You not who I thought you was and I'm not who you think I am either. Let's just stop right now before somebody get hurt."

"Before somebody get hurt? What is you talking about? I only been with you since I been out. Everything that you seen ain't what you think it is. Stop so we can talk."

She stopped to face me, anger blazing in her eyes. "You telling me that when I walked in the church, Tasha wasn't giving you 'I wanna fuck you eyes' and rubbing on your chest?"

"She was but that's not what it was."

"What about the woman I just seen. What did she want?"

If I told her Shawntale was trying to give me her number, she would walk away. So I didn't say nothing. Charlene convicted me for remaining silent.

"Yeah. Like I thought, playa-playa." She rolled her eyes. "And I bought a house with my boyfriend on twenty fifth street. Go back to your life and I'ma go back to mine."

The words about buying a house with her boyfriend punched me in the chest and left me speechless. Did that mean she wasn't leaving him? Were they still together? Was she lying to me all along? Thoughts of being deceived by another woman pissed me off. When she walked away, I let her go.

Chapter 23

Charlene

I couldn't stop thinking about Bobby. I liked him. A lot. And I missed him way more than I thought I would. I wondered if I was wrong for not hearing him out. What if there was a reasonable explanation for the women at church? What if everything was innocent and I was overreacting? But I knew what I seen. Tasha was rubbing his chest. There was something between them. And there was also something with the other one after church. His silence was admitting guilt. I didn't know I could be so jealous but seeing him interacting with other women did something to me. I wanted to call him but I couldn't get up the nerve to dial his number. Not because of the women but because of the look on his face when I told him me and Klan owned a house. He was hurt that I lied to him. If I called, I would have to answer all of the questions about my relationship with Klan and I wasn't ready to do that. So I mourned the relationship that could've been as I drove home from work, preparing myself to spend another night alone. After parking and locking my car, I let myself in the house and got the biggest shock of my life. My living room was filled with teddy bears, balloons, and flowers. The scene took my breath away and I immediately thought of Bobby. He must've followed me home. But how did he get in my house?

"Honey, I'm home."

When I heard the voice, my body turned ice cold like I was standing soaking wet in the middle of a blizzard. Klan. I turned and seen him walking out of the bedroom smiling. He held a single rose in his hand. My worst fear had come to life.

"Why you looking like that? You ain't happy to see me?"

I was shocked numb. Speechless. I wasn't happy to see him and I couldn't pretend. "When did you get out?"

"This morning. They dropped all my charges."

He walked towards me to give me the rose but I took a step backwards. "How did you get out? I thought you had a P.O hold."

"I told you I wasn't going back to jail. I did what I had to do. That's how it is out here. You do what you gotta do to get what you want and keep yo ass out of them people jail. But what's up with you? You ain't happy that I'm out? You look like you wanted me to stay in jail."

"Klan, I told you that-"

He closed the distance between us quickly. "Oh, you thought you was leaving a nigga? You thought blocking my calls was gon end the last three years?"

I took another step back and hit the wall. I had run out of room. "I don't want to do this anymore. I don't want to be controlled and told what to do. "

He got mad. "So, what the fuck is you sayin, Charlene? Huh? Say it, nigga. Say it."

Tears burned down my cheeks as I gathered the courage to stand up to him. "You had the police break down my door and treat me like a criminal. They tried to rape me. Do you really think I'm supposed to act like everything is all good? I'm done, Klan. I'm done."

He cocked his head to the side and mean mugged me. I thought he was about to hit me but he wrapped me in his arms and held me. "I'm sorry for everything I put you through. I know I been fucking up but I promise I'ma change."

I didn't know what to say or do so I remained stiff as a board as he held me. I wasn't expecting him home nor did I expect the apology and promise to change. But I had heard all this before. The change would last less than a week and then I would be miserable all over again. I couldn't keep playing this game. I had to end it.

"I can't do this no more, Klan. I'm done."

He stumbled back like my words had wounded him. There was a deep sadness on his face. "So, you sayin its over?" The pain in his eyes and in his voice touched a place deep inside me that would always love Klan. But I was done.

"It's over."

His head drooped down until his chin was touching his chest. He let out a couple deep exhales and I waited on edge to see how he was going to respond. When he looked at me again, a fiery rage burned inside his eyes. "You fucked somebody while I was locked up?"

I almost choked. The question came out of the blue and I wasn't expecting it. I took a split second to figure out if I should tell him the truth. And that small pause was enough for him to make me guilty.

"Bitch, I'ma kill you!"

He wrapped both hands around my neck, lifted me in the air and squeezed. I tried to pry his hands lose but he was too strong. He had me suspended in the air choking the life out of my body. I looked in his eyes and the Klan I knew was gone. A monster was staring back. His eyes told the hurt, betrayal, and hate that his lips couldn't speak. When the air ran out of my lungs, my face grew hotter and my chest started burning. I kicked him a couple of times but it did nothing. My body started going limp and I was on the verge of passing out. Then he let me go. I hit the ground like dead weight and sucked in deep breaths. I was too weak to move so all I could do is watch as Klan destroyed everything in the living room. He flipped over couches, broke tables, lamps, and the TV. Punched holes in the walls. Then he stood in the midst of everything that he destroyed and stared down at me like he wanted to kill me. It reminded me of King Kong tearing up New York City.

"Get the fuck out before I kill yo bitch ass."

"Please, Klan-"

He grabbed a chair and threw it at the wall. "Bitch, get the fuck out!"

I grabbed my phone and keys and got the hell out of that house.

Chapter 24

Nephew

I spent most of the next day trying not to think about Charlene. That's how I found out I wasn't as strong as I thought I was. I thought Simone breaking bad got me over being sick about a female but it didn't. I wasn't in love with Charlene nor was I heart broken about how things ended, but I did miss her. She was cool as hell. Not being able to talk to her made me feel some type of way. I wanted to call but the comment about buying a house with her boyfriend made my mind wander and kept my fingers from dialing. She lied about living with her parents and didn't tell me that she owned a house with her boyfriend. If she would be deceitful this early there was no telling what she would do later. She probably wasn't even really leaving him. That's why she didn't want me to know where she lived. Simone, Jasmine, Tasha, and Charlene had all shown me that females were scandalous. The last thing I needed was another lesson. The phone ringing pulled me from thoughts of being betrayed by women. It was my mom. Her and Jamie had gone to some new soul food restaurant. I didn't feel like going out so I let them go alone. She was probably calling to see if I wanted them to bring me something home.

"Hey, ma."

"Bobby, they shot him!!"

Her words sent a chill through my body. "What you talking about?"

"Somebody shot, Jamie," She cried. "Oh my God, somebody shot Jamie."

I shot up in bed. "What happened? Where you at?"

"We at the gas station waiting for the ambulance. I can't believe they shot him, baby."

"What gas station y'all at?"

"On Hopkins and Hampton. Oh, my God. Hang on, Jamie. Hang on. Please don't leave me."

I jumped up and ran to the living room to find my moms keys. "I'm on my way, mama. I'm on my way."

I hopped in the RAV4 and drove like I was a NASCAR racer. Jamie got shot at the same gas station that Jewels tried to kill me at. I wondered if he somehow knew who my people were and got at them because he couldn't get at me. Or was this random? Milwaukee was dangerous and the streets didn't care if you were a civilian. When I pulled up to the gas station the police had the scene taped off and were talking to witnesses. I didn't see my mom or Jamie. I called her to find out where they were. "Bobby, where you at?"

"I'm at the gas station. Where y'all at?"

"We in the ambulance on the way to Saint Josephs."

"Okay. I'm on my way. What happened?"

"We stopped to get some gas. I was in the gas station and I heard shooting and when I looked outside somebody was pulling off in Jamie's car. I came out and seen him laying on the ground. I can't believe they shot him over the car."

When she broke down crying, I felt her pain in my soul. "Its gon be a'ight, mama. How many times they shoot him."

"Twice in the chest. They got him hooked up to tubes and trying to stop the bleeding. I need to call the pastor. Come to the hospital."

I thought the worst during the drive. A chest shot could kill him. If Jamie died, it would crush my mother. He was the only man she had been with since my father. The only man I knew as a father. I never thought this would happen to us. I thought once I changed my life things would become easy. But that wasn't the case. Life was harder for me now than it had ever been. I just hoped Jamie survived.

My mother was in the waiting room when I got to the hospital. She was crying and covered with Jamie's blood. She ran over and buried her face in my chest. "Oh my, God, Bobby, it was so much blood. I don't know what I'ma do if I lose him."

"Where is he?"

"He in the surgery. Oh my God. Oh my God."

I hated when my mother was in pain. It pissed me off and made me want to find whoever did this and bring them pain. Pastor Sims and other members of the church began showing up to offer up prayers and support. Four hours later a bald brown skinned man wearing a white coat approached our family. We all stood.

"Mrs. Andrews?"

"Yes."

"Hi. I'm Doctor Thamus. I operated on your husband. I'm afraid to tell you that he lost a considerable amount of blood and we did everything that we could to save his life." He cleared his throat, leaving us hanging. "Excuse me. That was a bad time to clear my throat. But, Jamie will be good as new in a few weeks. The bullets missed all of his major organs and vessels and arteries. His lungs were punctured but he'll be fine. He just needs to rest."

"Oh, thank God!" My mother cried.

We all praised and thanked God.

"When can we see him?" I asked.

"He's being taken to the room as we speak. When everything is ready, the nurse will come get you. I'm afraid that only immediate family will be able to see him tonight."

"Thank you so much, doctor. God bless you, sir," My mom cried while shaking his hand.

When the doctor left we said another prayer with the church family before they left. A male nurse came to get us a few minutes later. We didn't talk during the elevator ride.

Nervous energy and the need for revenge filled me. We walked in the room and found Jamie asleep. There were a couple of wires hooked up to his chest and an IV in his arm. He had always looked young and strong but now that death had almost took him, he looked old and weak. I sat in the chair next to the bed while my mother curled up next to him and cried. The nurse said he was going to be out for a while because of the medications so I got comfortable and eventually fell asleep. I woke up when my mom screamed.

"Hey, baby. Oh my God! Bobby, Jamie is awake."

"Hey, baby. Did you miss me?" Jamie asked weakly.

"We thought we was gon lose you, baby."

"And get rid of me that easy. Never," he cracked, trying to make light of the situation.

I got up and walked over to the bedside. "Hey, man. How you feeling?"

"Like hell but I'll live."

"What happened? Did you see who did it?"

"I was pumping gas and then the next thing I know this light skinned dude walks up, pulls out a gun and told me to give him my car. I told him calm down and I'll give him a ride to wherever he wanna go. Then he just started shooting me."

Hearing the story pissed me off even more. "Do you know what he looked like? Tattoos or something?"

"He was really light skinned like he was mixed with something, about our height, had gold teeth, and some brushed waves that was really spinning. And he had a gold gun. That's what surprised me was the gun."

My insides boiled as I listened to Jamie describe the man that shot him. The gold teeth and light skin could've been anybody in Milwaukee. But the gun told it all. I remembered B-Eazy shooting at Jewels with the golden gun. And the gas station on Hopkins and Hampton was his stomping grounds. Jamie went on to thank God for saving his life but I wasn't feeling thankful. I wanted to hurt B-Eazy.

"I'ma run to the cafeteria and grab something to snack on. I'll be right back," I said.

Jamie and my mom were so focused on thanking God that they didn't see the murder in my eyes. I hopped in the RAV4 and drove back to the gas station. During the drive I thought of a plan. The police were gone so that meant the goons were back outside. I parked on the side of the gas station and waited to see if I would run into someone from my past. Ten minutes into the wait a short skinny dude dressed in all black walked up. Recognition flashed in his eyes. Part one of my plan was about to fall into place. I flicked my lights and rolled the window to get his attention.

"Corey, this Nephew. Come holla at me."

He smiled as he walked over. "Nephew, what's good, my nigga?"

"I'm good. Just seeing what's going on out here. Get in and let me holla at you."

"I hear you livin out that good book now," he said as he hopped in the passenger seat.

"News travel through the hood fast, huh?"

"Yeah. B-Eazy said you almost got whacked out here a while back. What happened?"

"I tore it up out here before I got knocked. Er'body don't respect change. I wanted to ask you about B-Eazy. You seen him?"

He laughed. "Fool just got the hood hot takin a nigga Benz. He out here flexin somewhere."

It took everything in me to not show my hand. I was boiling inside but I kept it under control. "Dog is a fool. You got a heat on you?"

He gave a suspicious look. "Yeah. Why? I thought you was living that righteous life now?"

"I am. But I need to hold that for a minute."

He laughed. "You joking, right?"

I looked him in his eyes and allowed him to see my pain and anger. "I'm not playing. I need that."

He paused, trying to decide what to do next. I knew the look. He didn't want to come off the pistol. In the hood, you didn't let nobody hold your banger. It was like an extension of you. An arm. Leg. Your heart. Without it you were naked. "Man, Nephew, you know you my nigga. I grew up watching you and the big homies get down. I know you a demon. And one thing yall taught me is to never give up my shit."

I respected what he said. That was the first rule of street. But I wasn't taking no for an answer. I went in my pocket and handed him five hundred dollars. "I need that heat, lil brah."

He counted the money and then looked at me, weighing his options. "You lucky you my nigga."

$$$

I glanced at the time on my phone. 10:22 PM. I had been looking for B-Eazy for almost three hours. I had gone through all his known hang out spots in the hood but no one knew where he was or how to find him. But I did learn that he was dipping through a chick named Amy's house. I didn't know her so instead of approaching her house, I stayed parked a couple houses away. I had been watching and waiting for a little over an hour. I would wait for as long as it took. Hours, days, months, or years. It didn't matter. I was getting my lick back. Wasn't nobody touching my family and getting away with it. An eye for an eye. Just like it said in the Bible. I sat in the truck caressing the black 9 milli like it was a super bad female. I didn't want to let it go. It felt good in my hand. Like it belonged. I could feel the power to take a life surging through the metal. I could also feel the conflict from wanting to kill surging through me. The Bible tells us to leave revenge for God. That he would fight our battles. But I couldn't let this go. I wanted to look in his face when I pulled the trigger. If I was caught, prison was sure. I hadn't even been out three months and I was about to do something that could send me back to Waupun with a life bid. Or I could die. My mom, Jamie, Pastor Sims, and our whole church family would be mad at me. They would all tell me to leave it to God. But I couldn't turn the other cheek. Not this time. B-Eazy had to get his. My phone ringing pulled me from thoughts of consequences. It was Little.

"Yeah."

"What's good, Nephew?"

I let out a long angry breath. "Man, Little. It's all bad, brah. I'm bout to kill this nigga."

"What is you talking about? What happened?"

"B-Eazy. He popped Jamie and took the Benz. Corey said he seen him in it."

"B-Eazy popped Jamie? Why would he do that to yo pops?"

"I don't think he knew who he was."

"Is he a'ight?"

"He good. But when I see B-Eazy, I'm puttin em down."

"Cmon, Nephew. We don't draw like that no more. We walking a different path."

"Man, Little... I can't let em get away with this one. I can't."

"Awe, cmon, brah. We better than this. You better than this."

"I'm not."

"Damn, brah."

We were silent for a moment.

"I can't let you do this by yo'self. Tell me where you at. We for life."

"I'm sittin in moms truck on 36th and Glendale."

"I'm on my way, Nephew. Don't do nothing til I get there."

I hung up the phone and went back to watching Amy's house. When the front door opened, my heart started beating faster. When B-Eazy stepped on the front porch, my whole body began to shake. Something dark started growing inside of me. I wanted to hop out the car shooting but I could miss.

Plus, he was strapped and that could lead to a shootout. I needed to get close so I could give him a facial. I wanted to see the fear in his eyes before he died and I wanted him to know I shot him. So I tucked the burner in my waist and hopped out the truck. He was walking down the porch steps when he spotted me and went for his waist.

"B-Eazy, this Nephew. Chill, fam," I called, never breaking stride.

"Awe, man, you can't be creeping up on a nigga like that. You know how it is out here," he slurred. "What's good, fool?"

"I need to holla at you."

"Them ribs must be touching," he laughed.

When I was close enough, I swung. He never seen it coming and the blow landed on his right temple. He stumbled backwards and reached for his waist. I rushed him and speared him like I was a wrestler. We fell on the grass and began rolling around. He was still trying to pull his pistol so I grabbed his arm with both hands and tried to take it. He punched me on the chin and rocked me a little but I never let him get the gun out. We rolled around in the grass until I got the advantage and climbed on top. I grounded and pounded him like I was a UFC fighter. He stopped trying to pull the gun and covered up. That's when I pulled my pistol and pointed it in his face. Terror lit his eyes.

"Nephew, what you on, nigga?"

I slapped him with the gun. "You shot my pops, bitch ass nigga!!"

"Fuck you talkin bout, nigga? I don't even know yo pops."

"You took his Benz, nigga."

Recognition flashed in his eyes. "I didn't know that was yo pops. The streets ain't got no sympathy."

His words triggered me. He almost killed the only man I knew as a father and the lack of remorse made it easier for me to pull the trigger. The world began to close in all around me and my senses were heightened. I could taste the air, smell B-Eazy's fear, and hear sirens screaming in the distance. A vision of Jamie in the hospital flashed in my head. I squeezed the trigger.

Click.

B-Eazy's eyes grew wide and then we both realized the gun jammed. I tried to cock the slide back but he punched me and bucked his hips, throwing me off. I reached to grab him but he rolled away and shot to his feet. He was going for the gold gun and I couldn't stop him. I cocked the gun and ejected the bad bullet. When I looked up, B-Eazy was pointing the gun at me. I froze up and he snatched the pistol from me.

"You should'da stayed in church, nigga."

He pointed both guns at me and I watched his fingers apply pressure to the triggers.

"Freeze! Put the gun down!"

The voice cut through the air like a torpedo through water. B-Eazy froze. I looked around and seen two police officers near the house next door pointing guns at B-Eazy.

"Put the gun down right now!" They ordered.

B-Eazy didn't turn around to acknowledge them. Instead he smirked and shook his head. He wasn't going to jail. He was holding court in the street. He spun around and started shooting at the police. They fired back. B-Eazy's body jerked as the bullets hit him in the chest and stomach. He fell to the ground next to me and started moaning.

"Don't move! Don't you fucking move!" The cops yelled as they approached.

I lifted my hands and turned to look at B-Eazy. He was choking on blood and it was beginning to soak his shirt. And then he was gone.

Chapter 25

Charlene

The murderous look on Klan's face popped into my head as soon as I opened my eyes. I thought he was going to kill me. I couldn't believe that he let me walk out of that house. I was so thankful to be alive. How could someone that claimed to love me bring me so close to death? I reached for my neck to rub the bruises left by his giant hands. They hurt and my voice was a little hoarse. What kind of love almost kills you? I sat up and looked around. I was in Lana's living room. I slept on the couch because I didn't want to go home. Klan could find me there. I also didn't want my dad to see my neck. He would've tried to kill Klan and I didn't want him to get hurt. I reached for my phone to check the time. 5:37 AM. Normally I would be getting ready for work but I wasn't going in today. I needed to take some time off for me. I needed time to heal. I texted my boss and told him that I had food poisoning then checked the missed calls and texts hoping to see one from Nephew. I had no such luck. They were all from Klan. I read a few. They started off angry but then turned to apologies. I blocked his number and then sat my phone down. I closed my eyes and replayed him choking me.

"Charlene, you woke?" Lana asked.

I opened my eyes as she sat next to me on the couch. "Yeah."

"How are you feeling?"

"I'm okay. My throat hurts."

"Do you need me to get you anything?"

"No. I'm good."

"I have to get ready for work. You can stay here for as long as you want. Are you sure you don't need nothing? I got some more muscle relaxers."

"Yeah, I'll take another muscle relaxer. I need to rest."

She touched the bruise on my neck. "I hope somebody fucks his ass up. I hate niggas that hit women. Fucking coward."

"I don't care what happens to him. I just want to be left alone."

"What you gon do about the house? I know you not about to let him have it. It's in your name. Sell it and keep the money. That's how much it cost to be with him for all those years. Make his ass pay."

"I don't know what I'ma do with it. I don't know nothing right now."

"I know you done with his ass. That's what really matters is that you done. Right?" She was looking at me to make sure I wasn't thinking about getting back with him.

"I'm so done."

"Good. I'm going to get ready for work. I'll grab them pills for you."

When Lana left, I popped another pill and drifted back to sleep. I was awakened around 3:30 by my phone. It was a text from my mom telling me to call her.

"Hey, mom."

"Klan came by the house and is calling around looking for you. What is going on?"

"We got into a fight last night and I left him."

"A fight? Did he hit you?"

"No, but he choked me."

"Oh, dios mio! Are you okay? Did you call the police?"

"No. I'm not trying to go that route. I just want to move on with my life."

"I thought he was going to be in jail for a while?"

"So did I but he got out yesterday. I came home from work and he was in the house. He worked out some kind of deal for them to let him out."

"Where are you? Why didn't you come home?"

"I didn't want him to find me so I spent the night at Lana's house."

"Well, your coming back home today and we're going to sit down with your father and talk about what to do next because you are done with him."

"I've been done with him, mom. I told him it was over while he was locked up and then again yesterday. He choked me because he figured out that I slept with Bobby."

"Do they know each other?"

"No. He asked me if I slept with somebody and I didn't answer fast enough so he figured it out and choked me."

"I hate that son of a bitch. He's going to get his karma. Did you talk to Bobby about this yet?"

"No. We aren't talking right now."

"Why? What happened?"

I let out a frustrated breath. "It's complicated, mom."

"More complicated than Klan choking you?"

"No. It's just that I got jealous of some girls he was talking to in church and we had words about it. I also never told him that I lived a few blocks from the church in the house that I bought with Klan until we were having those words. The first time we went out he picked me up from your house and I told him that's where I lived. He was kinda hurt when he found out the truth."

"Who were the girls in church?"

"The girl Tasha was rubbing his chest when I walked in and the other one tried to talk to him after church was over. He said it was all a misunderstanding and that Tasha is about to marry somebody. But I know what I saw. I think there is something between them."

"It does sound complicated. But she's about to get married. What if it really was a misunderstanding? Do you think he is a player?"

"I don't know. He said I was the only girl that he slept with since he got out. I kind of believe him."

"Well, I think you should probably take a little time to figure out you before you get into another relationship. And I also think that you should hear his explanation. It could be a misunderstanding. If you think he is bullshitting, just move on with your life."

"Yeah. I'm going to think about it."

"Do that. Also call your dad and tell him what happened. If you don't, I will. And bring your butt home."

After hanging up with mom, I decided to text Bobby.

'Can we talk?'

I chipped the paint from my fingernails as I waited for him to call back. After five minutes and no response, I checked to see if he looked at the text. He hadn't. So I called. He didn't answer. I stared at my phone screen trying to decide what to do next. Was he still mad? Was it really over before it began? All because I didn't tell him I lived with Klan? But he didn't seem vindictive or the type to hold a grudge. He was nice, understanding, and calm. But what if he didn't like liars? His track record with women hadn't been that good. What if he was comparing me to the ones that did him wrong? I needed to explain myself and hear what he had to say about the women at church. I needed to know if God created these opportunities for us to be together. So I cleaned up, jumped in my car, and drove to his house. There were no cars in the driveway, and nobody answered the door. He got off work at three o'clock and it was already past four. Since I didn't have anything else to do, I sat in the car and waited. After thirty minutes and no one came home, I decided to try my last resort. The City of God Church. I was nervous about going so close to my house knowing that Klan was out and about but I did it anyway. I needed to talk to Bobby. I parked in the back of the church and looked around nervously as I tried the back door. It was locked so I went around to the front door. It was open. The sanctuary was empty so I headed for the offices down the hall.

"Can I help you?"

I turned and seen Tasha. She had come from the bathroom and the way she was looking at me told that she knew who I was. "Hi. My name is Charlene. I was wondering if anybody has seen Bobby?"

She looked me up and down like women do when we judge one another. "And, how do you know him?"

"We're friends."

She sucked the back of her teeth, jealousy in her eyes. "Did you try calling him?"

I wanted to snap at her for asking me a dumb ass question. Like I wouldn't try to call him before popping up in church on a Tuesday. I seen the type of games she was playing so I got on her level. "Yeah. He didn't answer. And I went by his house but him nor Mr. or Mrs. Andrews was home."

Her top lip twitched a little. She didn't like that I dropped names. "Oh. Well, since you know the whole family, how come you don't know that Jamie got shot last night and Bobby is in jail?"

My heart almost jumped out of my chest. "What?"

She gave a devilish smile. "Yeah. Bobby back in jail. Sad too cause he letting all of that go to waste."

She looked happy to deliver the bad news and that pissed me off. Especially because we were in church and she was supposed to be a Christian. "Why you seem so happy that he locked up? What's wrong with you?"

She rolled her eyes. "Girl, that boy ain't who you think he is. He got all y'all fooled but not me."

"What does that mean?"

"Ask yo man."

I thought about punching her but a man came from one of the offices. "Hey, baby. I thought I heard somebody out here. Who is that?"

Tasha lost all of her attitude. "Hey, honey. I was coming to surprise you when I ran into Bobby's friend, Charlene. She was looking for him."

"Hi, Charlene. I'm Greg. Tasha is my fiancé," He introduced, extending his hand. "What happened to Bobby and his family is tragic."

I wanted to tell Greg the truth about his fiancé but Bobby and his family was more important. "What happened? "

"Well, I don't know too many details but Jamie got carjacked and Bobby went to confront the man that did it. There was some kind of altercation, and the police killed the car jacker."

"What? So, why is Bobby locked up?"

He shrugged. "That's all I know. We're still waiting to hear more."

I was stunned. "Um, do you know how to reach Bobby or his family?"

"Yeah. They're at Saint Josephs. I'm sure you can visit. Tell them you're from the church."

"Thank you so much, Greg. You're an angel."

"It's no problem. They are a good family."

I looked at Tasha. She smiled at me but I could see the true hate in her eyes.

"Aren't you about to get married?"

She showed her ring. "Yes."

I turned to Greg. "She doesn't deserve you."

He smiled, thinking I was giving a compliment. "No. I actually don't deserve her."

I shook my head. "No. She doesn't deserve you. She's not who you think she is. Ask her about Bobby."

Tasha looked like she wanted to kill me.

Greg's eyes grew wide and he turned to his fiancé. "I knew there was something going on with you and Bobby."

I walked away and left them to deal with their issues.

I left the church and drove to Saint Joseph's Hospital. I talked to the woman at the help desk and she told me what room Jamie was in. I was nervous as hell about going to see Bobby's stepdad. I didn't know if they talked about me or if I would be welcomed. But I had find a way to talk to Bobby. I needed answers about Tasha, answer any questions he had for me, and find out when he was getting out of jail. Jamie was on the third floor. I tapped on the door lightly.

"Come in." He was sitting up in bed watching TV and looked surprised to see me.

"Hi," I waved.

"Hey. Charlene, right?"

"Yes."

"Have a seat. You're looking for Bobby, huh?"

"Yes. I've been trying to get in contact with him all morning so I went to the church and Greg and Tasha told me what happened. Are you okay?"

He opened the robe to show the bandage on his chest. "I'll be okay. Fool car jacked me. Doc says I'll heal. I'm more worried about Bobby. He has a couple years on parole and we don't know if he's being charged with anything. He could go back to prison for a long time."

"Have you talked to him?"

"He called this morning to tell us that he was locked up and needed a lawyer. That was it."

"When he calls again, will you tell him to call me?"

"I will." He looked at the bruises on my neck. "You okay?"

"It's part of what I wanted to talk to Bobby about."

"What happened?"

"I had a fight with my ex yesterday. I broke it off with him and he got violent."

"You were seeing him and Bobby at the same time?"

"No. My ex was locked up when I started talking to Bobby. He got out yesterday but I didn't know. When I got home he was in the house. We bought it together and he has keys. I want to be with Bobby but we haven't talked since church on Sunday."

"Yeah, I heard a little bit about that. He says you lied to him about living with your ex."

"I did. But that was because he had his friends watching my house and I didn't want them to run into Bobby. They rob people and I didn't want your son to get involved with them so I told him that I lived with my parents. I lied to protect him. It was wrong, but I wasn't trying to be deceitful."

"That sounds like a good reason to lie. I hope that y'all can work out whatever issues you are having because my son really likes you. He thinks God brought y'all together."

That made me smile. "Really?"

He nodded. "He told me some of the things you have in common and that he knows your dad. The one thing that we know is that there is no such thing as coincidences in Christianity. God's plan is perfect. If you two are meant to be together, you will."

Chapter 26

Bobby

I couldn't believe I was back in jail. All of the changes I made and all of the people that I let down who had been praying for me rang in my head like a bell on top of the church. I swore that I would never see the inside of a jail cell again when I left Waupun. But less than 90 days after my release I was sitting on a hard concrete bench inside of a holding cell. I stared at the wall in front of me and continued thinking about B-Eazy. Even though death had been calling his name for a long time, I was the reason he finally met the reaper. If I hadn't tried to get revenge, his blood wouldn't be on my hands or staining my conscience. I didn't pull the trigger but I might as well had. I wanted to kill him. I wanted him dead for what he did to Jamie. And now he was. I had killed him. The clicking of the lock on the door pulled me from my thoughts. A police officer stuck his head in the room.

"Peterson, your lawyer is here."

I got up and followed the cop down the hall to a small room. A short female with blonde tipped dreadlocks sat at the table. When I walked in she stood up and extended a hand.

"Hi, Bobby. My name is Marissa Connely. Are you okay?"

"I'm good."

"Your parents hired me. Have a seat. I talked to the detectives, but I want you to tell me what happened."

I shook my head as thoughts of Jamie in the hospital bed and B-Eazy laying on the ground flashed in my head. "B-Eazy carjacked my pops. I went to confront him and we started fighting. He was about to shoot me but the police killed him."

"Did you have a gun?"

I paused and wondered if I should lie. Admitting to having a gun would get me sent to jail for sure. But as a Christian I had to tell the truth. "Yeah."

"Did you tell the police that you had a gun or did anybody see you with the gun?"

"No. I didn't talk to the police and wasn't no witnesses."

She cocked her head to the side and lifted an eyebrow. "So, you didn't have a gun?"

I shrugged, unsure how to answer.

"We only admit to what they can prove. If nobody seen you with a gun or they didn't catch you with one, then you didn't have one. Right?"

I liked the way she thought. "Right."

"So, the victim had two guns. Give me some history? How did you find him? Did you know him?"

"I'm from the neighborhood. We used to run together back in the day. I changed my life around when I got locked up but I had a run in with him the second day I got out. He saved my life. Somebody that I robbed seen me at the gas station and was about to shoot me but B-Eazy started shooting at him. When my pops described the person that shot him and that he had a gold gun, I knew it was him. He had the same gun when he saved my life. So I went to look for him. I asked around the hood and they told me that he be kicking it at Amy's house. I waited until he came out and confronted him."

She nodded and took notes. "Okay. So, I'm going to try to do what I can to get you out of here. Right now they just have you on a P.O hold and are trying to figure out if they can charge you with anything. I can't do anything about that because your parole officer has to do their investigation and I can't represent you for that. But I am going to talk to the police to see if they can just wash their hands with you and not charge you with anything. You didn't have a gun or break any laws. Basically all you did was confront the guy that shot your dad. That's not a crime. Sit tight."

When Marissa left, I was put back in the holding cell. I prayed and paced until she showed up at the door an hour later and told me the police weren't charging me with anything. If I didn't have the parole hold, I would be free. That was a bittersweet moment. I was happy not being charged with anything but pissed that I was still locked up. When she left, I was taken to the booking room and booked into the county jail. After being fingerprinted I went to the phone banks to call my parents and tell them the news.

"Hey, son." Jamie answered. "Your mom is right here."

"You okay?" my mom asked.

"Yeah. They not charging me with nothing but I got a P.O hold. I wasn't supposed to have no police contact. They could send me back to prison."

She sounded outraged. "For what? You didn't do nothing?"

"I don't know. I guess that's just how they do, ma. I need you to call my P.O and see what's up."

" We will as soon as I get off the phone with you. They better not send you back to jail. We ain't going for that," Jamie said.

"I feel you. But I just can't stop thinking that I got him killed. Even though he shot Jamie, I still feel bad about it. Watching him die is having some kind of effect on me."

"Don't let it affect you, son. For one, you didn't get him killed. He did that to himself. And for two, he shot my husband so we shouldn't feel bad for him. He got what he had coming. God took care of that."

"Your mom is right, Bobby. He was a proud sinner and you know the streets only get you two things. In jail or dead. He made his own bed."

"I hear y'all but it just feel kinda heavy on me."

"Let it go, son," mom said. "Pray about it and let it go."

"You can't change it. What's done is done. Dwelling on it won't change nothing. Do like your mom said. Pray about it and let it go."

I knew they were right but watching someone die wasn't easy to let go. "Okay."

"Oh, and Charlene said to call her. She came by to visit me a little while ago."

Hearing her name made my heart beat faster. "She came by the hospital?"

"Yeah. She had been trying to call you and then went by the church and they told her what happened. She had some bruises on her neck so y'all have a lot to talk about."

That surprised me. "What that mean? What were the bruises from?"

"Her ex boyfriend. Said she broke up with him and he got physical."

The explanation made me feel some type of way. "She told me he was locked up."

"He was but somehow got out. Give her a call and hear her out."

After talking to my mom and Jamie, I took a moment to get my thoughts together before calling Charlene.

"Hi, Bobby. How you holding up in there?"

"I been in here before. Nothing I can't handle. How are you?"

"I'm worried about you. Are they going to let you out?"

"I don't know. I got a P.O hold. Police contact is a no-no. They gotta do they investigation. The good news is I don't got no charges."

"I hope they let you out. That'll be so wrong if they keep you for confronting the guy that shot your dad."

"I hope they let me out, too. I haven't even been out for three months. I swore that I was never coming back. I can't believe I'm back in here. I was so blinded by anger that I couldn't think straight. Now that everything is settled, I regret leaving the hospital and going to find him. I should've let God deal with it all."

"We live and we learn."

We were quiet for a moment. I fished. "How have you been?"

She let out a breath and took her time responding. "I'm still trying to figure that out."

"What does that mean?"

"I'm talking about you."

I waited for her to say more but she didn't. "Jamie told me you got into it with your ex-boyfriend. I thought he was locked up."

"He was but got out. I don't know how either. He was supposed to have a P.O hold but somehow he was in the house when I got off work yesterday. I told him it was over and he asked me if I messed around with anybody while he was locked up. I guess I didn't answer fast enough because he started choking me. I thought he was going to kill me. Right before I passed out, he let me go."

"Did you call the police?"

"No. I don't want to go that route. Klan is really in the streets. If I call the police, I think he might kill me."

Hearing the explanation pissed me off. It angered me even more that I was locked up and couldn't do anything to help her. "So, what are you going to do? Don't you own a house with him?"

"I do. But I don't know what to do about it. For now I'm going to move back in with my parents until I figure it out."

"Are you really done with him?"

"Yes, I am. He put his hands on me and he's been controlling and abusing me for years. I'm done-done. I've been done. That's why I slept with you. I'm sorry that I lied about where I lived but I did it to protect you. He had his friends watching my house and I didn't want you to run into them. I wasn't trying to be sneaky. His friends came over before and he threatened to have them come over while he was locked up."

I took a moment to digest what she said. She was making it clear that things between her and Klan were over. I also believed the reason she lied was to protect me. "Okay. I believe you."

"And now that I've told you the truth, I need you to tell me the truth about you and Tasha. I seen her at church earlier today and she was acting like there is something between you and her."

"Man, Tasha is a real-life nasty freak. She been tryna get with me since I got out but I didn't want to cross that line because that's Pastor Sims daughter. I went by their house to meet with the pastor and almost got with her but I canceled at the last minute. My conscious wouldn't let me do it. But she did um, swallow my seed."

"Wait. She did what?"

"During dinner she had her foot between my legs. It had been a while since I got off and it happened at the dinner table. "

Charlene bust out laughing. "Are you for real?"

"I'm serious. I went to the bathroom to clean up and she bust in and damn near tried to rape me. I didn't let it happen so she grabbed my boxers and licked some of my nut. That's all that happened between us. That's my word."

She bust out laughing again. Laughed way harder than I thought was necessary. "Oh my God, Bobby. That is so funny. And nasty too. I was not expecting to hear that but, okay. As long as you're not lying about sleeping with her, we're good. But what about the other one? The one that approached you after the service?"

I was feeling good that she believed me so I cracked a joke. "I didn't know shorty but she was definitely feeling me."

"Really, Bobby. You got jokes when this is a serious moment?"

"I'm sorry but I couldn't help. It was good to hear you laugh and I wanted to make you laugh some more. I need to laugh too so I can keep from crying about being back in jail. But in all seriousness, her name is Shawntale and I never seen her before that day. Tasha tried to hook me up with her and another girl before the service. But I don't want none of them. I feel like God brought me and you together for a reason and I want to find out what it is."

She laughed again. Not a funny laugh but a relieved one. "That's good to hear, Bobby, because I think the same as you. God don't make no mistakes, right?"

"God is perfect."

Chapter 27

Charlene

A week had gone by since I moved in with my parents and to my surprise and relief, Klan hadn't come looking for me. A part of me felt like he got the hint and let me go but another part of me didn't want to let my guard down. He was Crazy with a capitol C and there was no telling what he was capable of. So I would continue to be careful when I was out and watch my back at all times. Another reason he probably hadn't come looking for me was because I gave him the house. I talked to a lawyer and had him draft up the paperwork for the transfer of property. The house was the only thing connecting us and I didn't want to fight him for it. He paid most of the money so he could have it. I just wanted to be free from him and move on with my life.

"I don't understand westerns, daddy. Why don't the police just take the people's guns so there won't be that much shooting?"

He looked at me like he wanted to push me off the couch because I just told him I was voting for Trump. My dad loved old western tv shows and movies. When he wasn't being a workaholic he binge watched them.

"Because its the wild wild west, baby. In those times everybody had a gun. Even the preachers. And they settled their problems according to the wild wild west code. The fastest gun wins."

"Its still like that today. If they would've took the guns back then we probably wouldn't have the problems that we have today."

"Yeah, you have a point. People out there killing each other like its going out of style. That's why I'm glad you moved back home and out the hood. We were worried about you some nights. That old boyfriend of yours was bad but ain't nobody badder than a bullet."

"Awe, daddy got a soft spot," I gushed, reaching over and hugging him.

"Now you done went too far. Get off me. Ain't nothing about me soft," he laughed. "But seriously, princess, I'm so happy that you got away from that no good thug. I still want to shoot him for putting his hands on you. He's lucky I promised your mother that I wouldn't."

"Thank you for not wasting your bullets on him, dad, or for ending up in jail. I don't know why I stayed with him so long. I guess I thought I could change him. I look at you and mom and I want that."

"Well, its hard to hit a home run the first time you go up to bat."

I had no idea what that meant. "What?"

"Sometimes with this love thing you don't get it right the first or second time. Took me three tries on the wheel of love before I found your mother and got it right. I know Latrell and Klan didn't work but maybe the next ride on the love train will lead you to true love and happiness."

"Dang, daddy. You killing it with the sentimental stuff tonight. Wait til mom come back home and hear how you been giving me lessons on love."

"Shoot, your mother knows all about my lessons on love. Why you think we been married for over twenty years. I puts it down, baby."

"Daddy!" I yelled, pushing him. "I don't need to hear nothing about what you be putting down. Ewww."

"I was just telling you about love, baby," he laughed.

My phone rang and gave me the much needed distraction from my dad's lessons on love. The screen said it was a call from Waupun. My eyes popped and pulse quickened. "Excuse me, dad," I said, getting up and heading for my room. My hands began to shake as I answered the phone. A recording told me that I was getting a prepaid call from Waupun Correctional Institution and to press 5 to accept. After a couple of deep breaths I accepted the call.

"Hello?"

"Is this Charlene?" Roland questioned.

Even thought I don't remember hearing his voice, it sounded familiar. "Yeah."

"Oh my, God. I can't believe it's you. Hey, baby girl. I've been wanting to talk to you for a long time."

"Hi, Roland," I said weakly, hoping he wouldn't ask why I didn't want to talk to him three years ago. "How are you doing?"

"I'm doing good now that I'm talking to you. I gotta be honest, Charlene. When I got that letter with your phone number I cried," he said, getting a little choked up. "I have been praying for this day for so long. God is good."

Hearing the emotion in his voice touched me. "Awe, Roland. You about to make me cry."

"Don't cry. I'm just a little emotional. And happy. So, I imagine you have a lot of questions, as do I. Where do you wanna start?"

I took a moment to think. "I guess we should start by talking about the man that made this happen. I met Bobby after he got out of Waupun. He was the one that told me about you."

"Are you talking about Bobby that we used to call Nephew?"

"Yeah. Him. He's my friend."

"Get out of here. You know Bobby? How is he doing? Is he still in the church?"

"Yeah. That's where we met. But he got locked up about a week ago."

"No. Bobby is back in jail?"

"Yeah. Somebody carjacked and shot his dad. He went to confront the guy that did it and they ended up fighting. The police killed the car jacker and locked up Bobby on a P.O hold. He's waiting for the revocation hearing."

"Awe, that is so sad. Do you talk to him?"

"Everyday. He's going to call again in the morning."

"Tell him I said what's up and that me and the rest of the brothers will be praying for him and to keep his head up. This is a small world. So, if you don't mind me asking, are you and Bobby dating?"

"Kinda, sorta, but not really."

"What does that mean?" He laughed.

"We're still figuring things out. We both believe that God made all of this happen for a reason and we're trying to get it right."

"Well, the one thing I know about God is that he don't make mistakes. What's supposed to happen will happen. Make no mistakes about that."

The words were a confirmation of everything that me and Bobby had been saying. It felt good to know that Roland thought the way we did. It made me feel a little more comfortable and want to know him more.

"Yeah. That's what we've been saying. Talking to you is like a confirmation of everything. When I first found out why you were locked up I prejudged you but now that I'm talking to you I'm seeing that I was wrong. I want to know more about you? Tell me how you grew up and about your side of the family."

I talked to Roland for thirty minutes and he answered every question that I asked. Even the hard ones about why he got life. His co-defendant shot the pregnant woman during a robbery. Both of them got life. I wanted to know more about him but we ran out of time. He promised that he would call back tomorrow and I was looking forward to the call. I was excited to get to know him. The doorbell ringing pulled me from thoughts about my biological father. I thought my dad would answer since he was in the living room watching TV but when it rang again I got up to answer. I seen that my dad wasn't in the living room as I walked to the door.

"Who is it?"

"Charlene, we need to talk."

Hearing Klan's voice stopped me stop in my tracks. I remembered him choking me and my body started trembling. I wasn't ready to face him. And the way I was feeling, I wasn't sure that I would ever be ready.

"Charlene?" He called.

I stayed stuck and looked around for my dad. I needed help. Then he appeared from the hall.

"Who's at the door?"

"Klan."

A snarl spread across my dad's face as he went for the door. "What is this fool doing by my house?" He snatched open the door and got in Klan's face. "What the fuck you want? Didn't she tell you it was over?"

Klan didn't look phased by my dad's aggressive demeanor. He stayed calm, glancing at me before looking my dad in the eyes. "I need to talk to Charlene."

"She don't got nothing to say to you. It's over. Leave her alone and don't come by my house no more. And if you ever put your hands on her again, I'ma put you down."

Anger flashed on Klan's face and he bit his lip like he was going to do something. Then he took a step back and calmed a little. "I'm sorry for what happened, Mr. Anderson. My anger got the best of me. But I just need to talk to her for five minutes. Please."

My dad looked at me over his shoulder then back at Klan. "She's standing right here. Say what you gotta say and then leave."

He looked past my dad. "Charlene, just talk to me for five minutes. I just need you to hear me out."

"You just told me that," My dad interrupted. "Say what you need to say or leave."

Klan stared at me and I could see the anger and frustration building in his eyes. If I didn't talk to him, he would probably snap. I didn't want that. "It's okay, dad. Let me talk to him."

"No. He is going to say what he has to say right now or get the fuck off my porch."

"Dad, please. Just let me do this."

My dad's face was a mask of anger. He didn't want to leave me alone with Klan. "Are you sure?"

"Yes. I'm sure."

He mean mugged Klan one more time. "I'm going to be standing in this living room window holding my 45. If you touch my daughter, I'm blowing your head off."

When my dad left, I stepped out on the porch and closed the door behind me. Me and Klan stared at each other for a moment. I could see regret and sorrow in his eyes.

"I need you to come back home, Charlene."

"I am at home. You can have the house. I'm done."

He looked towards the window. My dad stood in the window brandishing the gun. "Dude is being real extra."

"You put your hands on me. What you expect?"

"And I'm sorry for that. I didn't come over here on that. I don't want no smoke with yo people. I just want you back. I'm sorry. I'll do whatever it takes to get you back. Just say it."

"I can't do it no more. I wasn't happy with you. You hurt me. You controlled me. I can't go back to that."

"I'm sorry for that. For real. I'll leave the streets and go to church. I'll change. I won't try to control you no more. Shit ain't been right since you been gone. My mind is slipping and it feel like I'm going crazy. I need you."

Listening to Klan express himself and hearing how hard it has been for him was tugging at my heart. "I've heard all this before. You almost killed me. How can you do that to somebody you love?"

"It was a mistake. You know I got issues."

"And what happens the next time you make a mistake?"

"It won't be a next time. That's my word. I love you. Come back home." He reached for my hand but I pulled away. The pain of rejection shown in his eyes.

"It's over, Klan. I'm done. I just want this to be over. Let me go."

"You don't mean that. Let me make it up to you."

"You can't."

He tried to grab my hand again and I took a step back.

"For real, Charlene?"

I stood strong. "Leave, Klan. It's over."

He stared at me. Surprise, anger, and hurt played across his face. Then he looked towards the window and nodded. "I'ma leave before I say or do something that I can't take back. But I ain't letting you go, Charlene. You gon always be mine."

A shiver rattled my body as I watched him walk away. The declaration of love was really a threat and I was terrified. When I walked in the house my dad left the window and tucked the gun in his pocket.

"You okay, baby?"

"I don't know. I did the right thing but something still feels wrong."

He wrapped me in a hug. "That's okay. You just need some time to get over everything. There is a rainbow on the other side of the storm."

Chapter 28

Klan

I wasn't the kind of nigga that do sucka shit for a bitch but losing Charlene was fucking with a nigga mental. I had only been in love once before Charlene. Eva. I thought she was my ride or die but when I found out she was riding Nitty's dick, I tried to kill both they backstabbing asses. Nitty was my day one. Knew this nigga since we was rocking Batman drawers. If I had it, he had it and vise versa. He bussed his gun for me and I rode for him. Then he turned around and fucked my bitch. The shit cut me so deep that I didn't remember what happened until they was both laying on the floor bleeding. I popped him in the stomach and beat her ass so bad that she almost died. Nitty lied to the police and wouldn't cooperate. Eva pressed charges and went back home to Dallas. If I ever see her ass again, she gone pay with her life for sending me to the bing. *Punk ass bitch.*

I swore that I wasn't gon ever fall in love again. Going to prison for having a sucka attack wasn't something I wanted to be known for. I'ma beast in the streets and niggas know I don't fuck around. The last thing I want attached to my name is some punk ass shit like that. Plus, I know these hoes ain't loyal. Eva taught me that. So I turned my heart ice cold and smashed and dashed. Then I met Charlene. She was different than any female I ever fucked with. I was used to that rachet shit. Females that worshipped money and would cut a nigga throat for it. But Charlene was pretty, educated, and humble.

310

I never met a baddie that didn't act boojie until I met her. Didn't give a fuck if a nigga was fucked up because she seen the potential. She was a rare gem. I wanted my diamond back.

"So, when you wanna move on this nigga, Klan. You know the squad need to eat. J-Dot is a lick."

I looked over at Jax sitting in the passenger seat. My nigga was a real life demon. No conscience. Put niggas down for talking shit about his favorite rapper, NBA Young Boy. Had more bodies than me. The nigga was blood thirsty and probably a psychopath. And he also looked like Jax from the Mortal Kombat video game. If he gained fifty pounds of muscle and got some metal arms, the whole world would be in trouble. The nigga would be a terrorist.

"I don't wanna rush it. This move got the potential to change niggas lives. A quarter M. We gotta make sure we find that safe house. Kidnapping the nigga ain't a guarantee that he gon give it up. And them shooters stay active. We gotta do it right."

"Man, fuck that nigga shooters. We got shooters, too. Take the nigga mama and I bet he give it up."

I had to laugh. "We gon get that nigga, my boy. Trust and believe that. We just need to take a lil more time. Squeeze n'em got eyes on him. We gon move when they find that house."

He didn't like my answer but accepted it. He respected my slot as the leader of TMT, Take Money Team. Niggas wasn't eating like that while I was locked up but I got out and put niggas on. Made sure everybody had enough to eat and play with.

"Shit taking too long but I know you right. I got a couple plays that I can make until we hit."

I took my eyes off driving to see if I could see why this nigga was running through his money so fast. We just hit for sixty gs two days after I got out and split it four ways. Twelve gs wasn't that much money but a nigga shouldn't be broke a few weeks later. Especially since he didn't buy a car or jewelry. "You tapped out already?"

"BMF. Blowin money fast."

"What you blowing yo money on? I ain't seen no new whips or bussed down pieces."

He gave me a sideways look. "What up with all the questions, fam?"

"You my nigga and I'm just checkin on you."

"I'm good."

I knew better. Tone-Tone told me about Jax's growing habits but I wasn't gon speak on it until he was ready. I turned my attention back to driving when something caught my eye. "What the fuck?"

Jax became alert. "What happened?"

We were heading down Fond Du Lac when I seen Charlene step out of a store called Monique's Boutique. I broke my neck to see where she was going as I sped towards the next intersection to make a U-turn. "That was Charlene."

Jax looked out the back window of my Tahoe. "She going to a white Benz. And a nigga just got out to open the door for her."

I damn near ran up on the curb as I struggled to look for her in the side mirror. The thought of her with a new nigga made it feel like I was having a heart attack. "It gotta to be the nigga she cheated on me with while I was locked up. Punk ass bitch."

"I want that Benz," Jax smiled, pulling his heat.

I spun around at the next intersection and punched it. The nigga had just walked around to the driver's side of the Benz and was about to get in the car. When I got close, I smashed the brakes, sliding the truck to a stop. The nigga looked terrified as Jax hopped out and put the banger to his face. I pulled my shit out and ran around to the passenger door and snatched it open. I yanked Charlene out by her hair only to discover that it wasn't Charlene. Shit.

"Oh my God!" She screamed.

"What's going on?" The man asked.

For a moment I was stuck. We fucked around and ran up on the wrong people. "Damn. It ain't her," I told Jax before letting the female go. "My bad. I thought you was somebody else."

"I still want the Benz," Jax said, keeping his gun in the nigga's face.

I walked back to my truck. "Nah. We can't do em like that. Let's go."

Jax didn't move.

"Young man, listen to your friend. We're not the people that you're looking for. I'm a pastor and this is my wife. If you want, we can pray for you. Please, just let us go."

I jumped back in the truck and called for Jax. "Let's go, brah."

He reluctantly let the man go and got in the truck. "That was a 750. I could'da bussed that bitch down and ate, fam."

"We good, my nigga. I don't wanna take nothing from no preacher anyway."

"Man, fuck them niggas. They be pimpin them mu'fuckas that go to they church anyway. That bitch did look like Charlene, though."

$$\$\$\$$$

After kicking it with my niggas for most of the day, I ended the night by my side bitch house. I was laying in her bed smoking a three-five and watching a porno that we made a couple days ago. She was laying next to me wearing a bra and panties and fucking with her social media. I had been fucking with Donna for like four months. She was a super baddy, too. Twenty-two years old with a pretty face and body like a stripper. She was also a super rachet ass bitch with three babies and three baby daddies. One of em was dead and the other two was locked up. I normally didn't fuck on bitches with them type of issues because too many baby

313

daddies can cause problems. But I kept shorty around since them niggas was locked up and she was bout that action. And the action I'm talking about was that freaky shit. Let me do all that nasty shit that some hoes won't let a nigga do. Nut on her face. Pull it out her ass and stick it right in her mouth. And she got a couple bad ass friends that she let me fuck on and have threesomes with. Long as I dick her down and bless her with some paper, she let me have my way.

"Hold this phone so I can make another twerk video on my Instagram," Monique said, passing me her phone.

I slapped them cheeks as she crawled in front of me and started making it shake, bounce, and jiggle. Then she posted the video and read the comments.

"Niggas love this ass, Klan," she bragged, recording herself sticking out her tongue and squeezing her titties.

My dick started getting hard as I watched her suck my dick in the porno. "I love that neck better."

Her eyes lit up and mouth dropped open. "You love me Klan?"

"Nah, that ain't what I said. I said I love that neck. Look." I showed her my phone screen.

"Ooh, I was doing that," she grinned. Then she straddled my lap to look in my eyes.

"What you doing?"

"I want to see how you react when I tell you that I love you."

I laughed. "What?"

She looked hurt. "For real? I tell you that I love you and you laugh?"

"Man, you tripping. Fuck is you on?"

She rolled her eyes, smacked her lips, and started making them noises that Cardi B make. "Hello? I just told you I loved you. Fuck you mean, nigga? I want the number one spot. I wanna have yo baby."

I just stared at her, trying to put my thoughts into words. "Listen, baby, you cool but I definitely ain't wifing you up.

We ain't doing that baby shit either. I don't know what you on, but we ain't on none of that."

She rolled her eyes and got dramatic. "So, you just wanna fuck me and have threesomes with my friends but you don't wanna make me yo bitch? For real though?"

"Yeah. That's exactly what we doing?"

Her eyes turned angry and she crossed her arms over her chest. "Well, I don't want to do that no more. I don't wanna be on the side no more so make a choice."

Hearing her try to change the rules pissed me off. "Bitch, shut the fuck up. You don't make no muthafuckin rules. Matter of fact, bitch, suck my dick."

"Fuck you, bitch ass nigga," she said, putting the palm of her hand in my face and muffing me as she tried to get up.

I grabbed her arm and slung her ass. She flew across the bed and rolled onto the floor. I jumped up, ready to stick my foot in her ass. "Bitch, you don lost yo mind puttin yo hands on me?"

She tried to scramble away but I was on her ass. I wrapped my hand around her throat and pushed her into the wall and started choking her. "Bitch don't you ever put yo muthafckin hands on me or I'll kill yo bitch ass. You hear me, bitch?"

She couldn't talk so she nodded. Her eyes bulged with fear as I squeezed harder. Then Charlene's face popped into my head and I let her go. She dropped to her knees and grabbed my legs while sucking in deep breaths.

"I'm sorry, daddy. I'm sorry, daddy."

I was suddenly disgusted with Donna. I didn't feel sorry for choking her like I did Charlene. Instead I felt hatred. I wanted to choke her again. I wanted to beat her ass. Who the fuck did she think she was to put her hands on me? Instead I shoved her out of the way. "Get cho fucking hands off of me," I snapped and went to find my clothes.

She ran over and grabbed me. " I'm sorry. I'll do whatever you want."

I pushed her away. "Move, Donna."

She grabbed me again. "Please, don't leave. I'll suck your dick all night."

I picked her up and slammed her ass on the floor. "Bitch, don't touch me no more!"

She lay on the floor and cried. I got dressed and went home.

I woke up the next morning and thought about how I treated Donna last night. I probably over reacted but that bitch shouldn't have put her hands on me. That's one thing I didn't play. Plus, I wasn't feeling that love and baby shit. Why would I get a thottie with three baby daddies my seed? She would do anything for some likes. Wasn't no way my first baby mama was gon be out there like that. The only female I wanted to have a baby with was Charlene. When I thought that was her with the nigga in the Benz yesterday, that shit made my chest hurt so bad that it felt like I was about to have a heart attack. Damn, she had a nigga soul. She had been gone for almost a month and I still couldn't believe that she left a nigga. I missed the shit out of her. She was a good woman. I wonder if I would've showed her that I could change, would she still be with me? I promised that I would go to church with her but never went. Maybe that's why she hit it.

Then I got a thought. What if I went to church? Nah, that shit wasn't for me. I didn't even believe in Jesus being the son of God. But what if that's what it took to get her back? What if all she wanted to see was some effort? I sat up on the couch as a newfound hope surged through my body. She said she went the church down the street. What if I didn't try to force it? Just showed up on some nice guy shit and acted like I was ready to change? Today was Sunday. This was the perfect opportunity. I checked the time on my phone. 7:38AM.

"Fuck it, Klan. What else you got to lose?" I told myself.

I took a shower and threw on the cloths that I wore when I took her to the private party thrown by the Bucks nigga. I hoped dressing up a little would bring me some good luck. Then I grabbed my pistol, because I didn't leave home without it, and went to church. I could hear the choir singing as I walked up to the big double doors at The City of God Church. I felt kind of bogus for bringing my heat to church but I had done too much dirt and I wasn't finna let a nigga catch me slipping. God was just gon have to forgive me for this one. I walked down a hallway and followed the sound of music to the inner part of the church where everybody did the worshipping. A choir stood on the stage singing and people in the congregation stood and clapped and sang along. I took a moment to search for Charlene but couldn't find her. A tall brown skinned nigga walked over.

"Good morning, brotha. Let me help you find a seat."

I followed him to a pew in the middle of the church. "Thanks, brah."

I sat and listened to the choir sing and found myself nodding my head. They were good. Then a couple people from the congregation got up to pray and read from the Bible. I kept looking around for Charlene but couldn't find her. I thought about leaving but then I heard a voice that kept me in my seat. He was a short old man but he had a voice that made you want to listen. Raspy and deep and filled with authority.

"Good morning, church. The Lord gave me a good word for you today. Can I tell it?"

"Go head. Tell it, pastor," the people shouted back.

The little back and forth made me smile. I had to hear this.

"Church, be careful what you ask God for. I'ma say it again. Be careful what you ask for because you might just get it. How many of y'all pray for humility and peace? How many for patience? For Wisdom? You ever ask yourself what it takes to gain these divine qualities? Well, to achieve these you have to go through a process. You don't just pray for it and wake up wise, humble, patient, or peaceful. You have to learn those things. Attaining these divine qualities ain't a walk in the park either. The process involves blood, sweat, and tears. Just ask brotha Bobby."

He pointed to a tall brown skinned nigga that sat up front.

"Bobby could teach us all a lesson or two in humility. This past month, this brother was tested and put through the fire. He suffered some lessons. Notice what I said. He suffered those lessons. The devil used his servant to attack his father, Jamie. Like most of us would, Bobby wanted revenge. He went looking for it and found it. A man was killed and he spent almost a month in jail. Even though he didn't shoot the man, he accepts some responsibility for the part he played in the man's death. That was his lesson in humility, church. A man died. Now the scripture, 'vengeance is mines sayeth the Lord', is real to him. And that lesson humbled him and will continue to do so."

I liked the preacher. Listening to him was a treat. He used the Bible to teach real life lessons that average people could use in their life. He didn't say anything that would make me change or become a Christian, but I respected what he was teaching. He was definitely a good preacher and I could see why Charlene wanted me to come listen to him. And even though Charlene never showed up, I stayed for the entire service. When it ended, I was making my way towards the door when me and Bobby crossed paths. We exchanged nods and kept it moving. Then I ran into the nigga that led me to my seat.

"Did you enjoy the service?" He asked.

"Y'all pastor is a beast, brah. I like the way he made the teachings in the Bible apply to the average person. Especially the lesson in humility. That was good."

"Yeah. That was a hard lesson." He extended a hand. "My name is Devin."

I shook. "Cedric."

"So, what brings you to The City of God?"

I wondered if I should tell him that I came for a woman? Nah. He might know her and what happened between us.

"Fam, I just wanted to see what this church stuff was about. I been living down the street for a minute and I always heard the music. I didn't know y'all preacher got down like that. Sometimes I felt like he was talking to me."

"That's how that word is. Pastor Sims knows how to teach those messages that touch everybody."

"Real talk," I agreed.

"Will you come back and see us again next Sunday?"

I didn't want to commit just in case something came up. "Lets play it by ear."

He grinned, knowing I was spinning him. "It's a lot of good people in here that can help you. You can make some real connections. Help you with work or school. Whatever you need."

I studied Devin for a minute and seen sincerity in his eyes. He really wanted to help me. "Can I ask you a question?"

"Yeah. What's up?"

"You know Charlene?" He thought for a minute. "Yeah. I think I do. As a matter of fact, brotha Bobby know her."

He waved over the nigga that Pastor talked about in his sermon.

"What's going on, fellas?" He asked, looking me over.

"What happened to that sistah, Charlene?"

"She running late. She coming to the next service. Why?"

I spoke up before Devin could blow me up. "I know her friend, Lana. She told me Charlene went to this church."

Bobby gave me a suspicious look like he knew I was lying. "Well, if you stick around you might run into her."

I wondered why he knew she was running late and the other nigga didn't. Then it hit me. This is the nigga she was fucking! A church nigga. My blood started boiling and I wanted to bust this nigga in his shit. If we wasn't standing in a church, I would'da got down on his ass. But I played it cool. "Nah, I'ma get outta here. Got some things I need to take care of. Y'all be smooth."

I went outside and posted up at the bus stop on the corner. Me and Charlene was finna talk whether she wanted to or not. I couldn't believe she was fucking a weak ass church nigga. I didn't have to wait long either. Her car pulled up about five minutes later and Bobby stepped outside to meet her. When I seen them hug and kiss, I snapped. I felt them same feelings that I did when I found out Nitty was fucking Eve. I could barely control the rage. That shit was threatening to take over me. "CHARLENE!"

She spun to face me, continuing to hug Bobby. Her eyes grew wide in fear when she seen me storming across the street.

"So this what we doing, huh? This the nigga you was fuckin while I was locked up?"

Bobby stepped in front of her, lifting a hand to stop me from getting too close. "Bro, this ain't the place for that."

"Fuck out my way, nigga." I slapped his hand out of the way and bussed him in his shit. He fell to the ground. I got in Charlene's face, wishing we was alone so I could choke the life out of her ass. "You don't wanna talk to me because you fuckin this nigga?"

Bobby moved faster than I expected. He jumped up from the ground and punched me hard as fuck. I stumbled and almost fell. And that's when I let the rage take over. This nigga was about to pay with his life for putting his hands on me. The next thing I knew I had my pistol out.

"No, Klan!" Charlene screamed.

I squeezed the trigger and hit Bobby in the chest two times. He went down and I was about to shoot him in the head when Charlene stepped in front of him.

"Stop it, Klan! Stop!"

"What the fuck, Charlene? Look what the fuck you made me do."

"Why did you come here? Why did you shoot him?" She cried. " I said it was over. It's over."

Seeing her tears sobered me up and allowed me to see what I had done. I just popped a nigga in front of a church. About twenty people stood around watching and more of them was coming outside. I was going back to the joint for sure. And it was over a female again. Fuck. I turned my heat on Charlene.

"Get in the car right now!"

"No. I'm not going nowhere with you."

Bobby made a noise and she bent down to try to stop the bleeding.

I pointed the gun in her face. "If you don't get in the car right now, I'm blazing you."

She looked at the gun and then up into my eyes. Her look was defiant. She made up her mind and was staying with Bobby. So I shot her in the face.

Epilogue

(1 year later)

Our most costly mistakes will bring the greatest lessons. I am thankful for every mistake and loss that I've suffered because those experiences gave me great gems of wisdom. I'm not glorifying doing bad things or minimizing the hurt and pain that my mistakes caused other people. I know that lives were changed or lost because of some of the choices I made. I must live with the knowledge of that for the rest of my life. And with all that said, I'm still thankful.

God protects those he plans to use.

Its been a year since Klan shot me. The doctors said I was lucky to be alive considering how much blood I lost and that the bullets missed any major arteries or organs. I disagreed that it was luck that kept me alive. I know where my blessings come from and it was only by the grace of God that I survived.

Out of our bruised and bleeding places will come our greatest strength.

Charlene survived but lost a chunk of her left jaw when Klan shot her. She thinks the scar and missing bone makes her ugly but I disagree. My wife will always be the most beautiful woman in the world. Her scars are her greatest strength. They not only tell of the tragedy that we survived but they also testify to the power of God. Klan could've killed us both, but God... Now we're expecting our first child in three months.

What you've done has no determination on what God can do through you.

Me, Charlene, Little, and Lisa make up the City of God Prison Ministry. Every Saturday we go to different prisons around the state to preach the word of God and save souls. The first place we visited was Waupun. It was amazing. I got to kick it with the choir and other brothers I had done time with. Charlene also got to meet her father.

The devil doesn't attack the people that he owns, but he uses them to attack the people that he doesn't.

Klan died a couple hours after he shot me and my wife. He took her car and went on a high speed chase that ended in a big shootout. He killed two police officers before they killed him. As I look back on my life, I can see that God has been walking with me. And when I couldn't walk, he carried me. And whenever I walked into trouble, He saved me. The lesson in all of that is even a gangsta can be saved.

The end...

Lock Down Publications and Ca$h Presents
Assisted Publishing Packages

BASIC PACKAGE	UPGRADED PACKAGE
$499	$800
Editing	Typing
Cover Design	Editing
Formatting	Cover Design
	Formatting
ADVANCE PACKAGE	**LDP SUPREME PACKAGE**
$1,200	$1,500
Typing	Typing
Editing	Editing
Cover Design	Cover Design
Formatting	Formatting
Copyright registration	Copyright registration
Proofreading	Proofreading
Upload book to Amazon	Set up Amazon account
	Upload book to Amazon
	Advertise on LDP, Amazon and
	Facebook Page

***Other services available upon request.
Additional charges may apply

Lock Down Publications
P.O. Box 944
Stockbridge, GA 30281-9998
Phone: 470 303-9761

Submission Guideline

Submit the first three chapters of your completed manuscript to ldpsubmissions@gmail.com. In the subject line add **Your Book's Title**. The manuscript must be in a Word Doc file and sent as an attachment. Document should be in Times New Roman, double spaced, and in size 12 font. Also, provide your synopsis and full contact information. If sending multiple submissions, they must each be in a separate email.

Have a story but no way to send it electronically? You can still submit to LDP/Ca$h Presents. Send in the first three chapters, written or typed, of your completed manuscript to:

LDP: Submissions Dept
P.O. Box 944
Stockbridge, GA 30281-9998

DO NOT send original manuscript. Must be a duplicate.
Provide your synopsis and a cover letter containing your full contact information.

Thanks for considering LDP and Ca$h Presents.

NEW RELEASES

BLOODLINE OF A SAVAGE **BY PRINCE A. TAUHID**

THE MURDER QUEENS 4 **BY MICHAEL GALLON**

THE BUTTERFLY MAFIA **BY FUMIYA PAYNE**

KING KILLA 2 **BY VINCENT "VITTO" HOLLOWAY**

BABY, I'M WINTERTIME COLD 3 **BY MEESHA**

THESE VICIOUS STREETS **BY PRINCE A. TAUHID**

TIL DEATH 2 **BY ARYANNA**

CITY OF SMOKE 2 **BY MOLOTTI**

STEPPERS **BY KING RIO**

THE LANE **BY KEN-KEN SPENCE**

MONEY GAME 2 **BY SMOOVE DOLLA**

THE BLACK DIAMOND CARTEL **BY SAYNOMORE**

CRIME BOSS 2 **BY PLAYA RAY**

THUG OF SPADES **BY COREY ROBINSON**

LOVE IN THE TRENCHES 2 **BY COREY ROBINSON**

TIL DEATH 3 **BY ARYANNA**

THE BIRTH OF A GANGSTER 4 **BY DELMONT PLAYER**

PRODUCT OF THE STREETS **BY DEMOND "MONEY" ANDERSON**

Coming Soon from Lock Down Publications/Ca$h Presents

BLOOD OF A BOSS VI
SHADOWS OF THE GAME II
TRAP BASTARD II
By **Askari**

LOYAL TO THE GAME IV
By **T.J. & Jelissa**

TRUE SAVAGE VIII
MIDNIGHT CARTEL IV
DOPE BOY MAGIC IV
CITY OF KINGZ III
NIGHTMARE ON SILENT AVE II
THE PLUG OF LIL MEXICO II
CLASSIC CITY II
By **Chris Green**

BLAST FOR ME III
A SAVAGE DOPEBOY III
CUTTHROAT MAFIA III
DUFFLE BAG CARTEL VII
HEARTLESS GOON VI
By **Ghost**

A HUSTLER'S DECEIT III
KILL ZONE II
BAE BELONGS TO ME III
TIL DEATH II
By **Aryanna**

KING OF THE TRAP III
By **T.J. Edwards**

GORILLAZ IN THE BAY V
3X KRAZY III
STRAIGHT BEAST MODE III
By **De'Kari**

KINGPIN KILLAZ IV
STREET KINGS III
PAID IN BLOOD III
CARTEL KILLAZ IV
DOPE GODS III
By **Hood Rich**

SINS OF A HUSTLA II
By **ASAD**

YAYO V
BRED IN THE GAME 2
By **S. Allen**

THE STREETS WILL TALK II
By **Yolanda Moore**

SON OF A DOPE FIEND III
HEAVEN GOT A GHETTO III
SKI MASK MONEY III
By **Renta**

LOYALTY AIN'T PROMISED III
By **Keith Williams**

I'M NOTHING WITHOUT HIS LOVE II
SINS OF A THUG II
TO THE THUG I LOVED BEFORE II
IN A HUSTLER I TRUST II
By **Monet Dragun**

QUIET MONEY IV
EXTENDED CLIP III
THUG LIFE IV
By **Trai'Quan**

THE STREETS MADE ME IV
By **Larry D. Wright**

IF YOU CROSS ME ONCE III
ANGEL V
By **Anthony Fields**

THE STREETS WILL NEVER CLOSE IV
By **K'ajji**

HARD AND RUTHLESS III
KILLA KOUNTY IV
By **Khufu**

MONEY GAME III
By **Smoove Dolla**

MURDA WAS THE CASE III
Elijah R. Freeman

AN UNFORESEEN LOVE IV
BABY, I'M WINTERTIME COLD III
By **Meesha**

QUEEN OF THE ZOO III
By **Black Migo**

CONFESSIONS OF A JACKBOY III
By **Nicholas Lock**

JACK BOYS VS DOPE BOYS IV
A GANGSTA'S QUR'AN V
COKE GIRLZ II
COKE BOYS II
LIFE OF A SAVAGE V
CHI'RAQ GANGSTAS V
SOSA GANG III
BRONX SAVAGES II
BODYMORE KINGPINS II
By **Romell Tukes**

KING KILLA II
By **Vincent "Vitto" Holloway**

BETRAYAL OF A THUG III
By **Fre$h**

THE MURDER QUEENS III
By **Michael Gallon**

THE BIRTH OF A GANGSTER III
By **Delmont Player**

TREAL LOVE II
By **Le'Monica Jackson**

FOR THE LOVE OF BLOOD III
By **Jamel Mitchell**

RAN OFF ON DA PLUG II
By **Paper Boi Rari**

HOOD CONSIGLIERE III
By **Keese**

PRETTY GIRLS DO NASTY THINGS II
By **Nicole Goosby**

PROTÉGÉ OF A LEGEND III
LOVE IN THE TRENCHES II
By **Corey Robinson**

IT'S JUST ME AND YOU II
By **Ah'Million**

FOREVER GANGSTA III
By **Adrian Dulan**

GORILLAZ IN THE TRENCHES II
By **SayNoMore**

THE COCAINE PRINCESS VIII
By **King Rio**

CRIME BOSS II
By **Playa Ray**

LOYALTY IS EVERYTHING III
By **Molotti**

HERE TODAY GONE TOMORROW II
By **Fly Rock**

REAL G'S MOVE IN SILENCE II
By **Von Diesel**

GRIMEY WAYS IV
By **Ray Vinci**

Available Now

RESTRAINING ORDER I & II
By **CA$H & Coffee**

LOVE KNOWS NO BOUNDARIES I II & III
By **Coffee**

RAISED AS A GOON I, II, III & IV
BRED BY THE SLUMS I, II, III
BLAST FOR ME I & II
ROTTEN TO THE CORE I II III
A BRONX TALE I, II, III
DUFFLE BAG CARTEL I II III IV V VI
HEARTLESS GOON I II III IV V
A SAVAGE DOPEBOY I II
DRUG LORDS I II III
CUTTHROAT MAFIA I II
KING OF THE TRENCHES
By **Ghost**

LAY IT DOWN I & II
LAST OF A DYING BREED I II
BLOOD STAINS OF A SHOTTA I & II III
By **Jamaica**

LOYAL TO THE GAME I II III
LIFE OF SIN I, II III
By **TJ & Jelissa**

IF LOVING HIM IS WRONG…I & II
LOVE ME EVEN WHEN IT HURTS I II III
By **Jelissa**

BLOODY COMMAS I & II
SKI MASK CARTEL I, II & III
KING OF NEW YORK I II, III IV V
RISE TO POWER I II III
COKE KINGS I II III IV V
BORN HEARTLESS I II III IV
KING OF THE TRAP I II
By **T.J. Edwards**

WHEN THE STREETS CLAP BACK I & II III
THE HEART OF A SAVAGE I II III IV
MONEY MAFIA I II
LOYAL TO THE SOIL I II III
By **Jibril Williams**

A DISTINGUISHED THUG STOLE MY HEART I II &
III
LOVE SHOULDN'T HURT I II III IV
RENEGADE BOYS I II III IV
PAID IN KARMA I II III
SAVAGE STORMS I II III
AN UNFORESEEN LOVE I II III
BABY, I'M WINTERTIME COLD I II
By **Meesha**

A GANGSTER'S CODE I &, II III
A GANGSTER'S SYN I II III
THE SAVAGE LIFE I II III
CHAINED TO THE STREETS I II III
BLOOD ON THE MONEY I II III
A GANGSTA'S PAIN I II III
By **J-Blunt**

PUSH IT TO THE LIMIT
By **Bre' Hayes**

BLOOD OF A BOSS I, II, III, IV, V
SHADOWS OF THE GAME
TRAP BASTARD
By **Askari**

THE STREETS BLEED MURDER I, II & III
THE HEART OF A GANGSTA I II& III
By **Jerry Jackson**

CUM FOR ME I II III IV V VI VII VIII
An **LDP Erotica Collaboration**

BRIDE OF A HUSTLA I II & II
THE FETTI GIRLS I, II& III
CORRUPTED BY A GANGSTA I, II III, IV
BLINDED BY HIS LOVE
THE PRICE YOU PAY FOR LOVE I, II ,III
DOPE GIRL MAGIC I II III
By **Destiny Skai**

WHEN A GOOD GIRL GOES BAD
By **Adrienne**

A GANGSTER'S REVENGE I II III & IV
THE BOSS MAN'S DAUGHTERS I II III IV V
A SAVAGE LOVE I & II
BAE BELONGS TO ME I II
A HUSTLER'S DECEIT I, II, III
WHAT BAD BITCHES DO I, II, III
SOUL OF A MONSTER I II III
KILL ZONE
A DOPE BOY'S QUEEN I II III
TIL DEATH
By **Aryanna**

335

THE COST OF LOYALTY I II III
By Kweli

A KINGPIN'S AMBITION
A KINGPIN'S AMBITION **II**
I MURDER FOR THE DOUGH
By **Ambitious**

TRUE SAVAGE I II III IV V VI VII
DOPE BOY MAGIC I, II, III
MIDNIGHT CARTEL I II III
CITY OF KINGZ I II
NIGHTMARE ON SILENT AVE
THE PLUG OF LIL MEXICO II
CLASSIC CITY
By **Chris Green**

A DOPEBOY'S PRAYER
By **Eddie "Wolf" Lee**

THE KING CARTEL I, II & III
By **Frank Gresham**

THESE NIGGAS AIN'T LOYAL I, II & III
By **Nikki Tee**

GANGSTA SHYT I II &III
By **CATO**

THE ULTIMATE BETRAYAL
By **Phoenix**

BOSS'N UP I, II & III
By **Royal Nicole**

I LOVE YOU TO DEATH
By **Destiny J**

I RIDE FOR MY HITTA
I STILL RIDE FOR MY HITTA
By **Misty Holt**

LOVE & CHASIN' PAPER
By **Qay Crockett**

TO DIE IN VAIN
SINS OF A HUSTLA
By **ASAD**

BROOKLYN HUSTLAZ
By **Boogsy Morina**

BROOKLYN ON LOCK I & II
By **Sonovia**

GANGSTA CITY
By **Teddy Duke**

A DRUG KING AND HIS DIAMOND I & II III
A DOPEMAN'S RICHES
HER MAN, MINE'S TOO I, II
CASH MONEY HO'S
THE WIFEY I USED TO BE I II
PRETTY GIRLS DO NASTY THINGS
By Nicole Goosby

LIPSTICK KILLAH I, II, III
CRIME OF PASSION I II & III
FRIEND OR FOE I II III
By **Mimi**

TRAPHOUSE KING I II & III
KINGPIN KILLAZ I II III
STREET KINGS I II
PAID IN BLOOD I II
CARTEL KILLAZ I II III
DOPE GODS I II
By **Hood Rich**

STEADY MOBBN' I, II, III
THE STREETS STAINED MY SOUL I II III
By **Marcellus Allen**

WHO SHOT YA I, II, III
SON OF A DOPE FIEND I II
HEAVEN GOT A GHETTO I II
SKI MASK MONEY I II
By **Renta**

GORILLAZ IN THE BAY I II III IV
TEARS OF A GANGSTA I II
3X KRAZY I II
STRAIGHT BEAST MODE I II
By **DE'KARI**

TRIGGADALE I II III
MURDA WAS THE CASE I II
By **Elijah R. Freeman**

THE STREETS ARE CALLING
By **Duquie Wilson**

SLAUGHTER GANG I II III
RUTHLESS HEART I II III
By **Willie Slaughter**

CHURCH IN THESE STREETS | J-BLUNT

GOD BLESS THE TRAPPERS I, II, III
THESE SCANDALOUS STREETS I, II, III
FEAR MY GANGSTA I, II, III IV, V
THESE STREETS DON'T LOVE NOBODY I, II
BURY ME A G I, II, III, IV, V
A GANGSTA'S EMPIRE I, II, III, IV
THE DOPEMAN'S BODYGAURD I II
THE REALEST KILLAZ I II III
THE LAST OF THE OGS I II III
By **Tranay Adams**

MARRIED TO A BOSS I II III
By **Destiny Skai & Chris Green**

KINGZ OF THE GAME I II III IV V VI VII
CRIME BOSS
By **Playa Ray**

FUK SHYT
By **Blakk Diamond**

DON'T F#CK WITH MY HEART I II
By **Linnea**

ADDICTED TO THE DRAMA I II III
IN THE ARM OF HIS BOSS II
By **Jamila**

YAYO I II III IV
A SHOOTER'S AMBITION I II
BRED IN THE GAME
By **S. Allen**

LOYALTY AIN'T PROMISED I II
By **Keith Williams**

CHURCH IN THESE STREETS | J-BLUNT

TRAP GOD I II III
RICH $AVAGE I II III
MONEY IN THE GRAVE I II III
By **Martell Troublesome Bolden**

FOREVER GANGSTA I II
GLOCKS ON SATIN SHEETS I II
By **Adrian Dulan**

TOE TAGZ I II III IV
LEVELS TO THIS SHYT I II
IT'S JUST ME AND YOU
By **Ah'Million**

KINGPIN DREAMS I II III
RAN OFF ON DA PLUG
By **Paper Boi Rari**

CONFESSIONS OF A GANGSTA I II III IV
CONFESSIONS OF A JACKBOY I II
By **Nicholas Lock**

I'M NOTHING WITHOUT HIS LOVE
SINS OF A THUG
TO THE THUG I LOVED BEFORE
A GANGSTA SAVED XMAS
IN A HUSTLER I TRUST
By **Monet Dragun**

QUIET MONEY I II III
THUG LIFE I II III
EXTENDED CLIP I II
A GANGSTA'S PARADISE
By **Trai'Quan**

CHURCH IN THESE STREETS | J-BLUNT

CAUGHT UP IN THE LIFE I II III
THE STREETS NEVER LET GO I II III
By **Robert Baptiste**

NEW TO THE GAME I II III
MONEY, MURDER & MEMORIES I II III
By **Malik D. Rice**

CREAM I II III
THE STREETS WILL TALK
By **Yolanda Moore**

LIFE OF A SAVAGE I II III IV
A GANGSTA'S QUR'AN I II III IV
MURDA SEASON I II III
GANGLAND CARTEL I II III
CHI'RAQ GANGSTAS I II III IV
KILLERS ON ELM STREET I II III
JACK BOYZ N DA BRONX I II III
A DOPEBOY'S DREAM I II III
JACK BOYS VS DOPE BOYS I II III
COKE GIRLZ
COKE BOYS
SOSA GANG I II
BRONX SAVAGES
BODYMORE KINGPINS
By **Romell Tukes**

THE STREETS MADE ME I II III
By **Larry D. Wright**

CONCRETE KILLA I II III
VICIOUS LOYALTY I II III
By **Kingpen**

THE ULTIMATE SACRIFICE I, II, III, IV, V, VI
KHADIFI
IF YOU CROSS ME ONCE I II
ANGEL I II III IV
IN THE BLINK OF AN EYE
By **Anthony Fields**

THE LIFE OF A HOOD STAR
By **Ca$h & Rashia Wilson**

THE STREETS WILL NEVER CLOSE I II III
By **K'ajji**

NIGHTMARES OF A HUSTLA I II III
By **King Dream**

HARD AND RUTHLESS I II
MOB TOWN 251
THE BILLIONAIRE BENTLEYS I II III
REAL G'S MOVE IN SILENCE
By **Von Diesel**

GHOST MOB
By **Stilloan Robinson**

MOB TIES I II III IV V VI
SOUL OF A HUSTLER, HEART OF A KILLER I II
GORILLAZ IN THE TRENCHES
By **SayNoMore**

BODYMORE MURDERLAND I II III
THE BIRTH OF A GANGSTER I II
By **Delmont Player**

CHURCH IN THESE STREETS | J-BLUNT

FOR THE LOVE OF A BOSS
By **C. D. Blue**

KILLA KOUNTY I II III IV
By Khufu

MOBBED UP I II III IV
THE BRICK MAN I II III IV V
THE COCAINE PRINCESS I II III IV V VI VII
By **King Rio**

MONEY GAME I II
By **Smoove Dolla**

A GANGSTA'S KARMA I II III
By **FLAME**

KING OF THE TRENCHES I II III
By **GHOST & TRANAY ADAMS**

QUEEN OF THE ZOO I II
By **Black Migo**

GRIMEY WAYS I II III
By **Ray Vinci**

XMAS WITH AN ATL SHOOTER
By **Ca$h & Destiny Skai**

KING KILLA
By **Vincent "Vitto" Holloway**

BETRAYAL OF A THUG I II
By **Fre$h**

CHURCH IN THESE STREETS | J-BLUNT

THE MURDER QUEENS I II
By **Michael Gallon**

TREAL LOVE
By **Le'Monica Jackson**

FOR THE LOVE OF BLOOD I II
By **Jamel Mitchell**

HOOD CONSIGLIERE I II
By **Keese**

PROTÉGÉ OF A LEGEND I II
LOVE IN THE TRENCHES
By **Corey Robinson**

BORN IN THE GRAVE I II III
By **Self Made Tay**

MOAN IN MY MOUTH
By **XTASY**

TORN BETWEEN A GANGSTER AND A
GENTLEMAN
By **J-BLUNT & Miss Kim**

LOYALTY IS EVERYTHING I II
By **Molotti**

HERE TODAY GONE TOMORROW
By **Fly Rock**

PILLOW PRINCESS
By **S. Hawkins**

CHURCH IN THESE STREETS | J-BLUNT

SANCTIFIED AND HORNY
by **XTASY**

THE PLUG OF LIL MEXICO 2
by **CHRIS GREEN**

THE BLACK DIAMOND CARTEL
by **SAYNOMORE**

THE BIRTH OF A GANGSTER 3
by **DELMONT PLAYER**

BOOKS BY LDP'S CEO, CA$H

TRUST IN NO MAN
TRUST IN NO MAN 2
TRUST IN NO MAN 3
BONDED BY BLOOD
SHORTY GOT A THUG
THUGS CRY
THUGS CRY 2
THUGS CRY 3
TRUST NO BITCH
TRUST NO BITCH 2
TRUST NO BITCH 3
TIL MY CASKET DROPS
RESTRAINING ORDER
RESTRAINING ORDER 2
IN LOVE WITH A CONVICT
LIFE OF A HOOD STAR
XMAS WITH AN ATL SHOOTER